K.V

JASMINE [CRESSWELL]

"Seat-of-the-pants tension... [...] twist make this fast-p[...]"
—*Publishers Weekly* on *The Daughter*

"*Secret Sins* is romantic suspense at its finest and places Jasmine Cresswell on the mantel with the great ones such as Jayne Ann Krentz and Judith McNaught."
—*Affaire de Coeur*

AMANDA STEVENS

"With enough twists and turns to keep you turning the pages... Stevens draws readers into her tightly woven web."
—*Romantic Times*

"Ms. Stevens weaves intrigue, believable characters, legends and emotion together seamlessly for an engrossing read."
—*The Best Reviews*

DEBRA LEE BROWN

"*The Mackintosh Bride* escalates in excitement just as a large rock speeds down a mountain... go along for the ride and you won't be disappointed."
—*Rendezvous*

"Debra Lee Brown makes her mark with *The Virgin Spring*, which should be read by all lovers of Scottish romances."
—*Affaire de Coeur*

Jasmine Cresswell is a multitalented author of over forty novels. Her efforts have gained her numerous awards, including the RWA's Golden Rose Award and the Colorado Author's League Award for the best original paperback novel. Born in Wales and educated in England, Jasmine met her husband while working at the British Embassy in Rio de Janeiro. She has lived in Australia, Canada and six cities in the United States. Jasmine and her husband now make their home in Sarasota, Florida.

Amanda Stevens was born and raised in a small Southern town, and frequently draws on memories of her birthplace to create atmospheric settings and casts of eccentric characters. She is the author of over twenty-five novels, the recipient of a Career Achievement award for Romantic/Mystery, and a 1999 RITA® Award Finalist in the Gothic/Romantic Suspense category. She now resides in Texas with her husband, teenage twins and her cat, Jesse, who also makes frequent appearances in her books.

Debra Lee Brown's ongoing romance with wild and remote locales sparks frequent adventures in the Alps, the Arctic—where she has worked as a geologist—and the Sierra Nevada of her native California. An avid outdoorswoman, Debra likes nothing better than to strand her heroes and heroines in rugged, often dangerous settings, then let nature take its course. Debra invites readers to visit her Web site at www.debraleebrown.com or to write to her at P.O. Box 214801, Sacramento, CA 95821.

JASMINE CRESSWELL

AMANDA STEVENS
DEBRA LEE BROWN

COLORADO CONFIDENTIAL

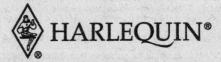

HARLEQUIN®

TORONTO • NEW YORK • LONDON
AMSTERDAM • PARIS • SYDNEY • HAMBURG
STOCKHOLM • ATHENS • TOKYO • MILAN • MADRID
PRAGUE • WARSAW • BUDAPEST • AUCKLAND

ISBN 0-373-83564-7

Special thanks and acknowledgment are given to Jasmine Cresswell,
Amanda Stevens and Debra Lee Brown for their contributions to the
COLORADO CONFIDENTIAL series.

COLORADO CONFIDENTIAL

Copyright © 2003 by Harlequin Books S.A.

The publisher acknowledges the copyright holders
of the individual works as follows:

PRIVATE EYES
Copyright © 2003 by Harlequin Books S.A.

KISS AND TELL
Copyright © 2003 by Harlequin Books S.A.

CENTENNIAL BRIDE
Copyright © 2003 by Harlequin Books S.A.

CONTENTS

PRIVATE EYES   9
Jasmine Cresswell

KISS AND TELL   171
Amanda Stevens

CENTENNIAL BRIDE   271
Debra Lee Brown

PRIVATE EYES

Jasmine Cresswell

CHAPTER ONE

FRANKLIN GETTYS slammed down the phone and swung around, fists clenched and cheeks flushed with anger. For a moment Helen thought he was going to hit her but, at the last second, he regained control of himself and stepped away.

"That phone call was from Charlie Quarrels at the Half Spur ranch," Franklin said. "My foreman tells me you drove out there on Friday and were poking around the place for most of the day."

"Well, yes, I was there," Helen admitted, wondering what she'd done wrong this time. "The spring sunshine was so great, I took a picnic lunch—"

She didn't have the chance to make any more excuses. Franklin stormed across the room and marched her backward until she was pinned against the bedroom wall, with his hands splayed on either side of her head. "Stop trying to elbow your way into every damn corner of my life," he said, his voice cracking with rage. "Don't try to defy me, Helen, because it won't work. You're moving way out of your league when you pick a fight with me."

"But I wasn't trying to pick a fight," Helen protested. She was trembling inside, but for once she didn't retreat into apologetic silence. For a moment she seriously considered doing something outrageous, like kneeing her husband in the groin so that she could break free of his hold, but sanity—or fear—prevailed. "I would never have gone to the ranch if I'd realized it would make you angry," she said apologetically.

"Then why didn't you tell me you'd been out there?" Franklin demanded. "Why all the secrecy if the trip was so innocent?"

Because you never bother to ask about what I've been doing while you're away in Washington, and it didn't occur to me to tell you, Helen thought. She didn't explain that to Franklin, though, because she was afraid it might sound like a complaint. Her husband didn't deal well with complaints.

"You were tired when you came home last night and we didn't talk much about anything," she suggested meekly.

Somewhat appeased, Franklin pushed away from the wall, releasing her. "Well, don't go behind my back again. I'm not just angry. I'm mad as hell."

"But why are you so mad?" Helen asked, finding a remnant of courage and not letting the subject drop as she would have done normally. "What's wrong with me visiting the Half Spur, since we own it? You've been in Washington for ten days, so it didn't interfere with your plans. I was alone here in Denver and it seemed such a long time since I'd been out of the city...."

"*You* don't own the Half Spur ranch," Franklin said cuttingly. "*I* own it. For the last time, keep your nose out of my private business affairs, Helen, and that's an order."

About to whisper an apology and sneak out of the bedroom, Helen suddenly despised herself for being such a coward. Franklin's behavior was totally unreasonable, so why in the world did she feel guilty? "I didn't harass the sheep, or interfere with the men working at the ranch," she said. "I barely spoke to them, in fact. You need to be more specific about what I did that was so terrible."

"You went where you weren't invited," Franklin snapped, slapping his fist into the palm of his other hand in a gesture that struck Helen as deliberately threatening. "Before you set off on your next wild-goose chase onto my property, ask my permission first. Do we understand each other?"

Helen nodded. Her view of marriage was practical rather than romantic, which was how she'd ended up married to Franklin in the first place. But she'd certainly never dreamed that she would one day find herself ordered to ask permission for something as simple as making a day trip out of Denver. How in the world had her marriage degenerated to this point, she wondered. How had she let herself slide into such a humiliating state of inferiority?

For the second time in as many minutes, Helen failed to share her thoughts with her husband. The past two years had taught her that Franklin's view of marriage was light years away from her own. Her husband wanted a relationship where all the power was his, and all the submission hers. Any attempt to carve out a more independent role resulted in outbursts of violent temper that reminded her all too vividly of her father and left her sick to her stomach.

It was true that Franklin gave her a generous monthly allowance and for a while, early in their marriage, her shiny new credit cards had created the illusion of freedom. She'd even congratulated herself on being sensible, and rejecting the lure of passion and romance offered by her relationship with Ryan Benton. But Helen soon realized that parting from Ryan hadn't just meant the loss of romance in her life. It had meant the loss of hope and fun and laughter as well. Franklin's money came with very long strings attached. He had stated many times that since he paid all the bills, he had the right to demand that she should obey him completely. The trade of freedom for financial security might have suited some women. Unfortunately, Helen didn't find shopping much of a substitute for having friends and an interesting job, much less for surrendering the right to a mind and opinions of her own, and for giving up on any chance of real companionship in her marriage.

She was bone weary of her unequal relationship with Franklin, Helen reflected. She was tired of being humiliated, tired of being made to feel inferior. Her stomach lurched as she confronted the fact that she had finally arrived at the end of her emotional rope. That rope had been long and thick, but this morning marked a turning point in her marriage to Franklin. After two years of nonstop retreat from confrontation, her back was pinned against the wall—figuratively as well as literally—and she had no choice but to stand up for herself and fight.

It took every ounce of her available courage, but she drew herself up and turned around so that she could look straight into her husband's eyes. "Franklin, we have to talk some more about this—"

"Not now," he said, sounding impatient. "I'm late, since you neglected to wake me up on time."

She could have reminded him that she'd tried to wake him twice, and he'd told her to get the hell away and leave him to sleep, but it seemed a waste of breath and energy. She knew he would merely twist her excuses around so that she would end up taking the blame not only for letting him oversleep, but for a bunch of other supposed marital sins as well.

"I need help, Franklin," she said, instinctively retreating into the placating tone which was her usual method of conversing with her husband. This time, though, the humility was false. He might not be aware of what was at stake right now, but she knew their future was on the line. She was offering her husband one last chance to suggest how they might get their marriage onto a healthy footing, a foundation that promised both of them at least a shot at happiness. Both of them, instead of just him.

"I'm feeling lost, Franklin, and I need your guidance," she said. "What am I supposed to do with myself all day? You don't want us to have children—"

He made a brusque chopping gesture and marched toward his walk-in closet. "For God's sake, don't start that pointless discussion again. I don't want kids. I never suggested we would have kids, and I haven't changed my mind. End of story. End of discussion."

"I'm not starting that discussion again," Helen said, aware that Franklin was correct, and this was a subject they'd beaten to death and beyond. She'd mentioned her desire for children on several occasions during their brief engagement and Franklin had simply failed to respond. She'd interpreted his silence as agreement that they would start a family soon after they married. In retrospect, Helen realized how foolish she'd been to make that assumption. On a subject as important as whether or not he wanted children, she should have confronted Franklin head-on, explicitly spelling out her own desire to have at least one child, and preferably two.

Unfortunately, in those early days of their relationship, she'd been so blinded with happiness that a man as important and famous as Franklin Gettys wanted to marry her that she hadn't cared to probe too hard into the roots of her happiness. It wasn't every day that a United States senator and former football hero asked a twenty-six-year-old casino dancer to marry him, and Helen had been floating on a cloud of euphoria from the time of their first date until the moment she said "I do."

She had spent the past two years learning the grim lesson that a handsome, rich husband was no great catch if he despised you. And even less of a catch when you realized you were beginning to despise him right back.

"I can't spend all day every day shopping, so what am I supposed to do with my time?" she asked, emboldened by desperation. "You ordered me to resign when I volunteered at the local homeless shelter. Same thing when I tried to raise funds and start a day-care center for single moms. You won't let me get a job—"

"You're not qualified for any job suitable for a senator's wife," Franklin said, opening a locked drawer in the dresser to select a pair of cufflinks. The drawer was kept locked because Franklin suspected Mercedes, their housekeeper, would rob him blind if given half a chance. Mercedes was an immigrant from Central America, and Franklin had instructed Helen never to trust her around money or valuables, because immigrants didn't share the values of "real" Americans.

Helen realized she was getting angry just watching her husband lock the drawer and return the key to his pocket. Mercedes didn't deserve the insult. In Helen's opinion, their housekeeper's ethical standards were a lot higher than Franklin's. But since she could only fight one battle at a time, she brought her attention back to the subject they were discussing. "I could help with your reelection campaign—"

"Doing what?" Franklin asked, sticking out his chin so that he could fasten the top button on his shirt. "Political campaigns require brains and education. You don't have either."

Helen flinched, but continued doggedly. "I could address envelopes. I could answer the phone. I'm used to dealing with people, and I think I could be friendly and polite, even in difficult situations. A waitress has to learn how to handle guests who are making unreasonable demands—"

"You think the fact that you were once a waitress qualifies you to talk to people calling my office?" Franklin laughed incredulously, then shook his head. "I wouldn't let you near any phone of mine. God knows what you might say to some important donor that would piss him off."

"Nothing rude or inappropriate, I'm sure." Helen was stung into defending herself.

Franklin rolled his eyes. "Right." He finished sliding polished ebony links into his shirt cuffs and began to knot his silk Givenchy tie. "The last time you chose to spout off your mouth at a fund-raiser, you started lecturing one of my biggest donors on the dangers of biochemical weapons. He happens to be one of the country's leading advocates of increased funding for biological warfare programs, and every damn thing you said offended him. I nearly lost him as a contributor to my reelection campaign, thanks to you.''

"I didn't lecture,'' Helen protested hotly, the injustice of the accusation making her burn inside. "Your donor suggested that the best protection against dictators with weapons of mass destruction was to manufacture a huge supply of our own biochemical weapons. And I simply responded that it could be dangerous for us to stockpile such potent weapons. A terrorist would only need to steal a vial of smallpox, or bubonic plague, and we could have a deadly nationwide epidemic in no time flat. Thousands of American citizens could die—''

"I'm sure my campaign donor was aware of the problems before you gave him the benefit of your ill-considered opinions.''

She gritted her teeth, ignoring the insult. "I don't believe your donor had given five seconds of thought to the problems of safe storage. He just wanted Congress to authorize a new weapons research program so that he could spend millions of taxpayer dollars on his pet project. He for sure didn't suggest any ways to solve the problems I'd raised.''

"Because you were talking garbage and it wasn't worth his time to correct all your mistaken conclusions. You need to keep your opinions on complicated subjects like this to yourself. Take a tip from me, Helen. Don't try to appear smart, and then you won't embarrass both of us by displaying your ignorance.''

Her husband certainly knew how to wound her, Helen thought, shriveling into silence. She was always painfully conscious of the fact that she had no college degree. However hard she'd tried to improve her general knowledge over the past couple of years, her constant reading was probably not enough. She was miserably aware that there could be gaps in her basic education that she wasn't even aware of, gaps that validated Franklin's opinion of her stupidity.

Tears burned at the back of her throat and she swallowed hard, banishing them before Franklin could be aware of how his jibes had hit home. Tears and self-pity never got a person anywhere worth going, Helen reminded herself. She'd learned that lesson years ago, when she was fourteen and her mother had died. Her father had just about drowned in grief and bitterness, leaving Helen to take care of the house, the bills and her desolate younger brother. Even at fourteen, she'd thought that her father's wallowing self-pity had been a pretty crummy way to honor her mother's memory.

Helen sighed, making one last effort to show Franklin how his various rules and edicts left her with a life that was empty of worthwhile activities. "If I can't even offer my honest opinion about important political issues, what is there left for me to do?" she asked. She hoped against hope that her husband would take the question seriously and make a constructive suggestion in response. "I want to help you, Franklin. I want to be part of your life. Just tell me how."

"You could start by showing a bit more enthusiasm in the bedroom," he said. "I'm sick to death of sleeping with a woman who doesn't even bother to fake orgasms anymore. Sex with you is about as exciting as taking a plastic doll to bed."

She blushed. "I'm sorry," she said huskily. "I realize I haven't been too much fun as a lover recently...."

"Fun?" He snorted. "There's an understatement if ever I heard one. You don't seem to know what the word means anymore." He shrugged into his blazer and stepped back to look at himself in the mirror. He was scornful of athletes who allowed their bodies to turn to fat when they retired, and he worked hard to keep himself lean and muscled. Giving a satisfied pat to his flat stomach, he tugged at the cuffs of his shirt until a precise quarter inch was showing. Then he swung around to look at Helen, who was sitting on the edge of the bed. His mouth curled in barely concealed contempt.

"You know what your real problem is, Helen? You've forgotten who's who in this marriage."

"No, of course I haven't—"

He cut across her words. "*I'm* the United States senator, for God's sake! You're a former exotic dancer from a second-rate casino who started out her career as a waitress. A waitress! How could you imagine I would have any interest in hearing your opinion about a complicated subject like bio-weapons research? Or any other political topic, for that matter. It would be laughable if it wasn't so insulting."

Helen dug the palms of her hands into the bed linens, where she could better conceal the tremors. "It's true I was a waitress and a dancer in a casino, but that doesn't mean I can't have opinions on current events. I read the papers and the weekly business journals. I watch news program on TV. And I was pretty smart in high school—"

"Sure you were." Franklin's voice oozed sarcasm. "Which, presumably, is why you ended up working as a waitress. There's a career that takes a real high IQ."

"Being a good waitress requires a lot more skill than you might think. Not to mention that it's incredibly hard work. I earned every nickel of my tips." Helen stopped short. They'd had this conversation before, and Franklin wasn't interested in hearing what he termed her excuses for not going to college. He didn't care that her father had lost yet another job due to his violent temper right as she was graduating from high school, with the result that money had been even tighter than usual in the Kouros household. With her father on unemployment, and making little effort to find a job, she'd given up her dream of going to college. Instead, she'd worked as a waitress to save money so that Philip, her brilliant younger brother, would have the educational opportunities she'd missed. But Philip was yet another touchy subject as far as Franklin was concerned, and so Helen steered away from it.

She drew in a steadying breath. "Franklin, I only want to make our marriage work better. Tell me what I can do to make things right between us—"

"Quit trying to be somebody you're not," Franklin said, striding toward the bedroom door. "Look, I told you already I'm late for a meeting. I don't have time for any more of this stupid discussion. Just keep in mind that if I'd wanted to marry a college professor, I sure as hell wouldn't have gone looking for my wife in the Swansong casino."

That sounded as if he'd been actively looking for a wife when he came to the Swansong, as opposed to being swept off his feet by her charms, which is what he'd claimed had happened. "What do you mean exactly?" she asked.

He made a dismissive gesture, brushing away her

question. "I mean that the way you can please me is to keep your opinions to yourself and fix a happy smile on your face whenever you're with me and my friends."

"I've been doing that for two years. My smile is wearing thin."

"Yeah, well, work on it, babe. And while you're at it, find something to wear to the reception tonight that isn't so damn dowdy. Show a bit of tit and ass, for God's sake. That's what my donors are interested in, not your brains. Such as they are." He walked out of their bedroom without waiting for her to reply, slamming the door behind him.

The noise of the slammed door reverberated around the plushly carpeted bedroom. Helen remained seated on the edge of the bed because her legs were too shaky to support her. She stared dry-eyed into space, her stomach churning. The soft, muted gold of the bedroom walls didn't provide its usual solace, and even the drapes with their interesting design of autumn leaves didn't cheer her up. Attractive surroundings were a very poor substitute for a friendly husband and a happy marriage, she reflected bleakly.

She'd been so excited and hopeful for the first six months of their marriage, determined to justify her decision to marry for security rather than passion. The freedom from a demanding work schedule had afforded her the time to read voraciously, and she'd been thrilled when Franklin had given her a charge card for one of Denver's most prestigious stores and told her to buy a new wardrobe. She was feminine enough to have enjoyed every minute of shopping for the clothes and accessories that she hoped would be part of the magic act that changed her from Helen

Kouros, casino dancer, into Helen Gettys, poised and elegant wife of the junior senator from Colorado.

Then there had been the pleasure of transforming Franklin's eight thousand square foot mansion in Cherry Hills into a home that was less garish and more welcoming. She studied every home decorating magazine she could lay hands on, spent hours in the public library researching theories of interior design, and toured furniture galleries searching for ideas. Franklin gave her permission to make whatever changes she pleased, and she strove to do him proud with a makeover that was both tasteful and pleasing to the eye.

She'd taken down the stiff draperies with their pouffy valences and tasseled tiebacks, substituting colorful linens that complemented the bright skies and almost permanent sunshine of the Denver area. She painted the stark white walls in soft, muted pastels to make the overall effect more tranquil, and warmed the main reception rooms by adding area rugs to the slate tiles and polished parquet floors.

She'd worked hard to keep her redecorating costs down and Franklin had never complained about the bills, giving her a false illusion of partnership in the marriage. But he'd never complimented her on the new decor, either, and she'd come to the conclusion months ago that her efforts to turn the house into a home had never especially pleased him. He was not a man who paid much attention to his surroundings, so provided she kept herself busy, didn't attempt to get involved in his public life and was available for sex whenever he slept at home, he didn't much care what she did with the rest of her time.

Helen could almost laugh at her naiveté when she

remembered the dreams she'd harbored about the life
she would lead when she became Franklin's wife. She
wasn't just going to be a perfect mother to their beautiful children, she was going to transform herself into
his political partner and become a brilliant hostess as
well. Best of all, she was going to be secure. No more
teetering on the brink of the financial abyss; no more
emotionally draining struggles to keep her brother
safe and hold her family together.

She'd imagined hosting intimate little dinner parties in their lovely dining room—dinner parties that
would become the high point of Denver's social
scene, with all the local luminaries competing for in-
vitations. She'd daydreamed about entertaining
Franklin's political colleagues, as well as local business leaders and interesting people from the world of
music, theater and the arts.

The intimate little dinners never happened, of
course. She had no idea what sort of parties Franklin
threw when he was in Washington, but here in Colorado he limited his entertainment to big cocktail parties, with hired caterers, plentiful booze and so many
guests that nobody ever actually had a chance to talk
to anybody else. Which was probably just as well,
since Helen was instructed before every event that she
was to keep her mouth shut except to smile. This
morning's instruction about finding a revealing dress
wasn't a new one, either. Franklin wanted people to
notice his wife, but not for her warm personality or
interesting ideas.

The sad truth was that she and Franklin had shared
a relationship for the past year that barely deserved
the name of marriage, but this morning's argument
had still caught Helen off guard, revealing the full,

sordid depths of the chasm between them. She forced herself to acknowledge reality: her marriage to Franklin Gettys, United States senator from Colorado, was a hollow sham, held in place by a rancid glue of threats and fear. Whatever she and Franklin had hoped to find in each other when they exchanged vows two years ago had long since vanished. The only question that remained was what she proposed to do with the rest of her life.

She would suggest to Franklin tonight that they should seek professional marriage counseling, Helen decided. She'd made the suggestion before and been scornfully rejected, but it was the only hope she could see for building something worthwhile out of the ruins of their current relationship. And what if he refused yet again? She drew in a long, slow breath. If Franklin refused to participate in counseling, she saw no alternative except to file for divorce.

Divorce was an ugly, frightening word, and Helen recognized that she wasn't nearly as strong a woman right now as she had been when she and Franklin married. Two years of listening to her husband tell her that she was ignorant and not very sexy had taken their toll. But she comforted herself with the knowledge that she'd managed to take care of herself since she was eighteen, and she could surely take charge of her life again if she set her mind to it. She wouldn't allow Franklin's constant put-downs to intimidate her into believing she was no longer capable of supporting herself financially. As for her appearance...well, Franklin complained all the time that she had no taste in clothes and didn't know how to make the most of what he termed her assets, but she wasn't hopelessly unattractive. Was she?

Almost scared at what might confront her, Helen walked over to the mirror and stared at her reflection. She pulled a face, not nearly as happy with what she saw as Franklin had been with his appearance a few minutes earlier. Her light brown hair was expensively cut and artfully streaked with blond highlights, but her gray-green eyes had lost the sparkle that had been her trademark at the Swansong casino. Her cheeks had no color and she was too thin—a better problem than being overweight, maybe, but she'd always liked the fact that her body was athletically fit rather than fashionably emaciated. She was twenty-eight years old, and the unpleasant truth was that she could only have been mistaken for a woman in her mid-thirties with no problem at all.

Helen turned away from the mirror, invigorated rather than depressed. Improving her physical appearance was surely one of the easiest tasks confronting her. Instead of lamenting that she looked a wreck, she needed to work on getting back the gleam in her eyes and the glow in her complexion. After all, how hard could it be to put on seven or eight pounds? Finding a way to consume more calories was surely a problem most women would love to have!

She grinned, her mood lifting further. She was an optimist by nature, and Franklin hadn't yet succeeded in leeching all the natural exuberance out of her. Later on this morning, she was having lunch with her brother, Philip, at their favorite Italian restaurant in LoDo. She would order ravioli with cream sauce, and tiramisu for dessert. That should make an excellent start on gaining back the missing pounds.

And tonight she'd lay down her ultimatum to her husband. Counseling or divorce. His choice, but it had to be one or the other. She'd finally stopped being a doormat, Helen decided. After two years of trying to transform herself into the meek, subservient slave Franklin Gettys wanted, she was going to abandon that destructive quest and become her own woman once again.

She felt better already.

CHAPTER TWO

PHILIP WAS ALREADY at the restaurant when Helen arrived. He'd taken advantage of the warm May day to request a table outside on the sidewalk, and he was studying the menu in the shade cast by a brightly-striped awning.

He was looking terrific, she saw with relief. His face had acquired the start of a summer tan, his thick brown hair shone and his huge dark eyes—so much like their mother's—glowed with animation. It was almost a month since she'd seen her brother and he appeared visibly fitter than at their last meeting.

"Hi, Nell, how's it going?" Philip stood up and gave her a quick hug before slouching back into his chair and trying to find somewhere to tuck his feet. He was tall, like her, with most of the length in his legs, and the small ironwork table didn't allow either of them much room.

"I'm fine, thanks." It was automatic for Helen to present a cheerful facade to her brother. He found his own burdens hard enough to carry, so she never attempted to have him shoulder hers as well. "How about you, Phil? You're looking great."

"I'm feeling pretty damn good, too." He shoved up the sleeves of his cotton sweater, then flexed his arms, displaying a modest set of biceps. "I've been working out, as you can see. In fact, I've been hitting the gym four or five times a week.''

Helen squeezed his forearm and rolled her eyes in mock awe of his new muscles. "Wow, I'm seriously impressed!"

"You should be." He flashed her a teasing grin, reminding her that he was heart-stoppingly good-looking when he was healthy. "You can call me Iron Man."

She groaned, but gave his forearm another admiring squeeze. "Schwarzenegger had better look out. You're about to steal his glory."

"Yeah, you're right." Philip's grin deepened. "With a couple of thousand more hours in the gym, I could be serious competition for good ole Arnold." He rolled down his sleeves and handed her a menu. "I'm going to order my own personal pan pizza with extra cheese. How about you? Are you sticking with your usual rabbit food?"

She shook her head. "Today I'm thinking pasta. Lots of pasta."

Her brother turned his thumbs up in silent approval, and tipped his chair back, enjoying the moment. His robust appetite was another positive sign, Helen mused. When he craved a hit, eating was just about the last thing on his mind, and at the height of his addiction, he'd become terrifyingly thin.

Her brother had been clean and sober for two years, ever since he'd checked himself into rehab just after her marriage, but Helen still hadn't forgotten the nightmare period when every phone call had set her heart pounding as she wondered if this was going to be the occasion when the police informed her that

Philip had skipped out of the latest residential program and was dead of an overdose.

Helen pushed the bad memories aside and twisted
around so that her back was to the sun and she could
study the menu. Her heart gave a little lurch when
she recognized the man sitting at a window table inside the restaurant. It was Ryan Benton, accompanied
by an exceptionally pretty young woman with fluffy
blond curls. She felt a spurt of totally irrational resentment of the blonde, which she turned into a silent
question. What was Ryan doing in Denver? She
hadn't seen him since the night she'd accepted Franklin's proposal, and it was disconcerting to realize how
her breathing quickened and her pulse raced at the
mere sight of him. It had always been that way when
she and Ryan were together. One glimpse was all it
took for her body to respond, reacting to some sub-
liminal sexual urge that was all the more powerful
because it was primitive, visceral and totally outside
the realm of rational analysis.

Unfortunately, an intense physical attraction was
pretty much the sum of what she and Ryan had
shared. When Franklin had first asked her out on a
date, Ryan had been disbelieving to hear that she'd
agreed to go with him to a reception at the governor's
mansion in Denver. Ryan's disbelief escalated to
scorn when she accepted Franklin's offer of marriage
a mere eight weeks after that first date.

Ryan had been scathing about her decision but
Helen knew that her motivation had been much more
complicated than just wanting a rich, successful husband. Even now, with her "sensible" marriage crumbling around her, she still believed that sex, however
fabulous and mind-blowing, wasn't much of a foun-

dation for any long-term relationship. Her goals in life had been quite different from Ryan's, and she still believed that you needed shared goals if a marriage was going to work out in the long term. Ryan had been dedicated to his career as small-town sheriff, and she'd yearned to live in a big city and make an impact on the world. He was casual, laid-back, easy going. She was intense, focused, goal-oriented. They hadn't shared any rapport outside the bedroom, and she'd told him as much when he asked her to marry him, a couple of weeks before she started dating Franklin.

"So we'll spend our lives in bed," Ryan had said, slanting her one of the smiles that made her heart melt and her toes curl. He'd wrapped his arm around her shoulders and Helen had felt herself weaken, snuggling against his chest, breathing in the scent of his skin and allowing a blissful sensation of homecoming to wash over her. Then common sense had returned and she'd been angry—with him and with herself. It seemed that Ryan only had to smile his sexy smile and all her own ambitions melted under the heat of his charm. She had never understood why he tempted her so much. She knew from bitter experience that life was a serious business, with difficult challenges waiting to ambush any married couple. How could she face those challenges with Ryan as a husband, when they never did anything when they were together except laugh and have fun? What kind of a basis was that for marriage?

She and Ryan had parted hurt and angry, and her feelings grew more raw, more painful as the days passed. It had seemed such a rewarding contrast when Franklin—*United States Senator Gettys*—asked her out on a date. Unlike Ryan, Franklin had no sense of

humor, and they for sure didn't spend much time together laughing or having fun. But Helen had seen
that as a plus. She was fascinated by Franklin's ref-
erences to his work in the Senate, and hypnotized by
his casual mention of great national figures like Senator Edward Kennedy, Supreme Court Justice
Thomas Clarence and Donald Rumsfeld, the secretary
of defense. How amazing it would be to meet such
important people face-to-face! Helen had been infu-
riated by Ryan's sarcastic comment that she needed
to blink the starshine out of her eyes so that she could
look behind the job title to the man himself. If Franklin Gettys hadn't been a senator, would she still be
interested in him, Ryan demanded.

She knew the answer to that question now, Helen
realized, suppressing a grimace, although it had taken
her much too long to realize the truth. She'd been
foolish enough to think that marrying a senator would
give her the sense of personal fulfillment she craved.
After two painful years of marriage she finally realized that fulfillment could only come from within. A
sense of purpose in life wasn't something you could
suck in from the outside because your spouse had an
important career. You earned fulfillment by your own
efforts. She sure had learned that lesson the hard way.

Helen was still staring at Ryan's profile—fortunately he hadn't noticed her—when she felt her
brother's hand closing over hers. "What's up, Nell?"
he asked quietly. "Not to beat around the bush, you
look like hell."

"I do?" Helen gave a wry smile, tearing her gaze
away from Ryan Benton and burying the erotic memories deep in the past where they belonged. "And I

thought this shade of moss green was especially flattering.''

"It's not your clothes," Philip said. "They look great. Very fashionable, as far as I can tell. It's you, Nell. Your eyes have got that look they had right after Mom died. Like you're lost somewhere real unpleasant between sad and haunted."

She was surprised that her brother had noticed anything amiss, partly because she'd always been good at hiding what she was feeling. Mostly, though, she was amazed that Philip had progressed far enough with his recovery that he was finally sensitive once again to the signs of another person's unhappiness. It had to be at least five years since he'd last been sufficiently outward-looking to pay real attention to subtle clues about her mood. Or anyone else's mood, for that matter.

Helen started to protest that she felt fine, just a little tired, then cut off the threadbare lies. If Philip was far enough into recovery to notice when she was upset, he deserved to hear at least a modified version of the truth about her crumbling marriage.

"It's been a rough morning," she said. "Franklin and I had a humdinger of a row, which is something we seem to be doing quite often these days. On the rare occasions when he's home, that is."

Philip held her gaze. "Anything I can help with?" he asked.

She managed a smile, although she was afraid it wasn't very convincing. "Thanks for the offer, but this is something we have to work out ourselves."

"Okay, but I make a real good listener." He gave a wry grimace. "All those years of expensive group therapy have to be good for something, you know."

Helen was surprised at how badly she wanted to confide in her brother, but habit won out and she shaped a bland response that barely hinted at the details of the morning's ugly scene. "I guess the short version is that Franklin and I have very different views about what it means to have a committed, caring relationship. I'm starting to get a little tired of making excuses and pretending things will work out in the end if I just have patience."

Philip's voice became husky with sympathy. "You've found out about the other women," he said quietly, as if stating the obvious. "I often wondered if I should tell you, and then I decided it wasn't my place to butt in. I'm glad I don't have to keep pretending anymore."

Helen put down the menu and stared at her brother in stupefied silence. What was Philip talking about? What other women? He seemed to be suggesting that Franklin had been unfaithful, not just once, but often.

Philip took one look at her and muttered a curse under his breath. "Damn, I've stepped right into it. You didn't know. You and Franklin were fighting about something else this morning. Jeez, I'm real sorry, Nell. Forget I said anything."

Her tongue finally unglued itself from the roof of her mouth. "You have nothing to apologize for."

"Yeah, sure I do. I should have made certain we were talking about the same thing before I shot off my mouth. Anyway, I'm probably mistaken." Philip started to talk at random about the menu, the weather and one of the kids he was tutoring at the drop-in center where he worked.

Helen finally cut him off, unable to bear his efforts to pretend he hadn't said what they both knew he'd said. "How do you know Franklin has been seeing other women?" she asked.

Seeing. There was a pathetic euphemism if ever she heard one.

"I know a couple of people who know people," Philip said vaguely, obviously reluctant to be more specific. "Some of the stories filter back to me because I'm your brother, I guess."

At gut level, Helen had depressingly little difficulty in believing that her husband had been unfaithful. But on a more intellectual level, it struck her as unlikely. Franklin counted on the support of conservatives who were big on family and traditional values. He simply couldn't afford to risk alienating such an important part of his constituency. Could he?

"It's most likely just rumors," she said. "Franklin's handsome and he has a friendly manner in a social setting. People might be mistaking ordinary friendship for something more."

"Yes, I expect that's it," Philip said. "You're right. Of course you are. People love to invent gossip and scandals."

His eagerness to agree with her had the perverse effect of convincing Helen that the stories he'd heard had been embroidered with more than enough colorful details to convince him they were true. Her heart started to pound in double time, but she covered her agitation with a rueful smile. "You are one lousy liar, little brother. You don't for a moment think these are false rumors, do you?"

"Here comes our waitress," Philip said, with almost comical relief at the welcome interruption. "I'm hungrier than a hibernating bear. How about you?"

Helen ordered mushroom ravioli, although she was

afraid it might choke her if she actually had to eat more than a token mouthful, and added an order of iced raspberry tea. Her brother ordered pizza and Coke.

Their server disappeared back into the restaurant. Ryan Benton, she noticed, had gotten up to leave with his companion. Instead of feeling relief at his departure, the knot of tension in the pit of her stomach tightened. Her emotional system seemed to be totally out of whack, unable to cope with the impact of too many shocks in too short a space of time. There was no justification for her crazy sensation of regret, much less for her sudden yearning to hear his voice again.

Hiding a sigh, she turned her attention back to her brother, ignoring the fact that he looked ready to slide under the table rather than answer her questions. "I know you're hoping I'll gloss over your comment about Franklin's extramarital affairs," she said. "Sorry, Phil, you're out of luck. I need to know the truth. Have you just heard vague rumors about Franklin being unfaithful, or are the stories more specific?"

Philip sent her a wry glance "You're not going to let this subject drop, are you?"

"Absolutely not, so you might as well put us both out of our misery."

Her brother stared into the distance for a few seconds, then spoke rapidly. "I'm good friends with Miranda Parton. She volunteers quite a bit at the center, and I don't think she's the sort of person who likes to spread malicious gossip for no reason."

"Miranda Parton? Isn't she one of Franklin's staffers at his office here in Colorado?" Helen asked. "I remember meeting her once. She seemed competent, and very nice, too."

"She is competent and nice. And, yes, she worked for Franklin in his Denver office."

"But she doesn't work for him anymore?"

"No, she quit." Philip didn't elaborate. "According to Miranda, Franklin has affairs all the time. Not long-lasting affairs and never with his staff. Just weekends in the Bahamas, or a quick ski trip to Aspen, that sort of thing. One of the women she mentioned him being involved with was Natalie Rodriguez."

"I see." Natalie was the weather forecaster for a local TV channel and a minor Denver celebrity in her own right. Trust Franklin to be smart enough to limit his adultery to women who were public figures and not likely to sue him for sexual harassment. Helen took a sip of ice water. "Doesn't it bother Franklin's staff that they're working for a man who preaches family values and yet is consistently unfaithful?"

"It's possible most of Franklin's staff doesn't realize what's going on," Philip said. "Miranda was responsible for his scheduling so she was bound to notice things that the others didn't."

"Senators have to leave phone numbers where they can be contacted in an emergency. Most of his staffers would surely know if Franklin was spending the weekend in the Bahamas, or escorting a perky ski bunny up to Aspen. Why would they cover for him? Why not leak a juicy story to a hungry journalist?"

Philip shrugged. "Political staff tend to be super-loyal, I guess. That's why they're hired in the first place—because they agree with the views of the man they work for."

"And you think staffers who support Franklin's conservative views on family values would remain loyal to him even though he's cheating on his wife at the same time as he's preaching to the media about the sanctity of marriage?''

"Maybe." Philip swirled the melting ice cubes in his glass of water, hesitant to meet Helen's eyes for the first time that morning. "The thing is, Nell, Franklin has spread the word far and wide that you're not willing to participate in his public life and your aloofness annoys his supporters. According to Miranda, he's often hinted that you're not willing to participate in his…um…private life, either, and so it's possible they make excuses for his sexual adventures on the grounds that you're not an…um…proper wife."

Helen felt fury bubbling up from deep inside. "Franklin tells people that I'm not willing to play any role in his public life?"

"Well, yes." Philip's eyes narrowed and he looked up from his ice-stirring. "Why are you sounding so annoyed, Nell? You know you hardly ever attend any political functions with Franklin. In fact, I was wondering myself if you would do more with him when he gets geared up for next year's reelection campaign."

It was too humiliating to admit that she wasn't allowed to attend most events because her husband considered her an embarrassment. Recalling how just this morning Franklin had summarily rejected her plea to be allowed to play a role in his political career, Helen fought to keep hold of her temper. The effort not to shout and yell left acid burning in her stomach.

"Franklin's exaggerating," she said with hard-won calm. "I attend quite a few functions with him when he's in Denver." Somehow she managed to sound like a sane person, instead of a foaming-at-the-mouth banshee, which was how she felt. ''In fact, I'm going to a huge fund-raising reception with him tonight. I sounded annoyed because I resent the implication that I'm not willing to do my share of handshaking, that's all. I attend every single function that Franklin ever invites me to.''

''I can see why the rumors that you're uncooperative would make you mad. I know how friendly and outgoing you are even if Franklin's staffers don't.''

Her reaction might be irrational, but Helen was almost more hurt that Franklin had distorted the truth about her willingness to be involved in his career than she was about the fact that he'd been unfaithful. When she recalled the dozens of times she'd begged to be allowed a role in his public life, his pretense that she refused to participate seemed as much of a betrayal as his adultery.

The waitress arrived carrying Philip's pizza still sizzling on a metal platter, and Helen's ravioli steaming in a colorful ceramic bowl. Helen was grateful for the excuse to remain silent during the ritual offering of freshly ground pepper and grated Parmesan cheese. She needed a few minutes to recover her equilibrium.

''Enjoy your lunch!'' the waitress said as she dashed off.

Helen stirred sauce into her pasta, giving her brother a decent imitation of a smile. ''This smells even better than it looks. I didn't get breakfast this morning, so I'm really hungry.''

''Don't, Nell.'' Philip spoke with sudden forcefulness. ''Don't pretend it doesn't matter that the bastard's betrayed you.''

Helen stared unseeingly at her meal, then forced herself to swallow a piece of ravioli as an excuse not to answer her brother right away. She gradually absorbed the knowledge that the anger she felt toward Franklin was intense, but it was barely tinged by grief. What a sad commentary on their travesty of a marriage, she thought, that she could contemplate its end with an emotion that felt closer to relief than anything else.

Philip wiped his fingers on his napkin, and rested his hand over hers once again. "Okay, Nell, lecture time. You're looking really down in the dumps, so I'll repeat the advice you've given me a hundred times. Don't blame yourself for other people's bad behavior. You're a good wife to Franklin, and you're not responsible for the fact that he's a lousy husband. The guy's a fool not to realize what a huge asset you could be to his political career, but you aren't to blame for his womanizing. No way, no how."

She smiled, albeit a little wanly. "Thanks for the reminder."

"You're welcome. The doctor is available for consultations any time." Philip took a hearty bite of a second slice of pizza and Helen concentrated for a few minutes on eating enough ravioli to prevent her brother taking her to task.

This was a major role reversal, she thought wryly. If there was any silver lining to the cloud of discovering that her husband had been routinely unfaithful, it would have to be the simultaneous discovery that Philip had his life so much together that he had been able to conceal from her any hint of what he knew about Franklin's adultery. Moreover, he was demonstrating the sort of care and concern for her well-being that she had never before been able to expect from him.

"Divorce him, Nell." Philip spoke into the silence. "I know it's not for me to tell you how to run your life, but you deserve somebody so much better than Franklin Gettys."

She was able to laugh at that, struck by how ridiculous Franklin would find it for anyone to believe that she—the former waitress and casino dancer—deserved a better husband than him—the rich and handsome United States senator. But her brother was right, Helen reflected. She deserved a better husband than Franklin Gettys, and tonight, after the fund-raiser, she was going to tell him so.

CHAPTER THREE

HELEN HAD BEEN SMILING with such determination for so long that she was afraid the muscles of her face must be locked in place by now. A portly man, with champagne in one hand and a stuffed artichoke heart in the other, nodded to her in greeting.

She read his name tag and nodded back. "Good evening, Mr. Tazio, thank you so much for coming out tonight despite the rain. I know how much Franklin appreciates your support."

"Great to be here. A good man, your husband. He's right on the money with his insistence that we need taxes cut across the board."

"He will be very pleased to know you approve of his position, Mr. Tazio." Smile glued in place, she moved on.

She greeted the CEO of one of Denver's largest companies, but slipped away before the woman could engage her in conversation. For once, Helen's efforts to avoid speaking to Franklin's guests had nothing to do with his instructions; she simply didn't trust herself to utter anything beyond total platitudes without spewing out some acid comment about her husband that she would later regret. If there was anything she owed Franklin at this point, she thought it might be the dignity of a quiet, hassle-free divorce.

Slipping around a tub of Norfolk pines to escape

the CEO, Helen found herself face-to-face with the dean of the Business School at the University of Colorado. Definitely a case of out of the frying pan into the fire. She found her smile again. "Good evening, Professor De Laurens, thank you so much for coming out tonight, despite the rain. I know how much Franklin appreciates your support."

The dean scowled. "I'm not sure your husband's going to have my support for much longer. I don't understand why he continues to endorse massive increases in funding for biological weapons. I've tried to discuss the issue with him on a couple of occasions, and he's just not willing to listen. Your husband can be a mighty stubborn man, Mrs. Gettys."

"Yes, I know he can!" Helen chuckled, as if Franklin were a lovable curmudgeon rather than a narrow-minded bigot. "I've lobbied him about biological weapons, too, professor. I'm hopeful that he'll shift his position before the next election. Just this morning, we were discussing the issue of safety risks, and the problem of protecting stockpiles of biological agents from terrorist attack."

Well, it was true they'd discussed it, Helen thought ruefully, even if Franklin had informed her that she didn't have the slightest clue what she was talking about.

"Protecting the stockpile is one of my major concerns, too," the dean said, looking at her approvingly. "Although I have problems with the ethics of this sort of weapon, as well. We're the most powerful nation in the world, with military technology that's at least five years ahead of the rest of the world. Why would your husband be such a strong advocate of weapons that move us back toward a type of warfare that was condemned as barbaric almost a hundred years ago, at the end of World War I? I'm no pacifist. I understand the need for a strong defense. But we need to be gearing ourselves toward twenty-first century weapons. We need more smart bombs and unmanned planes, weapons that can destroy tactical targets and government buildings. We don't need to be using germ warfare to wipe out innocent populations who are probably more opposed to their tyrannical governments than we are.''

"That's exactly how I feel," Helen said, momentarily forgetting that she wasn't allowed to give voice to her opinions. "Believe me, professor, I share your views. In my opinion, the inherent risks of the project outweigh the advantage of high-tech jobs for our state."

"Well, I'm sure you're the most effective lobbyist I could ever have for my cause," the dean said, giving her a quick smile. "How could Franklin possibly resist such a delightful combination of brains and beauty?"

It had been so long since a man had paid her a compliment that it took Helen a moment or two to absorb the praise. Then it registered. The dean of the business school had said she was brainy! Flustered, she was still searching for an appropriate reply when she heard the sound of Franklin's voice, booming behind her.

"Now what mischief are you and my wife brewing up, Thomas?" he asked.

The dean shook hands with Franklin. "No mischief at all. Your charming wife was just assuring me that I can hope for a modification in your position on bio-weapons research before we get to the end of the political year.''

''Was she now?'' Franklin smiled broadly, but the glance he shot toward Helen was hot with fury. ''Well, I can't argue with a lady now, can I? Especially when that lady is my wife.'' He gave a chuckle that sounded amazingly good-humored, although Helen wasn't deceived. She'd not only disobeyed instructions about talking to the guests, she'd broached the subject of biochemical weapons, which seemed an especially sore spot with Franklin for some reason.

Fortunately, he was too smart to insult her in public. Instead, he half turned so that he could draw forward a man who had been standing slightly behind his left shoulder. She recognized that he was making the introduction to put an end to her conversation with the dean, but nobody else would have realized the motive for his maneuver.

''Helen, honey, this is Ryan Benton. He's not only a detective with our wonderful police force right here in Denver, he's from Silver Springs, where you and I first met.''

Her heart started to race and she felt hot color rise into her cheeks. More than two years had passed since she last saw Ryan, and now she'd seen him twice in one day.

''What a coincidence,'' she murmured, keeping her gaze fixed firmly on Franklin. ''It's a small world, isn't it?''

''Sure is, honey.'' Franklin beamed at her as if he thought she was the most beautiful, talented woman in the world. He had the politician's knack for displaying whatever emotion he thought would please his audience, and since Thomas De Laurens approved of her, he expressed approval, too. "Ryan, meet my lovely wife, Helen."

Helen had about ten seconds to adjust her expression to one of polite neutrality. "Mr. Benton, it's a pleasure to meet you."

Ryan stepped forward to shake her hand. He was still tall, still lean and he still had thick, light brown hair and hazel eyes, but she knew at once that it was only the physical characteristics that remained the same. The man standing in front of her had lost his easygoing, laughing approach to the world's folly, that much was clear. Next month he would be thirty-five years old, and he looked as if he'd been stripped of any last tiny remnant of youthful indiscretion years ago. It was impossible to imagine this austere-faced man lying in bed next to her, smiling as he suggested that they could spend the rest of their lives right there, in each other's arms.

"Mrs. Gettys is forgetting that we already met," he said coolly. "We knew each other before she married you, Senator."

"Is that so?" Franklin's gaze narrowed.

"Oh, of course! He was the sheriff of Silver Springs," Helen said hurriedly, hoping her voice didn't shake. "How are you, Ryan? It's been a long time."

"I'm well. Enjoying my job in the big city. How about you, Helen? Is life as Mrs. Franklin Gettys everything you hoped for?"

"Everything and more," she lied, avoiding Franklin's gaze. Despite Ryan's expression of cool courtesy, she could feel tension shooting back and forth between the two of them with such force that she could only assume everyone else would be equally aware of it. She should learn to be more careful of what she wished for, Helen reflected wryly. At lunchtime she'd been yearning to hear Ryan's voice again. Now she wished fervently that she could have avoided this encounter.

"Being a senator's wife is very challenging," she said, with what she hoped was just the right amount of casual sincerity. For some reason, it seemed very important not to let Ryan know what a total screwup she'd made of her life.

"And I'm sure you rise beautifully to all the challenges," Thomas De Laurens said, smiling at her. "You're a lucky man, Franklin, to have such a lovely and intelligent wife."

"So Helen keeps telling me." Franklin laughed to show that he was making a little joke.

"I've been trying to persuade your husband that we need more cops on the beat in big cities," Ryan said, his eyes directed straight at her. "I've been trying to persuade him to throw his weight behind a bill that's currently languishing in the Senate—one that would provide extra funds directly to cities."

Helen looked at her husband because that was safer than continuing to gaze hypnotically at Ryan. "And do you plan to support the bill, Franklin?" she asked.

"I haven't decided," Franklin said curtly, his public good humor wearing thin at the edges. "Obviously I'm proud of the great work done by our Denver police officers, and I know they could use more help. On the other hand, the citizens of this country already shell out too much of their hard-earned money paying taxes to the government. We have to think long and hard before we politicians decide to spend more of John Q. Citizen's money."

"Maybe our government could stockpile fewer military weapons and use the money to pay for more police officers," Helen suggested. What the hell. She was going to get in trouble anyway, so she might as well say what she really thought.

"Excellent suggestion," Thomas De Laurens said. "You should listen to your wife, Senator."

If looks could kill, the one Franklin shot at her would have been instantly lethal, Helen decided. Without speaking to her directly, or responding to the dean's comment, Franklin put his arm around De Laurens's shoulder and guided him away with the excuse that he wanted to introduce him to somebody from the mayor's office.

Helen was relieved that Franklin had moved on without making a public scene, but she wished he hadn't taken the dean with him. Being left alone to face Ryan Benton came pretty close to the top of her list of activities to be avoided. Not because she expected Ryan to be cruel or sarcastic, despite his earlier coolness. Rather she was afraid of the opposite, that he would be too kind. Right now, she was balanced on such a knife edge of emotional tension that she was afraid kindness might send her flying into the abyss.

She needn't have worried. The two years since her marriage to Franklin had apparently changed Ryan as much as they'd changed her. In the past, his hazel eyes had always been warm, with laughter lurking not very far beneath the surface. Earlier his gaze had been courteous, if distant. Now his gaze raked over her with a cynicism that was entirely alien to the open and friendly man she'd known back in Silver Springs.

"You're looking...elegant," he said finally. "You

have that high-gloss, polished look that women only manage to acquire when they're spending a fortune on their appearance.''

"You make high-gloss and polished sound like insults.''

"I did? I apologize. Believe me, Mrs. Gettys, that was entirely unintentional.''

The sarcasm in his voice provoked a welcome flash of anger. Welcome because anger was a much more comfortable emotion than regret. "Did you come here tonight merely to insult me, Ryan, or was there some more worthwhile purpose to your visit?''

"I came to see you,'' he said. "My sister wanted me to let you know that she's just landed her first dancing role on Broadway. She's in a new musical that's opening at the end of this month, and she says you were her role model and her inspiration, so she owes you big time.''

"Becky's landed a job on Broadway! Oh my God, that's such fantastic news!'' Helen was so excited she forgot all her inhibitions and worries about how she had to behave now she was Mrs. Gettys. She flung her arms around Ryan's neck and hugged him tight, laughing up at him as if the past two years had never happened. "I always knew Becky would make it. You and your mom must be so proud.''

"Not so as you'd notice,'' Ryan said, his coldness dissolving into one of his once-familiar smiles. "Mom's only spent every day for the past two weeks trying to find the perfect outfit to wear for opening night.''

Helen laughed. "Oh, I wish I could be there for opening night. It would be such fun.''

"We'd love to have you join us if you can find the time to get away. Becky would be thrilled."

Helen felt a surge of such intense longing that it was physically painful. If only Ryan knew how badly she wanted to accept his invitation, she thought. If only he knew how absolutely impossible it was for her to do something so harmless. What would he say, she wondered, if he realized that in the two years of her marriage, she'd only left Franklin's house in Cherry Hills to attend a few political fund-raisers and to go shopping? All other outings were forbidden, as she'd found out to her cost when she visited the Half Spur last weekend.

She suddenly became aware of the fact that she was still in Ryan's arms and that several nearby guests were looking at them with undisguised interest. Not to mention the fact that she could feel a prickle at the back of her neck that meant her husband was staring at her from across the room. She quickly stepped out of Ryan's arms, the happiness and laughter draining out of her as she transformed herself once more into the "senator's wife."

"What is it?" Ryan asked. "Is something the matter?"

"No, nothing." She found her professional smile again, and flashed it at Ryan. "Will you please tell Becky how delighted I am for her success? I am truly thrilled. I'll be looking forward to reading the reviews."

"Yes, of course." He was retreating as fast as she was into cool formality. Helen tried not to feel regret for the lost moment of intimacy.

"Will you excuse me, Ryan? It's been wonderful to see you again, but Franklin is sending me one of those silent husband-and-wife messages to please come and rescue him. I have to go.''

Ryan's expression took a step further toward polite neutrality, and he inclined his head in an impersonal parting gesture. ''The senator is lucky to have you available for rescue duty. Goodbye, Helen. See you in another couple of years, maybe.''

''Or sooner I hope.'' She smiled blindly and walked away, wondering if he had even the faintest clue what it had cost her to produce that seemingly casual parting remark.

CHAPTER FOUR

IN CONTRAST to his fit of temper that morning, Franklin wasn't in an especially bad mood as he got ready for bed. The fund-raiser had been successful, adding a welcome hundred thousand dollars to his campaign coffers, and his speech had been well received. Basking in the afterglow of the applause and the compliments, his tone of voice was quite mild as he listed Helen's misdemeanors. Confident that she would be suitably submissive, he didn't even bother to check that she was paying attention as he wandered back and forth between the walk-in closet and the bedroom, sipping at a small snifter of brandy as he undressed.

Helen discovered it was almost soothing to let Franklin ramble on now that she had no interest in pleasing him, or putting things right between the two of them. Listening with less than half her attention, she occupied herself nipping off dead leaves from a philodendron plant she had placed to catch the morning sun in the deep bay window. It was hard to take Franklin's complaints seriously when his chief gripe seemed to be that she refused to dress like a bargain-priced whore. She wondered why in the world she had ever felt obligated to please a man who wanted her to display her breasts as a come-on for political donors.

Helen wrinkled her nose in silent disgust, waiting for her husband to pause so that she could get a word in edgewise. When she finally had an opening she spoke quickly, before he could start droning on again.

"Franklin, I want a divorce."

He swung around to stare at her in mute astonishment. He'd just taken off his shoes and he stood on one foot, with a black dress sock dangling from his hand, frozen by shock. His expression couldn't have been more amazed if he'd discovered a space invader with a deadly ray gun standing beside his bed.

"A divorce?" he said finally, as if he'd never heard the word and didn't understand what it meant. "What are you talking about?"

"I want a divorce," Helen said. "I'm sure you do, too—"

His shock gave way to anger. "What the hell have you been smoking? How dare you ask for a divorce? Have you lost your mind?"

"On the contrary," she said with amazing coolness. "I believe I've just come to my senses—"

"It sure doesn't sound like it! If you want a divorce, you need to see a mental health specialist! You're obviously too messed up to know when you have it easy!"

She shrugged, refusing to be intimidated. "Seriously, Franklin, when you think about the time we've spent together over the past eighteen months, we've barely had a single pleasant conversation. You're disappointed in me as a wife and, to be honest, I'm disappointed in you as a husband. The truth is, our views about marriage don't mesh too well."

She didn't specifically mention his infidelity, perhaps because Franklin's extramarital affairs were merely the final prod that had pushed her over the edge. They were a symptom of everything that was wrong with their marriage rather than the root cause of why she wanted the marriage to end.

Franklin balled his sock and tossed it in the direction of the laundry hamper, the action full of suppressed fury. He stormed across the room, his arms outstretched and his hands fisted. Helen jerked back, becoming aware of the fear lurking just beneath her calm facade. She licked her too-dry lips, and realized she was vibrating with tension. She had been psyching herself up all evening to tell Franklin that she wanted a divorce, and she'd dreaded the possibility that he would lose control. Franklin had never been physically abusive, but she'd been worried for months that the potential for violence was there, only a fraction beneath the surface.

His lips tightened when she flinched, but whether in annoyance or because he felt guilty about his aggressive gestures, she wasn't sure. He drew in a harsh breath, seeming to fight for mastery of his surging temper.

"You're not being reasonable," he said finally. "Why would you want a divorce? Do you remember what you were doing when I met you? For Christ's sake, do you remember what a hard, miserable life you were leading?"

She shook her head. "That's your perspective, Franklin. I didn't find my life hard or miserable. I love to dance. I enjoyed every minute of my work at the Swansong Casino—"

"I made you the wife of a United States senator, for God's sake! I gave you credit cards so that you can buy whatever clothes you want. Your financial future is secure—''

''My future is empty,'' she said flatly, noticing that Franklin mentioned money, but not companionship, much less love. ''You won't let me play any role in your life—''

''This is about the fact that you want to have children, isn't it? You're starting that damn fool argument again.''

''No, far from it.'' Helen shook her head vehemently. ''This has nothing to do with my desire to have children one day. In fact, the last thing I want right now is to complicate our situation by getting pregnant. This isn't a ploy on my part to change the terms of our marriage—''

''Then what is it?''

''A courtesy to you,'' she said quietly. ''I want to be upfront with you about my plans. I'm going to see a lawyer tomorrow and find out what steps I need to take to get a divorce. You don't have to worry about negative publicity. I promise I won't say anything to the media except that we remain good friends.''

In retrospect, she could only be thankful that Franklin had always been so adamant in his refusal to start a family. If they'd had a child, the decision to end their marriage would have been infinitely more complicated. As it was, the only lives that would need to be pieced together again were hers and Franklin's, which meant that the divorce would be painful, but not shattering for some innocent child caught in the middle of an adult disaster.

''I'm not willing to give you a divorce,'' Franklin said curtly. He took a monogrammed dressing gown from his closet and tied the tasseled belt with a vicious tug, seeming to feel that he needed to be clad in more than underclothes and a single sock in order to give weight to his words.

"But why not?" she asked, bewildered. "We're hardly ever together, and when we are, we fight. You can't possibly be happy with our relationship, Franklin."

"It suits me well enough," he said tersely.

"How can it? You complain all the time about how incompetent I am—"

"I'm not complaining. I'm trying to educate you, so that you can play an effective role as my wife."

"What role is that?" Her bewilderment was tinged with exasperation. "For Heaven's sake, Franklin, face reality. You have more of a relationship with your office assistants than you do with me!"

"What has that got to do with anything?" He gave a bark of disbelieving laughter. "If you think I'm going to allow myself to be divorced by a *waitress,* you can think again."

Of course! The lightbulb clicked on and Helen finally understood why Franklin was so resistant to the prospect of ending their marriage. He was furious that *she* was rejecting *him.* In their relationship, he was supposed to be the person who called all the shots and his opposition to the idea of a divorce was knee-jerk rather than reasoned. With luck, by tomorrow morning he'd be sighing with relief at the prospect of getting rid of a wife who'd proven so inadequate to his needs.

"I don't want to make things difficult for you," she said truthfully. "I'll find a discreet lawyer, and I'll tell him we want to file on the grounds of irretrievable breakdown of the marriage. I won't even tell the lawyer about your affairs—"

"What the hell are you talking about? What affairs? You know how dedicated I am to the values of clean family living. Who's been stuffing your head full of garbage about me having affairs?"

"There's no point in lying," she said, too disgusted to be angry. "I know you haven't been faithful, Franklin."

His face suffused with angry color. "Have you been following me?" he demanded. "Have you hired a private detective to spy on me? Is that why you went out to the Half Spur over the weekend?"

What in the world did the ranch have to do with their divorce? What bee did Franklin have buzzing around in his bonnet in regard to the Half Spur? "No, of course I haven't hired a detective—"

"Then don't leap to conclusions that aren't justified," he said.

"My conclusions are entirely justified." Helen still felt more weary than angry. "You can't keep taking women on vacations to the Caribbean, or up to your ski lodge in Aspen, and expect to keep your activities a permanent secret."

"The fact that I need a break from my demanding schedule doesn't mean I've been unfaithful—"

"Don't." She held up her hand, warding off his lies. "It so happens that Miranda Parton is an old friend of my brother's, and she confided the truth about why she'd left her job—"

"Because she was fired for incompetence," Franklin barked, but he gave a guilty start at the mention of Miranda's name. "Your brother needs to learn to keep his nose out of other people's business," he added.

"And you need to learn to keep your fly zippered if you're going to continue raking in the cash from all your conservative, family values friends," Helen shot back.

He stared at her in mute bewilderment, reminding her of what a doormat she'd been for the past two years. Unable to cope with a wife who answered him back, he gave up on his protestations of fidelity and changed the subject.

"You're not going to walk away from this marriage with any of my money, in case you have dreams of a fat alimony settlement. I trust you haven't forgotten you signed an ironclad prenup—"

"I hadn't forgotten. I don't care about your money, Franklin. I just want out of this sham of a marriage."

He was silent for a couple of minutes while he finished his brandy, and when he spoke again his manner was surprisingly conciliatory. "You're determined about this, aren't you?"

"Yes. Our marriage has been over for months." In any real sense, there had never been a marriage, Helen thought sadly. She gave a tiny sigh, full of regret for the might-have-beens. "Getting a divorce just makes the truth of our situation into a legal reality."

"I guess you're right," Franklin said slowly. "You're not the woman I thought you were when we married, so it's best if we end it. You've been a real disappointment to me. Totally inadequate for the role of my wife."

Franklin was already heaping the blame for the failure of their marriage on her, but Helen had anticipated that. She was just relieved to see that he was coming around to the idea of splitting up now that he'd gotten over his initial shock.

"Would you be willing to wait until next Friday before you make an appointment with your lawyer?" he continued, sounding almost mellow. "I could free up a couple of hours on Friday morning and we could have an initial consultation together. After all, as you mentioned, we both want to keep this breakup as low-key as possible. You don't want to be fending off the media any more than I do, right?"

"Right." It was one thing for Franklin to accept that divorce was the best choice for both of them, but Helen was mystified by his sudden eagerness to cooperate, even to the extent of coming to the lawyer with her. What was she missing here? Why the heck was he suddenly being so agreeable?

Perhaps he was afraid there were loopholes in the "ironclad" prenup she'd signed, Helen conjectured with a cynicism that was new to her. However, since she had no intention of making a fuss, claiming alimony or generating negative publicity for him, she had nothing to worry about. In fact, it would be in her own interests to cooperate as much as possible because she really didn't want to generate a lot of media attention. She just wanted to leave quietly and get on with rebuilding her life.

"If you think it would be helpful, I'll wait until Friday to start proceedings," she said, opening a drawer and taking out a clean nightgown, anxious to escape to another bedroom. "I'll let you know my lawyer's name tomorrow—"

Franklin spoke quickly. "You haven't chosen an attorney already, then? Or had any consultations about the terms of the divorce?"

"No," she said. "I haven't discussed the possibility of getting a divorce with anyone. I thought you should be the first person to know."

"I appreciate that," Franklin said. "An early appointment on Friday morning with the lawyer would be best for me," he added, his manner oddly abstracted, as if his thoughts were somewhere else.

"Then I'll arrange the appointment for nine or ten," she said.

"Thanks." He registered that she had taken a nightgown from the dresser drawer—by chance she'd pulled out something black and transparent she hadn't worn in months—and his eyes gleamed with sudden desire. "How about one last night of sex before we call it quits?" he asked, his voice thickening.

With difficulty, Helen managed to prevent herself shuddering with distaste. "I'm sorry…" No, that was a lie. She wasn't in the least sorry. "I don't think that would be a good idea," she said, her voice carefully neutral.

Franklin's eyes narrowed, but instead of launching into a tirade of abuse, all he asked was where she was going to sleep.

"I planned to use one of the guest rooms. But I could move into a hotel if you'd prefer that," she suggested.

"No!" His reaction was swift and forceful. Realizing that he'd raised his voice, he gave her a conciliatory smile and spoke more softly. "It's silly to waste money on a hotel, and people might gossip. This house is big enough that we never need to speak to each other even if we both continue living here until the divorce is final. We have three guest bedrooms. Pick whichever one you like."

The longer they talked, the more Franklin's reaction struck Helen as completely out of character. She hadn't expected him to feel deep sorrow at the ending of their marriage, but she would have expected him to make everything as difficult for her as he possibly could. Instead, he was being more agreeable than he'd been in months. Why?

She gave a mental shrug, dismissing the question. When you got right down to basics, she didn't really know very much about what made her husband tick. Obviously she'd never understood the first thing about his attitude toward relationships and commitment, or they would never have married.

Relieved and grateful that the divorce had been agreed upon with so little yelling and almost no hurtful recriminations, she said an awkward good-night and headed for the solitude of the most distant guest bedroom, where she cried herself to sleep, mourning the death of their marriage. A marriage, she realized in retrospect, that had never been much more than a wistful dream.

CHAPTER FIVE

THE PHONE CALL from her brother came early on Wednesday evening, while Helen was exploring the contents of the freezer in search of something for dinner. She had no idea where Franklin was, or what his plans were for the night, but she often hadn't known that sort of thing even before they agreed to divorce, so his absence wasn't surprising or bothersome.

She picked up the phone, her attention focused on whether to microwave frozen chicken casserole or lasagna with Parmesan topping. Since she'd decided to gain a couple of pounds, the lasagna was the way to go, she decided.

"Hello," she said, using her hip to close the freezer door.

"Nell? Thank God you picked up the phone." Philip's voice cracked with anxiety. "I'm at the police station in North Denver near 56th Avenue. Please, Nell, you have to get here right away."

Her stomach tied itself into an immediate knot. "What's the problem?" she asked, her voice hard. She couldn't manage to say anything more, or use a more reassuring tone. Why was her brother calling from a police station? *Please don't let him tell me that he's been doing drugs again.*

His hesitation was audible. "I've been arrested for dealing coke," he said finally.

Dealing coke? Helen's stomach plunged. That was a terrifying new departure. Even at the depths of his addiction, Philip had only used, never dealt. She closed her eyes, her hand gripping the phone so tightly that her fingers ached.

"How much coke?" The answer to that would affect the charges her brother was facing.

"I'm…not sure."

"You must know—"

"No, I don't. The cops haven't told me…."

That struck Helen as such an obvious evasion she didn't even bother to call him on it. "When were you arrested?" she asked, wondering if Philip found the roster of questions as wearily familiar as she did.

"This afternoon. The cops came to the Youth Center and they had a warrant to search my locker." Philip's voice rose, his panic barely controlled. "Nell, I didn't do it, I swear. I've been set up—"

"Don't!" she commanded. "Don't lie and make excuses, Phil. I can't bear it when you lie." She'd already had more than enough of that from Franklin and she wasn't ready to endure more of it from her brother.

"I'm not lying." His voice lowered with despair. "Nell, please come. You're the only hope I have right now. Please get here as soon as you can. They say I have to hang up the phone now, but I'm counting on you to straighten out the mess."

She was sure he was, Helen thought with unusual bitterness. She replaced the receiver in the phone cradle, her stomach cramping with worry and disappointment. For once in her life, she wished she could count on her brother to be there for her instead of the other way around, but that was clearly a fantasy not likely to be fulfilled in the near future. Maybe never.

Helen shoved the lasagna back into the freezer, slamming the door with all the force of her pent-up frustration. She couldn't believe that only a couple of days earlier she'd been congratulating herself on the giant strides toward total recovery that Philip seemed to be making. Good grief, how in the world had he managed to fake her out so completely? She could usually see right through his efforts at deception.

She went upstairs to the guest bedroom, so that she could freshen her makeup and change out of jeans into something more formal. She'd learned over the years that if she could look well-groomed and neatly put together, she had a better chance of persuading the police to process her brother into a rehab center rather than through the criminal justice system, but she was getting mighty tired of having to manipulate the system on his behalf. Maybe she'd be doing him a favor if she let the criminal justice system take its brutal course, she reflected tiredly.

Tough love was all very well in theory, but hard to put into practice. She'd been mothering Philip for fourteen years—more than half his life—and the habit by now was ingrained. Surrendering to the inevitable, she quickly checked through her selection of suits, choosing one that was a soft shade of gray with a subtle sheen of heather woven into the silky fabric. The skirt was short, too, which was an added advantage, especially when coupled with a pair of high-heeled shoes. Franklin had a fully equipped exercise room in the house, so she still had her shapely dancer's legs, and she was willing to exploit whatever assets she could come up with to help Philip.

What a complete hypocrite she was, Helen mused, shrugging out of her jeans. She wasn't willing to strut her stuff on behalf of her husband, but if flashing a few inches of thigh could improve the mood of the cop who'd arrested Philip, then she was willing to provide him with whatever eye candy she could come up with.

It was amazing that her brother could still deceive her after all these years, Helen thought, flicking a comb through her hair and giving her makeup a final check. She'd really believed him at lunch when he'd told her that he was working out and generally getting his life together. She'd even believed that he was about to resume his studies at medical school. Obviously, she should have known better.

Squaring her shoulders and mentally preparing herself for what was ahead, she grabbed her car keys and headed for the depressingly familiar terrain of yet another police station.

"THERE'S A WOMAN here to see you," Detective Josie Frutt said, setting a paper cup of Starbucks double-espresso on the desk beside Ryan Benton, her partner.

Ryan looked away from his computer, where he'd just pulled up a list of prior arrests on Philip Kouros. "I'm trying to get the paperwork finished on this afternoon's drug bust so I can go home. Who is it? Can somebody else deal with her?"

"It's Helen Gettys. And she's busy reminding everyone that she's married to United States Senator Franklin Gettys, so we'd better all get our butts in gear and pay attention to her."

Ryan frowned, concealing a crazy little shock of desire at the mention of Helen's name. So much for his often-repeated mantra that he was over her. It seemed the mere mention of her name could cause his mind to go blank and his stomach to knot. Ever since the arrest this afternoon, he'd been wondering if she would follow her usual pattern and turn up to rescue her brother. Now he had his answer, and it seemed she was still firmly on the disastrous path of enablement.

Even though he considered Josie a close friend, his past relationship with Helen was something he'd carefully avoided discussing, and this wasn't a good moment to reveal that he knew the sister of the perp— intimately. He disliked lying to Josie, even by omission, but he had no choice unless he wanted the case to be taken away from him. And of course, he didn't want that because handling the processing of Philip Kouros gave him an excuse to exercise his masochism and spend time with Helen. Jeez, he was pathetic.

Josie poked his shoulder. "Hello, earth to Ryan Benton. Mrs. Gettys is tapping her elegant foot, waiting for us to jump to attention. Are you going to deal with her?"

Ryan looked up, his expression schooled to reveal nothing more than mild curiosity. "What the hell is Mrs. U.S. Senator doing here? And why does she want to speak to me?"

"She wants to talk to you because you're the detective working her brother's case."

"Her brother?" Ryan said, as if he didn't understand.

"Yeah. Apparently Philip Kouros is her younger brother."

"Well, that's a surprise." Uncomfortable with deceiving his partner, Ryan pushed away from his desk and rose to his feet, which gave him the excuse he needed to avoid Josie's gaze. "I guess I'd better go talk to her right away or she'll be calling the commissioner to complain about our incompetence."

Josie gave him a friendly thump on the shoulder. "Keep your eye on the prize, Benton. Mrs. Gettys clearly knows how to make the most of her assets. Not only is she flashing the senator's name, she's flashing her legs, too. She's wearing a skirt short enough to distract any male still breathing."

Ryan managed a carefree grin as he headed toward the reception area, espresso in hand. "Don't worry, partner. Mrs. U.S. Senator is about to discover I'm *real* good at holding my breath."

He'd spoken too soon and much too confidently, Ryan realized when he saw Helen standing by the dusty window in the crowded reception area, the sun shimmering behind her, burnishing her hair with a subtle gold fire. Jesus, she was more lovely every damn time he saw her. At the reception for her husband, she'd appeared in her element, surrounded by people of elegance, power and wealth. Here in the shabby police station, she stood out like a perfect water lily in a pond choked with algae.

Ryan pulled himself back from the romantic imagery. Helen Gettys was not only the brother of a suspect, she was also a married woman, he reminded himself. And not just any married woman: Helen had rejected his offer of marriage only weeks before she became engaged to Franklin Gettys. That put her triple-time off-limits and Ryan didn't believe in wasting valuable time fantasizing about a woman who was unattainable. He had once been a starry-eyed country bumpkin, but Helen herself had cured him of that. Nowadays he was strictly big city sophisticated. He liked his women uncomplicated and uncommitted, with no emotional baggage to get in the way of hot sex and the occasional friendly date for dinner and the movies.

Still, it required more effort than he cared to acknowledge for Ryan to drag his gaze away from Helen's entirely amazing legs and focus on her face instead. Not a significant improvement, he discovered, since he should have remembered that she had the most ravishing eyes he'd ever seen, and at the moment they were clouded with worry. To his chagrin, the sight of that worry provoked an urge to protect her—which for sure wasn't an emotion he cared to feel toward a woman who had rejected him in favor of a man whose chief qualification as a husband seemed to be the fact that he had scads of money.

Get a grip, Benton. You're not the first man to discover that women like rich men better than poor ones. Time to stop drooling over Helen's unavailable attractions and concentrate on the all-too-real crimes of her brother.

Ryan had learned over the years that adopting a low-key, laid-back attitude often lulled suspects and witnesses into a sense of security that produced valuable results when building a criminal case. He saw no reason to change this assessment just because he'd spent some of the most amazing moments of his life in bed with the woman he was about to interview.

Adjusting his expression to display nothing more than bland courtesy, he crossed the room to Helen's side. It was disconcerting to discover that the closer he got, the harder he had to fight the urge to wrap his arm around her too-thin frame and assure her that everything was going to be fine.

Which it almost certainly wasn't.

He halted while he was still a couple of feet away from her. "Helen." He held out his hand, and she shook it quickly, giving him a smile that appeared warm, sweet and a little hesitant, just as she'd looked two nights earlier at the god-awful reception for her husband that he'd been dragged to by the chief of police. Ryan's heart skipped a beat, before he reminded himself that Helen had been married to Franklin Gettys for over two years, and Gettys was a consummate politician with vaulting ambitions. Helen seemed thrilled to assist her husband in any way she could. She probably had a morning exercise routine that included ten minutes of practicing sweet, innocent smiles in front of the bathroom mirror.

Ignoring his thumping heart, he returned her smile with a cool nod. "I wondered if you'd come to your brother's rescue," he said.

She looked away, not responding to the implicit rebuke in his words. Before Franklin Gettys arrived on the scene, the only subject they'd ever argued about had been her overprotective attitude toward her brother.

"I didn't realize you worked in this precinct," she said.

"I've been here ever since I left Silver Rapids, which was two years ago."

"I thought you despised big city police departments after your experiences working with the Denver police ten years ago. I thought you always wanted to work in a small town. I seem to remember you told me that you'd be quite happy to be town sheriff until the day you retired.''

"Circumstances change, and people, too." He'd left Silver Rapids in something mighty close to a temper tantrum after she'd rejected him. He'd come back to bury his hurt in the brutally hard work of being a big city cop only to discover that he actually preferred being at the center of the action. But Ryan didn't want their conversation to start wandering down dangerous byways into the past, and he brought her back to the present with brusque efficiency.

"You've probably been told that I'm the detective assigned to your brother's case. I executed the search warrant at the Youth Center this afternoon.''

"I didn't know that until I arrived here," she said softly. "Philip didn't tell me when he called.''

She sounded sad and tired and…lonely. Annoyed with himself for reading way too much into her words, Ryan held open the door to an interview room and gestured for her to go inside. It was disconcerting to discover that after so many years in law enforcement, he was still having such a hard time separating his personal feelings from his job responsibilities.

"We can be more private here than at my desk. Can I get you a cup of coffee? We have bottled ice water, too." He made the offers mechanically, concentrating on getting back into investigative mode. Think Mrs. Franklin Gettys, he lectured himself. Think *married woman*. Forget Helen Kouros, sleepy-eyed and sexy in his bed. That woman didn't exist anymore.

"No, thank you." Helen sat down, crossing one exquisitely long leg over the other. Ryan gulped and directed his gaze to an unattractive black smear on the wall above her head, staring as if he'd never seen it before, although in fact it had been there for at least a year. He wondered if Helen realized that the prim neckline on the jacket of her suit made the short skirt even more eye-catching than it might have been in a more blatantly sexy outfit.

Of course she realized, he thought cynically. This was a woman who'd captivated the attention of every man working at the Swansong Casino—and been the most popular dancer with customers, too, even though she had no professional training and got by on charm and vivacity rather than expert dancing technique.

Shape up or ship out, Benton, he warned himself. He needed to pull himself together or take himself off the case if he couldn't keep focused on the facts of Philip's crime rather than the attractions of Philip's sister. He cleared his throat. "What information do you want from me, Helen?"

She got straight to the point. "My brother called and told me he'd been arrested on a drug-dealing charge…that you found cocaine in his locker at the Youth Center. What exactly are the charges? And what grounds do the police have for believing that my brother has been dealing drugs?"

"We received a tip-off yesterday that your brother was using his work at the Center as a cover for dealing drugs," Ryan said, choosing his words carefully. "Specifically that he was dealing cocaine in large quantities. Since there are a lot of at-risk young people who use the Center as a supposedly safe place to hang out, we obtained a search warrant immediately, and I searched the premises with the assistance of two uniformed officers. Drugs were found in your brother's locker, inside a small duffel bag that he identified as his.'' He paused for a moment, then gave her the bad news. ''We found almost five hundred grams of cocaine, Helen—''

''Five hundred grams!'' she exclaimed. She sounded appalled, which was no surprise. She had enough experience with drug busts to know that five hundred grams equaled more than a pound of cocaine. Far too much for Philip to claim it was strictly for his personal use, and more than enough to get him convicted of drug trafficking charges.

''My God! Where did Philip get his hands on such a huge amount of coke! How could he even pay fo—'' She broke off, realizing that sounding horrified wasn't the best way to help her brother. ''What did Philip say when you confronted him with the stash of coke?'' she asked, recovering her composure.

''He said he'd never seen it before,'' Ryan replied, not bothering to conceal his cynicism. ''He said he'd been set up.''

Helen dropped her gaze to her lap. ''Philip might be telling the truth…. How can you be sure the drugs weren't planted?'' Her voice wasn't steady, and Ryan was quite sure she didn't believe her brother's claims of innocence any more than he did. They both knew Philip was an addict with a long history of cocaine use. He wished he didn't have to confirm her fears, but Philip was following a depressingly familiar pattern, even if he was the brother of the woman Ryan had once loved and wanted to marry.

''It's difficult to imagine how the drugs could have gotten into your brother's locker without his consent,'' Ryan said. ''There are heavy-duty combination padlocks on all the staff lockers at the Center. The padlock on Philip's locker was intact, which means whoever put the drugs there didn't have to break it to gain access. If the lock hasn't been tampered with, and it's your brother's locker, he's not just the logical suspect. He's the only suspect.''

"Maybe he didn't adjust the combination dial on the padlock to close it properly—"

Ryan shook his head, not allowing her false hope. "The lock's self-closing.''

"But you must need to click it. Philip might have forgotten to click it shut. Or maybe somebody else at the Center knew his personal access code.''

Ryan felt like a brute as he squashed one hope after another. "Your brother himself admitted that he hadn't told anyone the combination for his padlock. We're left with the entirely logical conclusion that Philip put the coke into that bag himself. It doesn't help that he has a long history of problems with drug abuse, and several prior arrests.''

"Okay, we both know my brother has a history of using cocaine,''. Helen conceded. "But you know as well as I do that he's always been a user, not a dealer. I swear he's never, ever dealt drugs before. Not when we knew each other, or since.'' She leaned forward, pleading her brother's case with passionate intensity. Ryan repressed the urge to go find Philip and beat some sense of remorse into his airy, coke-filled head.

"You know Philip was a medical student, one of the most brilliant in his class, before his drug use got the better of him. He's always been really conscious of not wanting to facilitate anybody else's habit. I know my brother, and I can't believe he'd start dealing. No way, no how.''

Ryan refrained from quoting the horrifying statistics on nurses, surgeons and other medical specialists who had problems with drug addiction. "The fact that your brother didn't deal in the past doesn't mean much," he said quietly, hiding his frustration at her ongoing reluctance to face up to the reality of her brother's addiction. "Using cocaine exacts a heavy toll on a person's moral standards, Helen—"

"But he hasn't been using anything for months, I swear!"

"Remember we got a phone tip that he was dealing," Ryan said shortly, feeling all his old frustration rebuild, although whether with himself, with Philip or with Helen he wasn't sure. "We're not just basing his arrest on the fact that we happened to stumble across the coke in his locker."

"Do you know who the tip came from?"

"No," he admitted. "But that doesn't mean anything. Tips about drug deals usually come from clients who've fallen out with their suppliers and we expect them to be anonymous."

"So you think the tip came from one of Philip's...drug clients?"

He nodded and she turned abruptly, hiding her eyes, but Ryan could tell that she was deeply distressed. Whatever else might have changed about Helen Gettys, it was clear that she still cared a lot about her younger brother. Probably too much for Philip's own good. The kid might have done better without a supportive sister to come running every time he screwed up.

"My recommendation is that you hire a good lawyer," Ryan said when she didn't speak. "Your brother is facing charges that could buy him serious jail time. But you know that already, I'm sure."

"My brother doesn't have any money."

He was surprised by her response. "Well, maybe not. But I assumed you would be hiring the lawyer on your brother's behalf."

"Oh. Yes, of course." She looked down at her hands, which were clasped in a death grip in her lap. When she looked up again, he saw that her face had lost every trace of color and she was biting her lower lip in an effort to keep it steady. She made no further reference to his comment about hiring a lawyer.

"I'd like to see my brother, please."

"Are you planning to bail him out?"

Her pallor vanished, replaced by a wash of crimson. She was clearly embarrassed, but he couldn't pinpoint the source. As an investigator, he wasn't doing too well in assessing what made Helen Gettys tick. Fact was, he was having a real difficult time separating his memories of Helen Kouros, naked in his bed, and Helen Gettys, sophisticated wife of Colorado's junior senator.

"I'm...not sure if I'll bail Philip out," she said. "But I definitely want to see him. I really need to talk to him and find out firsthand what happened today."

Her beloved kid brother had been caught dealing cocaine, that's what had happened today. Ryan suppressed a sigh. It seemed that Helen was still acting the role of enabler, a role he'd tried to persuade her to abandon years ago. She would try to extract a promise of reform from her brother before agreeing to bail him out. Ryan debated telling her that she would be a complete sucker if she believed her brother's promises, or fell for his likely excuse of having been set up by some unknown enemy, probably the cops. He decided to save his breath. He and

Helen had been down that same frustrating road too many times already and there was no point in going there again. Philip Kouros was a smart guy and an addict, which meant by definition that he had a real good line in stories that blamed everyone in the universe for his problems except himself.

"I'll arrange to have you escorted to the holding cells," Ryan said, getting to his feet to prevent himself getting dangerously involved. "Goodbye, Helen. I'm sorry that we had to meet again under such unpleasant circumstances."

She acknowledged his remarks with nothing more than a brief nod of her head, but even though seeing her again had messed with his head to the point that his emotional radar was almost nonfunctional, Ryan understood that she wasn't being standoffish. He realized she was simply holding herself under tight control for fear that she would fall apart if she relaxed even a tiny bit.

Stifling a rush of sympathy that there was no appropriate way for him to express, Ryan turned sharply, anxious to escape from a situation that offered no good outcome for either of them. Helen was married, her brother was an addict and he was a cop. Three points of a triangle with no good way to connect the dots, especially in view of their past, failed relationship.

"Wait here," he said, suppressed emotion making his voice curt. "I'll send a uniformed officer to escort you to the cells."

"Thank you." Her voice was husky. "I appreciate your help, Ryan."

"You're welcome. I'm sorry I happened to be the one to make the arrest." It seemed an inadequate response, but it was all he could offer her. He left the interview room without looking back.

Whether because Ryan had taken pity on her and pleaded for special consideration, or else because the cops were impressed by the fact that she was the wife of Franklin Gettys, Philip was locked in a holding cell by himself, and Helen was allowed to go inside with him.

She entered warily, keeping her distance. "Hi, Phil. How are you doing?"

Her brother didn't rush over to hug her, or even thank her for coming. Standing in the corner of the cell, fists clenched, he spoke with low-voiced passion.

"I didn't do it, Nell. I've been set up."

Her temper, rubbed raw by the events of the past few days, snapped. "Oh for goodness sake! For once in your life can't you just take responsibility for what you've done? Ryan's a decent man and a great cop. Why would he arrest you unless he had real cause?"

Philip glanced down at his scuffed sneakers. "I deserve that," he said quietly. "I know I let you down a lot of times in the past. But not this time."

"You're in jail, charged with dealing cocaine. You haven't just let me down, Philip. You've let yourself down."

Her brother's voice deepened, throbbing with urgency. "I didn't do it. I haven't done any drugs in almost two years, since just after you got married. I haven't even had a beer. I'm stone-cold sober and have been for months." He walked across the cell and grabbed her by the arms. "Look at me, Nell. For God's sake, *look at me!* You know what I'm like when I'm using. *I'm not using.* Check it out for yourself. You have to believe me."

Helen finally forced herself to meet her brother's gaze in critical assessment. His eyes were clear and focused, she saw, although his body vibrated with a toxic combination of despair, rage and tension. His nostrils weren't inflamed, and his nose wasn't dripping. For the first time since she'd received his phone call, she allowed herself a tiny flicker of hope. Was it possible that the cops had made a mistake? That Ryan had jumped to conclusions based on his prior knowledge of her brother's problems with drug addiction? If Philip really was innocent, she felt she could cope with all the rest.

"The drugs were in your duffel bag inside your locker," she said, not allowing herself to overlook facts despite her desperate wish to believe in his innocence. "According to Ryan, the padlock hadn't been tampered with, and you admitted that nobody else knew your combination number. How did the drugs get inside your duffel bag if you didn't put them there?"

"I didn't speak directly to Ryan," Philip said. "And the cops are either deliberately misrepresenting what I told them, or they weren't listening closely enough. Kids often stand around talking to me when I'm at my locker. It's true that I'd never *told* anyone what the combination is for my padlock, but it wouldn't have been all that difficult for someone to watch me open the lock and take a mental note of the number sequence."

"Did you explain that to Ryan?" Helen asked.

He shook his head. "I told the uniformed cop who found the coke, but not Ryan. I think since Ryan knows me he wanted another cop to take my statement. But the bottom line, Nell, is that it wouldn't be hard for somebody to have gotten into my locker and plant those drugs.''

''But why would anybody want to set you up?''

Philip shrugged, not interested in a question that he found irrelevant. ''Could be any one of a dozen reasons. Maybe the real dealer got a tip-off the cops were coming and needed somewhere to hide his stash. Maybe some kid is pissed off at me and I don't know it. Maybe some cokehead zoned out and shoved his supply into my locker by mistake—''

''This mythical cokehead was too zoned out to remember where his own locker is, but he remembered your combination?''

Philip grimaced. ''Weirder things happen when you're high. All I know for sure is that I was the unlucky bastard who got stuck with a damn great bag of coke I'd never seen before in my life.''

His explanations were all reasonable, but her brother had a stratospheric IQ. How difficult would it be for him to invent credible lies? Helen held his gaze, willing him to be truthful. ''Phil, I want to believe you, but it's hard, given what's happened in the past. Tell me one more time. Do you know anything at all about these drugs and how they came to be in your locker? In the long run, it's going to be better for everyone if you tell the truth.''

He spoke with fierce intensity. ''I know nothing about the drugs, except that somebody else put them in my locker.'' He smiled bitterly. ''You want to hear something funny? I was so damn certain I had my drug problems under control that a couple of months ago I reapplied to medical school. The University of Colorado accepted me to start in January, giving me three semesters of credit for the courses I've already taken. I've even got the financing worked out.''

Helen stared at her brother, momentarily speechless. "Oh my God, that's wonderful!" She pulled him into a bear hug, tears clogging her throat. "Congratulations! Why didn't you tell me, Phil? I'm so thrilled for you.''

"I was saving the news for my birthday next weekend.'' He attempted to give a casual shrug and failed miserably. "Well, I guess today's events take care of my chances of ever starting medical school again.''

"We won't let it ruin what you've worked for,'' Helen said fiercely. "We'll beat these charges, Phil.''

"How?'' he asked simply. "Even you assumed I was guilty.''

"That was before I spoke with you.''

Philip gave her a pitying look. "The cops aren't going to be persuaded because I talk a good game. They have all the evidence they need. A tip-off recorded on the drug hotline. A plastic bag stuffed full of high-grade coke and a witness who's willing to swear I sold drugs to his friend. I don't think my protestations of innocence are going to win the day, especially since Ryan Benton thinks I've talked myself out of trouble way too many times already.''

"There's a witness to you making drug deals?'' Helen's stomach gave another lurch downward. "What's his name?''

"Shawn Johnson. He's one of the few kids at the Center that I don't like. He'd sell his grandmother for a hundred bucks, and his mother for fifty, so his word is basically meaningless.''

"What does that mean?''

"It means Shawn has been bought. Still, with my

record what hope do I have of convincing the cops I was set up?''

She frowned in thought. "We have to find out who persuaded Shawn Johnson to provide false testimony. Once we have a lead, I bet Ryan would follow up on it. He was always conscientious to a fault when I knew him in Silver Springs.''

"That's a great plan," Philip said wryly. "The concept's terrific. Unfortunately, I can see a couple of problems with the practical details. Such as how the hell we're going to persuade Shawn Johnson to admit that he lied?''

Money would be the quickest way, Helen thought. Unfortunately, she didn't have any of that available for bribing Shawn. A credit card good at a fancy boutique couldn't provide ready cash. "I didn't say it would be easy," she said, hiding her worry. "But there must be some way to put pressure on Shawn to give up a name—''

"Yes, we need to bribe him." Philip echoed her thoughts. "The trouble is, I have no money, Nell.''

"None?" she asked ruefully, although she wasn't surprised. Working as a counselor at a youth center might be spiritually rewarding, but the pay was lousy.

Her brother shook his head. "I have five hundred bucks in a savings account, maybe another two hundred in checking. That's it. And seven hundred bucks isn't going to buy any useful information from Shawn Johnson.''

"Are you sure? That's a fair sum of money for a teenager.''

"Yeah, but you have to count in the fear factor. Presumably he was paid off by a big-time coke dealer, which means that telling the truth is going to put him at serious risk of getting beaten up. Or worse. I don't think seven hundred bucks will persuade Shawn to risk dying.''

Helen wished with all her heart that she had some money of her own to offer her brother. Quite apart from bribing Shawn to tell the truth, they needed money for a lawyer, and maybe a private investigator. Not to mention bail money, so that Philip could get out of jail while waiting for his trial. Even if they went to a bail bonds outfit, they'd need ten percent in hard cash.

"I'll ask Franklin to loan me the money," she said, sounding a lot more confident than she felt.

Philip shook his head. "No, you won't, Nell. I know damn well that Franklin's forbidden you to give me any money and that he checks all your accounts and bills and receipts to make sure you're not slipping me cash on the side. I'm not going to be responsible for putting you into that man's debt. No way, no how."

"Franklin will understand this is a different situation," Helen said, hoping she was telling the truth. "He disapproves of me giving you money because he believes that earning your own living is an important part of your rehabilitation." That was a somewhat liberal translation of Franklin's edict that she was to stop throwing good money after bad on her no-good asshole of a brother.

"I'll talk to Franklin tonight, and see what we can come up with," she said, determinedly optimistic. "After all, he's a senator. He must know a couple of really top-notch lawyers, don't you think?"

"Probably," Philip said, trying to sound cheerful and not mentioning again what they both knew, which was that Franklin most likely wouldn't be willing to offer any help at all, especially not financial help.

"I really appreciate all you do for me, Nell." Philip ducked his head in awkward gratitude. "Thanks for believing in me one more time. You've done so much for me since Mom died—"

"I'm your sister. Of course I want to help."

"I wish you didn't have to keep hauling me out of trouble. That was one of the worst parts about being arrested this afternoon…I hated to disappoint you. I couldn't bear for you to suspect I'd thrown it all away again. I didn't, Nell, I swear."

"I believe you." Helen gave him another quick hug, then stepped back before either one of them broke down. "I'll be back as early as I can tomorrow morning. Keep your spirits up, Phil. We'll straighten out this mess, I promise."

Leaving the police station, breathing in the fresh night air with a sensation of profound relief, Helen could only hope that she'd be able to make good on her promises. First she had to find Franklin. Then she had to persuade him to provide her with a loan of several thousand dollars. A loan that would take months to repay, even after she got a job.

All this when they were about to start divorce proceedings. Plenty of men more generous than Franklin might think twice about helping a wife who was about to apply for a divorce. Especially when the purpose of the loan was to bail out a brother-in-law he'd always despised.

The timing of Philip's arrest couldn't have been worse, Helen reflected, but there was nothing for her to do right now but go home and grovel to Franklin.

She was not looking forward to the task.

CHAPTER SIX

FRANKLIN'S BMW was in the garage, suggesting he had come home while she was at the police station. That was a relief, Helen thought. For all she'd known to the contrary, he could have flown back to Washington, which would have made the rescue of her brother a lot more difficult. A sudden image of Ryan Benton sitting across the table from her flashed into her mind. He'd looked so honest and dependable, she thought wistfully. If only she could ask him for help instead of Franklin, she'd be a lot more optimistic that her brother would soon be free.

Dismissing the hopeless wish, she entered the house through the door from the garage into the laundry room. Dropping her purse onto the kitchen counter, she shucked the high-heeled shoes she'd donned to impress the cops. The shoes were new and she wriggled her toes gratefully before setting off in search of her estranged husband.

On the rare nights he spent at home, Franklin liked to watch a sporting event on the TV in his study. Padding along the polished parquet floor of the main hallway, Helen made her way toward the study. She was still several yards from the entrance when she heard the sound of men's voices.

Hoping to find out how long she might have to wait before she could plead her brother's cause, she stopped and listened for a moment, knowing that she would be ruining her chances of success if she interrupted Franklin when he was with a friend or business colleague. The prospect of a long delay was nerve-racking. Truth be told, she was absolutely dreading the discussion and wanted to get it over with as soon as she could.

"It's lousy timing," she heard a man say. "Quite apart from the negative media coverage, we don't want anybody looking over your financial assets right now." The speaker had a distinctive, gravely sound to his voice, and she recognized it as belonging to one of Franklin's most important financial backers, a man called Lio. Helen didn't know Lio's last name, or his profession, but that wasn't surprising since Franklin rarely bothered to make more than perfunctory introductions. All she knew was that Lio must be a close friend as well as a generous political supporter because he came to the house more often than any of Franklin's other associates.

"I'm well aware of the problem," her husband said, sounding defensive.

"Then take care of it." Lio was giving an order, not making a suggestion. How odd, Helen thought. She wouldn't have expected Franklin to tolerate the company of anyone who spoke to him in such peremptory tones.

"I have taken care of it," Franklin replied. "In fact, I wasted most of yesterday dealing with the problem. Trust me, she's going to change her mind about wanting a divorce real soon."

Helen's heart began to beat in double time. Franklin and Lio were apparently discussing her decision to seek a divorce, which was surprising in itself. But even more surprising was Franklin's conviction that she was going to change her mind about wanting out of their marriage. What possible grounds did he have for believing something so unlikely?

Lio spoke again. "Make sure she does back off, Franklin. Things are moving forward at the Half Spur and I don't want any fancy, high-priced divorce lawyers out there poking around—"

"Why would they?"

"Because she'll go after your money and her lawyers will want to find out how much the property is worth in a settlement. I sure as hell don't want anybody to link ownership of the Half Spur to one of my corporations. I've gone to a lot of trouble to hide the fact that you and I are joint owners of the ranch. One nosy divorce lawyer could blow us both out of the water."

"That's not true," Franklin protested. "Helen has no claim to the ranch. She has no claim to any of my assets, for that matter. I've told you before, Lio, we have an ironclad prenup that Helen signed before we ever married."

Lio gave a hoarse laugh. "And I've told *you* before that your prenup isn't worth the paper it's written on. You might as well flush it down the toilet now. Take it from a man who's been divorced three times and is finally smart enough to realize marriage is strictly for losers. There isn't a prenup ever written that can stand up to attack by a lawyer who knows his trade. Besides, in this case it isn't what the judge decides at the end of the day that matters. It's what Helen's lawyers might discover while they're sniffing around, requesting notarized statements from everybody and their dog."

"Yeah, well, we have no worries. Helen isn't going to divorce me."

Like hell she wasn't. Helen resisted the urge to burst into the study and tell Franklin that he was delusional if he thought she was going to change her mind about splitting up. As for Lio, she'd always disliked the man, and his sordid advice to Franklin merely confirmed her bad opinion. They'd sounded like a couple of Mafia dons discussing their illegal business deals, she thought disgustedly.

She heard the sounds of the two men rising from their chairs, the squish of air returning to leather cushions, and the rolling of castors across the oak-plank floor. Very quietly, she turned and ran back to the kitchen. Then she put her shoes on again and emerged noisily into the hallway, creating the impression that she'd just walked into the house.

Her timing was perfect. Franklin and Lio came out of the study at the same time as she *tap-tapped* out of the kitchen. "Why hello, Franklin." She gave him a smile instead of the snarl she'd have liked, and turned to his companion. "And Lio, too. I didn't see your car. It's good to see you again."

"Likewise. My car's around the front." Lio shook her hand, his gaze hot as he made a leisurely survey of her body. She'd learned on previous visits that the man was a letch of the worst type, and she always took care not to be alone with him.

Lio gave her a brief, insincere smile. "Well, I'm sure you and the senator have things to discuss and I need to get home. Take care, Helen."

"Where is your home, Lio?" Helen hoped she made the question sound casual, but she was suddenly very curious about exactly who Lio was and what his relationship was with her soon-to-be-ex-husband.

Lio's eyes narrowed. "I have a home right here in Denver," he said, pausing by the front door. "Good-bye, Franklin." He nodded to Helen. "And you, too. Enjoy your evening."

After Lio had left, Franklin didn't escape back into his study as might have been expected. Instead he turned to Helen with an oddly self-satisfied smile. "Was there anything you wanted to talk to me about?" he asked. "Where have you been at this late hour, my dear? You look as if you're dealing with a crisis."

Franklin's taunting manner, combined with his comments to Lio suddenly made sickening sense. The truth exploded into Helen's consciousness with the force of a rocket launch. Good God, how could she have been so thick-witted for so long? There was no need to go searching for some disgruntled addict to find out who had set Philip up. Her brother was in prison right now because Franklin Gettys had arranged to send him there.

Helen felt as if she might suffocate. She could barely tolerate being in such close proximity to a man who could exploit her brother in such a despicable fashion, but ranting and raging wouldn't get Philip released. With a single furious glare at her husband, Helen turned and stalked into the formal living room. If she'd needed confirmation of her suspicions, Franklin provided it by following her into the room without being asked.

It had to be eighteen months at least since he'd followed her anywhere, she thought acidly. If she'd wanted to capture her husband's wandering attention, it seemed there could be no better method than telling him she wanted a divorce.

Helen walked over to the empty fireplace before swinging around to confront him. "You wanted to know where I'd been. I'm sure you won't be surprised to hear that I've just come back from the police station in North Denver."

Franklin cocked his head in pretense of an inquiry, but his gloating smile gave him away. "Why would you go there, my dear? A police station isn't a very pleasant place to spend the evening. I do hope you're not about to start off on one of your do-good schemes again."

The endearment set her teeth on edge, but she ignored it. "Okay, let's cut to the chase. What's your deal, Franklin? What do I have to do in order to get Philip out of jail?"

"Your brother's in jail?" Franklin went to the built-in bar, took ice from the automatic ice-maker and poured himself a vodka on the rocks. "What's he accused of this time?"

"Exactly what you arranged for him to be accused of," she said bitingly. "Possession of five hundred grams of cocaine with intent to deal." Franklin started to speak but she cut him off, literally sick to her stomach at the prospect of participating in his cat-and-mouse play.

"I'm not interested in hearing any more of your fake expressions of shock and surprise, Franklin. Let's quit the perverted games and move straight to the bottom line. What do I have to do in order to get the charges against my brother dropped?"

"What makes you so sure that I can make the charges go away?"

Helen's stomach dropped away into the abyss. Had she misjudged? Not that Franklin had set her brother up—she was a hundred percent sure of that. But had her husband set Philip up simply as a form of revenge with no way to spring the trap? Then she remembered Franklin's boast to the mysterious Lio and was somewhat reassured. Her husband had arranged for Philip to be arrested in order to force her to comply with his wishes. That meant there was a way to get her brother out of jail.

"You can make the charges go away if you want to," she said, with more certainty than she felt. "You set Philip up, so I'm damn sure you can spring him. Just tell me the deal, Franklin."

"All right, I will." He took a long swallow of his vodka. "I want you to drop this crazy nonsense about getting a divorce. If you agree that we're going to stay married, I'll do my best to get the charges against your brother dropped."

She shook her head, feeling a hundred years older and wiser than she had been only a couple of days earlier. "No, Franklin, that's not the way it's going to work. First you have to spring my brother from jail and make sure all the charges against him are dropped, and then I'll agree not to divorce you."

The angry look he shot in her direction was tinged with admiration. "Playing hardball, my dear? I didn't expect it from you. But the short answer is, no deal. Who the hell do you think you are, laying down conditions to me?"

She was nearly suffocating with fright, but Helen hid her panic and managed a shrug. "Who do I think I am?" she asked, hoping Franklin couldn't hear the shake in her voice. "Well, I guess I'm the woman you want to keep as your wife. I'm also the woman who can ruin your political career if I decide to do so. All I have to do is give a friendly reporter the details of some of your extramarital affairs, and there goes your support among all the family values folk who helped put you in office."

"You bitch!" Franklin cursed viciously for almost a minute. Helen waited for him to draw breath, then spoke quickly.

"I may be everything you say, but I hold the winning cards on this deal. I'm sure some of the women you've seduced and discarded will be more than happy to go public with their stories, so it's not just my word against yours." She paused for a few seconds to let her threat sink in, then added a threat that she didn't understand, but guessed would be potent. "And if your affairs aren't enough to shake Philip loose from jail, then I'll tell the reporters to take a good look at what's going on at the Half Spur. Now, would you like to reconsider springing my brother from jail?"

Franklin was staring at her as if he didn't know her and she couldn't blame him. Right at this moment, Helen hardly recognized herself.

"You deceptive bitch," he said. "What the hell were you doing out at the Half Spur last weekend? Who sent you there?"

"I was having a picnic," she said, her voice taunting. In other circumstances, she thought it might have been amusing to know that telling the absolute truth could seem so threatening to Franklin's peace of mind.

For a moment she wondered if she'd gone too far. Franklin literally looked murderous. By great good fortune, the phone rang at that moment. She snatched up the receiver and heard a telemarketer offering her a free weekend at a resort in the Rockies.

"Hi, Mary!" she responded, as if the woman were a lifelong friend. "I can't talk right now because Franklin and I are in the middle of a discussion, but I'll get back to you in twenty minutes, okay?" She hung up on the telemarketer in midpitch.

"Are you ready to work out a deal in regard to my brother?" Helen said, turning back to face Franklin.

The phone call had given him time to calm down. "I can get the charges against your brother dropped," he said. "But don't imagine that as soon as he's out of jail, you can renege on our deal and walk away from our marriage. I have cops on my payroll, and the charges against your brother will all come back with a vengeance the day you try to divorce me."

Helen's gaze narrowed. Franklin was obviously desperate to keep her inside the marriage, she reflected, and she would love to know precisely why. What had Lio meant about this not being a good time to subject Franklin's financial affairs to scrutiny? Was he somehow laundering illegal campaign contributions through the ranch accounts? It was the sort of thing she could imagine him doing and it would explain why Lio—probably an illegal campaign contributor—was so anxious to avoid having a divorce lawyer demand to see a statement of the ranch's finances.

There was no chance that Franklin would admit the truth, so she didn't squander her bargaining power—already pretty weak—by asking why he was so desperate to prevent her from seeking a divorce. But she sure as hell planned to use the next few weeks to discover a little bit more about what her husband and Lio were up to, especially at the Half Spur.

"Here are my terms," she said. "I'll keep up the facade of being married to you if that's what it takes to save my brother, but I'm not going to have sex with you ever again, or sleep in the same bed—"

"Is that a threat or a promise?" Franklin asked with heavy sarcasm.

"Neither. It's a simple statement of fact."

"Supposing I say that I want sex, or no deal?"

"Then my brother can rot in jail. There are limits to what I'm prepared to sacrifice for Philip." Helen produced the lie in clipped tones that—she prayed—carried conviction. To her overwhelming relief, Franklin seemed to believe her. Besides, she was sure that his determination to stay married had nothing to do with wanting to keep her as a sexual partner, so it wasn't such a big deal for him to concede. She had no doubt that he'd continue being unfaithful, so he wasn't going to be sexually deprived.

She hit home her point. "I want my brother out of jail by tomorrow afternoon," she said. "Otherwise I'm going to the media with a few juicy stories about the women you've been bedding—"

He grabbed her by the arm, his face turning almost purple with rage. "Don't threaten me," he said. "You were nobody until I made you Mrs. Franklin Gettys, and don't you ever forget that."

She ought to have been frightened by his rage, but it seemed that she'd finally found the backbone that had been missing for the past eighteen months. "I was Helen Kouros before I married you, and she was one hell of a strong woman. I want Philip out of jail. You want me to stay married to you. We've got a

Mexican standoff here, but don't ever again make the mistake of thinking you can intimidate me. Get my brother released from jail, or I'll blow you and your cronies right out of the water."

Helen wasn't at all sure that her bluster would work, but for all the shouting that followed, she knew that Franklin had basically surrendered. She decided to back off and act humble, since that was the course of action that seemed most likely to secure her brother's release.

But the humility was an act, even if Franklin wanted to believe that he'd reasserted his mastery. Because if there was one thing Helen was absolutely determined about, it was this. Once her brother was released from jail, she was going to find a way to keep him safe, probably by encouraging him to leave the state. And then she was going to divorce Franklin Gettys.

CHAPTER SEVEN

BY THE TIME Philip was processed out of the system, Helen was beginning to wish he was less sensitive to other people's emotions, not to mention a lot less smart. Her brother instantly saw through the holes in the story she'd concocted to explain why, thirty-six hours after he was arrested, he was suddenly being released, all charges against him dropped.

Unfortunately, she couldn't risk telling her brother the truth until she had him safely out of the state, far removed from Franklin's reach. If Philip guessed that Franklin was blackmailing Helen to stay married, he might feel compelled to fight for justice by remaining in jail and attempting to expose her husband's corruption.

Helen was all in favor of exposing Franklin's corruption, but the past few days had taught her some hard lessons in the exercise of raw power. She no longer believed that just because Philip was innocent and Franklin dishonest, then her brother would go free and her husband would face the punishment he deserved. She was quite sure that Franklin had a backup plan already in place that would enable him to shake off any accusations she and Philip could make. In fact, Franklin was more than capable of twisting their accusations into a weapon that would boomerang and destroy both her and her brother.

"For once, Phil, just be thankful that I'm married to a senator, and that Franklin knows some people who could make things happen," she said as they finally walked out of jail, with Philip still hounding her with questions.

Philip frowned. "I'm trying, but I don't understand how he did this. And I hate to sound ungrateful, but I'm having real trouble picturing Franklin going out of his way to help me, of all people. The guy loathes me."

"Well, he did help you," Helen snapped, disliking the lie, but seeing no alternative. Right now, she was focused on getting Philip back to his apartment so that she could persuade him to pack up and leave the state before Franklin found another way to screw him over.

"Sometimes, it's smart not to probe too deeply into the hows and wherefores," she said, hurrying toward her car, which was parked in a corner of the precinct lot. "Just go with the flow, okay?"

"That doesn't sound like you, Nell. In fact, it's so out of character in terms of advice that it strikes me as real ominous."

"It's not ominous at all. Why can't you accept that Franklin called in a few heavy-duty favors? He persuaded the police to double-check with the witness and Shawn admitted he invented the story of seeing you deal drugs because he wanted to get back at you as vengeance for being dropped from the basketball team."

Philip rolled his eyes in disbelief, and Helen could see why. "Okay, somehow the cops lost their star witness," her brother said. "But there are five hundred grams of coke sitting in the evidence room that still need to be explained away. Why the hell are the police turning me loose just because Shawn back-tracked on his story?''

Helen squirmed. There was no way for her to feel comfortable about Franklin's manipulation of the justice system, even though she assumed he had only pulled the same corrupt cop strings to make the drugs vanish as he'd used to get them planted in the first place.

"Why are you looking so damn guilty?" Philip demanded. "Come on, Nell, cough it up.''

"Actually…um…the drugs seem to have disappeared from the evidence room."

"What?" Philip stared at her.

"Be grateful for the bureaucratic screwup. You got lucky.''

He snorted in derision. "There's only one way Franklin could have made that coke disappear, and it isn't a lucky screwup. He must have bought off a cop. Or more than one, in fact.''

Philip was clearly on the brink of demanding an explanation she wasn't willing to give, and she tried to think of a way to distract him when the sound of a man's voice calling her name provided a welcome diversion. Supremely grateful for the excuse to change the subject, she turned and saw Ryan following them across the parking lot.

A pleasant warmth unfurled in the pit of Helen's stomach as she waited for the detective to catch up with them. Her whole body suddenly felt more alive. Her reaction was crazy, she realized, not to mention inappropriate. Not only was she still a married woman, at least technically, but Ryan had no reason to harbor friendly feelings toward her, given that he believed she'd rejected his proposal simply because a richer and more famous man had come along.

Even with the advantage of hindsight, Helen knew she hadn't been as shallow and grasping as Ryan assumed. In retrospect, though, she realized she'd been misled by her own past experiences. When her mother died of ovarian cancer, her father had gone to pieces, devastated by the loss of the woman he loved. He'd drunk too much, cared too little about his home and kids and taken out his grief in explosions of temper against his fellow workers. He'd been fired from job after job, leaving Helen to worry about paying bills and putting food on the table. Worst of all, in her opinion, her father had used his grief to justify beating up on her younger brother for a long list of imagined sins, when his only true offense had been that he looked too much like their dead mother.

With those experiences in her past, the passion she'd felt for Ryan hadn't struck her as a solid basis for marriage. Her father's behavior convinced her that sexual passion and starry-eyed romance led nowhere good. The fact that Ryan moved through life with such confidence, and found laughter in the simple events of daily life, didn't reassure her. On the contrary, she worried because everything about her relationship with Ryan was way too easy and too much fun. Life wasn't fun, it was deadly serious, at least in her experience.

She worried about what would happen when she and Ryan hit the first real bump in the road. The fact that Ryan was forever advising her to quit cosseting her brother warned her how he would most likely respond. He'd be like her father. At the first hint of real trouble, he'd walk away, at least emotionally, if not physically. If his advice was to walk away from her brother, why would his response to other problems be different?

Franklin Gettys had seemed the antithesis of all that was worrisome about her relationship with Ryan. He certainly didn't take life lightly. In fact, he was downright pompous, but Helen had found his pomposity comforting. Moreover, he was powerful, socially prominent and rich enough to provide the security she craved. Only people who'd never known the fear of facing an empty food cupboard could afford to dismiss the importance of having enough money. She didn't want her marriage to be about love and romance. Her parents had been in love and look what happened to them. She wanted her marriage to be about making a secure home, so the fact that she wasn't sexually attracted to Franklin and that he had no sense of humor didn't bother her in the least.

When you got right down to it, Helen thought with a wry smile, she'd agreed to marry Franklin because absolutely nothing about their relationship had seemed fun or frivolous. In hindsight, those had to be among the least sensible reasons for getting married that she'd ever heard.

Her rueful amusement must have shown on her face. Ryan drew up a couple of feet away from her, his brows drawn together in a ferocious scowl. "I'm glad you find the situation humorous," he said, his teeth visibly clenched.

Why in the world was he looking so angry? "I'm sorry—" Helen pulled herself up short, her pleasure at the unexpected encounter vanishing. Dammit, she was through with apologizing to men when she had no reason to. That destructive pattern had started with

her father, been brought to a fine art with her soon-
to-be-ex-husband, and wasn't about to continue with
Ryan Benton, even if she'd once been in love with
him and he was still the best-looking cop she'd ever
seen.

She could have ignored him and walked away. But
she was through with avoiding confrontation, too.
From now on, the world was going to see a whole
new Helen Gettys. Strike that. A whole new Helen
Kouros.

She held out the car keys. "Philip, could you go
start the car, please? I'll be right with you. Ryan and
I need to talk for a moment."

Somewhat to her surprise, her brother took the keys
and walked off without comment, leaving her free to
respond to Ryan's remark. She tilted her head back
so that she could stare straight at him. "Last I heard,
there was no law that said citizens aren't allowed to
smile. Not even citizens unlucky enough to find themselves at a police station, confronting a pissed-off detective."

"Maybe there should be." Ryan Benton looked as
if he meant it. "I'll admit you had me fooled, Helen.
Despite your marriage, I had you figured for a woman
of integrity who—"

"I am a woman of integrity."

Ryan gave a hard laugh. "Sure you are. That's why
you paid somebody to get rid of five hundred grams
of coke in the evidence room."

She blushed scarlet. "I...didn't pay off anybody."
It was a feeble excuse, but how could she explain the
truth?

"I'm sure you didn't. Not in person. Why would
you get your elegant fingers dirty?"

"You don't know what you're talking about, Ryan, so back the hell off. My brother was set up—"

"Don't!" he said angrily. His voice lowered, and he looked at her with less anger and more sympathy. "You're doing Philip no favors by springing him from jail. Drug addicts have to learn to take responsibility for their actions. How many times did I tell you that already? Trust me on this, Helen, and do your brother a big favor. Let him hit bottom, because that's the essential first step on the road to recovery. He sure as hell won't turn his life around as long as you keep buying him out of trouble."

"You're mighty free with your advice," she said, her feelings raw with accumulated stress. "For your information, Philip is innocent of the charges you're trying to stick him with. He hasn't been near a drug deal in over two years, either as a buyer or a seller. And you can go to hell."

Ryan ran his fingers through his hair, his expression grim. "That seems to be exactly where I'm headed."

"Good. I'm sure you'll fit right in with the other residents." Helen swung on her heel, breathing fast. Her fury was illogical, she knew. She should have been able to show some sympathy for Ryan's frustration. After all, he had been the arresting cop, and from his point of view, Philip's release from jail was a travesty of justice. Money, power and insider contacts had been used to corrupt the judicial system and Ryan had no way of knowing that the system had been corrupted twice, resulting in the release of a man who hadn't deserved to be imprisoned in the first place. Somehow, though, she wasn't willing to empathize with Ryan's frustration. To hell with him, anyway.

Why should she care what he thought about her? Their relationship had finished years ago, in another lifetime.

"Not so fast." Ryan grabbed her arm and swung her around again. Helen held his gaze, shaking not only with rage and the traumatic upheavals of the past few days, but also with an emotion she was mortified to identify as sexual desire. It was humiliating to know that her physical attraction to this man remained so powerful.

"Let go of my arm, Detective." Her voice was low-pitched, and throbbing with the intensity of her feelings.

"Or what?" he asked tauntingly.

She sought wildly for an answer. "Or my husband will be forced to demonstrate his displeasure with your behavior."

Ryan looked as if he'd been kicked in the stomach, but he didn't loosen his grip. "Don't threaten me, Helen. Your husband is a dud weapon as far as I'm concerned."

"Are you sure of that, Ryan?"

"I'm one hundred percent sure." Instead of dropping her arm, he almost shoved it against her body. For an endless moment they stared into each other's eyes, generating emotional heat that had very little to do with her brother's release from jail. Then Ryan turned away, striding toward the station house without saying anything more. When Helen realized she was staring with hypnotized fascination at his retreating back, she jerked her gaze away and almost ran the last few yards to her car.

"What was that all about?" Philip asked as she

slid behind the wheel. "The pair of you looked as if you were about to come to blows."

She ought to have been grateful that her brother's attention had been temporarily diverted from the disappearance of five hundred grams of coke from the evidence room. Perversely, Helen discovered that she wanted to discuss Ryan Benton even less than she wanted to discuss the true reasons behind her brother's release.

"The detective was annoyed that his case against you went up in smoke," she said, trying to end the discussion before it began.

"Was he? After the stories I heard during the past twenty-four hours, I assumed he wouldn't care."

Helen frowned, concentrating on easing out of the parking lot into the heavy flow of rush hour traffic. Against her better judgment, she probed her brother's remark. "Why did you think Ryan wouldn't care?"

Philip hesitated for a moment. "I know you used to date him for a while in Silver Rapids—"

"That was over before Franklin and I were married. These days he's barely even an acquaintance."

"That's good. I was afraid you might have bribed him to get me out of jail."

"Bribed *Ryan Benton?*" Helen stopped reversing to stare at her brother.

"Yeah." Her brother paused.

"You know something you're not telling me."

Philip shrugged. "I heard some weird insider stuff from the guy in the cell next to me last night. He's a regular jailhouse inmate and told me there's a huge corruption scandal brewing in the precinct."

Helen was oddly surprised, despite the fact that her brother's arrest was living proof that all was not as it should be with the police department. Still, as big city police departments went, Denver was known for honesty and integrity. "How would some crook in a jail cell know that? I haven't seen a whisper about police corruption on TV or in the newspapers."

"The guy is a street crook," Philip said. "Rap sheet miles long, all for petty offenses. He's currently a runner for one of the drug gangs, and the cops use him as an informant. Every so often, they haul him into jail and leave him there for a couple of nights, just to remind him what could happen if he doesn't cooperate. Anyway, this guy said something about a rumor out on the street that Ryan Benton is about to be brought up on corruption charges as a result of an investigation by Internal Affairs."

"Say that again," Helen ordered, then had to slam on the brakes to prevent the car rolling backward into a bush because she wasn't concentrating. "Ryan Benton has been investigated by the police disciplinary department? He's *officially* suspected of being corrupt?"

"Yeah. At least according to the guy in the next cell." Philip nodded. "Apparently Ryan was involved in an earlier corruption scandal ten years ago, so he's an automatic suspect. At that time, his partner, Colleen Wellesley, got kicked off the force but he was allowed to resign. I guess they didn't have enough evidence to bring charges or he'd never have been hired as sheriff in Silver Rapids. Or hired back on here in Denver. Kind of surprising, isn't it?"

Incredible, Helen thought. She'd never in a thousand years have figured Ryan Benton for a bought cop. The possibility that he might be in Franklin's pay hadn't once crossed her mind, even though he'd been the arresting officer on Philip's case, and even though she knew that Franklin had to be bribing somebody in the precinct. She drew in a deep breath, fighting a sudden wave of nausea.

"What exactly is Ryan accused of doing?" she asked. "Did your informant explain?"

"He's not been formally accused of anything so far, but apparently he and his partner are both accused of taking bribes to look the other way at crime scenes. Guess he fooled me, even though he was the one who busted me on a phony charge." Philip shook his head. "Ryan looks an honest, down-to-earth kind of guy. To be truthful, I kinda liked him. Insofar as you can like a cop who's busting your ass."

"It just shows how looks can be deceiving." Helen managed to sound casual enough, but the nausea wouldn't go away. Her stomach was churning with so much acid that she thought she might actually throw up.

"You didn't get any hint he was dirty when you were dating him?" Philip asked.

"Not a thing, or our dating days would have been over." At least she could answer that honestly. "I never heard or saw anything to suggest he was dishonest. He was the town sheriff, you know, and his reputation in Silver Rapids was just about golden."

"Maybe the big city got to him."

"Maybe."

The lying hypocrite, Helen thought, putting all the facts about Ryan Benton together and coming up with a new and unpleasant picture. The mealy-mouthed bastard had dared to complain to her about Philip's release from jail when all the time he was part of the very corruption he appeared to condemn. Her con-

versation with him took on a different significance
once she considered the likelihood that Ryan was
dirty, and his parting remark suddenly struck her in a
whole new light.

Your husband is a dud weapon. Helen had taken
that to mean that Ryan was an honest cop who refused
to be intimidated by the power of Senator Franklin
Gettys. But if Ryan was already in Franklin's pay, his
remark might mean simply that he had nothing to
fear. In fact, she reflected grimly, Ryan and Franklin
could well be allies. The idea made sense. Ryan had
made the bust, so nothing could have been easier than
for him to cook up the case against Philip in the first
place.

Seething with outrage, Helen added up the indict-
ment against Ryan. Franklin had been talking to him
at the cocktail party the other night. Why else would
her husband waste his time with a lowly detective
from one of the city's less affluent neighborhoods unless the guy was in his pocket? Add to that the fact
that Ryan had been the arresting cop when her brother
was set up on a fake charge, orchestrated by her husband, and it began to seem more and more likely that
Ryan had been paid off to do Franklin's bidding.

Helen felt a disappointment that was painful, even
if irrational. Until a few days ago, she and Ryan
hadn't spoken to each other in two and a half years,
so there was no reason for her to feel as if she'd been
personally betrayed. Still, it was yet another lesson
learned in a week that was already too full of difficult
lessons. How many times did she need to have it ham-
mered home that you couldn't judge the heart of a
man from his handsome exterior?

"You okay, Nell?" Philip touched her lightly on the arm.

"Yes, sure. I'm fine now you're out of jail." With considerable effort, she dragged her attention away from Ryan Benton and back to her brother. Right now, all that mattered was that she should get her brother out of state, far away from Franklin and his corrupt cronies. And then, as soon as Philip was safely out of reach, Helen could fight for her own freedom from a marriage that had turned into the worst sort of prison.

She was counting not just the weeks or the days, but the hours and the minutes.

CHAPTER EIGHT

Seattle, September, 16 months later

LABOUR DAY was barely past, but Seattle had already given up on summer sunshine. Helen shivered as the drizzling rain trickled under her umbrella and soaked through her linen jacket. Her clunker of a car was in the shop—again—so she'd been forced to take the bus to and from her work at Nordstrom's flagship department store.

She was cold and soaked through, but Helen didn't mind the discomfort. She was human enough to heave an occasional nostalgic sigh for the BMW sports coupe that had vanished along with her marriage, but taking the bus every so often seemed a small price to pay for the glorious gift of freedom from Franklin Gettys. She hadn't realized how desperately unhappy she'd been in her marriage until it had ended and she had headed west to join her brother in Seattle.

Her idle days in the lonely Cherry Hills mansion were a fast-fading memory that brought only relief, not regrets. Nowadays, she lived in a rented row house and worked long hours for modest pay. An outsider might think that her life had taken a sharp turn for the worse. Helen knew it had taken a fantastic turn for the better.

She sidestepped a puddle, missed, and was rewarded with water sloshing inside her shoes. Her life

might be better in a general sense, she reflected with
an inward smile, but right at this moment she was
looking forward to getting home and enjoying a hot
bath, scented with something luxuriously seductive.
That is, if bath oil bought at a discount drugstore
could be considered luxurious. Helen grinned. At
least she'd bought the cheap pink stuff herself, and
that made the perfume incredibly sweet.

Her steps and her thoughts both slammed to an
abrupt halt as a trench-coated woman blocked the
sidewalk in front of her. The woman was holding a
mike, which she thrust out under Helen's nose.

"I'm Desiree Shelton from Eyewitness News," she
said. "You are Helen Gettys, the former wife of Senator Franklin Gettys, right?"

"I have no comment about anything," Helen said.
Belatedly—very belatedly—she realized there were
half a dozen people clustered outside the modest row
house that she and Philip rented. There was also a
minivan with the logo of a local TV station parked
right across from their rickety front gate.

What the hell had Franklin said or done now, Helen
wondered wearily. She was so tired of her ex-
husband's seemingly endless need to make her the
butt of stories leaked to the media, designed to show
her as an adulterous alcoholic, and himself as the
wonderful man who'd struggled to bring her to sal-
vation, failing only because of Helen's willful refusal
to accept his loving help.

Whatever story he'd concocted this time, she
wouldn't dignify it with a denial. If there was one
thing she'd learned in the months following her divorce, it was that there was absolutely nothing she
could say to the media that would cause them to slant

their stories in any way other than the direction they'd always intended—usually negative to her and praising Franklin to the skies.

"Excuse me, please." She tried to pass the Eyewitness News reporter. "It's been a long day at work and I'd like to get inside my own home. You're blocking my entrance."

"Would you care to comment on the kidnapping case of baby Sky Langworthy, Mrs. Gettys?"

Helen reared back and stared directly into the reporter's eyes. "Why on earth are you asking me about the Langworthy kidnapping?" she asked, startled out of her standard no-comment response.

"You haven't heard about the statement your brother made earlier this morning?"

Helen shook her head in bemusement. Was it possible that Philip had commented on the kidnapping of the three-month-old baby grandson of a former governor of Colorado? That seemed not just incredible, but bizarre. Why would her brother make a statement? And who would care if he did?

Young man who has no insider information, knows none of the parties involved, and lives a thousand miles away from the scene of the kidnapping, makes public statement about the Schyler Langworthy kidnapping.

Yep, she could sure see how that would bring all the press hounds salivating.

Helen was media-savvy enough not to utter a single word of what she was thinking. "I haven't heard anything about any statement my brother might have made," she said, hoping that she sounded calmer than she felt. "We've never discussed the kidnapping. Excuse me, please. I have no comment to make at this time.''

"But you'll have a statement to make later, Mrs. Gettys?'' the reporter asked eagerly.

Helen shook her head. "I have nothing to say now, or at any time in the future. Oh, and by the way, my name is Helen Kouros. I'm sure you are aware that Senator Gettys and I are no longer married.''

She dodged around Desiree What'sHerName and sprinted up the path to the front door. Thank goodness Philip must have been watching from inside the house, because he tugged open the door before she had even started looking for her key, and dragged her inside.

Helen slumped against the inside of the door, umbrella dripping onto the worn linoleum floor. The house had been built in the nineteen forties, when Seattle was practically a frontier town, and had a minuscule entrance hall with doors that opened to a tiny parlor on one side and an even smaller dining room on the other. Right now, she was glad the hallway had no windows. It was good to be shielded from prying eyes, and she felt pleasantly cocooned in the enclosed space, a comforting contrast to the harassment waiting on the outside of the door.

"What in the world was that about?'' she demanded, too stressed even to take the necessary few steps into the parlor. "Why do we have a TV crew camped out on our doorstep?''

"Haven't you heard?'' Philip's smile was bitter. "I'm the media's latest hot suspect in the kidnapping of the Langworthy baby.''

Helen almost laughed. Almost. "Why in the world would anyone suspect you of kidnapping the Lang-

worthy baby?'' Helen was glad she had the front door
to hold her upright. ''Are they nuts? Quite apart from
anything else, you're here in Seattle and the baby was
kidnapped from his crib in Denver—''

''Yeah, you're right. Unfortunately, the baby was
snatched on the Fourth of July—''

''And so?''

''That's when I was camping in the Colorado
Rockies.''

''Oh no! Oh damn!''

''Oh yes,'' Philip said bleakly. ''I was gone for a
week, remember?''

''But you were camping with friends! They can
provide an alibi for you.''

Philip shook his head. ''I was only with friends for
the first five days. On the Fourth, the campground was
swarming with tourists, so the other guys went home
a day early and I hiked way up into the mountains
and slept out for the night.''

There was no way her brother could have guessed
what a rotten idea that would turn out to be. Helen
damped down her frustration. ''Okay, but you weren't
alone all the time, were you? Somebody must have
seen you.''

''Yeah, I guess people saw me,'' Philip said,
sounding gloomy. ''But it's more than three months
later. I bet there's not a chance of finding a witness
who could swear they saw me in the Arapahoe National Forest at the time Schyler was taken from his
crib. The reporters have it all worked out, it seems.
They claim I had enough time to hike down out of
the forest, drive into Denver and snatch the baby.''

''Then they're nuts! You were miles away from
Denver.''

"I had a rental car, remember, so it's physically possible I could have done the deed, although even the FBI agrees I must have had an accomplice helping me because I didn't have any baby with me later that evening when I met up with another friend for dinner."

"The FBI?" Helen said, her voice sharpening with worry. "Don't tell me that law enforcement is paying attention to this latest load of media garbage?"

"They're paying enough attention for two agents to come out to the college campus this afternoon and question me for three hours. Although they didn't hold me when I kept saying I knew nothing at all about the kidnapping. I guess that's one minor blessing."

"And who does the FBI believe is your accomplice?" Helen asked, although she was afraid she already knew the answer to that question.

"Well, since Franklin Gettys is undoubtedly the bastard who leaked this bullshit to the media, I'll give you one guess about who they suspect."

She swallowed. "Me?"

"Bingo. Give the lady a prize. That son of a bitch you were married to has stuck it to us again."

"Oh my God." A wave of pessimism washed over Helen, even though she knew the media interest in her couldn't hold up. She'd been at a barbecue on the Fourth right here in Seattle, and she could prove it. But the prospect of fighting off the press again really depressed her. She should have known the past ten months living in Seattle had been much too peaceful after the tumultuous period of her divorce from Franklin Gettys.

Sighing, she pushed her hair out of her eyes. She

couldn't afford fancy haircuts anymore, and she'd let it grow long so that she could wear it swept back into a chignon—the cheapest of all styles.

"Let me get out of these damp clothes," she said to her brother, needing a few minutes to grasp the full implications of what he'd told her. "Then we'll have a family conference and decide how we're going to handle this—"

"Actually, we have a visitor."

"Cathie's here?" Helen said, her mood perking up a little. Philip had been dating seriously for the past five months, and Helen thought that in Cathie, a nurse with a graduate degree in obstetrics, her brother might have found the perfect future wife. Not to mention a sister Helen would love to have.

Philip shook his head. "Not Cathie, although I'm going over to her apartment later tonight. Ryan Benton's come from Colorado to see us. He's waiting in the parlor."

Ryan Benton was here, in her house? Helen forgot all about changing out of her damp clothes. She pushed open the door and marched into the parlor, where Ryan Benton was indeed waiting. He rose to his feet, looking tall and dominating in the tiny room. He also looked spectacularly handsome, but she did her best not to notice that annoying fact. In her opinion, one of the few things more despicable than a crooked politician was a dirty cop, and she had no intention of allowing her physical attraction to Ryan Benton to override her ethical standards.

"What are you doing here?" she demanded.

Ryan gave an infuriatingly controlled smile, his gaze traveling slowly upward from her mud-splattered shoes, past her damp jacket and skirt, and coming to rest on her disheveled hair. "It's nice to see you, too, Helen."

By the time he'd finished his inspection, she felt as elegant and put-together as something the cat had dragged out onto the back stoop to finish eating. She pushed a strand of damp hair behind her ear, ignoring the drips onto her neck. She drew herself up to her full height, which meant that she was still seven inches shorter than Ryan's six foot two, and glared up at him.

"I assume you have a reason for being here. Please state it and then leave."

"I'm investigating the kidnapping of Schyler Langworthy—"

"Then you're in the wrong place, because Philip and I know nothing about the kidnapping. Goodbye."

"I think you can help me with my investigation—"

"I know you're not a cop anymore, Ryan, so how can you be investigating a kidnapping?" Helen didn't want to listen to him lie, so she told him what she knew. "I heard all about the corruption charges made against you and your partner. I know you both left the police department under a very large black cloud. There were lengthy reports about you and your partner in the Denver newspapers at least two months before I moved from Colorado to Seattle."

If anything, Ryan's expression became more bland. "The newspapers didn't give an entirely accurate account of what happened. Despite the lurid reporting, my partner and I were never formally accused of anything. The truth is, we chose to resign."

"In other words, you made your escape one step ahead of the law." Helen had been a victim of distorted media reporting often enough that she ought to have been willing to give Ryan and his partner the benefit of the doubt. But for once everything she knew personally backed up the published reports. She knew for a fact that Ryan had been bribed by Franklin Gettys to frame Philip for drug dealing. She would never forgive him for that injury to her brother.

Her caustic comment caused the faintest tightening of Ryan's mouth. Maybe he wasn't quite as indifferent to her barbs as his neutral expression might suggest. Helen was obscurely pleased to know that she had the power to get under his skin, even if only marginally.

"Are you planning for us to spend the next few minutes trading insults?" Ryan asked. "If so, I can give back as good as I get. Or should we simply take the insults as a given and move on to the real reason why I'm here?"

"We should move on," she said tightly. But there was a definite appeal to the idea of trading insults. Her skin felt prickly with irritation at Ryan's presence here in her new home. She was tired of the way he kept popping back into her life, disturbing her equilibrium. Most of all, she despised the way her body reacted to his physical attractions, despite what she knew about his moral worth. Or lack thereof. Apparently marriage to Franklin Gettys hadn't rammed home the elementary lesson that good looks had nothing to do with character.

"Okay, then. We'll skip the insults." Ryan was definitely losing some of his cool. He drew in a sharp breath and spoke with visibly hard-won calm. "As I started to explain, I'm helping to investigate the disappearance of Schyler Langworthy. A member of the baby's immediate family has hired my company to help find him.''

"Hired your company?" Helen asked. "Do you work for a firm of private investigators, then?"

Ryan nodded. "Yes, I do. When I was sheriff of Silver Rapids, I worked on a case with a woman called Colleen Wellesley. She started her own investigative agency some years back, and she invited me to come and work for her at Investigations, Confidential and Undercover. She needed the extra help." He gave a tight smile. "Investigating sleazy activities seems to be a recession-proof business."

"Yes, there's always plenty of sleazy activity to go around, isn't there?" Helen said sweetly. She was surprised Ryan and Colleen Wellesley had managed to get their detective company licensed. Or perhaps she wasn't. After all, they had corrupt friends in high places. No doubt Franklin Gettys and his cronies found it useful to keep gofers who had their fingers on the pulse of Denver's criminal underbelly. If Franklin couldn't have Ryan operating from inside the heart of the police force, having him on tap as a private investigator was probably the next best thing.

"That still doesn't explain what you're doing here in my house," she said. "If you believe my brother and I have anything to do with Schyler's disappearance, I can only tell you one more time that you're entirely mistaken."

Ryan looked unimpressed by her vehemence. "Mistaken or not, you're both going to face a lot of questions. Channel 12 broke the story of Philip's possible involvement yesterday afternoon. I followed up with the FBI, expecting them to tell me I should pay no attention. Instead, the FBI agent in charge of the case confirmed that Philip was 'a person of interest' to the investigation. Given our firm's involvement in the case, I had no choice but to come out here and investigate why the bureau believes your brother can help them with their inquiries.''

Helen smothered a flare of anger at the FBI agent who could so casually toss her brother to the wolves. ''The bureau has a bad habit of identifying 'persons of interest' who later turn out to have nothing at all to do with the case they're investigating. If the bureau truly believes Philip is involved in the kidnapping of Schyler Langworthy, then they're dead wrong. I'm sorry for the Langworthy family and what they're suffering, but we can't help them. In fact, I can't imagine why my brother let you into our home. We have nothing to say to you or to the FBI, and I'd appreciate it if you'd leave.''

Helen jumped to her feet and pointedly held the parlor door open. She wanted Ryan out of her sight before she started to recall too much about the happy times they'd shared in Silver Rapids during the nine months they'd dated. In her memories, the days unfolded as a fun-filled G-rated movie, accompanied by a soundtrack filled with laughter, music, and light-hearted conversation. The nights blurred into a triple X-rated movie with a soundtrack of heavy breathing and low moans of sexual pleasure.

Helen blinked, hurriedly returning her attention to the present. If she carried on with that train of thought much longer, her damp clothes would soon be steaming.

''Goodbye, Ryan,'' she said, with a firmness that was as much for herself as for him. ''Have a safe flight home to Colorado.''

"Not so fast," he said, not moving. "Let me remind you I'm in this house at your brother's specific invitation."

"Then I can only assume some alien has swooped down and taken possession of his body because my real brother would never invite you into our home." Helen remained by the door, fingers tapping on the handle.

"Well, here he comes. Ask him yourself." Ryan gestured toward Philip, who was entering the parlor at that moment, carrying a tray with three steaming mugs of coffee mixed with hot milk—his homemade version of café latte. Three mugs, Helen noted. It seemed Ryan was correct in claiming that her brother had invited him to stay for a while. What's more, her brother looked positively friendly as he came into the parlor and aimed a smile in Ryan's direction.

Possession by space aliens began to look more and more likely. How else to explain Philip's amiability? After her divorce, she'd told her brother the truth about the drug charges that had been brought against him, including the fact that Ryan was the cop who'd helped Franklin to set him up. Not surprisingly, her brother had been outraged. If Ryan hadn't already been dismissed from the force, her brother would have launched a one-man crusade to get him convicted of corruption. And now here Philip was, suddenly all smiles toward the man he'd sworn vengeance against less than nine months ago.

"How far did Ryan get in telling you what's going on?" Philip asked, handing his sister a mug of coffee. "Here Ryan. You don't take sugar, right? Did you already explain to Nell why you're here?"

"We barely got started," Ryan said smoothly, taking his coffee with a murmur of thanks. ''Your sister and I were still catching up on a few personal details.''

Philip dropped into his favorite chair, draping his long legs over the arm. That left Helen nowhere to sit except on the sofa, next to Ryan. Spine ramrod straight, she perched as far away from him as space allowed, wrapping her hands around the warm mug. Just because her brother had taken leave of his senses, there was no need for her to do the same. She'd listen to Ryan's excuses for being here and then she'd show him the door.

For some reason better left unexamined, the prospect of his departure didn't make her as happy as it should have.

CHAPTER NINE

FAR FROM SHOWING animosity toward the man who'd arrested him, Philip seemed entirely relaxed and friendly as he sipped his coffee. "We'd better fill Helen in on the details of the Langworthy baby's disappearance," he said to Ryan. He smiled affectionately toward his sister. "She's such a softie that she hasn't been following the case very closely. She says it's too painful to imagine what the baby's family is going through, so she prefers to avoid hearing the details. That way, her imagination can't go into overdrive."

"Then here's a really condensed version of what happened," Ryan said, turning on the sofa to face Helen. "Schyler Langworthy was kidnapped from his crib on the morning of July 4. He was three months old at the time. His mother is Holly Langworthy, and she's a single parent—"

Helen nodded. "And I remember that Holly's father is Samuel Langworthy, who was the governor of Colorado most of the time I was in grade school."

"And now Holly's half brother, Joshua, is running for governor in the upcoming election," Ryan said. "Governor Forbes, the incumbent, went into the election campaign with quite a few negatives to overcome, but he's proving a surprisingly difficult opponent to beat."

"He's a good campaigner," Helen conceded. "I met the governor on a couple of occasions when I was married to Franklin, and he's a tough old bird." She hadn't been very impressed with Todd Forbes, she reflected, who had seemed big on charm and short on genuine warmth—a similar personality to Franklin, in fact. She knew from TV and newspaper commentaries that her ex and Governor Forbes were political allies who shared an enthusiasm for bio-weapons research that they both tried to pass off as nothing more than a desire to bring high-tech jobs to Colorado. Given their personalities, Helen suspected that job creation was low on their list of priorities. What they both wanted was the power that would come from controlling a new weapons program.

"As you can imagine, there are a lot of high-powered people desperate for Schyler to be found," Ryan said, sipping his coffee. "The baby's disappearance is not just a tragedy for the Langworthys. It's giving the local cops a severe attack of heartburn, and creating a ton of unfavorable publicity for the FBI. The press commentary has gotten so scathing that the FBI director sent an official letter of rebuke to the Denver FBI office. As you can imagine, they're not happy about that, to put it mildly."

Much as Helen disliked thinking along such lines, the absence of progress in the case seemed to suggest that baby Schyler might already be dead. She shuddered in sympathy for what Holly Langworthy was going through. She couldn't imagine a worse nightmare than having your baby snatched from his crib, followed by months of silence about his fate.

"From what little I know about the case, the public's been very supportive," she said, trying not to dwell on the disturbing image of Holly's grief. "Aren't the police getting any tips on their hotline?"

"There have been plenty of tips," Ryan said. "But they've all petered out, and right now the agent in charge admitted to me that the case is on a high-speed track to nowhere."

Philip folded a paper napkin to make a coaster for his coffee mug. "Meanwhile, the cable TV channels are blanketing the airwaves with around-the-clock coverage, so every kook with an ax to grind can find an outlet to get publicity for his nutty theory. Naming me as a suspect is just the latest flaky theory in a long line of them."

"And the rival political camps in the governor's race aren't helping," Ryan said. "The two camps are hurling accusations at each other, each one claiming that the other guys are trying to make election capital out of the baby's disappearance."

Helen felt another wave of sympathy for Holly Langworthy, who was coping not only with the devastating disappearance of her son, but also with media speculation that was downright vicious. "I *despise* the way politicians manage to make even a tragedy like the kidnapping of a baby into campaign propaganda," she said.

"Yeah, it's been depressing to watch," Ryan said. "Especially since Josh Langworthy has some interesting new ideas to put to the electorate. It's a shame he's not getting a chance to campaign on the issues, instead of constantly being asked about his missing nephew. However, you two can't afford to spare any sympathy for other people. Right now, you need to look out for yourselves because unless you act fast, you're going to be dragged front and center of the media circus—''

"I don't see how," Helen said. "Surely to goodness this interest in Philip is going to be a one-day wonder on the cable news channels and then all the speculation in us will die down again."

Ryan shook his head. "You're not going to escape that easily. My contact at the bureau told me their sudden interest in your brother wasn't just fueled by media hunger for new suspects. It seems the bureau received an anonymous package that contained detailed information outlining how and why Philip was involved in kidnapping Schyler Langworthy."

"That must have been a slender package," Helen said tartly.

"The evidence is circumstantial but it fits convincingly together," Philip said, scowling into his empty coffee mug. "They even have a motive as to why I might have done it. They claim I have a crazy, drug-induced desire to get back at Holly Langworthy."

"But you don't even know Holly Langworthy!" Helen exclaimed.

"I do know her a little," Philip admitted. "Or at least I did. I dated her years ago, but for less than a month—it was when you were working at the Swan-song Casino, Nell, so you weren't often in Denver, which is why you didn't know about it."

"You're right, I had no idea you'd ever set eyes on her, much less dated her." Helen said. "Is the FBI correct? Did she dump you?"

"Yep, she dumped me all right," Philip said wryly. "I was heavily into cocaine at the time, so I don't remember all the details of our traumatic parting scene, but I know it was related to my drug use and

I'm sure I deserved whatever insults she heaped on my spaced-out head. As for wanting to get back at her...well, that's nuts. To be honest, I hadn't thought about Holly from the day we split up until the day I heard Schyler had been kidnapped. The fact is, I never really knew much about her, except that she was real pretty and a cool date to take to a party."

"Did you explain all this to the FBI?" Helen asked.

"Yeah, but straight-arrow FBI agents aren't the types to have much personal experience with the highs and lows of drug addiction. It's hard for them to grasp how superficial my relationships were back then, and how little connection I feel nowadays to that part of my past. They think I'm holding back information, when really I don't have any to give them."

Helen counted off on her fingers. "Okay, so you have no alibi, the media is pursuing us and the FBI seems to be considering both of us as possible suspects—"

"The FBI aren't going to arrest Philip, much less you," Ryan said. "As soon as they run a serious investigation of the accusations, they'll realize they don't have a case."

"Great," Helen said. "So we won't get arrested, we'll just get convicted by the media. Are we going to sit around and wait for our lives to be destroyed before we get serious about demonstrating that these crazy theories have no basis except in my ex-husband's desire for vengeance?" Instinctively, she turned to Ryan as she spoke.

"Are you asking me?" he said quietly.

She hesitated for a moment, realizing the incongruity of looking for help from a man she had no reason to trust. "I guess I am," she said finally. "You're the detective, after all."

"I'm a detective you accused of being corrupt only a few minutes ago."

Helen pushed at the loose strands of her hair again, as if taming her hairstyle would somehow enable her to make sense out of her muddled thoughts. Ryan leaned toward her and caught her hand, keeping it in his clasp.

"Let's face facts, Helen, even if they're uncomfortable. We can't work together unless the two of us get some personal issues out on the table."

"What sort of personal issues?" Helen asked, instantly wary.

"At a minimum, issues about honesty and integrity," Ryan said. "Not just mine, but yours, too. I came here believing I had good reasons to distrust you and your brother. Ever since Philip escaped so easily from that drug dealing charge, I've blamed you. I convinced myself you were so overprotective where he was concerned that you'd lost your judgment. I believed you were willing to use your influence with Franklin Gettys to corrupt the system and get the drug charges against your brother thrown out—"

"Well, you were right," she said. "I did exactly that, but for a valid reason. The charges against Philip were false." Confusion made her voice harsh. "You of all people should know that."

"I know it *now*," Ryan said. "That's because Philip spent the two hours before you arrived home from work filling me in on the details of how Franklin blackmailed you into staying with him. But I had no idea your brother had been set up when I arrested him last spring. At the time I didn't have a clue what was going on, I swear it. I was a victim of Franklin Gettys every bit as much as you and Philip.''

Ryan sounded so honest, so sincere. So goddamn *trustworthy*. Helen jerked her hand out of his grasp, curling it into a fist because it required real physical effort not to touch him, not to give in to the temptation of taking him at his word. She so much wanted to believe that he could be trusted. Out of the blue, the thought sprang into her mind that Ryan might have been sent here on Franklin's orders, with instructions to worm his way back into her confidence. Her stomach heaved in revulsion at the thought.

''You may have convinced my brother that you didn't know the score when you arrested him, but I have the best of reasons for believing that you were a dirty cop,'' she said. ''I didn't just pull the accusations out of thin air. I know my husband was paying you off.'' Her voice lowered as she admitted the truth. ''I wish I didn't.''

She wasn't angry anymore, Helen realized, simply sad. When she was with Ryan, it was so hard to believe that he was one of the bad guys.

''The accusations against my partner were false,'' Ryan said tersely. ''And even the department didn't attempt to bring corruption charges against me. They knew they'd be laughed out of court. As for the accusation that your husband was paying me off…what evidence do you have for suggesting that?''

''The best. Before our divorce was finalized, Franklin flat out admitted to me that you were in his pay, and that you were the cop he'd bribed in order to get Philip arrested. In other words, I have proof right from the horse's mouth.''

''And you believe Franklin's accusations?'' Ryan

asked, his voice harsh. "Knowing me as well as you once did, you still believe your ex-husband's words over mine? Did it never occur to you that Franklin might have reasons to lie about which cop he was paying off?"

"Why would he lie about something like that? What advantage would there be to him in that?" But even as Helen asked the question, she realized the answer.

Ryan shot her an incredulous glance. "Why would Franklin Gettys make a false accusation against me?" He laughed without mirth. "Gee, off the top of my head, I can't come up with more than a half dozen reasons. Here's one. He accused me because he was protecting somebody else on the police force. Somebody who was in a much more powerful position than me, and much more useful to him."

"With all the hundreds of cops in Denver, why did Franklin just happen to pick on you to accuse?"

Ryan shrugged as if the answer to her question were obvious. "Partly because he found out you and I had once been lovers and I'm sure it gave him a lot of satisfaction to get me in trouble. I don't think you ever realized just how jealous Franklin was of you, and especially of the popularity you'd achieved in the Silver Rapids community. But there was an even more important reason. I had begun to suspect who the dirty cops might really be and I was working to collect evidence to present to Internal Affairs. Not to mince words, Josie and I were beginning to scare the shit out of your ex-husband."

"Which cops do you suspect of being dirty?" Helen asked.

Ryan shook his head. "We have no proof that

would stand up in court and I'm not willing to make accusations that I can't back up. There's been way too much of that happening recently.''

"So I'm just supposed to take your word that you never accepted a bribe?"

"Yes, you are." Ryan leaned toward her, reaching for her hands again and folding them into his. "I'm asking you to trust me, Nell. Is that so impossible?"

When he used that gentle, coaxing voice, he could probably have convinced her that Santa Claus was going to be late delivering toys this year because of an industrial dispute with his elves.

His thumbs stroked across her knuckles. "Before Philip's arrest, however messed up our relationship was, you never had any reason to doubt my integrity, right? So the major reason you suspect me of being corrupt is because of your ex-husband's accusations, right?"

She nodded.

"Consider everything you know about Franklin and everything you know about me. Think about it, Nell. Who is more likely to be telling you the truth?"

Only two people in the world ever called her Nell. One was her brother, and the other was Ryan. Helen's resistance melted some more under the heat of remembered passion. She stared at Ryan's strong, lean hands wrapped around hers and wondered how in the world she was supposed to make rational judgments when all she wanted to do was lay her head against his shoulder and count the world well lost for love.

Getting honest cops thrown off the police force in order to divert suspicion from the real culprits fit the pattern of everything Franklin had done since the day she'd asked for a divorce, Helen reflected. But was that an objective assessment or an expression of her own prejudices? The temptation to believe in Ryan was so strong that she was afraid to give in to it, and she forced herself to make one more protest.

"You have no way to prove that you weren't being paid off by Franklin Gettys," she pointed out.

"No, I don't, but how does anybody prove a negative? It can't be done." Ignoring the fact that Philip was still in the parlor and was watching them with considerable interest, Ryan crooked his finger under her chin and tilted her face up so that she was looking straight into his eyes.

"Sometimes you have to trust your instincts, Nell, and that's always been tough for you. I can't shake the accusation that I'm corrupt without bringing the real dirty cops to justice, and so far we haven't managed to find the evidence for that. It's difficult working from outside the force, especially since the suspects I'm targeting hold such senior positions. But you're in the same situation as me, aren't you? You have no proof that Franklin orchestrated your brother's arrest on drug charges, and no way to prove that he's deliberately making false accusations about the Langworthy kidnapping, so the two of you are stuck under a cloud of suspicion, with no way to dispel the media attention. It's a mess, but unless you and I find some way to trust each other, Franklin Gettys will win."

"Even if we decide to trust each other, Franklin remains more powerful than either of us."

"Don't be so sure of that. I have some powerful friends myself." Ryan touched her lightly on her cheek. "Don't let him win, Nell. Trust me, not him.

For once in your life, listen to you heart, not your head.''

She'd listened to her head when she rejected Ryan's proposal. She'd listened to it again when she'd agreed to marry Franklin. Ruefully, Helen acknowledged that her head had made bad mistakes on both occasions. Why not trust her feelings for once? The screwup that might result surely couldn't be any worse than what had already happened.

She let out a long, unsteady breath and took a flying leap into unknown territory. ''I do trust you, Ryan.''

''Wise woman,'' he said softly. ''Smart decision.''

Helen only realized how hard it had been to cling to her suspicions about him when she felt her entire body go limp with relief. After almost eighteen months of telling herself that Ryan Benton was as crooked as they come, it should have been difficult to transform her mental images of him from dirty cop to just another victim of Franklin's machinations. Instead, it was one of the easiest things she'd ever done. Despite all the apparent evidence, she'd never managed to fit Ryan into the role of corrupt cop because it went against the grain of everything she knew about him. Franklin in the role of liar and manipulator, on the other hand, was a smooth and easy fit.

''I just wish that trusting each other made a real difference to Franklin's power to create mischief,'' she said.

''It makes all the difference in the world to me,'' Ryan said simply.

''It doesn't bring you any closer to finding Schyler Langworthy.''

''With your help, I may even have an idea or two

about that. We need to pool our information and see if that doesn't give us a new and better perspective. To be honest, what puzzles me most right now is why Franklin is wasting so much time and energy on blackening your reputation. I never had the impression that Franklin was deeply in love with you, but was I wrong? Is he so brokenhearted that he isn't able to be rational?''

''Franklin's heart never played any role in our marriage,'' Helen said. ''He married me for political convenience, that's all.''

''That answer just raises more questions. Why did Franklin find you such a convenient wife? If it's convenience he wanted, wouldn't he have done better to marry a woman who was already active in politics? Or at least a wife who could bring him lots of money to help out with his campaigns?''

''On the surface, you might think so. But Franklin only looked around for a wife because he had to, not because he wanted to. His fortieth birthday was long gone and he was getting too old to remain single—''

''Too old to be single?'' Ryan queried. ''You mean because he campaigns as a conservative, with a big emphasis on traditional family values?''

She nodded. ''Exactly. His core constituents are suspicious of middle-aged bachelors, so he needed to marry. But from Franklin's point of view, that need was a real pain. To be fair, he works hard, for long hours, and his schedule is erratic, making it difficult to coordinate his comings and goings with another person. Plus, he likes living alone. He enjoys eating all his meals in restaurants and going out every night with business colleagues. He also likes having sex with lots of young women he barely knows, and he doesn't want children. How does a wife fit into this picture?''

"Not easily," Ryan said.

"Not at all, in fact." Helen picked up her mug, realized the coffee was all gone, and set it down with a thump, still angry with herself for having been such an easy dupe. "Franklin never planned to be sexually faithful, and he didn't intend to let his wife share the political limelight. Even the need to please the voters wasn't enough to persuade him to have children, or change his lifestyle in any significant way. So he married me, the next best thing to having no wife at all. He figured he had me captive since I had no money, no high-powered friends and no dazzling career to fall back on if I got tired of being a doormat.''

"Not to mention your pain-in-the-ass younger brother who had a problem with cocaine," Philip interjected. "I wouldn't be surprised if Franklin saw blackmail opportunities in my addiction problems right from the start. I'll bet he always saw your love for me as something that could be exploited to keep you in line if you ever got too independent.''

"What a fool Franklin Gettys was," Ryan said softly.

"Yes, he is. As far as he's concerned, love is a weakness." Helen stared blindly at the hearth but, for a moment, what she saw wasn't the cozy parlor, but the formal living room of Franklin's house in Cherry Hills, where the two of them had shared no more than a dozen evenings in two years of marriage. She shivered at the bleak memory.

"I understand why Franklin married you and why he didn't want you to divorce him," Ryan said. "But I still don't understand why he's going after you now that the marriage is over. Why does he spend so much time blackening your reputation with the media?''

"His assessment of me has changed," Helen suggested. "I think...maybe...he's a little afraid of me and he wants to make sure the threat I present is neutralized."

"What threat do you represent?" Ryan demanded. "You said yourself that he's the person with all the power."

"Most of the power, not all, otherwise we'd still be married," Helen corrected. "Once Philip was safe here in Seattle, I began looking for a blackmail weapon to use against Franklin. I decided I needed information—something damaging that I could threaten him with. I knew he'd only agree to a divorce if it was more trouble to keep me in the marriage than to let me go—"

"I suggested she should collect a file with the names of all the women who'd had affairs with him and take it to the media," Philip said.

"But I decided that wasn't fair to the women," Helen said.

"Hell, you're more generous than I would have been," Ryan said. "They were women who'd been committing adultery with your husband—"

"Yes, but I'm sure he told them I was a total bitch who made his life hell, so they have some excuse."

"Not much of a one," Ryan said.

"Maybe not. But more to the point, the fact that Franklin had been unfaithful didn't strike me as formidable enough to be a real weapon. Even his conservative friends might have forgiven him a few episodes of adultery, given the unflattering picture he's managed to paint of me. An alcoholic wife who refuses to sleep with her husband or to share in his political career doesn't generate much sympathy.''

''So what did you find to use against him, if not his adultery?'' Ryan asked.

''I found the Half Spur,'' Helen said. ''It's a ranch near Granby, where Franklin runs two thousand head of Merino sheep—''

''I'm very familiar with the Half Spur,'' Ryan said. ''The ranch attracted the attention of my partners months ago. We even have a scrap of evidence from the ranch that possibly links Franklin as a suspect in the Langworthy kidnapping.''

Helen looked up quickly. ''Could Sky be at the ranch, do you think? It's a pretty big place, with lots of convenient trailers and huts where you could hide a baby.''

Ryan shook his head. ''We had the same idea, but there's no evidence we can find that Sky's ever been taken to the ranch, much less held there.''

Helen gave a half nod. ''On second thought, I can't imagine that Franklin would take the risk of hiding the baby at the Half Spur, even if he is involved in the kidnapping. He's absolutely paranoid about keeping outsiders away from there.''

''I notice that you don't seem shocked by the idea that Franklin might be a kidnapper.''

Helen was silent for a moment, realizing how horrifying it was that she'd accepted the idea of her ex-husband as a brutal kidnapper without a murmur of protest. ''No, I guess I'm not surprised or shocked,'' she said finally. ''It seems perfectly credible to me that Franklin would kidnap a child if it suited his purpose. And if he thought he could get away with it, of course.''

Ryan leaned toward her, so focused that Helen felt the intensity of his concentration as a physical presence. ''You had the inside track where Franklin Gettys is concerned, Nell, and that means you had access to information that our organization couldn't hope to find. Tell me what you discovered about the Half Spur.''

Helen was only too happy to oblige. The burden of what she suspected about her ex-husband's activities had been heavy for a long time. ''Luckily, Franklin was so convinced of my stupidity that he was careless about safeguarding his secrets from me even after he knew I wanted a divorce. He left his laptop on the desk in his office without ever bothering to lock it away, and I soon found out that the password to his confidential files was *Superbowl.* I saw him type it in once, and after that I had free range of his computer.''

''The guy should have stuck to playing football,'' Philip muttered. ''He was pretty good at that.''

''You were taking a huge risk in accessing Franklin's secret files,'' Ryan said grimly. ''He's not only a powerful man. It's my belief he's a dangerous one.''

There had been plenty of occasions when Helen had been terrified of what would happen if Franklin discovered her in his study. She hadn't been unaware of the risks she was running—just desperate.

She shrugged away the remembered fear. ''I survived, thank goodness. That's the advantage of spying on your own husband—you know his habits and you can act accordingly. He always took his laptop with him when he left home, of course, but when he was home, I'd get up very early in the morning and spend an hour checking out various files. Franklin would still be sleeping long after I'd shut down the laptop and made myself breakfast. I was never tempted to push my luck and spend longer than an hour because I knew I could always come back the next day, or the one after that.''

''It took Nell a while to figure out what she was actually seeing,'' Philip said. ''She was fixated on the idea that the ranch was a tax haven, or a cover for illegal contributions, and none of the charts and graphs seemed to make financial sense.''

''I was getting very frustrated,'' Helen agreed. ''I quickly found out that Franklin had a silent partner in the Half Spur, but I never could fathom who it was.''

''Do you know now?''

With regret, Helen shook her head. ''Not for sure.''

''But you have suspicions?''

''There was a man called Lio who used to hang out at the house a lot, and I suspect he's involved, but I can't prove it. I don't even know his full name. If Franklin's partner is this Lio person, he's hidden his ownership behind a facade of dummy corporations. I managed to unravel the trail back as far as an import-export company located in Nigeria, of all places. That was a complete dead end, though, so I was stymied in both aspects of my investigation. I couldn't confirm that Lio was Franklin's partner in the Half Spur, and the data I'd copied didn't tie in with my theory that the ranch was being used as a cover for illegal campaign contributions—''

''So I asked her to send me the files to see if I could come up with any insights that she was over-looking,'' Philip interjected. ''But sending me the data was difficult—''

''I couldn't risk downloading the files onto a disk,''

Helen said. "Something I once overheard Franklin say suggested there might be a security protocol on his computer that would warn him if anyone tried to copy the Half Spur files."

"It was smart of you to be cautious," Ryan said, flashing her an approving glance. "So how did you get the data to your brother in the end?"

"I wrote it all down by hand." She gave a wry smile. "As you can imagine, that took a while. Fortunately, like I said before, time was one of the few things on my side. In the end, I just sat at Franklin's desk each morning and copied an hour's worth of data by hand, using regular old pen and paper. Then, when I had everything relevant, I mailed the data to Philip."

"And?" Ryan asked.

Helen smiled at her brother. "Since Philip didn't share my fixation with the idea that the ranch was designed as an operation that could launder illegal campaign contributions, he recognized at once that we were looking at medical records—"

"Not for people," Philip said. "But for the sheep Franklin keeps at the Half Spur. My eighteen months of med school didn't exactly equip me to be a brilliant medical detective, so I showed a sample of the data to one of my professors and asked him what we were looking at. He suggested it was research on some sort of self-replicating virus, possibly part of a test for an experimental vaccine. It seemed important information, but we had no idea what to do with it."

"Your professor's conclusion would tie in with everything my partners and I suspected." Ryan drew in a sharp breath. "My God! This could be really important, Nell. Precisely how long ago did you access these records?"

"More than a year ago. Between the end of June and the beginning of September last year, in fact. I'm sorry my data isn't more recent—"

"Don't apologize. The fact that your information dates from last year is what makes it so interesting." He looked at her intently. "Did you tell Franklin what you'd done, and what you suspected was going on at the Half Spur?"

Helen nodded. "That was how I got my divorce," she said simply.

Ryan drew in a shaky breath. "You're lucky Franklin didn't kill you. And I don't mean that as a joke."

"Don't worry, we had the precise same thoughts," Philip said.

"When I told him that I'd copied all his files about his operations at the Half Spur, I warned him that I'd made a statement about everything I knew, and that I'd sent the resulting documents to my lawyer and the Greek Orthodox priest from the parish where I grew up, along with copies of the data from Franklin's computer. And that the envelopes of information were currently sealed, but the lawyer and the priest had instructions that they were to be opened and delivered to both law enforcement and the media the moment the priest and the lawyer heard I was dead. It was a little hokey, I guess, but it worked."

Philip shot her a smile. "Here she is, you see. Alive and a free woman."

Ryan looked as if he wanted to make a comment to the effect that she was only alive and free until the moment Franklin found a way to wriggle out from the noose she'd constructed, but he restrained himself.

Probably because he realized she was well aware of the fragility of her protection.

"And we don't believe the experiments at the Half Spur have stopped, of course," Philip turned toward Ryan. "We're guessing that's why Franklin keeps spreading rumors about Nell's mental health, and her supposed problems with alcohol. We figure Franklin is terrified she'll reveal what she knows, and so he's laying the groundwork to make sure that if either one of us goes public with our accusations, we're going to be dismissed as two more wackos with a crazy vendetta against a famous person."

Helen stood up, needing to stretch muscles that were cramped with tension. "Every time Franklin leaks some horrible new rumor about us we reconsider telling the media what we know," she said.

Philip ran his hand through his hair so that it stood up in spikes. "To be honest, I talked Helen out of going public on a couple of occasions. If we make accusations against Franklin and they don't stick, I'm afraid we'd be in real trouble. I honest to God think he's capable of ordering a hit on both of us out of sheer rage. And the documents Helen left with the priest and the lawyer wouldn't protect her anymore because they simply repeat the same information that already hadn't been sufficient to bring him down."

Ryan grimaced, his expression bleak. "I agree with you. Franklin Gettys is potentially capable of violence and you were probably smart to keep quiet about what you know. But that's where I come in. I'm sure my organization can help."

"How?" Helen asked bluntly.

"The only way you'll ever be truly safe is when Franklin Gettys is behind bars. We need to build a case against him, and I think the data you collected may provide the link we need to tie several threads from separate investigations together. There was an unusual outbreak of a disease with flulike symptoms in Silver Rapids early in the summer. It wasn't reported in the national press, so I doubt if you heard anything about it.''

Helen and Philip shook their heads. "No, nothing,'' Philip said.

"Our clients and cases are confidential, so I can't provide details about how we did this, but our agency managed to identify viruses in the blood samples taken from sheep at the Half Spur and link them to the blood samples taken from the victims of the epidemic in Silver Rapids.'' He turned to Helen. "With his usual capacity for wriggling out of trouble, Franklin managed to convince the authorities that the similarities were coincidence. But now you have a completely separate set of data, dating from long before the epidemic, that might help us to establish a link he can't explain away.''

Helen felt a spurt of relief that quickly dissipated. "But there's no way to prove I copied the information directly from Franklin's laptop, is there? And that means it's going to be my word against his, and you know who's going to sound more credible.'' She felt a surge of the sort of bitterness that had been absent from her life since the divorce. "There's never a way to pin anything on Franklin, dammit.''

"Don't be so sure of that,'' Ryan said. "If you'll agree to send the data you collected to my partners back in Denver, I think we might be able to forge a real link between your ex-husband's sheep ranch and the epidemic in Silver Rapids.'' Helen could tell from his expression that he felt a growing excitement. "I have resources I can tap—people with extensive medical training—who'd do a great job of interpreting whatever information you can provide."

"You bet we agree," Helen exclaimed, exchanging a glance with her brother. "Philip and I are both sick to death of living in the shadow of Franklin's threats of vengeance."

Philip walked over to the phone and picked up a message pad and pencil, which he handed to Ryan. "Give me the address where you want the data sent. I transcribed all Helen's handwritten notes onto my computer months ago, so I can e-mail it right now to your office."

"This is great. I appreciate your willingness to help—"

Philip shook his head. "It's definitely my pleasure. I can't wait to see that scumbag nailed."

Ryan scribbled a few words and handed the page to Philip. "That's the e-mail address for Colleen Wellesley. Write a covering note telling her you've sent this information on my behalf and that it's extremely confidential, okay? I'll give her a call and explain what it is and how you acquired it."

"Okay, will do. See you in a bit." Philip headed for the stairs and his bedroom, his fast pace underscoring his eagerness to take some action against Franklin.

"Do you think there's a chance you can pool my information with yours and come up with enough evidence to get Franklin indicted?" Helen asked Ryan.

"That's the plan, but we have a way to go before we're at that point." He took out his cell phone. "But you've provided a valuable new angle for us to investigate, and our organization has the resources to keep digging until we discover exactly what's going on.''

He gave her a surprisingly cheerful grin as he keyed in the numbers to reach Colleen Wellesley. ''We'll nail the bastard, Nell. Count on it.''

RYAN WAS STILL on the phone to Colleen Wellesley when Philip came back downstairs to report that the files had been e-mailed as promised. Leaving Ryan engrossed in his conversation, Helen and her brother carried the empty coffee mugs out to the kitchen.

''I have to get going,'' Philip said, setting the mugs in the sink. ''I promised Cathie I'd be at her house hours ago. We've decided to leave early tomorrow morning for her parents' vacation cottage out on Anderson Island. We figure we should be safe from reporters there, not to mention the cops, the FBI and anybody else Franklin decides to send after us.'' He pointed to a scrap of paper stuck to the fridge door with a ladybug magnet. ''That's the phone number if you need to be in touch.''

''Thanks, although I doubt I'll need it.''

''I'm hoping for a call saying that Franklin Gettys is in jail.''

''You and me both.'' She sighed. ''It's not going to happen this weekend, though, so you and Cathie should relax and enjoy the break.''

''We will. Neither of us has taken a vacation in months.'' Philip was halfway out the door when he turned back toward her, laughing.

''Share the joke,'' she said.

''It just struck me how annoyed Franklin would be if he realized that setting the media on my ass actually ended up helping you and Ryan get back together again.''

Helen joined in his laughter. ''Yes, you're right. There's definitely a twisted pleasure to be derived from that thought.''

Philip sobered, giving her arm a light squeeze. ''You know I'm only ducking out on you so that your slimy ex-husband can't use me to bring you any more grief.''

''Yes, of course I realize that.''

Philip shot her a speculative side glance. ''And I want to give you and Ryan the chance to be alone for a day or two.''

Helen was smart enough not to react to that unsubtle piece of brotherly prying. ''Thank you,'' she said with admirable cool. ''Ryan and I will enjoy catching up on old times.'' She gave Philip a quick hug before he could probe any more. ''Tell Cathie I'll look forward to seeing her soon, okay?''

''Will do. Take care, Nell. I'm outta here.'' Philip touched his hand to his forehead in a mock salute. ''I'm counting on you and Ryan to bring that creepy-crawly ex of yours to justice. Go get the bastard, and hang him out to dry.''

CHAPTER TEN

RYAN HAD COME to Seattle at the insistence of his colleagues in Colorado Confidential, the top-secret government agency that worked undercover behind the screen of the detective agency known as Investigations, Confidential and Undercover. He was as driven as his partners to find Sky Langworthy, but he had always thought this trip to Seattle was a wild-goose chase as far as Philip's involvement with the kidnapping was concerned. He'd only agreed to waste so much time because the trip provided a perfect excuse to see Helen again. It was way past time, he'd decided, to get Helen Kouros out of his system, once and for all. Unfortunately, instead of discovering she'd lost her power to enthrall him, he'd discovered that she was more desirable than ever.

When she'd stormed into the parlor, eyes flashing and hair flying, she'd looked nothing like the sleekly groomed society wife he'd seen at the Franklin Gettys's reception eighteen months earlier. Instead, he'd been confronted by a disheveled, sexy, luscious woman, with rain-dampened wisps of hair tumbling haphazardly onto her forehead. Her tousled hair and flashing eyes had reminded him all too vividly of the last morning he'd woken up with her in his bed. It had also reminded him—forcefully—that he wanted her back in his bed as soon as humanly possible.

The prospect of bringing down Franklin Gettys was one of the few things in the world currently capable of turning his thoughts from the splendor of Helen's legs and the length of time remaining before he could realistically expect to feel those legs wrapped around his naked body. Exerting maximum self-control, he focused one hundred percent of his attention on giving Colleen Wellesley a succinct account of everything Helen and Philip had told him, and answering his partner's volcanic eruption of questions.

Colleen was optimistic that the data Helen had copied from Franklin's computer would enlighten Colorado Confidential's experts as to exactly what experiments were being conducted on the sheep at the Half Spur, and she was hopeful they would be able to penetrate the barriers that screened Franklin's shadowy partners from discovery.

Even over the phone, Ryan could tell that Colleen was as excited as he was. His trip to Seattle was producing no immediately useful leads in the Langworthy case. But if baby Sky remained stubbornly lost, at least it seemed that there was finally a crack in the facade that Franklin Gettys presented to the world.

Ryan had just finished his call when Helen returned to the parlor carrying a tray of cheese and crackers, along with a bottle of wine and two glasses. "Philip has gone to his girlfriend's place for the weekend," she said, setting down the tray and reaching for a cracker. She added a cube of cheese and ate with evident pleasure. "Are you hungry? I'm starving. For some reason, rain always makes me hungry."

"Then you must be permanently in need of food," he said. "As far as I can see, it's always raining in this town."

She laughed, opening the wine with the efficiency of a former waitress. "No, the sun shines quite often. Truly."

"Sure. At least once a month. Maybe twice in August."

"Well, okay, the sky here tends to remain on the cloudy side. But rain's good for keeping the grass green. And the women here all have great complexions."

"Yeah. Especially if you like a bloom of mold on your cheeks."

She laughed again, a low, contented chuckle, and handed him a glass of wine. "This is from a local Washington vineyard. I was saving it for a special occasion, and I guess this is it." She lifted her glass in a toast, eyes sparkling. "To special occasions."

"And old friends reunited," he said, touching his glass to hers.

It had been a while since he had seen Helen looking so happy, Ryan reflected. In fact, the dazzling smile that had made her famous with regulars at the Swansong Casino had vanished almost as soon as she met Franklin Gettys. Until this moment, Ryan had believed that what he missed most about Helen was the incredible sex. Now he realized that, much as he yearned to make love to her again, of everything he missed about her, it was the absence of their shared laughter that had left the biggest gap in his life.

He was going to make damn sure that nothing ever happened to take the laughter away again, Ryan swore to himself. But he needed to move slowly, not rush her into making commitments that she wasn't ready for.

Helen returned to her previous seat on the sofa,

pulling the coffee table closer so that they could reach the platter of cheese. Ryan debated no more than a second or two before he sat down next to her. Hell, there was a difference between moving slowly and acting downright retarded.

He was close enough to smell her perfume, a subtle mix of fresh air and lavender shampoo. He crunched on a cracker, struggling to say something coherent other than *For God's sake, make love to me.*

Fortunately, Helen rescued him by inquiring about his sister. "Tell me what's happened with Becky's dancing career," she said. "I read that the show she was in closed after six months on Broadway. That was a pretty decent run."

"Enough to pay off her credit cards, which made her very happy. She was hoping it would last longer, of course, and make her world famous."

"Has she found another dancing job, or is she back to waiting tables?"

"She's just started touring with a new show," he said. "*Ipanema Express.* The out-of-town reviews have been great and the backers are planning to bring it to Broadway early next year, so Becky's ecstatic. One Broadway job might be considered sheer good luck, she says. Two mean she's a pro."

"That's fantastic news." Helen's face lit up. "If ever anyone deserved their professional success, it's your sister. Does the tour schedule include Seattle? I'd love to see her dance professionally."

"I'm not sure if they're coming here," he said. "But wait until the show makes it to New York next year and come see it with me."

She looked up at him, clearly startled by the invitation. "That would be lovely," she said, after a tiny pause. "I've never actually seen a live Broadway show."

"It's an experience you shouldn't miss. But be warned, it's addictive once you get started. You'll be planning trips to the Big Apple every year."

"Not unless I win the lottery." She pulled a face, but sounded perfectly cheerful, as if the lack of money didn't bother her much. "How about Becky's wedding plans?" she asked. "I know she and Jeff were talking about setting a date. Are they still engaged?"

"Who knows?" Ryan gave a wry grin. "They're still talking about getting married one day, but Jeff's dancing in Chicago right now, and Becky's in a different town every week. I don't know if they're ever going to reach the point where getting married is a priority for them. They're both pretty much obsessed with their careers."

Helen poured more wine into their glasses. "Then they're smart to postpone getting married, don't you think? It's probably not a good idea to get married chiefly because you both have a spare weekend in your schedules."

"I agree." He seized the chance to steer the conversation in a more personal direction. "What about you? Has your experience with Franklin turned you against the idea of marriage?"

Helen shook her head. "No. Almost the opposite, in fact. Going through the divorce helped me to see a lot of emotional stuff more clearly."

He aimed for casual and hoped he found it. "Care to share what you discovered?"

She was silent for a moment, searching for the right words. "When I agreed to marry Franklin I was way too hung up on what I thought I'd seen happening in my parents' marriage. I realize now I probably didn't see the truth. Kids usually don't. Besides, most of what I saw was my dad being a lousy parent, not a lousy husband. I guess I've wised up to the fact that Franklin and my dad are simply two messed-up individuals and I shouldn't make sweeping rules about men and relationships on the basis of their bad behavior.''

Ryan was relieved that Helen's marriage hadn't left her with a general bias against men. He searched for a response that would prove he was a caring, sensitive, honorable person who should never be confused with a loser like her father, or a badass like Franklin Gettys. Unfortunately, his supply of warm and friendly social chitchat had apparently run dry. Bone-dry.

Maybe he should suggest taking her out to dinner, except that he had no desire to eat when it meant breaking the fragile bonds of intimacy growing again between the two of them. In truth, he wasn't in the mood either for food or conversation. Instead, his brain drummed out the message that right now they were alone in the house. Just the two of them. Alone.

His body absorbed the message.

Ryan reminded himself yet again that he needed to go slowly, that nothing good was likely to be achieved by rushing things. They needed time to explore the many and subtle changes that had occurred in the years since their separation. Maybe he should suggest dinner after all.

But he didn't make the suggestion. Instead, his head bent toward Helen, who was looking up at him, lips slightly parted and cheeks flushed. She was so incredibly beautiful, he thought, with skin like fresh blossoms on the magnolia trees in his grandmother's garden, creamy white with a heavenly tinge of pink. And where the hell did that poetic comparison come from? He was a man trained to think in terms of cold, hard fact, not flowers and metaphors.

His head dipped lower, and still lower. Then she was in his arms and his mouth was covering hers, and his body felt as if he'd stepped on a live electric wire.

Jesus, she tasted good! Her lips were soft and yielding and even more wonderful than he remembered. Her body molded against his, fitting within the circle of his arms as if they'd exchanged their last kiss only yesterday, instead of more than three years ago. He drowned in the taste of her, letting the scent of her soak into his skin. He felt as if a starved place deep inside him was slowly reviving after years of drought. How had he survived without her, he wondered. How in hell had he done it?

When she left him for Franklin Gettys, Ryan had been so furious that she could do something so crazy—so totally insane—that pure rage had carried him through the first few weeks of their separation. Eventually, though, his anger had died away, and he was left with a painful awareness of how bitterly he missed her.

He resigned as sheriff of Silver Rapids, moved to Denver, signed on as a cop, and dated other women. Lots of other women, although what he was trying to prove he hadn't been quite sure. Now he knew. He'd always recognized that the hurt of separating from Helen had been severe, but even he hadn't realized how deeply the hurt had gone. He'd grown so accustomed to the ache of her loss that it had become part of the furniture of his life, something that couldn't be moved and so had to be accommodated. He'd tried to smother his pain in a cushion of other women.

Now, with Helen in his arms once again, with her mouth open beneath his, her legs twined around him, and her breasts pressed against his chest, he could see just how devastatingly hollow the years without her had been. When she'd left him, Ryan had sworn he'd never allow himself to be vulnerable to a woman again.

It was a good vow, he thought wryly. Pity that with Helen back in his life, he didn't have a hope in hell of sticking to it.

They broke apart, mostly because he needed to draw breath. But it was also a pathetic attempt to prove to himself that he was still enough in control of his emotions to do it. Helen looked up at him, and the light from the floor lamp by the hearth made her eyes appear almost golden. She was the one who spoke first.

"I used to think making love came too easily for us," she said, her voice husky. "We never had to work at our relationship. It was just—there, right from the start."

"Most people would consider that a miracle."

"But not me." Her voice filled with self-mockery. "Smart woman that I was, I figured that what we shared couldn't be worth much or it would demand more effort from us." She shook her head in bafflement. "How could I have been so...ignorant? I wasn't sixteen. I was twenty-seven and old enough to know better. I can't believe I threw away something so incredibly valuable."

Ryan took her hand and pressed a kiss into her

palm, about all he could trust himself to do at this precise moment. "Is that why you married Franklin Gettys? Because loving me was too easy?"

She flushed, embarrassed. "That sounds crazy."

"Yeah, I'd have to say pretty much."

She smiled, but there were shadows around the smile. "It *was* crazy, as I soon found out. I married Franklin because I thought he represented stability and security and everything that was practical and rational about choosing a lifetime partner. What I learned..." Her voice died away.

He took her face and framed it in his hands. "What did you learn?" From the darkness in her eyes it was obvious that the lesson had been hard won.

"I guess I learned that security in a marriage comes from loving and trusting your partner, not from marrying someone who has a respected position or a large income. But even more important, I learned that if you're ever lucky enough to find romance and passion and happiness and laughter in the company of another human being, you should grab on to the relationship with both hands and never let go."

That sounded promising, Ryan thought. "When you talk about grabbing a happy relationship and hanging on tight, are you talking in general terms here, Nell, or are you being specific?"

"I'm being specific. Sort of, anyway." She drew in a shaky breath. "I realize you may have moved on, Ryan. I mean, why wouldn't you? I know there must be a zillion women out there that you could date. And...and marry, if that's what you want to do. You're an incredibly sexy man—"

He was certainly pleased to hear that she thought so. He pressed his forefinger against her lips, his emotions nearly as tumultuous as her words. "Nell, honey, I'm having trouble translating. What exactly are you trying to say?"

For answer, she bit the pad of his finger and linked her hands behind his neck, pulling his head down to hers. "I'm trying to say…I missed you, Ryan. I missed you a lot. Kiss me again. Or better yet, take me to bed and make love to me for the rest of the night."

He spoke against her mouth, his hands already working on the buttons of her blouse. "Honey, I can't remember the last time I was so delighted to oblige a lady."

"Woman…" she murmured, as he pushed her shirt off her shoulders. "I'm a woman, not a lady."

"That's good news, because I'm sure as hell not feeling much like a gentleman." Ryan bent to nuzzle her breasts, his hand searching under the hem of her skirt and moving upward.

"Oh my God," she murmured.

"Yeah," he said. "My thoughts exactly."

Her hand reached for the buckle of his belt and then for the zipper of his jeans. He groaned, but held her gaze. "Oh my God."

"Yeah," she whispered, laughter in her eyes. "My thoughts exactly."

It was the last thing either of them said for a very long time.

CHAPTER ELEVEN

HELEN STIRRED LAZILY in the bed, swimming up toward consciousness through a warm, tropical sea of sensation. Gradually her drowsiness dissolved into full awareness of her surroundings: Ryan's hand resting on her hip, the repletion of her body, the soothing splatter of raindrops against the window panes. She nestled closer to Ryan and found the perfect place for her head on the crook of his outspread arm.

"It's raining again," she mumbled, still half asleep.

He traced a lazy pattern over her neck and shoulders. "What a surprise."

She gave a soft laugh. "It makes a great excuse not to get out of bed."

"I can think of better ones." He leaned over and kissed the hollow of her neck in the precise spot that was guaranteed to drive her wild. Her breath caught and her skin flushed with instant heat, although a few hours ago she had been so sated from their lovemaking that she'd assumed it would be days before she felt real desire again.

"Do you miss the Colorado sunshine?" Ryan asked, his thumb stroking tantalizingly across her nipple.

"Sometimes, especially the clear skies and the brilliant colors.'' She stirred beneath his touch, trying to hold on to the thread of their conversation when her body was already trembling with anticipation. "Seattle's a wonderful city and I love being close to the ocean, but I guess I'm a Coloradan at heart.''

"Come back to Denver with me,'' he said, his hands suddenly still.

Her heart skipped a beat. "For the weekend?''

"Forever.'' He raised himself on one elbow and looked down at her and the intensity of emotion she saw in his eyes made her heart skip a beat.

"I love you,'' Ryan said. "And I'm pretty sure you love me.''

Her smile deepened. "I think I may have mentioned something about that a couple of times last night.''

His hand trailed lower to draw the shape of a heart on her stomach. "It doesn't count when you're begging for sex. Say it again now, when you aren't desperate to have me inside you.''

"I love you,'' Helen said, her voice husky. She looked up at him, laughing. "Especially when I'm begging for sex.''

He kissed her on the tip of her nose, but his gaze remained serious. "We've already wasted almost four years of our lives living apart,'' he said. "I can't think of a single reason to waste any more time. Can you?''

She raised her hand and cradled it against Ryan's cheek. "Not a one.'' They'd both grown and changed, Helen reflected, but that didn't mean they'd changed in ways that had driven them apart. She realized now that the passion she and Ryan shared was a rare gift, almost as rare as the comfortable intimacy they were already beginning to recapture. She'd thrown that gift away once before but she wasn't going to make the same mistake twice.

They made love again, with a slow sweetness that built to a climax of shattering power. She was still drifting back down to earth when Ryan sat up and moved around the bed until he was kneeling in front of her, the sheets rumpled across his knees.

"Marry me, Nell."

The last time he'd proposed to her they'd been in Silver Rapids's fanciest restaurant, dressed in formal clothes, and he'd been holding a blue velvet jewelry box open to display a diamond solitaire engagement ring. Helen liked the setting for this proposal much better.

She sat up and knelt facing him, laughing as she threw her arms around his neck, kissing him hard and long. "Yes, yes, Ryan. Of course I'll marry you."

Ryan remained rigidly unmoving for about ten seconds. Then the reality of her acceptance sank in and he dragged her off the bed, sweeping her into his arms and waltzing around the tiny bedroom.

The ring of his cell phone on the nightstand beside the bed interrupted their impromptu dance. "Damn!" he said. "I have to get that. Only people at work have the number." He flipped open his phone. "Yes, this is Ryan."

He listened intently, then turned to give Helen the thumbs-up sign. "They've already started working on your data," he said, covering the mouthpiece. "They're ecstatic about how much information you've given them."

"I'm glad it's useful."

"I'll be back in the office on Monday," he said into the phone, taking his hand away from the mouthpiece. He paused to listen. "No, I can't come back today. I'll fly out of here either Sunday night or Monday morning."

Helen couldn't hear what the caller was saying, but he or she obviously asked what was keeping Ryan in Seattle.

Ryan's eyes lit up with silent amusement as he replied. "I'm making arrangements to get married," he said and shut the phone, tossing it onto the bed.

"That was Colleen Wellesley," he informed Helen.

The phone rang again before he could say anything more, sending him rummaging through the bedcovers to find it.

"Yes?" he said, flicking it open.

Even from the other side of the bed, Helen could hear the torrent of words gushing from the caller.

"Colleen, stop asking questions long enough for me to reply." Ryan kept a straight face, but his voice hovered on the edge of open laughter. "First answer: Helen Kouros. Second answer: As soon as she'll set the date. Third answer: We're dancing naked around the bedroom. Fourth answer: No, because I'm not answering the phone any more today. I'll check in again tomorrow morning. Fifth answer: Goodbye."

He shut the phone and put it on the nightstand. "Be grateful that Seattle is a thousand miles away from Denver," he said. "Otherwise Colleen would already be in her car by now, en route to visit us. Probably trailing half the office staff behind her."

Helen smiled, slipping on her robe. "I wouldn't mind. I'm looking forward to meeting your partners."

"They're interesting people," Ryan acknowledged, pulling on his jeans and the sweater he'd worn the day before.

"What did Colleen originally call about, before she got sidetracked into being amazed by the news that you're getting married?" Helen asked as they made their way downstairs in pursuit of breakfast.

"She wanted to let me know that she considers the information you've provided, combined with everything we already know, the beginning of the end for Franklin Gettys," Ryan said with quiet conviction. "Bribing cops and corrupting the justice system is only the tip of the iceberg as far as his criminal activities are concerned, I'm sure of it. It may take us a while longer before he's behind bars, but we're going to bring him down."

She wanted Franklin brought to justice, but Helen was astonished at how irrelevant his activities seemed to her now, despite his fifteen months of constant harassment. Why would she choose to stay mired in the past, a captive to Franklin's vindictive schemes, when she could walk into the future with Ryan?

She stared at him as he poured water into the coffeemaker, overcome by a sudden rush of emotion. "What is it?" he asked, searching her face. "What's wrong?"

"Nothing," she said. She laughed, her breath catching, and moved into his arms. "I just realized that I really, really love you."

He framed her face with his hands. "What took you so long?"

"Just a slow learner, I guess."

"Good thing I'm a patient man." His kiss was tender and rich with promise.

"Look," she said, her head on his shoulder. "The sun's come out. It's going to be a fine day, after all."

"It sure is," Ryan said. "A very fine day."

EPILOGUE

The offices of Colorado Confidential at the Royal Flush Ranch, Four days later

HER SECURITY MONITOR BEEPED, warning Colleen Wellesley that a car had just crossed the electronic perimeter fence and turned into the Royal Flush driveway. She recognized Ryan's dark blue Pathfinder, and quelled a sudden flare of nervousness. This was going to be her first meeting with Helen Kouros, and for Ryan's sake, she wanted it to go well.

She opened the file containing a printout of the material that had been e-mailed to her by Helen's brother on Friday night. She leafed through the forty pages of closely packed data, astonished all over again that Helen had managed to acquire so much confidential information without Franklin's knowledge. Colleen could only imagine the difficulty of writing out so many columns of figures by hand, with painstaking accuracy, and she admired Helen's persistence, not to mention her skill in avoiding detection.

The material from Franklin's laptop had turned out to be a treasure trove of vital insights into the illegal experiments being conducted at the Half Spur. Combined with information already in the possession of Colorado Confidential, Colleen was hopeful that a compelling criminal case could be built against

Franklin Gettys. After two years of trying, it seemed they were finally getting the facts to back up their suspicions.

Despite her gratitude to Helen, Colleen still harbored some doubts as to whether a woman who had been married to Senator Franklin Gettys could ever make a suitable wife for Ryan Benton. She discounted the rumors she'd heard about Helen's drinking problems and her numerous affairs because she knew those rumors had been circulated by Franklin Gettys and that automatically made them suspect. Still, she'd seen Helen at a couple of fund-raisers when she was still married to the senator, and Colleen hadn't been favorably impressed. Helen was certainly beautiful, with lovely facial features and a dancer's lithe and supple body, but Colleen hadn't detected a trace of warmth or spontaneity in her. You would expect a man as smart and insightful as Ryan Benton to realize that it would be no fun to marry an ice princess, but Colleen had learned from experience that men had a hard time paying attention to a woman's character flaws when they came wrapped in a package as enticing as Helen's.

The security system delivered another warning. Ryan was escorting Helen through the outer offices of the Royal Flush ranch and approaching the secret meeting room where Colleen waited to greet them. Her gaze fixed on the monitor, Colleen studied Helen while Ryan keyed in the code that would cause the wine rack to swing inward and give him access to the offices of Colorado Confidential.

Until now, Colleen had never seen Helen dressed in anything except expensive evening gowns, but today she was wearing jeans and a lemon-yellow cotton sweater and she still managed to look fabulous. On her, the everyday outfit looked like a high-fashion statement. The monitor was clear enough to show that she was wearing almost no makeup, and her hair was pulled back from her face in a loose and rumpled chignon. On most women, that sort of hairstyle looked a mess. On Helen, the wisps and haphazard strands looked like a style favored by movie stars who didn't want to appear as if they'd just spent five hours with their hairdresser.

The woman was seriously sexy, Colleen decided. More than attractive enough to screw with Ryan's mind.

Ryan came into the meeting room, his arm around Helen, his eyes glowing. "Okay, Colleen, here she is, fresh off the plane from Seattle." His voice was full of pride, his body language replete with love. "This is my fiancée, Helen Kouros. Honey, this is my boss, Colleen Wellesley."

Helen smiled, not the professional smile Colleen had seen at the senator's fund-raisers, but a warm smile, tinged with just a hint of shyness. "It's such a pleasure to meet you," Helen said, holding out her hand. "While we were driving out from the airport, Ryan told me more about the case you're trying to build against Franklin Gettys. I'm hoping so much that the information I copied from his laptop has provided you with some useful leads. Has it?"

Colleen was hard put to believe that this soft-spoken woman was the same person she'd seen standing stiff and unapproachable at Franklin Gettys's side. Belatedly, it occurred to her that in view of everything Colorado Confidential now knew about the senator's criminal activities, it was no wonder that Helen had always seemed so cool and withdrawn. Living as the wife of Franklin Gettys would be enough to drive any sensitive, openhearted woman into a state where total repression of her true feelings was the only way to retain her sanity. Her attitude toward Helen thawed the final few degrees.

"The information you provided has been invaluable," Colleen said. "But first things first. It's great to have you here, Helen. May I get you something to drink? Or something to eat? I know they never feed people on flights nowadays."

"Nothing for me, thanks," Helen said, shaking her head.

"How about you, Ryan?"

"Thanks, but we're going out to dinner as soon as we leave here," Ryan said, pulling up a chair for Helen, and looking as if it required all his willpower not to lean over and kiss her.

"We're going house-hunting after we've eaten," Helen explained. She dragged her gaze away from Ryan, her cheeks suddenly flaring with heat.

Good grief, Colleen thought in silent amusement. *They're about ready to tear each other's clothes off.*

"Then I'll try to keep this as brief as possible," she said, pretending not to notice the sudden increase in sexual tension that flooded the room. She turned to look directly at Helen. "The charts and statistics you copied from the senator's computer were more valuable than we could possibly have hoped or imagined. They filled in some vital blanks in other information that we'd recovered from various sources, and the bottom line is that—based on the package of information we've been able to provide—the local FBI office is launching an official investigation of Franklin Gettys—''

"That is truly good news." Helen's body slumped with relief. "Is my brother right about what Franklin was doing? Was he using the sheep as part of some sort of unauthorized medical experiment?"

"In a way," Colleen said. "Although we believe he was involved in something much more threatening than that. We believe the sheep at the Half Spur are part of an experiment involving biological weapons."

"My God!" Helen gulped. "Biological weapons?"

"That's what we think," Colleen acknowledged.

Helen appeared unable to grasp the enormity of it. "I know Franklin is always preaching that the only way to protect ourselves from maniacs like Saddam Hussein is to have the same sort of weapons capability that he did, but I still can't believe Franklin would take the law into his own hands like that."

"Believe it," Ryan said, his voice grim. "Remember the flu epidemic in Silver Rapids that I mentioned to you?"

Helen nodded.

"Well, we think that Franklin, either accidentally or purposely, ran a test that ended up infecting the people of the town."

Helen was quiet for a few seconds, and the happy light in her eyes died away. "I was married to a monster," she said finally. "How could I not have known that he was such a terrible person? How could I have stayed married to him for three weeks, let alone nearly three years? Why didn't I sense the darkness in him right from the start?"

Ryan took her hand and held it cradled in his.

"Don't blame yourself," he said. "Put the blame where it belongs, which is squarely with Franklin Gettys. Here's a man who had everything—a great career as a college athlete and then as a professional footballer, followed by the honor of winning election to the United States senate. Most people would have been overwhelmed with gratitude for their good fortune, but not Franklin. Instead of striving to serve the people of Colorado to the best of his ability, he turns around and uses his office as a power base to pursue his insane vision of bio weapons that can be unleashed on the unsuspecting world."

"You have nothing to blame yourself for," Colleen said, adding her own reassurance to Ryan's. "Remember, without the information you copied from Franklin's laptop, there would be no FBI investigation and virtually no chance that the senator might soon be indicted."

"At least that's some consolation," Helen said. "I guess."

"And there's more," Ryan said. "About the kidnapping of Sky Langworthy—"

"Oh, have you found him? That would be truly wonderful." Helen's expressive face shone with hope, and Colleen wondered how she could ever have imagined that this woman was aloof and unemotional.

"We haven't found Sky yet." Colleen permitted herself the luxury of a sigh. Their continued failure to locate Holly Langworthy's baby ate at her soul, day and night. "As you know, the data you copied from the senator's laptop predates Sky's disappearance by several months. But there is some very interesting e-mail correspondence between your ex-husband and a man called Lio—"

Helen nodded. "Yes, I copied that because I'm sure Lio is at least part owner of the Half Spur with Franklin. Unfortunately, I have no idea who Lio is, or what he does, or where he lives—"

"We might be able to fill in some of the blanks for you," Colleen said. "We believe that Lio may in fact be Helio DeMarco—"

"Helio DeMarco?" Helen queried.

"The organized crime boss," Ryan explained. "We knew DeMarco was operating in Colorado, and we suspected there might be some involvement with Sky's disappearance, but your computer notes give us a totally new lead to explore. Thanks to you, we're more hopeful of a break in the Langworthy case right now than we have been in several weeks."

"All in all, we're in your debt," Colleen said, smiling. "Thank you, Helen."

"No, it's the other way around," Helen said, rising to her feet. "I'm deeply in *your* debt. The knowledge that I might have contributed something useful to solving the Langworthy kidnapping and getting Franklin Gettys put behind bars makes me feel a lot less angry about those final months of my marriage. Perhaps they weren't the terrible waste I've always assumed."

"And on that positive note, we're out of here." Ryan put his arm back around Helen's waist, and she melted against him. He looked down at her, his gaze tender, then turned back to Colleen. "Okay, we're off in search of dinner and a new home."

"We've decided we'll get married as soon as we find the right house," Helen added.

They looked so happy together that it made Colleen

feel wistful. "Good luck with your house-hunting," she said.

Ryan and Helen left the meeting room and the secret door slid back into place. Picking up the latest field reports, Colleen redirected her attention to the demanding task of finding Sky Langworthy. Whatever it took, she was going to give Holly back her baby and bring his kidnappers to justice. That was a promise.

KISS AND TELL

Amanda Stevens

CHAPTER ONE

"WE HAVE REASON to believe that sometime during the course of your campaign, possibly within the next few days, an attempt will be made on your life."

"So that's the reason for this little cloak-and-dagger meeting." Joshua Langworthy studied the man and woman seated across from him in a back booth at Shorty's, a hole-in-the-wall restaurant in downtown Denver where nobody came to be seen. "This isn't the first threat my office has received since I announced my candidacy for governor. Every campaign brings out the nuts. What makes you think this one warrants special attention?"

"For one thing, the threat didn't come to your office. It came to us through an informant," Wiley Longbottom, director of the Colorado Department of Public Safety, explained. "What we'd like to do is add an extra security detail to your campaign—"

"Does this have anything to do with my nephew's disappearance?" Josh cut in.

Wiley hesitated. "We don't think so."

"Then the answer is no."

Wiley exchanged an uneasy glance with the woman seated beside him. He'd introduced her as a colleague. Fiona Something-or-other. Josh assumed she was a DPS officer, possibly a high-ranking one by the way she was dressed. Dark suit, crisp white blouse, blond hair pulled back and fastened at her nape. Professional all the way.

"No extra security," he said slowly, his gaze still on her.

"Don't be hard-headed about this," Wiley advised. "We're here to help you."

"If you have officers to spare, then for God's sake, put them on my nephew's case. He's the one you should be worried about."

Wiley expelled a heavy breath. "Everything that can be done is being done to find your sister's baby."

Josh's voice hardened. "I'd like to believe that, but Schyler was taken from his nursery three months ago, and none of you people—not the Denver PD or the FBI or the DPS—none of you has been able to come up with a solid lead."

When the DPS director had called to request a private meeting away from Josh's office, his hopes had surged that there had finally been a break in his nephew's case. Since Schyler's disappearance, the waiting had been agonizing for the entire Langworthy family, but especially for Joshua's younger sister, Holly, the baby's mother. She was an emotional and physical wreck, and there wasn't a damn thing Josh could do to help her.

And to make matters worse, Josh's opponent—desperate to knock a dent in Josh's popularity—had tried to capitalize on the tragedy. In addition to portraying Josh as some sort of thirty-something playboy unfit to hold public office, Governor Houghton's minions had subtly inferred to the media that Josh might have masterminded the kidnapping in order to snare the sympathy vote. After all, if it had worked in Missouri for the widow of a senatorial candidate, why couldn't it work in Colorado?

And the hell of it was, it *had* worked. With little more than a month until the election, a recent poll conducted among likely voters showed Josh pulling away with a seven-point lead over the incumbent.

It was now his race to lose, but Josh wasn't about to take anything for granted. The campaign was likely to get even dirtier from here on out. The Houghton camp would use any means necessary to defeat Josh, and he wondered what they would make of this meeting, how they would try to spin a threat against Josh to their advantage.

He glanced at the unlikely couple across from him, not sure he even trusted them. For all he knew, they could be on Houghton's payroll. Although he doubted it. Longbottom had a reputation for being a straight-shooter. He didn't seem the type of man who'd play politics with something as potentially serious as this.

"Who's your informant?" Josh asked.

"We're really not at liberty to say much more than we already have," Wiley hedged. "I'm sure you understand that our sources have to remain confidential." He leaned forward, his gaze anxious. "I can tell you this much. According to the information we received, the threat could be coming from someone close to you."

An uneasy chill rode up Josh's spine. "How close?"

Wiley shrugged. "Could be someone inside your campaign. Or even a personal connection. We just don't know. But we're taking the threat seriously, and you should, too." He eyed Josh for a moment as if to assess his reaction. "What we'd like to do, in addition to an added security detail, is put someone on you—"

Josh waved a dismissive hand. "I already have bodyguards assigned to the campaign."

"I'm not talking about a bodyguard. I'm talking about someone who could investigate from inside your campaign—and inside your personal life, for that matter—without attracting undue attention or suspicion."

"I don't follow."

Wiley pulled a newspaper clipping from his jacket pocket and slid it across the table. "Remember this?"

Josh groaned inwardly as he scanned the first few lines of the article. The item had appeared a few weeks ago in a gossip column that ran in a local paper. According to eyewitness accounts, he'd been spotted coming out of Denver's most exclusive jewelry store where a sales associate—who wished to remain anonymous—later confirmed his purchase of a five-carat diamond engagement ring. The piece had breathed life into the persistent rumor that there was a new woman in Josh's life and that now, according to the article, they were secretly engaged.

In reality, he'd picked up the ring as a favor to a friend who'd been delayed out of town and wanted to propose to his long-time girlfriend that night. But, of course, the explanation never made it to print, and for a full week after the story ran, reporters anxious to break the secret engagement story had bombarded Josh as he stumped through the state.

Secretly, Josh wondered if someone in his own campaign might have fanned those flames a bit in order to detract from the playboy image his opponent was trying to pin on him.

He looked up from the article with a scowl. "I fail to see what this has to do with a death threat. Or with anything else, for that matter."

"Supposing the rumors about your engagement turned out to be true."

"But they're not," Josh said impatiently. "And unless you get to the point, I don't see that we have anything further to discuss."

"The point is to use this article to our advantage. What we'd like to do is have someone pose as your fiancée."

Josh stared at the man as if he'd taken leave of his senses. "You can't be serious."

"Oh, we're serious, all right. Dead serious. And I think you'll see the merit of the plan once you give it some thought. Even though we haven't been able to link the threat to your nephew's kidnapping, there's always the possibility that the two are connected in some way. We nab the person behind the threat, he— or she—could lead us to little Schyler."

That stopped Josh cold. He'd do anything to find his sister's baby, but this whole scenario had the smell of a setup. "You said earlier you didn't think the threat had anything to do with the kidnapping."

"It's a long shot," Wiley admitted. "But if there's even a slight chance the two are connected…" He trailed off, letting Josh come to his own conclusion.

But he had Josh where he wanted him, and they both knew it. "What is it you want me to do?"

"Nothing yet. Just sit tight and wait to hear from us. We'll take care of the details. But there is one thing I need your word on. Nothing of what we've said can leave this table. That means no confiding in your friends or associates, or even your family, for that matter. If we're going to pull this off, you have to be convincing in your private life as well as in public.''

''I take it you already have someone in mind to pose as my fiancée?''

Wiley nodded. ''Ms. Clark here has agreed to help us out, and you'll be in good hands with her. She's a highly skilled security expert. She trained at Quantico.''

Josh's gaze narrowed on the woman. ''You're FBI?''

''Not anymore. I left the bureau last year. Now I work for a private investigation firm here in Denver.''

It was the first time Josh had heard her speak, other than a polite murmur when they'd been introduced, and he was taken aback by the sound. Her voice was crisp and clear and just the tiniest bit frosty, like an unexpected snowfall in June.

He turned to Wiley. ''If you think this threat is so credible, why bring in a civilian? Why not use a DPS officer or an undercover cop?''

''Because Fiona—Ms. Clark—has worked dozens of kidnapping cases for the FBI. None of my officers can touch her experience or expertise. Besides, an intrepid reporter would undoubtedly expose the ruse if we tried using an undercover cop. Ms. Clark's credentials are genuine, and they have the added bonus of providing an excellent cover story. You two met when her company was called in to consult on the security for your campaign. You kept the relationship out of the media because you both value your privacy, and later, out of respect for your sister.''

''How am I supposed to explain our decision to go

public now with the engagement?'' Josh asked with a frown.

"You don't explain it. We'll devise a scenario where the two of you will be caught in a compromising situation, shall we say. We'll make it seem as if you have no choice but to go public.''

"It seems you've thought of everything,'' Josh muttered, his gaze shifting back to Fiona Clark. Her eyes were brown, he noticed. He would have expected them to be blue with her fair coloring, but then, he had a feeling the woman might have a lot of surprises up her sleeve.

"What makes you think a ridiculous scheme like this could possibly work?'' he asked her.

Fiona Clark lifted her chin, her lips curving in a smile that sent a thrill of awareness—or warning— down his spine. "Because I'll make it work. I'm very good at what I do, Mr. Langworthy. All you have to do is trust me.''

"DID HE TAKE THE BAIT?'' Colleen Wellesley asked anxiously when Fiona returned to the office a little while later.

"He didn't at first.'' Fiona sat down in a chair across from her boss's desk. "In fact, he was adamantly opposed to adding any kind of security to his campaign, but he seemed to reconsider once Wiley pointed out there's a remote chance the kidnapping and the threat against his life could be related.''

"Which could mean one of two things.'' Colleen tucked a strand of dark brown hair behind one ear. "He's either innocent and genuinely wants to help find his nephew—''

"Or that's what he wants us to think,'' Ryan Ben-

ton put in. Years ago, he and Colleen had been partners in the Denver Police Department. Now they were
working together on a new venture.

To the outside world, Investigations, Confidential
and Undercover was a successful private detective
firm. In reality, the downtown Denver office had become a front for Colorado Confidential, a covert and
highly specialized division of the Department of Public Safety. Fiona had been recruited into the fledgling
operation on the recommendation of Whitney Romeo,
who headed up a sister Confidential organization in
Chicago.

Having just come off a six-month training regimen
at Colleen's ranch, the Royal Flush—which also
served as headquarters for Colorado Confidential—
Fiona was itching for more action. The surveillance
of Joshua Langworthy was her first major assignment
for CC, and she was determined to use it to get her
new career started on the right path—namely, in proving to her male colleagues that she was their equal in
every respect. She'd watched too many promotions
slip through her fingers because the FBI was still very
much a good ol' boys network. Fiona wasn't about to
let that happen again.

The tip from an anonymous source about a possible
threat on Langworthy's life had given her the opportunity she'd been waiting for—a way to get inside
Langworthy's campaign and inside his family. In co-
operation with the DPS, Fiona would investigate the
death threat against Josh while in turn gaining access
to the man himself. If he was connected in any way
to his nephew's kidnapping, Fiona was determined to
expose him.

The only problem was…she hadn't counted on her

reaction to the man. She'd observed him from afar for a couple of weeks now, but up close and personal was a whole different ball game. She'd been shaken to the core by the rock-star charisma that had practically oozed from every pore of his gorgeous body.

"I sense some hesitation on your part," Colleen commented. "You aren't having second thoughts about this assignment, are you?"

Fiona shook her head. "No, of course not. But I guess I do have to wonder why a man in Langworthy's position would go so far as to have his own sister's child kidnapped in order to further his political ambitions."

Colleen lifted a brow. "After all the kidnapping cases you worked on while you were with the FBI, nothing should surprise you anymore."

"That's true," Fiona agreed. "I also know that appearances can be deceiving. But the Langworthys have been an important family in this state for generations. Why risk everything for the sake of one political campaign? Much less put someone as fragile as Holly Langworthy appears to be through such emotional torture."

"Does the name Edward Kingsley mean anything to you?" Colleen asked suddenly.

Fiona shook her head. "No, I don't think so. Why?"

"The Kingsleys were once to Tennessee historically and politically what the Langworthys are to Colorado. Back in the late sixties, one of Edward's twin sons was kidnapped from his nursery during a heated political campaign. He wasn't found until years later, after he was grown. Iris Kingsley, the matriarch of the family, had arranged the whole thing. She planned her own grandson's abduction in order to ensure her family a political victory.''

"And don't forget that case in Chicago just a year or so ago involving a senator," Ryan said. "Similar situation. There's plenty of precedence for this sort of thing, Fiona. We're not investigating Joshua Langworthy just for the hell of it.''

"I know that. And I'm willing to do whatever it takes to find that baby and bring his kidnapper to justice. If the trail leads to Joshua Langworthy, then so be it. Just tell me how you want to proceed.''

Colleen opened a folder on her desk. "In addition to Langworthy, keep your eye on his inner circle of advisors. He has three that he's particularly close to. The media call them the Iron Triangle.'' She pulled out three photographs from the folder and placed them in front of Fiona. "You may recognize these people from your surveillance, but it won't hurt to go over their dossiers again.''

The first subject was a dark-haired female in her late thirties. Fiona picked up the photograph and committed the woman's features to memory. She was beautiful and sophisticated, but a hard gleam of cynicism radiated from her blue eyes.

"That's Nell McKenna, Langworthy's campaign manager," Colleen said. "She's been on the political scene for a number of years, and word around town is she's looking to use Langworthy's election as a springboard to the national stage. But she's already got two losses under her belt. Congressman Wellstone's re-election bid and Fitzhugh's mayoral race. If she lets this one get away, she'll have three strikes against her, and she can pretty much kiss a high-profile career goodbye. No one wants to hire a loser, particularly in the high-stakes game of politics. So she's got a lot riding on this campaign."

Fiona picked up the next picture. The subject in this photo was also a dark-haired, thirty-something female, but this woman had none of Nell McKenna's polish and sophistication. In fact, she looked downright mousy with her pixyish haircut and dark-rimmed glasses that overpowered her thin face and nondescript features.

"Dana Severn," Colleen said. "Langworthy's assistant. She's worked for him since his days in the Justice Department. When he moved over to the Public Defender's office, he took her with him, and she's been with him ever since. We don't know much about her background, but our sources tell us she's extremely loyal to Langworthy. She'd do anything to help him get elected."

Fiona glanced up. "Even kidnap a baby?"

"That's what we need you to find out."

Fiona picked up the third picture.

"Robert Smith, Langworthy's media advisor. He and Langworthy were roommates in college and by all appearances have remained close friends. Strange thing about that guy, though. He once worked for the ad agency that's been hired by the opposing camp. We don't know if he still has connections to his old firm or not, but he bears watching. Even best friends can hold secret grudges and resentments, sometimes for years. Especially against a golden boy like Langworthy."

Colleen placed a fourth picture on the desk. Fiona's stomach quivered when she saw who it was. Those gorgeous eyes. That sensuous mouth…

"The threat against Langworthy could very well be

genuine," Colleen said. "And if it is coming from someone close to him, it's imperative you keep your eyes and ears open and report any suspicious activity or behavior in that regard directly to the DPS.

"However, our main objective is Langworthy himself. A man with his wealth and power could easily hire someone to snatch a kid with very little risk of getting caught. That's where you come in, Fiona. You have to watch his every move while making sure he doesn't suspect your real motive."

"He won't," Fiona said with a little more confidence than she actually felt. She had a feeling pulling the wool over Josh Langworthy's eyes would be no easy feat.

"While Langworthy is our primary target," Colleen continued, "virtually everyone in his campaign and even certain family members remain suspects. By going in as his fiancée, you'll not only have access to Langworthy's staff, but to his friends and family as well. It's a tall order, Fiona. To operate effectively on the inside, it's crucial that everyone connected to Langworthy be convinced that you and he are engaged. Are you prepared for what that means?"

"Of course."

But a shiver eased up Fiona's spine as a sudden image of Joshua Langworthy formed in her head. She could almost feel the power of his presence, the intensity of that magnetic blue gaze.

And for the next several weeks, she would have to pretend that she was in love with the man.

It was a dirty job, but somebody had to do it.

CHAPTER TWO

AFTER A CLOUDY MORNING, the afternoon turned crisp and clear, the kind of brilliant fall day that carried both a memory of summer and the promise of winter in the chilly air. Snowfall in late September wasn't unusual in the higher elevations, but so far the autumn had remained mild and dry, and rather than an exhilarating snowmobile ride up the mountain, Josh had been forced to make the long trek to the cabin on horseback.

Not that he minded. The scenery was spectacular this time of year.

He stood on the porch of the cabin, one hand propped on a wooden brace as his gaze scanned the endless blue sky, broken only by the powerful thrust of the majestic snow-capped Rockies. And all around him, a yellow sea of aspens.

The setting was so calm and pristine that Josh was almost, but not quite, able to forget the ugly confrontation he'd had with his campaign manager before he'd left the office that morning. He'd already been fairly wired from his meeting with Wiley Longbottom and Fiona Clark, and the last thing he'd needed was to tangle with a hothead like Nell McKenna.

"You're *what?*" she'd all but screamed when he'd called her into his office and told her of his plans. "Tell me this is some kind of bad joke."

"It's no joke." Josh purposefully kept his voice low and reasonable in order to offset her quick temper. "I'm taking a couple of days off. I'll be back first thing Monday morning, but in the meantime, you won't be able to reach me."

Nell sucked in a sharp breath, her blue eyes simmering with fury. "Have you lost your mind? You can't just disappear for two whole days. You think Houghton is going to roll over and play dead while you're gone?"

"No, I don't. I'm sure Governor Houghton will continue to campaign just as he has been," Josh said. Which meant his opponent would continue to sling mud as fast and as furiously as he could.

Nell leaned forward, her black hair sweeping across her smooth cheeks as she planted her hands on his desk. "Campaigns are won or lost in the weeks between Labor Day and the second Tuesday in November. You risk our momentum by taking off two hours let alone two days at such a critical time."

"I'm not asking for your permission," Josh snapped, his own temper flaring. "My mind is made up. I'm doing this. When I get back, I'll throw myself into the campaign twenty-four hours a day. I'll glad-hand my way across the state and back if I have to. But right now, I need you to cut me some slack, Nell."

"I wish I could do that, but my job is to get you elected governor. And I can't do that if you decide to go traipsing off to God knows where just when I need you the most." When Nell saw that her argument was falling on deaf ears, she pounded her fist on the desk. "Damn it, this isn't just about you, Josh, and what *you* need. My reputation is on the line here. If we lose this election, I'm through in this state. No one will hire me.''

"I never made you any guarantees when you signed on," he reminded her coldly. "You knew the risks."

"Yes, but I never thought you'd pull a stunt like this just weeks before the election. My God, do you have any idea the kind of hours I've been putting in? The stress I've been under?''

"For which you've been well compensated."

Her dark eyes glittered with hurt. "I thought we were partners in this."

Lately, Josh had come to believe that his idea of a partnership differed a great deal from Nell's. He sensed she was starting to hope for something more than a business relationship, and the last thing he wanted was to give her the wrong impression about their future.

"We'll talk about this when I get back," he muttered. "Right now, I'm out of here."

He'd walked out of the office without another word, but he knew that wasn't the end of it. When Nell got a burr under her saddle, she could get downright nasty. But he'd deal with her when he returned on Monday morning. He'd deal with Wiley Longbottom, as well, and a certain blonde named Fiona Clark who, for whatever reason, had agreed to the DPS director's absurd scheme.

For the next two days, Josh planned to do nothing but bask in the quiet beauty of the mountains. The cabin had always been a place that kept him grounded, kept him focused, kept him humble. He'd been born into a life of wealth and privilege, but in the wilderness, he was just an ordinary man.

Not that he wasn't grateful for all his advantages. There'd been a time when he'd fully appreciated the fact that Langworthy money could acquire for him the fastest cars, the hottest girls and entrée into the coolest nightclubs in the country.

Then had come a cold dose of reality. With all that wealth and privilege came expectations and obligations. By the time he'd turned eighteen, his father had had Josh's whole life mapped out for him. Four years of an ivy league university, followed by Harvard Law School, and then a position at one of the most prestigious law firms in Denver where he would be groomed—not for the courtroom, but for his first run at public office.

All the preparations, of course, were building toward the culmination of Samuel Langworthy's hopes and dreams—the governorship of Colorado, perhaps an eventual U.S. Senate seat, and then, if all went as planned, a run at the White House.

Unfortunately, Josh hadn't shared the same vision. He'd enrolled at the University of Colorado, and when his father threatened to cut off his funds, he'd taken a construction job during summers and on weekends to put himself through school.

The manual labor had been an eye-opening experience and had given him a whole new perspective on life. It had made him aware, for the first time, of an entirely different world, one that didn't revolve around sports cars and ski seasons and the trendiest nightspots.

Those years had taught him a lot about himself and about the kind of person he wanted to be. They'd also taught him a lot about his father, and how far he was willing to go to get what he wanted. Josh had eventually gone to Harvard Law, but on his own terms. He and his father had made a tentative peace over the years, but the chasm that had developed back then had never completely been bridged.

And so it was strange, Josh supposed, that somehow, in spite of all the clashes, they'd come full circle. He was doing exactly what his father had always wanted him to do.

Five years ago, or even one year ago, Josh could never have envisioned himself in politics. But when he'd been approached by a group of local businessmen, the prospect of unseating Todd Houghton had intrigued him.

In Josh's opinion, Houghton was a disaster waiting to happen to Colorado. He'd spent the past six months lobbying Congress for a repeal of the 1972 Biological and Toxic Weapons Convention Treaty with an eye toward bringing a government-funded research lab to the state.

Such a lab, he argued, would infuse the depressed economy with jobs and federal monies. But Josh knew that it could also unleash the kinds of horror that had only existed in Stephen King novels until now. Houghton had managed to cleverly gloss over the risks, and Josh had felt a fierce obligation to call him on it.

But it wasn't for entirely altruistic reasons that he'd decided to throw his hat into the ring. He was his father's son, after all, Josh thought grimly.

He put up a hand to shade his eyes as the *whop, whop, whop* of a helicopter sounded over the treetops. As his gaze lifted, something flashed in the distance, like sunlight bouncing off a mirror.

Or a rifle scope, he thought suddenly.

Then he brushed the concern aside as he watched the helicopter top a ridge and fly directly toward the cabin.

For a moment, he thought the chopper might actually try to land, but it continued on an easterly course, straight up the face of the mountain.

Sightseers, he decided, but for some reason, a flicker of unease traced along his backbone. He scanned the slope again. This time, there was no flash of light. No discernible movement at all. No one was there.

But Josh couldn't shake the notion that someone had followed him up the mountain and was out there even now, watching him from a distance.

To what end, he could only imagine.

FIONA HELD HER BREATH as she watched the chopper's approach. It was flying low, as if searching for a place to land, and for a moment, she wondered if Colleen and Ryan had been right after all. Josh Langworthy was feeling the heat from the meeting this morning and he'd come here to rendezvous with whomever he'd hired to kidnap little Schyler.

The inaccessibility and remoteness of the cabin would make it the perfect place for such an assignation, but Fiona couldn't help feeling a measure of relief when the helicopter flew over the cabin and headed straight up the mountain.

She refocused her binoculars on Josh Langworthy. From her position two hundred yards from the cabin, she could observe his every move, even the slight flicker of his very long and very curly eyelashes. The powerful lenses brought him up close and personal, so to speak. Fiona had no trouble at all discerning the clear blue of his eyes, the classic contours of his jaw and chin, the firm yet slightly erotic set of his mouth.

The impact of the man's charisma through the binoculars was only slightly less devastating than being in the same room with him.

So what was she going to do when she was *alone* in the same room with him? Fiona wondered.

Cross that bridge when you come to it, a little voice advised.

Right now, she had to keep herself focused on the task at hand. Observing Josh Langworthy. Every gorgeous inch of him.

He'd changed clothes before heading off to the mountains. Instead of the expensive business suit he'd had on earlier, he now wore jeans, rugged boots and a faded jean jacket over an ordinary white T-shirt. Very cool. He hardly looked the part of heir to the Langworthy throne, but even the rustic attire couldn't detract from the air of confidence and privilege that seemed to surround him.

Fiona watched him watching the helicopter, and after the chopper had disappeared into the glaring sunlight, he turned suddenly to gaze at the mountains. For a moment, she could have sworn he was looking directly at her, and she quickly shrank back against the rocks. She could still see him through a crevice between the boulders, and she let out a long breath of relief when he turned and went back inside the cabin.

After he was out of sight, she kept the binoculars trained on the cabin, then slowly lifted the glasses and scanned the countryside. The craggy face of the mountain provided dozens of hiding places, as did the thick woods that surrounded the cabin. But Fiona had been at her post even before Josh arrived, and other than the chopper, she'd seen nothing out of the ordinary. Nothing at all suspicious. If a would-be killer—or a kidnapper—lurked somewhere nearby, he'd managed to elude her.

Governor Houghton's accusations aside, Fiona still had a hard time believing that Josh would have anything to do with his nephew's kidnapping. But as Colleen and Ryan had both pointed out earlier, such a scenario wasn't without precedence. If there was a chance, no matter how slight, that he could lead them to little Schyler, then it was imperative they keep him under close surveillance.

And that was why Fiona was here.

After the call had come in to Colleen's office that Josh was on the move, Fiona had rushed home to pack a bag and then had been whisked off to DPS headquarters where a chopper had flown her to a rendezvous point a few miles down the mountain from the cabin. She'd continued to her destination on horseback in order to better conceal her approach.

Shifting into a more comfortable position, she settled in for a long wait. Surveillance had never been her strong suit. The monotony wore on her nerves and blunted her sharpness.

At some point, she'd make contact with Josh. But not yet. More than likely, if a rendezvous with the kidnapper had been planned, it would take place by cover of darkness. By then, other night creatures would be on the prowl as well. Wolves. Coyotes. Bears.

Fiona was a city girl through and through. The idea of wild animals roaming about was more than a little disconcerting.

A twig snapped behind her.

She whirled, automatically whipping her gun from the back waistband of her jeans.

But she was too late. Josh Langworthy had gotten the drop on her.

CHAPTER THREE

"OH, HELL," Fiona muttered. She hadn't heard a sound until he was right on her. There was no excuse for such sloppiness.

But the tableau wasn't without comic appeal, she had to admit. There they stood, each with a bead drawn on the other—Josh in designer denims that made him look hip and cool, if a bit Ralph Lauren-ish, and Fiona in her faded and torn bell bottoms that made her look, well…underpaid.

Josh, however, didn't appear to appreciate the absurdity of the moment. He kept her firmly in his rifle sights, which Fiona did not take as a good sign.

"Looks like a standoff to me," she quipped. "Why don't we call it a draw and put away our weapons?"

She held up her hands in good faith, letting her gun dangle from one finger, then slowly returned the weapon to her waistband. To her relief, Josh lowered the rifle to his side. But his icy stare alone could have dropped her at twenty paces.

"How did you find me?" he demanded.

His voice, deep and sexy in spite of the chill, sent a thrill up Fiona's spine. "I followed you."

He seemed momentarily taken aback by her candor. Something flickered in his blue eyes. Fiona wanted to believe it was uncertainty, but she didn't think Josh

GET 2 BOOKS FREE!

MIRA

To get your 2 free books, affix this peel-off sticker to the reply card and mail it today!

MIRA® Books, The Brightest Stars in Fiction, presents

The Best of the Best™

Superb collector's editions of the very best books by some of today's best-known authors!

★ **FREE BOOKS!** To introduce you to "The Best of the Best" we'll send you 2 books ABSOLUTELY FREE!

★ **FREE GIFT!** Get an exciting surprise gift FREE!

★ **BEST BOOKS!** "The Best of the Best" brings you the best books by some of today's most popular authors!

GET 2

HOW TO GET YOUR
2 FREE BOOKS AND FREE GIFT!

1. Peel off the MIRA® sticker on the front cover. Place it in the space provided at right. This automatically entitles you to receive two free books and an exciting surprise gift.

2. Send back this card and you'll get 2 "The Best of the Best™" books. These books have a combined cover price of $11.98 or more in the U.S. and $13.98 or more in Canada, but they are yours to keep absolutely FREE!

3. There's no catch. You're under no obligation to buy anything. We charge nothing – ZERO – for your first shipment. And you don't have to make any minimum number of purchases – not even one!

4. We call this line "The Best of the Best" because each month you'll receive the best books by some of today's most popular authors. These authors show up time and time again on all the major bestseller lists and their books sell out as soon as they hit the stores. You'll like the convenience of getting them delivered to your home at our special discount prices . . . and you'll love your *Heart to Heart* subscriber newsletter featuring author news, horoscopes, recipes, book reviews and much more!

5. We hope that after receiving your free books you'll want to remain a subscriber. But the choice is yours – to continue or cancel, anytime at all! So why not take us up on our invitation, with no risk of any kind. You'll be glad you did!

6. And remember...we'll send you a surprise gift ABSOLUTELY FREE just for giving THE BEST OF THE BEST a try.

SPECIAL FREE GIFT!
We'll send you a fabulous surprise gift, absolutely FREE, simply for accepting our no-risk offer!

Visit us online at
www.mirabooks.com

® and TM are registered trademarks of Harlequin Enterprises Limited.

THE BEST OF THE BEST™ — Here's How it Works:

If offer card is missing write to: The Best of the Best., 3010 Walden Ave., P.O. Box 1867, Buffalo, NY 14240-1867

BUSINESS REPLY MAIL

FIRST-CLASS MAIL   PERMIT NO. 717-003   BUFFALO, NY

POSTAGE WILL BE PAID BY ADDRESSEE

THE BEST OF THE BEST
3010 WALDEN AVE
PO BOX 1867
BUFFALO NY 14240-9952

NO POSTAGE
NECESSARY
IF MAILED
IN THE
UNITED STATES

Langworthy had ever had a moment's self-doubt in his life. "How did you get here?"

"On horseback, just like you." She didn't bother to explain that an informant at the stables in the tiny hamlet of Crystal Falls where the Langworthys boarded some of their horses had called to let them know that Josh was on his way there. Armed with that information, it was an easy matter to project that the cabin would be his ultimate destination.

"You must have had a tail on me in Denver," he said coldly. "For how long?"

"We're concerned for your safety, Mr. Langworthy," she evaded. "Someone may want to kill you. It's our job to keep him—or her—from succeeding."

He gave her a long appraisal. "You know, there's one thing I don't understand about this whole scheme. What's in it for you?"

The resentment in his voice made Fiona wince. "What do you mean?"

His jaw hardened. "Just what I said. You're not a cop or a federal agent any longer. What are you getting out of this?"

She shrugged. "My salary plus expenses."

"Who's paying those expenses, Ms. Clark? Who's your client? My opponent?"

"Of course not."

"My father, then."

The contempt in his voice shocked Fiona. "Your *father?* Why would you think that?"

"I have my reasons," he said bitterly. "Is it true?"

"No, it's not true. Look, you already know why I'm here. But if you have doubts about my experience or my credentials, I suggest you take them up with

Wiley Longbottom. Or with my boss at the detective agency. Her name is Colleen Wellesley. I'll even give you her number.''

''Don't bother. I spoke to her on my way up here. I've also spoken with the special agent in charge of the FBI field office in Chicago.''

As they'd known he would. ''And?''

''You come highly recommended,'' he said grudgingly.

She gave him an approving nod. ''So you had me checked out. That's good. Now you know why I'm uniquely qualified for this assignment. I was with the FBI for eight years. During that time, I worked dozens of kidnapping cases. They became something of a specialty for me. That's why Wiley Longbottom came to me for help. Given the circumstances, I would think you'd be grateful for my expertise, as well.''

But gratitude was not exactly the emotion glimmering in his eyes, Fiona noted.

He cocked his head slightly. ''So you do think there's a connection between the threat on my life and my nephew's kidnapping?''

''That's what I'm here to find out.''

''By posing as my fiancée.''

The blatant sneer in his voice prodded Fiona's temper. ''We're on the same team here, Mr. Langworthy. We have the same objective—to find your nephew and bring him safely home. And if we can keep you alive in the process, so much the better. I'm good at what I do, but it would make my job a whole lot easier if you would lose the attitude.''

He didn't say anything for a long moment, merely

stared at her with those cold blue eyes. Then he said, almost matter-of-factly, "Where's your horse?"

She nodded over her shoulder. "Tied up in the woods. I didn't want anyone hearing me ride up."

His gaze narrowed, but he didn't comment. "There's a barn behind the cabin, but you'll have to take care of your own horse. No stable hands. No room service, either, for that matter. Up here, we rough it."

Fiona smiled. "No problem. I'm hardly accustomed to room service. And if you call that roughing it..." she nodded toward the spacious cabin "...you've led a very cushy life, Mr. Langworthy."

WHEN FIONA CAME IN from the stables a little while later, Josh showed her to the back bedroom, the one farthest from his. She'd brought in a backpack so he assumed she'd come prepared to stay for as long as he did. Obviously, she planned to take her undercover duties seriously.

But...was that really why he was so annoyed with her? The fact that she'd barged in on his weekend, making it next to impossible to say no to this whole setup? Or was there something more at play here?

The way she'd gotten under his skin so quickly was both puzzling and irritating. Josh didn't understand it.

Earlier that morning at the restaurant, he'd found her extremely attractive, but her cool remoteness had enabled him to dismiss his momentary interest without the slightest hesitation. She wasn't his type, nor, apparently was he hers.

But now she was like an entirely different woman. She'd traded the rigid business suit for a pair of faded jeans—bell bottoms, of all things—and her blond hair, falling past her shoulders, was all messy and wind-blown from the ride up the mountain. Rather than untouchable, she now seemed…earthy. Sensual. The kind of woman a man would not only want to take to bed but to a ball game. Like a blond Sandra Bullock.

The change had caught Josh completely off guard, and he'd been struggling ever since to regain his equilibrium. Now, all of a sudden, Fiona Clark wasn't so easy to dismiss.

A door opened and closed down the hallway, and he turned back quickly to the pot of chili he had simmering on the stove. He pretended he didn't hear her approach until she said almost rapturously, "Oh, *man,* that smells good!"

He glanced at her over his shoulder. When he tried to look away, he couldn't. Her hair was damp and wavy, as if she'd taken a quick shower before changing into a fresh pair of low-rider jeans and a T-shirt that said Get Ready on the front.

Get ready for what? he wanted to ask her.

"It's just chili," he said, trying to tear his gaze from the front of her T-shirt. "There's plenty for both of us if you're hungry."

"I'm starving. And since we don't have room service up here…" She gave him a disarming grin. "I believe I'll take you up on that offer."

"Have a seat then." He turned back to the stove.

"Sure I can't help?"

"No, everything's done. All I have to do is dish it up." He ladled out the chili, then carried the steaming bowls to the table and set them on the placemats.

Returning to the kitchen, he opened the refrigerator door and peered at the contents. "I'm having a beer, but we've got juice or soda if you prefer."

"Beer's fine."

But when he placed the icy bottle in front of her, she made no move to touch it. She did, however, attack her chili without hesitation. After several enthusiastic bites, she said in surprise, "This is really good. Spicy but good. I never would have pegged you for the domestic type."

He shrugged. "Why should you? You don't know anything about me. Not the real me, anyway."

Fiona sat back and blotted her mouth with her napkin. "That's true. And I've been thinking about that. Maybe it would be a good idea for us to use this time to get better acquainted. It might make our situation a little less awkward."

He grimaced. "I don't think anything could make this situation less awkward. I can't even believe I'm seriously considering going along with such an idiotic scheme."

She hesitated, as if choosing her words very carefully. "I can understand how all this might seem a bit unorthodox to you, but undercover assignments are nothing unusual in law enforcement. And this scheme, as you call, has been carefully planned, right down to the smallest detail. It'll work if you let it."

He glanced up at her. "And exactly how far are we supposed to go to convince my colleagues and constituents, not to mention my family, that our engagement is genuine?"

She didn't take the bait, but merely shrugged. "I guess we'll have to play that one by ear." She leaned toward him slightly. "Look at it this way. At least you'll be doing something concrete to help find your nephew."

And that was the only reason Josh would even consider cooperating. He'd never felt so helpless in his life as he had since Schyler disappeared. At least this way, he would be taking an active, if peripheral, role in the investigation. It wasn't much, but it was something.

"Can I ask you a question?"

He shrugged. "What?"

"Why did you come up here so suddenly after our meeting this morning?"

"I needed to get away for a couple of days, have some time to think." He rubbed the back of his neck, trying to relieve the tension that had been building for months. "This place has always helped me keep my head on straight."

She turned to stare out the window. "I can see why. It's beautiful up here. But…" Her expression turned reproachful. "Considering the circumstances, it probably wasn't the greatest idea to come up here alone. Besides, this close to the election, I would have thought every second on the campaign trail counted."

"Now you sound like Nell," he muttered, getting up for another beer. He checked Fiona's as well, but the bottle had barely been touched. He supposed she considered herself on duty.

"You're referring to Nell McKenna?" Fiona asked.

"You've done your homework, I see."

"It pays to in my line of work." She gave him a

careful glance. "Your relationship with Ms. Mc-Kenna is strictly professional, I assume."

"If you want to know whether or not I'm sleeping with her, the answer is no," Josh said coolly. "But I fail to see the relevance."

She shrugged. "Spurned lovers carry grudges. It's as simple as that."

Josh sighed. "Is that how this is going to play out? You're going to look for secret motives in everyone around me?"

Fiona's expression sobered. "The informant said the threat is coming from someone close to you, so, yes, everyone in your life is pretty much under suspicion. We can't afford to overlook any possibility. One of your closest friends could have a secret vendetta against you and your family. Someone you least expect may want you dead."

"And isn't that a cheery little thought?" Josh said grimly. But she was right. Of course, she was right. After Schyler's disappearance, family, friends, business associates, everyone had come under scrutiny by the police. Initially, they'd all been suspects, and Josh wouldn't have had it any other way. But it sure as hell hadn't made life pleasant. And now this.

"Look, I admit this all seems a bit...intense," Fiona said. "We've both been thrown into a situation that's bound to cause some friction between us. That's why I thought it would help if we got to know one another better. Why don't you tell me something about yourself?"

Josh wondered if she realized how much like a bad pickup line that sounded. "What do you want to know?"

She sat back, amusement glinting in her dark eyes. "Why do they call you the playboy candidate?"

"My opponent called me that once," Josh said with a scowl. "Unfortunately, it made a good sound bite so it picked up steam in the media."

"The press does seem to have a curious fascination with your love life," Fiona said. "Has it occurred to you that having a fiancée could actually benefit your campaign?"

"And has it occurred to you that I might not like deceiving the public?" Josh shoved aside his bowl, having suddenly lost his appetite. "I don't like pretending to be something I'm not. That's not the way I want to get elected. And besides, what happens when your assignment comes to an end? What are the voters supposed to think when one day I have a fiancée at my side on the campaign trail and the next day I don't?"

Fiona nodded. "I agree that could be a problem for you, but when we blow the case open, you can tell them the truth. Or you can simply tell them that things didn't work out between us and we called it quits. Whatever you decide, I'll back you up."

He gave a mirthless laugh. "And that's supposed to make me feel better about pulling a fast one on the voters?"

"Look, I understand how you feel," Fiona said. "But it's for a good cause. You're trying to do everything in your power to find your nephew. I don't think anyone can fault you for that."

"Sure they can," Josh said bitterly. "It's called spin."

"You seem to have a pretty cynical view of politics," she observed.

"No. I'm just a realist. I've learned the hard way that politics is all about power and how far a candidate is willing to go to get it."

"Does that include you?"

Their gazes met and held for the longest moment before Josh shrugged and glanced away. "Even if you go into it with the noblest of intentions, your integrity can quickly become lost in all the backroom deals and the hype and the mudslinging. It's an ugly business."

"If you really feel that way, I'm surprised you decided to follow in your father's footsteps," Fiona said.

"I can assure you, my running for governor has nothing to do with my father." But that wasn't true. Samuel Langworthy had everything to do with Josh's political ambitions, whether Josh wanted to admit it or not.

"Sorry," Fiona murmured. "I didn't mean to hit a nerve."

"You didn't. But enough about me." Josh eyed her for a moment. "If we're going to make people believe we've secretly been engaged for the past several weeks, then I should know something about you as well."

She lifted a shoulder. "Sure. Ask me anything you like. I don't have any secrets." But there was something in her eyes, something mysterious, that made Josh wonder what she might be hiding.

"Where did you grow up?"

"Chicago. Born and raised there. I graduated from Northwestern."

"How did you come to work for the FBI?"

"They recruited me right out of graduate school."

"What was your major?"

"Psychology."

He almost groaned. "Don't tell me. You wanted to be a profiler. You had dreams of becoming the next Clarissa Starling."

She shook her head. "Nope. I liked working in the field."

"Then why did you leave?"

"Oh, I don't know. After eight years, it was time for a change."

"That seems a little vague."

"You have to understand something," she said with a frown. "For all its modern technology, the atmosphere at the bureau is still very much the way it was in Hoover's day. In some field offices, female agents, no matter how talented, are still considered subordinate to their male counterparts."

He lifted a brow. "Were you harassed?"

"Not so much harassed as ignored. It was as if I didn't exist." She gave another shrug. "I don't know. It's bad enough when you never quite measure up at work, but when you get that same attitude at home…" She trailed off. "I have four brothers who are cops. For all my training and experience, they've never been able to see me as anything but a kid sister who needs protecting from the big bad world."

Josh had a hard time picturing her in that light. From what he'd been able to tell, Fiona Clark was more than capable—and perfectly willing—to take on that big bad world.

"It was humiliating enough that they had to interrogate all my dates back in high school, but they still give the third degree to any man they think I'm interested in. And if they think he might get out of line with me…'' She shuddered. ''It can get ugly.''

''So let me get this straight,'' Josh said slowly. ''If a man made a pass at you, he'd have to contend with your four cop brothers?''

''No,'' Fiona said with an intriguing little smile. ''He'd have to contend with me.''

CHAPTER FOUR

AFTER THE FOOD was put away and the dishes cleaned up, Josh disappeared into his bedroom. Fiona used the time to study the layout of the cabin.

To call the house a cabin was a bit deceiving, she decided, because it was far from small and far from rustic as the term usually implied. Each of the five bedrooms had its own private bath and spectacular view of the mountains, but there were no phones, fax machines or computers anywhere on the premises. Without cell phones, they would truly be cut off from civilization.

The living area, kitchen and dining room were combined in one large space that was decorated, on first glance, more for comfort than style. But on closer examination, the sofa and chairs arranged around a large stone fireplace were made of the supplest of leather, and the artwork on the walls looked original and expensive. Subtle touches were everywhere, and Fiona decided that it had probably taken an expensive designer with lots of time and an unlimited budget to achieve such casual elegance.

Her inspection of the house completed, Fiona settled down in front of the fireplace to wait for Josh. But the cabin was so quiet, the setting so serene, that she almost immediately drifted off to sleep.

She awakened sometime later with a start. She

didn't think she'd been asleep for all that long, but the sun was setting and the cabin had grown cold and shadowy. Almost unnaturally quiet.

She shivered uneasily as she got up and hurried down the hallway to Josh's bedroom. Knocking on the door, she waited a few seconds before calling out his name. When she still heard no response, she rapped a second time, then opened the door and called his name again.

Flipping on the light switch, she saw in a glance that the bed was neatly made, the room in perfect order.

Had he given her the slip while she lay sleeping? Had he gone off to meet an accomplice?

Or...had something happened to him?

Whirling, she hurried down the hall and rushed toward the front door. Throwing it open, she stopped dead in her tracks.

Josh was on the front porch, gazing at the mountains. When he heard the door open, he glanced over his shoulder. "Something wrong?"

Fiona gulped down her relief. "No. I guess I must have dozed off. When I woke up, I didn't know where you'd gone off to."

It was dark outside, but she thought she could see surprise flash across his features. "Why would you think I'd gone off somewhere?"

She shrugged. "I just...wanted to make sure everything was okay."

He didn't say anything for a moment, but turned back to the mountains. "I want to show you something," he finally said.

Fiona closed the door behind her as she walked out to stand on the porch beside him. He was still staring at the mountains and the sky, and Fiona followed his gaze. And drew in a sharp breath. "It's so beautiful up here. So...overwhelming." The mountains. The sky. Fiona suddenly felt puny and insignificant in the face of such grandeur.

He nodded, as if he understood precisely the way she felt. "That's why I keep coming here," he murmured. "It helps me keep things in perspective. Reminds me that we're all a part of something much greater than ourselves."

Fiona turned to stare at his profile. From the outset of the investigation, she'd assumed him a man of great style, but little substance. An arrogant, self-absorbed politician whose background of wealth and privilege gave him very little in common with the constituency he sought to represent. But there was more to Josh Langworthy than met the eye, Fiona thought with a shiver. So much more.

"You're cold," he said and slipped off his jacket. "Here, put this on."

"No, I'm fine," Fiona protested, but he was already wrapping the coat around her shoulders. His knuckles grazed against the bare skin of her neck, and Fiona suddenly went still with shock. Then she quickly reached up and pulled the jacket around her as she took a step back. "Thanks," she said awkwardly, wondering if he'd noticed her rather bizarre reaction to his touch.

If he had, he chose not to show it. He rested his hands on the porch railing, his gaze going back to the mountains.

After a moment, Fiona said softly, "Can I ask you something?"

He shrugged. "That's your job, I guess."

She hesitated, uncertain how to phrase her question, and even more unsure how he would take it. "Earlier when you mentioned your father, I sensed some tension. Or was that just my imagination?"

He glanced at her then, but she couldn't read his expression in the darkness. "Why do you want to know?"

"I need to know about your relationship with everyone close to you."

"You can't honestly think the threat against me is coming from my father?"

"I don't think your father is a threat to your life, no," she replied obliquely.

He straightened from the rail, gazing down at her. "Then what do you think?"

She met his gaze in the darkness. "How badly does your father want you to win this election?"

She still couldn't make out his expression, but she knew that he had suddenly tensed. She could feel it in the very air between them. "What are you getting at?"

"If the voting public became aware that there's been a threat against your life, you might garner a great deal of sympathy."

"So that's it. You think this is all some kind of publicity stunt," he said in disgust. "And I'm in on it, I suppose."

He'd hit so close to the truth that Fiona had a difficult time keeping her voice even when she said, "If Wiley Longbottom wasn't taking the threat against your life seriously, I wouldn't be here. But at the same time, we can't afford to overlook any possibility. Your father has made no secret of the fact that he thinks that the Langworthy legacy is riding on this election. Without a Langworthy in public office, your family stands to lose a great deal of its political clout.''

To his credit, Josh listened without interrupting, but once she'd finished, it seemed as if he could barely hold his anger in check. ''Let's make one thing very clear here. I don't give a damn what my father thinks is riding on this election. My running for governor has nothing to do with him. Or anyone else in my family, for that matter. My reasons for running are my own.''

''I understand. But you need to understand something, too. I'm not asking these questions out of some sort of perverse curiosity. If I'm to do my job, then I have to know about your relationships with the people who are closest to you. That includes family, friends, business associates, people who are working on your campaign. I need to know if there's anyone from your past or present with an ax to grind against you or your family. But even apart from that, I need to know about all these people because a fiancée would know. If I'm to be convincing—''

He turned suddenly, stopping her in midsentence. ''It always comes back to that, doesn't it? Convincing the people closet to me that you and I share an intimacy. But have you given much thought to what that will entail?''

''Of course, I have.''

''Really? Because an engaged couple would behave in a certain way, you know. The way they look at each other, the way they touch, kiss...''

Fiona caught her breath on that last word. ''When we're in public—''

''Even in public, a certain amount of affection will

be expected. But tell me something, Fiona." It was the first time he'd used her first name, and the way he said it, the way he lingered over the syllables caused her pulse to race. "When I put my jacket around you, you tensed the moment I touched you. And even now…" He took a step toward her, and Fiona automatically moved away. "See what I mean? You've been concerned about how well I'll play my part, but you're the one you should be worried about."

"I'll do whatever necessary when the time comes," she assured him.

"How do you know?"

She could feel his gaze on her in the dark, and the intensity sent shivers up and down her spine. "Because I've worked undercover before."

"As someone's lover?"

"Who said we were lovers?"

He gave a low laugh. "According to Wiley's scenario, we've been engaged how long? A few weeks? Months? We're neither one the patient type. We're lovers, Fiona."

He was deliberately doing this, Fiona thought. Deliberately seducing her. Deliberately making her picture the two of them together…intimately…passionately…

She lifted her chin. "Whatever. It doesn't matter as long as we get the job done."

"I think it does matter." He reached out and cupped the back of her neck, gently pulling her to him. "Because if we're going to be *convincing* as lovers…"

Fiona tensed, resisted.

"You can't do that," he murmured, "when I do this."

The moment his lips touched hers, Fiona's first instinct was to resist again, and her second was to relax. To go with the flow. To enjoy the gentle but demanding pressure of his mouth on hers.

Fiona went with the second. She couldn't seem to help herself. She hadn't been with a man…in that way…in a very long time. Hadn't been kissed by a man as handsome and sexy and accomplished as Josh Langworthy…ever.

He knew what he was doing, too. Knew how to make her feel as if they were the only two people in the world at that moment.

He could seduce her. Quite easily. In the back of her mind, Fiona heard the sound of a warning bell, but she chose to ignore it. Just for the moment. After tonight, she would be on her guard with him. She would. But for now…

She put her hands flat against his chest and kissed him back. Kissed him as if they *were* the only two people in the world at that moment. Kissed him with an erotic intimacy that made him—for just a split second—hesitate in surprise.

Then he upped the ante. Moved in for the kill.

His hands slipped inside the jacket, and he pulled her to him, pressing her body against his as he deepened the kiss, making Fiona think of old-fashioned words like "swoon" and "ravished." Words that any self-respecting undercover agent would never have in her vocabulary.

Maybe this was all part of his grand plan, she thought. To keep her so dazzled that she wouldn't see the truth about him if it hit her in the face.

Steeling her determination, she pulled away from the kiss. Josh held her for a moment, then let her go.

"You were right," he said softly. "You *are* good at what you do."

FIONA COULDN'T STOP thinking about that kiss. Even as she made her rounds that night, checking to make sure the cabin was secure before turning in, her mind was on that kiss. When she said good-night to Josh outside his bedroom door, her mind was on that kiss. When she showered and crawled into her own bed, her mind was on that kiss.

And now, hours later, she lay wide awake, staring at the ceiling and wondering what it was about Josh Langworthy that had gotten to her in a way that could only lead to trouble.

He was attractive, of course, but she'd known plenty of attractive men. He was wealthy, charming, charismatic…quite a catch, actually, but it was more than that. It was something inside him. Something deep within his soul that lured Fiona to a dark and tempting place. That made her, for the first time in her career, want to toss caution to the wind.

But as she lay there, thinking about Josh Langworthy in a very unprofessional way, she remembered her conversation with Colleen earlier. *After all the kidnapping cases you worked on while you were with the FBI, nothing should surprise you anymore.*

If Joshua Langworthy wasn't a viable suspect, then Colorado Confidential wouldn't be wasting time and money investigating him. Fiona had to remember that. She had to remain objective at any cost, because it wasn't just her career on the line. A baby's life was at stake.

Rolling over to her side, she fluffed her pillow, then settled into a comfortable spot and was just drifting off when a noise outside the cabin catapulted her upright in bed.

She couldn't say exactly what the sound had been. The barn door closing?

Had a wind come up since she'd turned in?

Getting out of bed, Fiona automatically reached for her weapon on the nightstand as she padded on bare feet to the window. Parting the curtains with the barrel of the gun, she peered out into the night.

All was still outside her window. Trees and darkness obscured the barn from her view, but Fiona stood watching for a long moment, her senses on full alert. She heard nothing else, but just as she was about to turn away, a shadow moved near the hot tub. Someone was stealthily making his way toward the back of the cabin.

Adrenaline kicking in, Fiona crossed the room, drew open the door, and hurried silently down the hallway. The door to Josh's room was closed, and she considered stopping for a moment to give him a heads up. But there was no time for that. The intruder would already have reached the deck.

Thankful she'd taken the time to absorb the layout of the cabin earlier, including furniture placement, she made her way unerringly to the back door, keeping away from the windows as much as possible.

Flattening herself against the wall, she watched as the back door slowly opened. She'd locked it herself earlier. Which could only mean—

Josh slipped inside, closed the door softly behind him, and then leaned his rifle against the wall as he bent to pull off his boots.

Whether he saw her or simply sensed another presence in the room, Fiona didn't know. But as he reached for the rifle, she lifted her own weapon.

His gaze on her gun, he let his hand drop slowly to his side. "Mind putting that thing away? I don't know how itchy your trigger finger is."

"Lucky for you, I'm the very epitome of self-restraint," she said dryly, lowering her weapon.

He mumbled something unintelligible as he bent to finish removing his boots.

"Where were you just now?" Fiona asked.

"I heard a noise outside."

"What kind of noise?"

"I couldn't pinpoint it exactly."

"So you went out to investigate it on your own?"

He shrugged. "There've been some bear sightings around here recently, not to mention the occasional mountain lion, so I went out to check on the horses." He let the remaining boot drop to the plank flooring with a loud thud.

In spite of herself, Fiona jumped. "Why didn't you wake me?"

"Why? So *you* could go out and investigate?" He straightened, and even in his sock feet he towered over her.

Suddenly, Fiona remembered the way she'd had to stand on tiptoes earlier to kiss him....

She tried to shake off the image. "It's my job to protect you."

"No, it's not." His gaze met hers in the darkness. "It's your job to find out if there's a connection between the threat against me and my nephew's kidnapping, but it is *not* your job to put yourself between me and danger. Let's be clear on that."

''That's what bodyguards do.''

''You're not a bodyguard. You're here to play a role so that you can investigate 'from the inside' I believe is how you put it. Anything beyond that and the deal is off as far as I'm concerned.''

''Don't you think you're being a little unreasonable?''

He shrugged. ''Maybe. But right now the discussion is tabled as far as I'm concerned. I'm going back to bed.'' He picked up his rifle and started across the room toward the hallway, then turned to glance over his shoulder. ''Are you coming?''

''In a minute.''

He stopped at that and turned back to face her. ''I wouldn't advise going out there alone with that peashooter of yours.'' He nodded toward her gun. ''It may work fine in an urban setting, but up here...'' He trailed off with a shrug. ''Grizzlies are mostly extinct in these parts, but you never know.'' And with that, he disappeared down the hallway.

Fiona waited until she heard his door close and then she turned to peer out the back window. She could go out and have a look around for herself, but honestly, what would that prove? Her bravery? It sure as heck wouldn't say much for her intelligence. She wouldn't be able to see a thing in the dark, and if something was out there...

Or someone...

Had Josh told her the truth? Had he really heard a noise and gone out to check on the horses?

Fiona had heard the barn door close herself, but what if Josh had gone out there to meet someone?

Had she missed her opportunity to blow this case wide open by fantasizing about a kiss that should never have happened in the first place?

CHAPTER FIVE

BY THE TIME Josh got up the next morning, Fiona had coffee and scrambled eggs waiting for him on the stove. She dished them up, and as they ate, he tried to ignore the full-blown sexual attraction that had suddenly sprung between them since that kiss.

This was ridiculous, he told himself sternly. He'd known women far sexier than Fiona Clark. Far more worldly and sophisticated.

But he couldn't honestly say any of them had ever laid one on him quite the way Fiona had last night.

And that body…

Whoa.

The contrast of soft skin and toned muscle…

He found himself getting aroused just thinking about that body moving against his…those lips…her tongue…

"Anything wrong?"

He looked up to find her gazing at him curiously over the rim of her coffee cup.

"No, just enjoying my breakfast," he said with a shrug. "The eggs are great, by the way."

She set aside her cup and folded her arms on the table. "I've been thinking about last night."

"That makes two of us."

He couldn't be sure, but he thought a faint blush touched her cheeks. "I'm talking about the noise you heard. I went out earlier to have a look around. I saw fresh hoof prints leading from the barn back into the woods. Someone was up here on horseback.''

Josh glanced up with a frown. ''How fresh?''

''No more than a day or two.''

''Could have been the caretaker. He looks in on the place at least once a week. Maybe he was up here yesterday before we arrived.''

''I didn't notice the prints when I put my horse away,'' she said.

''No, but were you looking for them then?''

Fiona shrugged. ''I guess I could have missed them. But under the circumstances, I think we have to assume that I didn't. Which means someone may have followed us up here.''

He put down his cup. ''If someone came up here to harm me—kill me, even—why didn't he just shoot me last night when I went out to investigate the noise?''

''Last night he—or she—may have been reconnoitering,'' Fiona said. ''Maybe you startled him away when you came outside unexpectedly. Plus, you were armed. Next time, you may not be so lucky.''

''So what do you suggest we do?''

She hesitated, her gaze going back to the window. ''We need to get off this mountain. I don't think it's safe to spend another night up here.''

After the kiss they'd shared last night and Josh's reaction to her this morning, he had to agree. ''When do you want to leave?''

She stared at him in surprise. ''Just like that? No argument?''

He shrugged. ''You're the expert. Besides, it's not

just my life on the line here. You could be in danger as well.''

"Your safety is my primary concern," she said. "But you're right. We could both be in danger. I think it would probably be a good idea to leave right after breakfast. No sense hanging around tempting fate.''

She certainly had a way with the double entendre, Josh thought dryly. "Why don't you start getting things organized in here, and I'll see to the horses." He started to stand, then paused. "Or would you rather go saddle up the horses?''

Something that might have been panic flickered across her features before she hurriedly rose and began gathering up their plates. "No, that's okay. I'm the one who made the mess in the kitchen. I should be the one to clean it up.''

SHE WAS TERRIFIED OF HORSES.

Well, perhaps terrified was too strong a word, but she definitely was out of her element, Josh thought as they mounted up a little while later.

She was competent enough. Someone had taught her the basics, but there was more to riding than skill. There was instinct, telepathy and a mutual respect between rider and beast.

Fiona had none of those. Oh, she had plenty of respect for her horse. She just didn't command the same in return. Luckily, the mare she'd hired was a gentle, soulful creature that didn't require much from her rider.

Still, as Josh took the lead, he couldn't help glancing over his shoulder every few minutes to make sure Fiona was holding her own.

It was a long ride, and although he'd enjoyed the leisurely pace he'd set the day before, now he felt anxious and wary. What if someone really had followed them up the mountain? What if that same someone had been watching the cabin last night, lying in wait? What if Fiona had been the one to go out and investigate?

What if she'd been shot...or worse...

He had to keep reminding himself that she was a trained professional. And ex-FBI agent. She knew how to take care of herself.

But she was also a woman, and his attraction to her made him protective. He couldn't help it. He was a man and certain feelings were instinctive even though he knew she would be the first to wave aside his concern.

He glanced over his shoulder, his gaze lifting for a moment to a flash of light back up the mountain. He stared at the spot for a moment, then, concluding it must have been sunlight dancing off rock, turned back to the trail.

And that's when it happened.

A gunshot fired from a high-caliber weapon somewhere behind them.

The sound echoed down the mountainside, shattering the serenity and sending both horses into a momentary frenzy. It was all Josh could do to control his own mount. Reining the horse in, he glanced back.

He had only a glimpse of the stark terror in Fiona's eyes before the mare reared back and tossed her to the ground with a bone-crunching jar.

CHAPTER SIX

THEY RODE DOUBLE down the mountain because Josh didn't know how badly injured Fiona might be, and he didn't want to risk her taking another nasty fall.

When he'd reached her side after the accident, she'd insisted she was okay, but Josh wasn't convinced. She'd hit her head on a rock, and though there was very little blood, she'd seemed dazed for several minutes afterward.

They'd taken cover behind a boulder and Josh had tried to check her out, but even though he was fairly certain she didn't have any broken bones, the head injury worried him. And there was always the possibility of internal bleeding.

He had to get her to a doctor, even though it meant exposing themselves to the gunman again.

But luckily, there were no more shots, and they made it without incident to the medical clinic in Crystal Falls. The doctor there had been cautiously optimistic about Fiona's condition. No broken bones, but the head injury worried him, too. He recommended that she go to a larger facility where she could get an MRI or EEG if necessary.

So Josh had whisked her off to the hospital in Aspen where for the past forty-five minutes he'd been cooling his jets in the emergency room waiting area, anxious for some word on her condition.

The waiting room was crowded, and he noticed people casting him curious glances from time to time. But if anyone recognized him, they didn't approach and he was thankful for that. He didn't feel like talking. He was much too worried about Fiona.

"Mr. Langworthy?"

He spun at the sound of his name.

A man in a white lab coat strode toward him. "I'm Dr. Stacey," he said briskly. "I understand you're Ms. Clark's fiancé?"

Josh opened his mouth to deny it, then merely said, "How is she?"

"Resting comfortably. She's suffered a mild concussion, but no broken bones so that's good news. And I've seen no evidence of internal injuries, but just to be on the safe side, I've ordered an MRI. I'd like to keep her here for the next twenty-four hours, but if everything goes the way I expect it to, she'll be good as new in a day or two."

"Can I see her?"

"I don't see why not. She's in Room 12. All the way at the end of the corridor and turn left. We'll be moving her upstairs in a little while."

"Thanks."

The nurse at the station gave him an inquisitive look as he walked by, causing Josh to wonder if she'd overheard his conversation with the doctor, if news of his engagement would be all over the hospital within the hour. He had a lot of friends in Aspen. He could imagine how quickly word would travel once it got out of the hospital.

The door to Fiona's room stood ajar, but he knocked anyway before going in. She looked relieved to see him. "The doctor found you, I see."

He walked over to her bed, trying to keep his expression even. But the sight of her in that hospital bed looking so pale and fragile did strange things to his insides.

"You told the doctor I was your fiancé," he said gruffly.

Fiona gave an apologetic shrug. "I was afraid he wouldn't let you in to see me if I didn't. Besides, I thought we could use this situation to our advantage."

"How?"

"I called Wiley. Someone from the hospital will leak to the media that Joshua Langworthy's fiancée was brought to the emergency room in Aspen following a riding accident. It should hit the news sometime tomorrow. Monday morning at the latest. I wanted to warn you so you can be prepared."

"I guess I'll need to alert my staff," he muttered. He should have been angry that she'd made the decision without consulting him first, but sometime during the last twenty-four hours, Josh supposed he'd resolved himself to the inevitable. This was going to happen.

"Hold off calling them until the news hits," Fiona said. "You're not supposed to know about the leak, remember?"

"Anything else I should or shouldn't know about?" he asked with a scowl.

"I filled Wiley in on the shooting. He's sending up a team of investigators to search the mountain."

Josh's scowl deepened. "I wish you hadn't done that. He won't have the manpower unless he pulls detectives off other cases to investigate what was probably nothing more than a coincidence."

Her brows rose in surprise. "You think that shot

was a coincidence? After the DPS received notice of a possible death threat?''

Josh ran a hand through his hair. ''That's exactly what I think. That shot wasn't even close. If the horses hadn't been spooked, neither one of us would have been hurt.''

''You can't know that for sure,'' she said.

''Think about it, Fiona. We were sitting ducks out there, both before and after the shot. If we'd been the target, the shooter could have easily picked us off. And why was there only one shot? My guess is, a hunter got a little close, panicked, and took off before we caught sight of him.''

Fiona hesitated. ''I admit I've been a little puzzled that the shooter only fired once, but we can't dismiss the possibility that you were the target. The incident has to be investigated.''

''And while it's being investigated, what happens to my nephew's case?'' he asked quietly.

''Everything that can be done is being done to find your sister's baby, Josh. I hope you know that. I hope you...'' She trailed off and glanced away.

''You hope what?''

She shook her head. ''Nothing. I just hope you'll have a little faith, that's all.''

Josh had the distinct feeling she'd meant to say something else entirely. Suddenly he remembered his first impression of Fiona Clark—that she was a woman with a few surprises up her sleeve.

She'd certainly surprised him last night with her response to his kiss. He couldn't help wondering what might be next.

JOSH LEFT THE HOSPITAL a short while later to shower and change at his family's condo in Aspen. When he returned, he brought a deck of cards, and he and Fiona played gin rummy to pass the time. They even managed to have a few laughs. Fiona couldn't remember the last time she'd been so relaxed in male company.

In her line of work, she always felt as if she had to constantly be on guard so that her femininity wouldn't be used against her. She'd long ago learned to suppress her softer side, both at home and at work, but Josh made her feel like a woman again. A cliché perhaps, but true.

And as the day wore on, she found herself falling more and more deeply under his spell. He was so different from the men she'd known in the past. Self-confident without a hint of arrogance. Articulate without being pretentious. If there was a bit of suspicion still lurking in the depths of his blue eyes, well, Fiona could understand that because, after all, she was still deceiving him. Her mission hadn't changed. She was still looking for a connection to Schyler's kidnapping, and if the clues led her to Josh, then she would have to bring him down.

It was as simple as that.

WHEN JOSH ARRIVED the next day to pick up Fiona, he expected the hospital to be swarming with reporters, but there was a kind of surreal tranquility about the place. The calm before a storm, he supposed as he rode the elevator up to Fiona's floor.

Her release papers were processed without a hitch, and within the hour, they were on their way back to Denver. All the way home, they listened to the news on the radio, but neither Josh's name nor Fiona's was mentioned in any of the broadcasts. They began to wonder if something had gone wrong and Wiley had changed his mind about the leak.

But when Fiona called, the DPS director assured them that everything was going according to plan and the bomb would drop sometime during the next twenty-four hours.

As it turned out, the bomb had already exploded by the time they drove into Denver late that afternoon, although Josh didn't know it until he let himself into his apartment after dropping off Fiona. The light on his machine blinked frantically, and when he played back the tape, three different reporters from three different newspapers had left messages requesting that he either confirm or deny the rumor that his fiancée had been admitted to an Aspen area hospital.

How they'd gotten his unlisted number, Josh had no idea, but he'd long ago given up any hope of privacy where the media was concerned.

He knew that he should call his staff and alert them of the whirlwind that was about to hit their campaign just weeks before the election. Any disruption could prove deadly at this stage of the game, but somehow Josh wasn't in the mood to deal with Nell. So instead, he erased the messages, unplugged the phone and headed off to the shower.

He went to bed early, but he was much too wired to sleep. He lay on his back and stared at the ceiling, his mind racing—not with thoughts of the campaign or the upcoming election, but of Fiona.

He thought about the way her mouth had tasted beneath his, the way her body had felt against his…and he wanted more of her. All of her.

He didn't want to feel this way. He didn't want this…thing between them, whatever it was. Attraction. Lust. Hell, maybe it was even something more than that. Something deeper. But he didn't want that, either. He especially didn't want that, because there was something about Fiona Clark he still didn't trust.

He couldn't shake the feeling that she was somehow out to get him. And that the moment he let down his guard, the moment he acted on his attraction, she would move in for the kill.

CHAPTER SEVEN

THE NEWS HIT the papers the following morning with the headline LANGWORTHY'S FIANCÉE RUSHED TO HOSPITAL.

The accompanying article went on to say that gubernatorial candidate Joshua Langworthy had rushed a young woman in her early thirties to the emergency room in Aspen following a riding accident on Saturday. According to unnamed sources, the woman sustained a head trauma and was admitted to the hospital for overnight observation. While being treated, she identified herself as Langworthy's fiancée. Witnesses reported that Langworthy seemed visibly shaken by the accident.

The article went on to remind readers of the rumors of a secret engagement, which had swirled around Langworthy's campaign several weeks ago. Josh, the paper said, had denied the rumors at the time, but was unavailable for comment concerning the more recent incident.

He arrived at his office early that morning amidst a cacophony of ringing telephones, humming fax machines and short-tempered campaign staffers.

Nell, Dana and Robert—the Iron Triangle—were already assembled inside his office, and Josh could feel the tension the moment he stepped through the doorway. He had no idea how long Nell had been waiting for him, but she'd already worn a path in the thick carpet with her pacing. She looked as if she could easily rip someone's heart out for a cigarette, but she'd quit several months ago and her willpower was only exceeded by her ambition.

Robert appeared on edge as well. Tall, lanky, with an often blasé demeanor that belied his keen, fertile mind, he stood at the window, jangling change in his pocket—a dead giveaway for him—as he stared down at the traffic on Main Street.

Only Dana appeared cool and collected. She sat in a chair directly across from Josh's desk, her dark head bent over her notebook.

Nell, with her political savvy and driving ambition, and Robert, with his advertising expertise and media contacts, were widely considered the powerhouses behind Josh's campaign, the two most influential sides of the Iron Triangle.

But it was Dana on whom he'd come to rely more and more as Election Day drew near. She'd always been a trusted and efficient assistant, but her calm and reasoned approach to the hundreds of daily problems that cropped up in the course of a campaign had made her indispensable. And the fact that she was an optimist in the face of Nell's eternal pessimism didn't hurt. She was worth every penny of her salary and then some.

She looked up from her notes as Josh strode around his desk and took his seat.

"I suppose you've all seen the headlines," he said.

Dana's dark gaze was still on him. Her expression was benign as usual, but there was something in her eyes, a wounded look, that made Josh curse himself for not having called her the night before.

She wasn't just a close advisor, but also a trusted friend. She'd helped him through the dark days after Schyler's disappearance, and she was one of the few people he'd confided in when he'd considered dropping out of the race. She was also the only one who hadn't tried to dissuade him. It was his decision, she'd said, and she would stand by him no matter what.

However, if she felt even a modicum of anger, or even annoyance, toward him along with the hurt, she managed to conceal it. Nell, on the other hand, made no such effort. She strode across the room and placed her hands flat on his desk. "Just tell me two things," she said bitterly. "Who is she and how much is it going to cost us to keep her from talking to the press?"

"She won't talk to the press," Josh said with a frown. He was amazed at how quickly and how naturally his defense of Fiona had sprung to his lips.

Nell straightened and gave a disgusted snort. "How naïve are you? They all talk to the press. She's probably already trying to figure a way to capitalize on her fifteen minutes of fame."

"As usual, you're putting the cart before the horse, Nell." Robert came over and took a seat next to Dana's. "The first question you should have asked was whether or not the headlines are true."

"Of course, they're not true." Nell gave Robert a withering look. "It's the same garbage the Houghton camp has been putting out since day one to keep us off message."

Robert turned his attention to Josh. "According to the papers, you're the one who took this woman to the hospital. Obviously, you two were together at some point over the weekend."

Nell answered for him. "So? Spending the week-end with a woman is a long way from an engagement. Josh got caught with his pants down, so to speak. These things happen during a campaign. They're called bimbo eruptions. I wouldn't be surprised if the whole thing was a setup. This woman could already be on Houghton's payroll."

"She's not," Josh said coldly.

Nell folded her arms. "How can you be so sure?"

"Because she *is* my fiancée."

Josh heard a gasp, but he wasn't certain whether it came from Nell or Dana. They both looked equally shocked while Robert merely looked...bemused.

Nell finally found her voice. "What are you talking about? You're not engaged. You can't be. You haven't even been dating anyone."

"Fiona and I met a few months ago when I hired her firm to consult on some security matters for the campaign. She and I have been seeing each other ever since."

"Then why keep it a secret?" Robert asked. "Un-less—"

"Unless what?"

Robert shrugged. "Unless she's, you know, already married or something."

"Oh, God." Nell put a hand to her forehead. "I think I'm going to be sick."

"She's not married," Josh said. "We kept our re-lationship private because we didn't know where it was going at first. And then later, after Schyler was kidnapped, it just didn't seem like the appropriate time to announce our engagement."

"Why now?" Robert asked. "This timing isn't the

greatest, either. There're only a few weeks left until election. Why not wait until then?''

''That's exactly what we were planning to do,'' Josh said. ''But someone in the hospital must have overheard us or saw Fiona's ring—''

''She has a *ring?*'' Nell looked as if she didn't know whether to scream or cry. ''How could you? How could you do this to—'' Catching herself, she amended whatever she'd been about to say. ''How could you do this so close to the election? You know what Houghton will make of this, don't you? He'll say it's a ploy to counteract his charges that you're nothing more than a vacuous playboy using your family's name and fortune to get elected.''

''She's right,'' Robert said. ''You can bet the Houghton camp is already planning a response. We need to get out ahead of this, have you explain the situation for yourself. If we call a press conference—''

''No, no press conference.'' Nell had started to pace again. ''The rumors of his engagement died down once before. Give it a news cycle or two, and the story will play itself out.''

''No, it won't,'' Josh said quietly, ''because from here on out, Fiona will be with me on the campaign trail. ''You may as well get used to it.''

JOSH HELD a press conference that afternoon to formally acknowledge his engagement to Fiona Clark. She stood with him on the podium, and after he read a brief statement, the two of them left hand in hand while Nell remained behind the microphone to answer questions. But from the eye daggers Nell had shot at Fiona earlier, she knew their betrothal hadn't exactly come as welcome news to Josh's gorgeous campaign manager.

Dana Severn, on the other hand, had graciously extended Fiona her best wishes and had offered to help in any way she could if Fiona ran into problems on the campaign trail.

Fiona had liked the woman immediately, although she suspected that behind Dana's quiet demeanor lurked a woman with a serious crush on her boss. Josh seemed oblivious to his assistant's feelings, but observing the two of them together, their closeness, Fiona was reminded of something Colleen had said on Friday about Dana.

We don't know much about her background, but our sources tell us she's extremely loyal to Langworthy. She'd do anything to help him get elected.

Even kidnap a baby?

That's what we need you to find out.

Fiona had yet to meet Robert Smith, the third member of the Iron Triangle, but she suspected she would get the opportunity that night. Samuel Langworthy and his wife, Celia, Josh's stepmother, were hosting a hastily arranged dinner party in Fiona's honor. Not only would she be able to observe Josh's top campaign advisors, but his family as well, including his two sisters, Holly and Marilyn.

By the time Fiona got home late that afternoon, she had a message on her machine from Josh, advising her that a meeting with some of the members of the Colorado legislature had run late and he'd have to send a car for her instead of picking her up himself.

Fiona didn't mind. The ride to the Langworthy mansion gave her time to prepare for the coming evening. The scrutiny would go both ways. Not only would she be able to observe Josh's family and staff, but they would be watching her carefully as well. The impression she made tonight could very well set the tone for the rest of her assignment. It was imperative that she get people to accept her, even, if possible, to trust her.

The Langworthy mansion was located in the Capitol Hill area of Denver, a neighborhood that had once been one of the most sought after addresses in Colorado. Time had taken a toll, however, and some of the homes had fallen into despair while others had been demolished to make room for high-rise condominiums and parking garages.

Staring out the window, Fiona caught her breath as the car pulled into the Langworthy drive, the gates swung open, and she got her first glimpse of the mansion. Lit up against the night, the beautiful Victorian reminded Fiona of something from a fairy tale. And when the car stopped in front and the driver came around to help her out, she experienced what could only be described as a true Cinderella moment. She had to keep reminding herself of who she was and why she was really there.

The driver escorted her to the door, and once she was inside, a maid took her coat. From the foyer, Fiona could see into the huge front parlor where perhaps two dozen people stood talking and laughing in small groups. They all seemed to notice her at once, and the room fell almost uncannily silent. Fiona was surprised by how nervous she suddenly was, how awkward the moment felt.

Then Josh, breathtakingly handsome in a formal dark suit and silk tie, excused himself from whomever he'd been talking to and strode across the room to greet her.

He bent and brushed his lips against hers, then murmured in her ear, "Relax. This is all part of the game, remember?"

Fiona's heart beat so hard she couldn't have responded if she'd wanted to. He took her left hand and slid something onto her finger as he lifted it to his lips. The maneuver was done so subtly that no one in the parlor would have noticed, but Fiona almost gasped when she saw the sparkle of the huge emerald-cut diamond on her finger.

"Don't stare at it," he said with a smile. "I would have given this to you weeks ago."

Why, all of a sudden, was he the expert and she the novice? Fiona wanted to know. Where was the cool-headed professional, the ambitious, determined agent who would stop at nothing to get her man?

But the way Josh looked tonight had caught her off guard. And then that kiss...

He'd merely brushed his lips against hers, but Fiona had felt the impact in her knees, in her stomach, in the heat that suddenly flooded her cheeks.

When he tucked her arm through his and whispered in her ear, "You look beautiful tonight," Fiona had to remind herself that that, too, was part of the game.

He led her into the parlor and made the formal introductions, presenting her first to his father. Samuel Langworthy took her hand in his and gave her a long, frank appraisal. He was a distinguished-looking man with thick gray hair and the most beguiling green eyes Fiona had ever encountered. She'd seen him before, but only from a distance, and like his son, up close and personal was a whole new ball game.

While he lacked Josh's youth and rock-star presence, the man was not without his own charisma. He reeked of power and old money, and looking into his eyes, Fiona was reminded of the Langworthys' long and distinguished history in Colorado. She suspected that legacy had held a commanding sway over Samuel Langworthy, and that a man in his position would do whatever necessary to ensure that his family's riches, both financial and cultural, continued to flourish.

His wife, Celia, was his opposite. Tiny and delicate, her faded beauty and southern accent conjured images of frosty mint juleps served on shady front porches in the heat of a Louisiana summer. Fiona knew that she was Samuel's second wife, and was Josh and his sister Marilyn's stepmother. She was Holly Langworthy's mother, making Holly Josh's half sister.

Celia took Fiona's hand warmly in hers as she beamed at her with undisguised delight. "Welcome to our home, Fiona. We're so happy you could join us tonight."

"Thank you for having me," Fiona murmured.

"So you two thought you could pull a fast one, did you?" Samuel was obviously not as taken with the idea of his son's engagement as Celia was. "What the hell were you thinking? Did you hear Houghton's sound bite on the six o'clock news? He's saying you got caught with your pants down, and now you're trying to cover your butt with the voters. And I don't mind telling you this all seems a little suspicious to me, as well—"

"Samuel," Celia admonished gently. "Can't we forget about the campaign for just one evening? This is supposed to be a celebration."

"There won't be any celebration if Josh lets the election get away from him because he couldn't keep his—"

"We'll talk about this later," Josh cut in coldly. "Come on," he said to Fiona. "I want you to meet my sisters." She could tell that he was angry. It was obvious he and his father rubbed each other the wrong way.

The question was, why? What had caused such a rift between them? Something to do with the election? The kidnapping?

Or did the animosity go back even further than that?

Fiona had no idea, but her mind grappled with the possibilities as Josh introduced her to his sisters. Marilyn, only three years younger than Josh, bore a striking resemblance to her and Josh's mother, Evelyn, who lived in Boston and whom Fiona had seen once or twice during her surveillance of Josh. They had the same regal blondness, the same aristocratic nose and the same cold, calculating eyes. Fiona didn't much care for the woman and sensed the feeling was mutual. She also sensed tension between Marilyn and her father.

Fiona was, however, instantly taken with Holly, Josh's younger sister. She couldn't have been more than twenty-two or twenty-three, much too young to have suffered such a terrible tragedy in her life. She was a lovely young woman, but the stark sadness in her eyes tore at Fiona's heart and made her want more than ever to find little Schyler and bring him safely home.

As she and Josh made the rounds, Fiona tried to commit names and faces to memory, tried to find out, without being too obvious, where those closest to Josh had been on the night of the kidnapping.

By the time dinner was announced, she'd met almost everyone present and was pleased to learn that she'd been seated next to Samuel and Robert Smith, both of whom she'd wanted to question a little more closely. Holly was directly across from Fiona, on Samuel's left, and Josh had been placed all the way at the other end, next to Celia and Nell.

"Josh tells us you're from Chicago," Samuel commented as the first course was being served.

Fiona smiled. "Yes, that's right."

"I know some Clarks who live in the Lincoln Park area." He tested his soup. "Vincent and Mary Clark. They're both attorneys. You wouldn't happen to be related to them, would you?"

"No, I'm afraid not. My family lives on the South Side." She named the blue-collar neighborhood where she grew up.

"The first Mayor Daly's old stomping ground," Samuel said, surprising Fiona.

"Sounds as if you're familiar with the city," she said.

"It's a great town. A lot of history and tradition. I appreciate a place that has a sense of itself. What made you decide to come to Denver?" His dark eyes burned into Fiona's, and she knew she was treading on very dangerous territory. Samuel Langworthy was nobody's fool.

"I was offered a job here."

"Josh says you work for a private investigation firm."

She nodded. "Investigations, Confidential and Undercover."

"I've heard of the outfit. It's run by a woman named Colleen Wellesley, if I'm not mistaken. She used to be Denver P.D., but I seem to recall there was some sort of scandal when she resigned."

His memory and knowledge of detail intrigued Fiona. "I wouldn't know. That was before my time."

Samuel blotted his mouth on his napkin. "So you and Josh met when he hired your firm to advise him on the security for his campaign." His gaze lifted to Fiona's. "Did I get the story right?"

Fiona met his gaze without flinching. "Yes, that's right."

"He says you're an expert in security matters."

"Well, I was with the FBI for eight years," she said carefully.

"Yes, that's what he said." Something flickered in his gaze that Fiona couldn't quite define. "Maybe I should have consulted with your firm about security for this house. Maybe then my grandson would still be with us."

Holly, who had been sitting quietly all through dinner, put a hand on her father's arm. "Dad, don't. Not tonight."

His expression softened as he turned to his daughter. "I'm sorry, honey. I spoke without thinking." He leaned toward her and said something no one else could hear. Holly nodded, and for several minutes, the two of them spoke in low tones. Fiona couldn't have heard them even if she'd tried, which she didn't. It was a private moment between father and daughter, and somehow she couldn't bring herself to eavesdrop.

Beside her Robert Smith gave a low chuckle. "That was some third degree. I don't know why he didn't just shine a hot light in your face and sweat it out of you.''

Fiona grimaced. "It did feel a bit like an inquisition. Now I know how it feels to be on the other side of an interrogation."

"I remember the first time I ever came here." He smiled, showing dimples at the corners of his mouth. Women would love that smile, Fiona thought. He was a handsome man, although he was nowhere near as good-looking as Josh. Fiona had a feeling he knew it, too.

"What happened?" she asked politely.

"The old man scared the crap out of me. Cross-examined me as if I was some kind of petty thief he'd caught in the act."

Fiona glanced around to make sure no one could overhear them. "You and Josh met in college, I understand."

"We were roommates. I was there on an art scholarship. I had no idea people like the Langworthys even existed outside of movies. I was pretty overwhelmed the first time Josh invited me here for a weekend."

"What was he like in college?" she asked curiously.

"Not as bad as you might think," Robert said with a grin. "That is what you want to know, isn't it? If he sowed his wild oats back then? I guess the first couple of years we were pretty much hell on wheels, but after that, Josh settled down."

"Settled down?"

"You sound surprised. But he's never been able to live up to his reputation, you know. No one could. I think Josh would have been perfectly happy to have been married all these years with a couple of kids to spoil. He's really a family man at heart.''

Fiona's gaze went to the end of the table, where Josh sat talking to Nell. He looked up at that moment, and their eyes met briefly before Fiona glanced away. But the eye contact had set her pulse to racing.

''Why is it he's never married then?'' she asked Robert.

''That's a dangerous question coming from his fiancée. How am I supposed to answer that?''

''As honestly as you like,'' Fiona said with a shrug. ''I'm not the jealous type.''

Robert's gaze dropped to the huge diamond on her finger. ''No reason you should be, I'd say. You're the first woman since…'' He trailed off and picked up his wineglass.

''I'm the first woman since…?''

He took a sip of his wine. ''I'm talking too much.''

''I like hearing about Josh's past,'' she said. ''He won't talk about himself.''

''All the more reason why I shouldn't, either,'' Robert said dryly. ''I sound like an old gossip.''

''Was there someone in college Josh was serious about?''

He stared into his wineglass for a moment. ''Her name was Theresa Santos. Teri.''

''What was she like?''

''Brilliant. Beautiful.'' He frowned into his glass, as if suddenly remembering something unpleasant. ''She and Josh were in pre-law together, and they fell in love.''

''What happened?''

Robert's gaze went to the man at the head of the table. ''Samuel Langworthy happened.''

"How do you mean?"

"Josh decided to enter the University of Colorado law school rather than Harvard, although, of course, that's where he eventually ended up. He didn't want to leave Teri. When Samuel figured out what was going on, he got rid of her."

Fiona stared at him in shock. "What are you saying?"

"Oh, don't look like that. I don't mean he pulled a Tony Soprano or anything. He bought her off. Made her an offer she couldn't refuse."

"So how did Josh find out about it?"

"He went over to her house one day, and she'd just packed up and left. Gone without a trace. Her roommate told him that someone in a limo had come to see Teri the day before, and that after he'd left, she was really upset and said she had to go away. The roommate never saw who was in the limo, but Josh figured it was his father."

"Did Josh confront him?"

"Sure, and the old man denied it. But who else would it have been?"

Fiona thought about that for a moment. "Did Josh ever try to find this girl?"

"It was a hopeless cause. Her grandmother raised her, and she died during Teri's second year of college. She didn't have any other family, so Josh pretty much hit a dead end when he went looking for her."

"He never saw her again?"

"Not that I know of. The roommate, Allison I think her name was, would come by every so often when she'd heard from Teri to let Josh know she was okay. But I never thought the roommate's motives were all that altruistic. She had a thing for Josh, but then, most girls did. And do." Was that an edge of resentment she heard in his tone? Fiona wondered. What was it Colleen had said in her office? *Even best friends can hold secret grudges and resentments, sometimes for years. Especially against a golden boy like Langworthy.*

Was it possible Robert had been in love with Teri?

"What made Josh decide to go to Harvard?"

Robert shrugged. "I think he wanted to get away from the memories here in Colorado. And maybe he just figured it was pointless to fight his old man."

He leaned toward Fiona. "Look, I'd appreciate if you wouldn't say anything to Josh about this conversation. I probably shouldn't have told you about Teri."

Fiona frowned slightly. "Why did you tell me?"

"Because you said you wanted to know about Josh. And because..." His gaze lifted to meet Fiona's. Something dark and disturbing flashed in his eyes. Something that made Fiona shiver. "I thought you should know the lengths Samuel Langworthy will go to get what he wants. Watch yourself, Fiona. Believe me, you don't want to get on the old man's bad side."

"WHAT ARE YOU DOING?"

Fiona let her hand slip from the door she'd been about to open and turned with what she hoped was a puzzled smile. "I beg your pardon?"

Holly Langworthy came toward her down the hallway. "That's my father's study. No one is allowed inside unless he's in there."

Fiona put a hand to her chest. "I'm sorry. I was looking for the powder room. The maid said second door on the left."

"Third door," Holly said, nodding down the hallway.

"I must have misunderstood her. I really am sorry."

Holly smiled. "No harm done. I didn't mean to snap at you. It's just been a terribly long day."

"I understand." She did look at the end of her rope, Fiona thought. The girl was thin almost to the point of gauntness, and her eyes were darkly shadowed underneath. She probably hadn't been able to eat or sleep since her baby had disappeared.

"May I talk to you for a moment?" Holly asked softly.

"Of course."

She took Fiona's arm and drew her down beside her on a thickly tufted bench. "I wanted to thank you and Josh for postponing your engagement announcement. It was a very thoughtful thing to do."

"You don't need to thank me," Fiona said. "It was the right thing to do. No one in your family is in the mood to celebrate right now."

Tears pooled in Holly's eyes. "Sometimes I still can't believe he's gone. I wake up in the middle of the night and go into his nursery before I remember that he's not there. And then I see his empty crib—" She broke off and turned away.

Fiona put her hand over Holly's. "Josh may have mentioned that I used to work for the FBI. I was involved in a lot of kidnapping cases back then. It's hard to explain, but there was always a feeling you got going into one of those cases. How it was going to turn out. Sometimes the feeling was based on the evidence and eyewitnesses or on the suspects, but other times it was nothing more than an intuition. An instinct. I've had a very strong feeling from the beginning that your baby is alive and that he'll be found very soon.''

The tears in Holly's eyes spilled over and ran down her cheeks. She squeezed Fiona's hand. ''Thank you,'' she whispered. ''Thank you for that.''

Fiona fervently hoped she hadn't given Holly false hope, but she'd spoken the truth. She had felt all along that Schyler was alive and well, and that it was only a matter of time before they broke the case.

''What's going on here?''

Fiona and Holly both glanced around to see Marilyn Langworthy striding toward them down the corridor. ''Holly, are you all right?''

Holly quickly drew a hand across her wet face. ''Yes, I'm fine. Fiona and I were just getting to know each other a little better. But now, if you'll both excuse me, I think I'll go up to bed. As I said, it's been a long day.''

Fiona rose, too. ''Of course. I'm glad we had this chance to chat.''

''So am I.'' Impulsively, Holly gave Fiona a hug. ''Thanks again for what you said. Maybe I'll even be able to sleep tonight.''

''I hope so.''

As she hurried off, Fiona turned to Marilyn, who gave her a cool, dismissive smile. ''Seems you've wasted no time in ingratiating yourself with my sister. But don't make the mistake of thinking I'll be as gullible.''

''I beg your pardon?''

Marilyn lifted her chin. ''Unlike Josh and Holly, I'm not so easily taken in. I know exactly who you are and why you're here. And if you think I'm going to stand by while you make a fool of my brother, you have seriously underestimated me. And what I'm capable of,'' she added with a sly smile as she turned and walked away.

CHAPTER EIGHT

THE NEXT TWO WEEKS passed in a blur for Fiona. For the first few days on the campaign trail with Josh, she created something of a sensation every time she appeared with him in public. But she soon became such a permanent fixture on the podium beside him that even the media grew bored with the story and moved on.

Meanwhile, Josh's popularity continued to soar. The week after he went public with the engagement, he received a bump in the polls and was now leading Governor Houghton by ten points. A feeling of euphoria settled over the Langworthy camp even though Josh cautioned his staffers not to get overly optimistic or complacent. A lot could still happen in the weeks leading up to the election. Todd Houghton was not the kind of man to roll over and play dead, and he could still have an "October surprise" up his sleeve.

But many of the volunteers working for Josh's campaign were college students, and with the scent of their first political victory in the air, their excitement was hard to contain.

While the campaign steamrolled toward Election Day, Fiona was not without concerns. There'd been no further threats against Josh, which was good news, but neither had she made much headway in the kidnapping investigation. If anyone in Josh's campaign, including Josh himself, was involved, they were keeping a very low profile.

But during her second week with the campaign, Fiona got her first break. Two things happened which made her wonder if someone close to Josh was trying to get rid of her.

The first incident happened in Boulder. Josh was to address a group of local businessmen, and there'd been some revisions to his speech. He'd asked Fiona to grab the final draft for him from his hotel suite, but somehow the folders had gotten switched and she'd given him a previous draft. Just seconds into the speech, Josh had realized the error and had had to ad lib much of his talk.

The second incident had occurred in Steamboat Springs. Josh was scheduled to visit a fifth grade class at a local elementary school, but before they'd left the hotel, Fiona had taken a call from the superintendent advising them that a last-minute change was necessary because of problems at the original school. When they arrived at the second location, the principal was completely caught off guard. It was an awkward situation, but again, Josh handled it with polished aplomb.

After that, Fiona began to think that someone was deliberately setting her up. Whether the gaslighting had anything to do with the threat against Josh or little Schyler's kidnapping, she had no idea. For all she knew, the incidents could be unrelated. She could very well be dealing with two separate crimes and three separate suspects, which meant that a complex investigation had just gotten a hell of a lot more complicated.

FIONA WALKED into the glittering ballroom of the Carlisle Hotel in Aspen, her gaze immediately searching the crowd for Josh. This was an important night for him. It was a fund-raising event masked as a formal reception for his closest friends and most generous donors. A way to say thank-you for their contributions while subtly reminding them that the race was still far from won, and their support—monetarily and otherwise—was needed now more than ever.

All the Langworthys were in attendance, and since Josh's mother and sister, Evelyn and Marilyn, were staying in the family condo, Josh and Fiona had gotten suites at the Carlisle, which had given Fiona a little more time to prepare for the evening.

Colleen had ponied up for a new dress, which Fiona had purchased at an exclusive boutique in Aspen. The sales clerk had assured her that the silk jersey halter top was the perfect dress for her figure. "Really shows off your assets. And it looks good from the front, too," he'd quipped. After that, there was no way Fiona could resist, and she'd even let him talk her into a pair of four-inch heels that made her feel positively willowy if not a bit wobbly.

She continued to scan the ballroom until she finally spotted Josh. He was talking to his mother and sister, and when he saw Fiona, he excused himself and headed across the room toward her.

His mother whirled to see who had caught her son's attention, and when she saw Fiona, her blue eyes narrowed in cold disapproval. Fiona had only met Evelyn Langworthy once since the engagement announcement, and like her daughter, Evelyn had made no secret of the way she felt about Fiona. She and Marilyn both seemed to think Fiona was a gold-digging opportunist out to seduce Josh for his money.

The idea of her as a femme fatale was so ludicrous to Fiona that she could almost find it amusing if she didn't suspect that Marilyn or Evelyn or both might have been behind the incidents in Boulder and Steamboat Springs. She wouldn't put it past either of them to try and make her look foolish and incompetent in Josh's eyes.

As he made his way toward her, Fiona saw Evelyn whip around and furiously whisper something to her daughter. Marilyn nodded, her frigid gaze still on Fiona.

And then she forgot about both mother and daughter because Josh was suddenly there in front of her, and Fiona found it difficult to breathe. He put his hands on her arms and bent to touch his lips to hers. It was an action that Fiona should have been used to by now. He did it every time they were in public. But she still went all weak in the knees when he kissed her, when he touched her, and her stomach fluttered at the mere sight of him. Certain men were born to wear a tuxedo, and Josh was one of them. And he always smelled so good. Fiona closed her eyes, drinking in the delicious scent of him.

The diamond glittered brilliantly on her left hand as he tucked her arm through his. "Get ready," he murmured. "We're in for a long night, by the looks of it. There are a lot of people here who want to meet you."

"Who want to meet Josh Langworthy's infamous fiancée, you mean."

"The way you look tonight, you could just stand

on the podium and the donations would come pouring in.''

Fiona warmed to the light flirtation in spite of herself. She was a woman after all. And Josh was an expert at bringing out the feminine side of her, not to mention all those deep, dark fantasies....

The ballroom was a sea of black, which was why Fiona had chosen to wear the dark color as well. She could easily blend in with the crowd if she needed to. Nell, on the other hand, had donned a red beaded gown that drew men to her side like a beacon.

When she saw Josh and Fiona, she parted the crowd of admirers and moved toward them. Entangling her arm with Josh's, she gave Fiona a brilliant smile. ''You don't mind if I steal Josh away for a few minutes, do you? There're some people he needs to speak with.''

''No, of course not.'' But Fiona found that she did mind. She watched as they moved across the floor and began to chat with a group of high rollers, all the while, Nell never relinquishing her grasp on Josh's arm. She clung to him almost obsessively, but Fiona had to admit, they made a striking couple. Tall, elegant, sophisticated.

A new dress, no matter how expensive, was never going to put Fiona in the same league as Nell McKenna. Not that she even wanted to be. She was happy with who she was and proud of where she'd come from.

But during the past two weeks, Fiona had sometimes found herself too caught up in the fantasy. She'd wondered, on more than one occasion, what it would be like to have a man like Josh fall hopelessly in love with her for real.

"You don't need to worry about Nell, you know."

Fiona turned in surprise. She hadn't even noticed the woman's approach.

But if she hadn't heard her voice, Fiona might not have recognized her. Dana looked so different tonight. She was dressed in a long-sleeve, form-fitting black dress that was very flattering to her slim figure. Her hair was different, too. Rather than lying flat against her head, she'd spiked it up a bit, and even the thick-rimmed glasses made her look hip and cool. Very un-Dana-like.

"Wow," Fiona said. "You look great. I hardly recognized you."

"Not my usual dowdy self, you mean," Dana said dryly.

"I didn't mean that at all. You just look so different." When Dana didn't respond, Fiona said, "You were saying something about Nell?"

Dana frowned slightly, her gaze moving across the room to where Nell and Josh stood arm in arm. "I never noticed until tonight how much she reminds me of someone I went to college with."

That wasn't what she'd said earlier, but the comment interested Fiona just the same. "Really?"

Dana turned with an anxious smile. "Will you excuse me, Fiona? I see someone I need to speak with."

"Sure."

An odd little conversation, Fiona thought as she watched Dana disappear into the crowd. She had the distinct feeling that Dana had approached her for a reason, maybe to share some information about Nell, but had changed her mind at the last minute.

Intrigued by the thought, Fiona wandered through the crowd searching for Dana until an arm wrapped around her waist and she looked up to find Josh smiling down at her. Without a word, he whisked her through one of the French doors and onto a lovely stone terrace draped with hundreds of tiny white fairy lights.

"Brrr." Fiona shivered. "It's freezing outside. What are we doing out here?"

Josh took off his jacket and wrapped it around her shoulders. "I thought we needed a moment alone."

Fiona gazed up at him. "Why?"

"Because if you really were my fiancée..." using the lapels of his coat, he tugged her toward him "...I'd want to do this..."

He bent and kissed her before Fiona had time to protest. Not that she would have. She'd wanted him to kiss her all night.

"This isn't a good idea," she murmured, when he finally pulled away.

"Sure it is. If anyone looks out, they'll think we're hot for each other, just the way an engaged couple should be."

"Josh—"

But she never finished her thought because he was kissing her again, and Fiona, God help her, couldn't resist him. He threaded his fingers through her hair as his tongue invaded her mouth, making her sigh deeply as she relaxed into the kiss.

When they broke apart, they were both breathing hard. Somehow they'd moved back into the shadows, and Fiona leaned weakly against a stone wall. Josh propped one hand over her as he bent to kiss her again, then trailed a finger down her throat.

"What are we doing?" Fiona asked on a ragged breath.

"Pretending to be in love."

But suddenly, it didn't seem so much like pretense. Fiona had a bad feeling that when all this was over, someone was going to be badly hurt, and she was pretty sure it was going to be her.

"Come upstairs with me," Josh whispered.

"We can't just leave. There're a lot of important people inside. They'll be expecting a speech from you."

"Fine. I'll say a few words, and then make my excuses. I had a long day today. I have to get up early tomorrow. Whatever. I'll be waiting for you upstairs."

"Josh, no. I can't. I have an assignment to carry out and you have an election to win. We can't... afford...to be..." she closed her eyes as he began kissing her neck "...distracted..."

"I'm already distracted. You're making me crazy."

"We'd better go back inside." Somehow Fiona summoned the willpower to push him away. "Look. I see Nell at the door. I think she's looking for you."

He murmured something Fiona didn't quite catch, but he released her and stepped back. "Okay. We'll go in. I'll do my duty, and then later...I'll be waiting for you in my suite."

"I'm not coming to your suite, Josh."

He curled a strand of hair around one finger. "That's up to you. But I'll be waiting just the same."

FIONA TOLD HERSELF that she wouldn't go to Josh's room that night. And then when she found herself outside his door, she told herself she wouldn't knock.

And then as her hand lifted, she told herself she'd only come to let him know that…she wasn't coming.

When he opened the door, Fiona's breath left her in a painful rush, along with her resolve. He'd removed his jacket and tie, and his shirt was untucked from his trousers and partly unbuttoned. He looked rumpled and sexy, as if he'd been waiting for her in bed.

"I didn't think you were coming," he said in a voice that melted Fiona's knees.

"I wasn't. I'm not. I just came to tell you that…"

And then somehow, before she could get all the words out, she was inside his suite, kicking the door closed with one of her new high heels as she flung herself into Josh's arms. His mouth claimed hers instantly as he picked her up and hauled her against him. Fiona's arms came around his neck, her legs around his waist as he pressed her back against the wall and they kissed as if there were no tomorrow.

They left a trail of clothing from the front door back to the bedroom. By the time they were settled beneath the covers, Fiona's body was in flames.

Josh didn't just know how to kiss, he knew where to touch her, what to say to make her writhe in ecstasy. He turned her, lifting her hair to kiss the back of her neck and then trailed his lips down her spine as his hands circled around her, cupping her breasts, skimming her waist, her hips, the insides of her thighs.

Fiona's breath came rapid and hard. She felt deliciously close to the edge as she arched her back and turned her head for Josh's kiss.

And then he was inside her, setting a furious rhythm as he drew her against him. Their bodies were hot, slick, straining. It was the way sex should be, Fiona thought. Out of control. Wild and messy.

Just the way she had known it would be with Josh.

As the first shudders pulsed through her, he held her close, whispered things in her ear, and made her feel as if she were the only woman in the world....

CHAPTER NINE

WHEN FIONA AWAKENED the next morning, Josh had already gotten up, showered and dressed. She could hear him moving about in the next room, ordering coffee from room service, turning on the TV.

She headed for the bathroom and took a quick shower, then slipped on one of the hotel robes hanging on the back of the door. Her clothes, for all she knew, were still scattered about the suite, and, morning after or not, she had no intention of walking out stark naked to retrieve them.

Josh had his back to her when she stepped out of the bedroom, and he didn't turn around to greet her. He was staring at the TV as if something on the news broadcast had captured his undivided attention.

And then Fiona suddenly knew why. "...A spokesman for the Houghton campaign claims to have learned from a reliable source in the DPS that gubernatorial candidate Josh Langworthy is now the primary focus of the investigation into his nephew's kidnapping. According to the spokesman, an undercover agent working inside the Langworthy campaign expects to gather enough evidence to convene a grand jury—"

Josh turned off the TV and turned slowly to face Fiona. "It's you, isn't it? You're the agent."

"Josh, you know why I'm here. The death threat—"

"Was a ruse. An excuse to plant you inside my campaign. And in my bed, evidently. All this time, you were after me. A gubernatorial candidate. A Langworthy. That'd be quite a feather in your cap, wouldn't it, Fiona?"

"It wasn't like that. I wasn't supposed to—"

"Sleep with me?" He gave a bitter laugh. "I asked you once how far you were willing to go to convince people you were my fiancée. I guess I have my answer."

Fiona's face heated with anger. "That's not fair. Last night had nothing to do with the investigation."

He lifted a brow. "Nothing? If I'd told you I had something to do with Schyler's kidnapping during pillow talk, you wouldn't have used it against me?"

She closed her eyes. "Of course, I would. But you didn't. And I've never really thought you had anything to do with the kidnapping."

"But that didn't stop you from investigating me, did it? That didn't stop you from lying to me at every turn. I said it once and I'll say it again." His cold, relentless gaze met hers. "You really are good at what you do."

THEY ARRIVED BACK in Denver late that afternoon. Josh went straight to the office along with Nell, Robert, Dana and several other close advisors to try and map out a strategy to contain the damage from Houghton's allegations. Josh had spoken briefly to the press earlier and told them that, while he was unaware of any specific investigation involving him, he assumed it was a matter of routine and he welcomed any new evidence that would help find his nephew.

He was calm, his demeanor serious but unconcerned. He'd presented exactly the right face to the reporters and to the cameras, but just how badly the allegations had hurt his chances might not fully be known until Election Day.

And as he and his advisors worked furiously behind the scenes, he all but ignored Fiona. The campaign was in such an uproar, she didn't think anyone had noticed their distance, but they would soon. And then there would be yet more questions.

Meanwhile, she had her own problems. A leak in either the DPS ranks or at CC was serious business. As soon as she arrived back in Denver, she went straight to the downtown office.

"Josh?"

He lifted his head and rubbed his eyes, realizing he must have dozed off at his desk. He glanced up. "What time is it?"

"Nearly two in the morning. Everyone else has gone home," Dana told him.

"What are you doing still here?"

She came into his office and closed the door. "I thought you might need someone to talk to. Someone who isn't concerned with whether you win the election or not."

He drew a long breath and released it. "I think I'm all talked out, but thanks anyway." He and his advisors had worked until well after midnight, trying to figure out the best way to handle the situation. Unfortunately, no matter what they did, there would be

a certain number of voters who would believe Houghton's allegations.

"That was one hell of an October surprise," he
muttered.

"Do you have any idea who the undercover agent
is?" Dana asked.

Josh hesitated. "No, not really. But I'm sure we'll
find out soon enough." He ran a hand through his
hair. "Why don't you go on home. It's been a long
day. We could all use some rest."

But instead, she came into the office and sat down.
"I was just thinking about that night after Schyler
disappeared. How you and I stayed up all night talking. Remember, Josh?"

"You've been a good friend," he said. "But go
home."

She looked as if she wanted to say something else,
then rose. "All right. I'll see you in the morning."

As she started for the door, Josh said, "Dana?"

When she turned, he stared at her for a moment.
"You look different tonight. Or am I just tired?"

She smiled. "I lost my glasses."

"You look like a different person. It's amazing."

She shrugged. "I know. But unfortunately, I can't
wear contacts, and I'm blind as a bat without my
glasses."

He nodded absently. "Do you need a ride home?"

"I have another pair in my car, but thanks anyway."

"Good night then."

"Good night. And, Josh? Everything will be all
right. I promise."

He stared after her for a moment, still marveling at

how different she looked without her glasses. Different…and yet oddly familiar….

THE DOORBELL awakened Fiona from an uneasy sleep. Grabbing her robe, she stumbled down the hallway and across the living room to the front door. She peered into the peephole, then drew back the door in surprise. "What are you doing here?"

"May I come in?"

"Is something wrong?" Fiona asked with a note of panic. "Josh—"

"Josh is fine."

The phone started ringing then, and Fiona glanced behind her. "Can you hold on a second? I'll be right back."

But the moment she turned her back, Fiona knew that she'd made a mistake. It was one of the first things she'd learned at Quantico. Never turn your back on a potential adversary. Lesson Number Two: Never underestimate the enemy.

A STRANGE PREMONITION had descended over Josh after Dana left, and he couldn't shake the uneasy feeling that something was wrong. He was too wired to sleep so instead of going home, he decided to drive around for a while, hoping it would clear his head.

He didn't have a destination in mind but wasn't really surprised to find himself driving down Fiona's street. He pulled to the curb in front of her apartment, and sat for a while, staring up at her window.

There was no good reason to feel so betrayed, he told himself. He'd known all along that she was working for the DPS. The relationship they'd cultivated had never been real. It had been pretend all along and he'd known that. He'd known the first time he'd kissed her. He'd known when they'd announced their engagement to the world. He'd known last night when he'd made love to her.

It had all been just make-believe, and yet last night...

Last night he'd convinced himself that it could be something more. He and Fiona had something special, something worth keeping after her assignment was over.

They could still have it, except...she was too damn good at her job. She'd played her part too well. How would he ever be able to trust her again? How would he be able to tell what was real and what was fantasy with her?

Reaching for the gearshift, he started to drive away, but then a shadow moved across her window, catching his attention. Someone was in the apartment with her.

Josh felt a rush of anger as he stared up at her window. It was after midnight. Except for a lover, who would she be entertaining at this hour?

WHEN FIONA CAME TO, she found herself lying on the floor, her hands bound behind her back. And now Dana was busily binding her feet, which told Fiona she'd only been out for a few minutes. She tried to struggle away, but it was too late. The ropes around her wrists and ankles were secure.

Dana rose and grabbed the gun from the floor.

"Why are you doing this?" Fiona asked softly, trying not to alarm the woman. The last thing she wanted was for Dana to panic.

"Because I want Josh to come to me, to need me the way he did after Schyler was kidnapped."

"You took Schyler?" Fiona whispered in shock.

"No, of course not. I'd never harm a child. But Josh came to me after it happened. He was so distraught. So stricken with grief. I'd never seen him like that. He was afraid someone had kidnapped Schyler to get back at him. He was thinking about pulling out of the race. And he came to me. To *me*," she said proudly. "Not to Nell. Not to you. He came to me. And I realized something that night. Josh always comes to me in moments of crisis."

"Like when he received a death threat," Fiona murmured. "That was you, wasn't it?"

Dana smiled. "And when Teri went away."

She was full of surprises, Fiona thought fleetingly. "You knew Teri?"

"I was her roommate in college. She and Josh met because of me. I saw him first. She knew I wanted him, but that didn't stop her from going after him. So I had to get rid of her."

"By calling Josh's father?"

She shrugged. "He offered her money, but she still wouldn't leave."

"So how did you get rid of her?" Fiona asked. "You killed her, didn't you? And when Josh thought she'd left him that gave you an excuse to keep in touch with him."

"I followed him to Boston when he went to Harvard. He never knew it, of course. I changed my name, my nose, got new glasses, a job with a law firm and waited for him to graduate. When he moved back to Denver, I came back, too, and applied for a

position with the Justice Department where he
worked. He never recognized me.''

"And all these years, you've waited for him to notice you."

"He would have, too, if people hadn't kept getting
in the way. First Teri, then Nell, and now you. I know
who you are, you know. I overheard you and Josh
talking at the cabin.''

"You followed us?''

"Of course. I've followed Josh for years. I've even
been in his apartment when he was home, and he
didn't even know. I'm very good at what I do.''

The irony was a little hard to stomach. "If you
know who I am,'' Fiona said, "then you know I'm
no threat to you. Josh and I aren't really engaged.''

"Yes, I know, except…I've seen the way he looks
at you. It's only a matter of time before he falls in
love with you. Maybe he already has.''

Fiona wanted to believe that. Oh, how she wanted
to believe it. "He despises me now,'' she said.
"There's no reason for you to do this.''

"When you're gone, he'll come to me for comfort.
And I'll be there for him—''

"Just like you always have been,'' a voice said
from the doorway.

Josh! She had no idea how he'd gotten into the
apartment. Dana must have left the front door un-
locked. Perhaps she wasn't as good as she thought.
And one mistake was all it took.

Fiona's frantic gaze rushed to his. He was unarmed.
Oh, God. He didn't know what he was walking into—

"I realize that now,'' he said softly. "I realize what
a good friend you've been to me, Dana. How much

you've come to mean to me. Put away the gun," he said. "So we can talk about this."

"No. You don't really mean that. You're just saying it to save her." She took a few quick steps back so that she could keep both of them in sight. She pointed the weapon at Fiona. "She's not who you think she is, Josh. She's trying to pin the blame for Schyler's kidnapping on you. But I won't let her. I won't let anyone hurt you, Josh."

She put both hands on the gun, and as Josh rushed toward her, she whirled toward him and fired. He might have been hit at pointblank range if Fiona hadn't managed to kick Dana's feet out from under her.

Dana fell sprawling to the floor and the gun went flying. Josh was on her in a flash, holding her down until the fight went out of her. "It's all over, Dana. Allison. Whatever the hell your name is."

"My name is Mrs. Joshua Langworthy," she said, and then began to laugh or sob hysterically. Fiona wasn't quite sure which.

CHAPTER TEN

"IT'S HARD TO BELIEVE that you can know someone for that many years, work with them that closely day in and day out, and still not realize how sick they are."

Fiona shuddered as she and Josh walked through the woods near the cabin. A week had passed since that night in her apartment, but in some ways it seemed like a lifetime. After Dana's arrest, everything had come out. Her stalking, the threat against Josh's life, Fiona's undercover assignment. Josh was no longer considered a suspect in his nephew's kidnapping, but whether the public would stand behind him was yet to be seen. He'd slipped in the polls. With the election only a few days away, the race was now virtually a dead heat.

"I'm sorry for the way things turned out," Fiona said. "I'm sorry you've been hurt by all this."

"A lot of people have been hurt. My sister most of all."

"We're not giving up the search, Josh. We'll find Schyler. I promise you that. But in the meantime…" She slipped off the engagement ring and held it out to him. "I guess I won't need this any longer."

He took the ring and held it up to the light. "When I first saw this in the jewelry store, it reminded me of you. All clean and clear and beautiful. I can't imagine anyone wearing it but you.''

Fiona gazed up at him. "I think that's the nicest thing anyone's ever said to me.''

He stared at the ring for a moment longer. "I think you should keep it.''

She gasped. "I couldn't. It must be worth a fortune. Josh, I couldn't—''

But he'd already taken her hand and was slipping the ring back on her finger. The fit was perfect. It always had been.

"I think maybe that's where it should stay,'' Josh murmured.

"What are you saying?'' Fiona's breath was coming so fast now, she could hardly speak.

"I think we should get engaged. Again. This time for keeps.''

"You're asking me to marry you?'' Fiona actually felt light-headed. He couldn't be asking her to marry him. Not after everything that had happened. Could he?

"Will you marry me, Fiona?''

"Oh, my God!''

"Shall I take that as a yes?''

"Oh, my God.'' She stared at the diamond.

"I'll take that as a yes.''

She lifted her gaze to his. "I do want to marry you. More than anything. I'm so in love with you.''

He reached for her then, but Fiona took a step back. "Wait. I have to tell you something first. You have to know…who I really am.''

A shadow flickered across his eyes. "What do you mean?''

"When I told you that I work for a private investigative firm, that's not altogether true. I'm an agent for a covert division of the DPS called Colorado Confidential. I was recruited by the man who heads up the Chicago office. That's why I left the FBI.''

"And you're first assignment was to investigate me," he said dryly. "Your future husband. That's something to tell our grandkids, I guess."

"Then you still want to marry me?"

"Of course I still want to marry you." He reached for her again. This time she didn't resist. "In fact, I think we should take this discussion inside. I'll even let you interrogate me if you feel you must."

"I'd have to frisk you first," she warned, running her hands inside his shirt.

He gave her a slow, sexy smile. "Take your time, Agent Clark. I've got all night...."

CENTENNIAL BRIDE
Debra Lee Brown

CHAPTER ONE

Colorado Territory, 1875

IN THE NEW YEAR Colorado would become a state and Jefferson Langworthy a statesman. The second generation cattleman saw his own success reflected back at him in the approving eyes of the prominent sheep ranchers he'd invited to the Bar L for supper.

"Brandy and cigars all around," Jeff said. As his guests helped themselves and settled in to enjoy the autumn sunset, he walked to the window and looked out on the high-country ranch land he'd inherited from his father.

Joshua Langworthy's dream had become his own. An obsession that, in a few short months, Jeff would see to fruition. By year-end he'd deliver the support of the local landowners, sheep and cattle ranchers alike, for Colorado's petition to statehood. In return he'd win himself a place in the new government, and one day he'd be a congressman.

The cattle ranchers had been easy to convince. Jeff had known them all his life. But the sheep ranchers had wavered, all the way up until this afternoon. He'd courted them for months, diffusing range wars and soothing skirmishes over water rights. As he turned from the window and faced his guests, their support now certain, he knew that his father, had he lived to see the day, would be proud.

"You've got a fine spread here, Jeff." Dan Chaitlain, one of the wealthiest sheep ranchers in the area,
smiled at him. Chaitlain was highly influential, both
in the territorial government and with the men gathered here today.

"Thank you, Dan. The cattle business has been
good to us." Jeff was referring to himself, his four
sisters, young brother and their widowed mother. The
Bar L would always be home, no matter how much
time he'd have to spend in Denver after the state con-
stitution was ratified.

"You'll be taking a wife soon, I suppose." Chaitlain's smile faded. "Politicians should be married.
Gives a more stable impression."

"I plan to be."

"Good." Chaitlain rose from his chair. "Anyone
we know?"

They did know her. Not her, but her father, a respected cattle rancher and Jeff's father's oldest friend.
It had been Joshua Langworthy's dying wish for him
to wed Cal McCall's daughter. Katherine was pretty
and likeable, so Jeff had agreed to the arrangement.
It was good for politics, and that was enough for him.
Besides, there was no one special in his life.

"As a matter of fact, Dan—"

Chaitlain dropped his snifter. It shattered on the
parlor floor, splashing brandy on Jeff's boots. Chaitlain pointed to the window.

A young woman with wide, frightened eyes stood
outside on the porch, clawing at the glass with broken, mud-caked nails. Bedraggled and soaked to the
skin, her blond hair clung to her in clumps. Blood
was streaked across her lower lip, and the front of her
gingham dress was torn across the bodice.

He approached the window, and her gaze, wild now with fear, locked on his. "J-Jeff," she mouthed, and pointed at him.

"Langworthy?" Chaitlain strode to the front door. The others followed him outside.

Jeff stood, mute, at the window, lost in the woman's eyes. They were *violet*, and that's what triggered the memory. The last time he'd seen Clarissa Mayberry he'd been a young buck and she a child, but he'd never forgotten those eyes.

Chaitlain got to her first. Jeff pushed through the throng of ranchers crowding the covered porch and reached her just as she collapsed. Chaitlain caught her.

"Jeff," she said, clutching at Chaitlain's jacket, her fear turning to panic. Again her gaze sought his. Again she pointed. "H-help me."

"Christ, Langworthy, what have you done?" Chaitlain lifted her onto the porch glider, then turned on him, accusation in his eyes.

"I've done nothing. She's my—"

"Neighbor," one of the sheep ranchers said. "Mayberry's daughter."

They were all looking at him now. Clarissa Mayberry shivered, pulled the shredded bodice of her dress together and stared at him, dazed, her face twisted in confusion.

"Yes," Jeff replied, still looking at her, and then it struck him.

All his life he'd had trouble with the Mayberrys, sheep ranchers and hell-raisers who owned a small spread flanking the Bar L. The father was a drunk, the mother a sharp-tongued harpy. The three sons, all about Jeff's age, were wild. They hated the Langworthys and had been jealous of their prosperity for as long as Jeff could remember.

Word got around, and Jeff suspected the Mayberrys knew just how important today was to securing the sheep ranchers' support at the territorial convention. It was just like those damned Mayberry boys to pull a stunt like this.

"Who put you up to it, Clarissa, your brothers?"

"No!" She pulled her legs up under her, scooting into a corner of the glider like a frightened mouse. "No, don't!"

"It's pretty plain what's happened here." Chaitlain knelt beside her and took her hand. "He did this to you, didn't he?"

"Wait a minute." Jeff grabbed Chaitlain's arm, but the rancher shook him off.

"Y-yes."

"That's a lie!" Jeff glared at her, but she wasn't looking at him anymore. She gazed off in the distance as if she were expecting someone to arrive momentarily.

"Well, hell," another of the ranchers said. "I was with you, Dan, on supportin' him, overlooking the fact he's a cattleman, but not after this."

"Wait just a minute!" Jeff followed the rancher to the steps. "This isn't my doing. It's a trick."

"The Mayberrys were never much in my book, drinkin' and thievin' and all, but they're sheep ranchers, and we stick together. You don't go roughing up their women, then lyin' about it, not if you want us to back you."

"Damned straight!" another one cried. They crowded around him, pushing and shoving him to the steps, and for a minute Jeff thought they were going to string him up over the young oak, right there in the front yard.

"Mr. Langworthy?" One of the women his mother employed to help out around the house stood at the far end of the porch, twisting her apron in her hands.

"There's nothing to worry about, Valentina," Jeff said. "Go on back to the kitchen."

She hesitated a moment, then vanished.

He'd never hated the Mayberrys more. The ranching accident that had killed his father eight years ago had always been suspicious in Jeff's mind. To this day he thought the Mayberry boys had had a hand in it, but he was never able to prove it. He turned on Clarissa and glared at her.

Chaitlain lifted her into his arms and tromped down the steps toward his buggy. "I'm taking her into town to see the doctor, and then I'm paying a little visit to the sheriff."

"I'm telling you, Dan, it's a trick, aimed at discrediting me. Surely you can see that. I haven't even seen the girl in years."

"Look!" someone cried.

Jeff followed Clarissa's widening gaze westward, across the rolling pastures, in the direction of the Mayberry spread. A lone horseman approached, and as he drew closer Jeff recognized him as one of Clarissa's brothers.

"No!" she cried, and twisted in Chaitlain's arms. He set her on her feet, and she turned to Jeff. "No, please!"

Chaitlain frowned in confusion as Clarissa threw herself into Jeff's arms. Jeff simply shrugged.

She was soaked to the skin and cold. It had rained that day, and now that he had a better look at her, he realized she must have walked the nine miles from her ranch to his. In good shape it would have taken her the entire day, but Clarissa Mayberry wasn't in good shape. He could see that now. She'd been more than roughed up, she'd been beaten. He brushed a thumb across her bloodied lip and felt something he hadn't felt in years. Rage.

She looked up at him. "Don't. Please." She clutched at his chest, pulling him closer, shielding herself. But from what, or whom?

His head throbbed with conflicting information, stray feelings he had no business entertaining, and a single question. Was this one of the Mayberrys' schemes, or was Clarissa's panic real? He didn't know, but he did know this: he needed Dan Chaitlain and the other sheep ranchers on his side. He'd worked too hard to lose them now.

Jed Mayberry rode right into the front yard and slid casually from his saddle. "Evening, gentlemen."

No one said a word.

Chaitlain narrowed his eyes, first at Mayberry, then at Clarissa. "What the hell kind of tomfoolery is this, Jeff?"

"The kind that ain't nobody's business." Jed Mayberry parted the crowd of sheep ranchers like Moses at the Red Sea, and swaggered up to where they stood, brass spurs clanking against his boots.

"What do you want, Jed?" Jeff could smell the liquor on him, and a month's worth of sweat. He wore a gun belt. It had been a long time since one of the Mayberry boys had dared trespass on his land.

"Ain't it obvious?" He grabbed Clarissa's arm.

She tensed, statue-still, and Jeff could swear he felt

a scream well up inside her, though she made no sound.

"Come on, little sister. It's time we're gettin' on home."

Clarissa clutched at him, and for the barest moment Jeff read something else in her eyes, a palpable fusion of hope and desire that faded as he let her brother lead her away.

"It's time we get going, too," Chaitlain said. The others murmured agreement.

"Wait a minute, Dan." Jeff tried to convince the ranchers to stay, but their minds were made up. The incident had cost him their trust. He knew this was a pivotal moment. His career hung in the balance, as did Colorado's statehood, but he couldn't concentrate to save his life.

His gaze kept straying to Clarissa Mayberry, who looked back at him as she clung to her brother atop his dappled mare. Jed Mayberry reined the animal west into the setting sun and spurred it home.

JEFF WAS STILL THINKING about her an hour later when his mother and sisters and little brother arrived home, late, from their Saturday trip to town.

"How'd your supper go? Did Valentina manage all right without me?" His mother watched him as he grabbed his rifle and went outside to saddle his horse. "And where are you off to so late?"

"There's something I need to borrow."

"What?"

"Trouble," he said as he mounted, then rode west into the night.

HE CAUGHT UP to them in a dry wash less than a mile from the Mayberry ranch. It had been the look in her eyes, that last long look, that had weighed heavy on his mind. Now that he saw her again, her hair, still damp, gone silver in the light of rising moon, her eyes brimming with relief, he knew he'd made the right decision.

"What do *you* want?" Jed Mayberry glared at him.

"Got a question." He slid from his horse, slipping his rifle out of its saddle holster, and walked toward them.

"Hold it right there." Jed placed a hand on his gun belt. "What's your question?"

"It's for her, not you." He looked at Clarissa. "Why'd you come to the Bar L? And don't lie to me."

Jed spat a wad of chewing tobacco on the ground near Jeff's boot. He ignored the provocation.

"I...I wouldn't lie."

"So why'd you do it? Did he put you up to it?" Jed laughed.

"N-no. I came on my own."

"Why?"

She looked with trepidation at her brother, and he shot her a menacing look.

"I...just wanted to. To see you."

"Why?" he said again.

"Go on, little sister. Tell him." Jed grinned at her, then at him.

"Tell me what?"

"She's in love."

"I am not!"

"The hell you ain't. Go on, then. I'm sick to death of you." Jed manhandled her down from the horse.

Jeff stepped forward out of habit, reaching out to

steady Clarissa as she dropped to the ground. She rubbed her arm where her brother had gripped it, then just stood there staring at the dead, trampled grass under their feet.

"You want to live with the damned Langworthys, go on, git! But don't be comin' back home, not ever." Jed viciously dug his spurs into the mare's withers, and the animal reared.

Jeff pulled Clarissa out of the way. "What's he talking about?"

She looked up at him, her eyes shining in the moonlight. For a moment he was reminded of the shy, skinny girl who used to haunt the upper pasture where he branded cattle as a youth. She looked away, and the memory vanished.

"I...I don't know. I just know I can't go back home. Not now."

Jed took off at breakneck speed, and they stood there together, listening, until the mare's hoofbeats faded.

"Well you can't go back tonight, at any rate. Come on." He turned toward his horse.

"Where will you take me?"

"Back to the Bar L." He returned his rifle to its saddle holster and mounted.

"You'd do that?"

"Why not?" Until he knew exactly what she and her brothers were up to, he wasn't about to let her out of his sight. Tonight's little drama had only confused him more. "Here, take this." He slid out of his rain slicker and tossed it to her. "You're wet. You'll catch your death."

She looked stunned, as if he'd just offered her his

last double eagle. Slowly she put it on. It was so big on her it looked comical.

"Give me your hand and I'll pull you up."

She hesitated, looking up at him, and he realized she wasn't that skinny little girl anymore. If you looked past the wet hair and mud and tattered clothes, she'd grown up into one hell of an attractive woman.

"Thank you," she said, and gave him her hand.

When she was seated behind him, her arms wrapped snugly around his waist, he had a bad feeling he'd been suckered. Both by her and her brother. As they settled in for the long ride across mountain meadows dotted with aspen, her heat at his back, the weight of her breasts pressing into him, other feelings flooded his senses.

He pushed them away, reminding himself he had work to do. He had sheep ranchers to woo. They'd eventually come back to the fold. Colorado's statehood was in everyone's best interest. It would take time, but Jeff was certain he could win back their trust and their votes. No, the sheep ranchers didn't worry him. What worried him was a sheep rancher's daughter.

"WHAT'S *SHE* DOING HERE?"

Clarissa recognized Jeff's eldest sister instantly. Agnes and she were the same age, eighteen. Agnes frowned at her as she slid out of Jeff's slicker and hung it on a peg in the Bar L's fancy kitchen.

Her whole life she'd dreamed of living here—with the Langworthys, with Jeff. And now here she was. She couldn't believe it.

Leftover barbeque sat on the stove in covered dishes. It smelled heavenly. The last thing she'd had to eat was a cold biscuit that morning before her brother Jed had beaten her and thrown her out. He'd had second thoughts that afternoon, and Mama had made him come after her. She'd feared another beating, and was just about to get one when Jeff had shown up and intervened. Lucky for her, Jed had let her go.

"She's wet and cold," Jeff said, "and Valentina's gone to bed. Why don't you fix her something hot to eat and find her some dry clothes? Can you do that for me, Agnes?"

His kindness touched her, but the tone of his voice made it clear he wasn't happy about her being here. He'd shot question after question at her on the ride back, and she'd answered them as best she could, but she knew he hadn't believed her.

Jeff's two youngest sisters crowded into the doorway behind Agnes, trying to get a look at her. She was embarrassed by her tattered clothing, the state of her hair, her nails, the mud caking her boots. The girls stared at her with saucerlike eyes, but said nothing.

Their little brother Abe squeezed past them, marched up to her and said, "Where you gonna sleep? We got a nice barn."

"We *have* a nice barn," Agnes corrected. "I'll get some blankets."

"That would be fine," Clarissa said, and risked a smile. The last time she'd seen Abe he'd been little more than a baby. All of them had grown, especially Jeff. He was taller now, more filled out. His rich brown hair was nearly shoulder length, and the boyish qualities she remembered had made way for a heart-stopping image that was all man.

"No one's sleeping in the barn." Jeff shot her a

sharp look, then turned to his sister. "Agnes, you move in with Mary and Frances, and Clarissa will take your room."

Agnes's mouth dropped open.

"Oh, no," Clarissa said. "I wouldn't dream of—"

"Why that's a fine idea." Their mother, Mrs. Langworthy, bustled into the kitchen and shooed her daughters out. "You, too, Abe. Time for bed."

Abe and the younger girls waved good-night to her and did as they were told. Only Agnes remained. Her face twisted into a nasty scowl, her eyes were bright green daggers.

"You, too, Agnes," her mother said.

"It's not fair!"

Jeff shot her a pointed look, and Mrs. Langworthy arched a brow. Agnes muttered something unintelligible under her breath, spun on her heel and quit the room.

"I didn't want to start trouble. The barn would be—"

"My lord, what's happened to you?" Mrs. Langworthy squinted at her through her spectacles, noting her torn clothing and swollen lip, then turned to her son. "Jeff?"

He explained how she'd wandered onto the Bar L that afternoon, and how Jed had come to retrieve her. "Her brothers tossed her out. So she says."

"He doesn't believe me." Clarissa fidgeted with the torn bodice of her dress. Mrs. Langworthy removed her shawl and wrapped it around her. "Thank you. You're very kind to take me in like this."

"What does he mean they tossed you out? Your own family?"

"Just Jed, really. But the others went along."

"Says she overheard them plotting against me, that they're out to ruin me before the territorial convention."

"I asked them to think about what they were doing, to reconsider, but they refused. Jed...beat me. The rest of them let him."

"You poor child!" Mrs. Langworthy pulled a chair out from the table and made her sit.

Jeff leaned against the kitchen's pie safe and just stared at her. "Maybe it's true and maybe it's not. Maybe it's some kind of trick."

"Oh, Jeff! Can't you see the poor girl's hurt? Here, let me see to that lip."

Clarissa looked up at him, and for a moment she thought she read remorse in his eyes. Green eyes, like his sisters', but different. Deep and thoughtful, exactly as she remembered them from when they were children. Then he snorted.

"What happened here today nearly cost me everything. Dan Chaitlain wasn't happy when he left."

"I'm sorry I ruined things."

"Don't you worry about that now," Mrs. Langworthy said. "I'll just go get some iodine for that cut. Then we'll take you up to Agnes's room and get you settled. Be right back."

She left, and then it was just the two of them. Jeff moved closer. "Let me see your face." He tipped her chin up, inspecting her split and swollen lip.

"I...fell when Jed slapped me. Is it bad?"

He grabbed a damp towel from the sink and dabbed at the cut. "Not so bad. Shouldn't leave a scar. You were lucky."

"Yes, I was."

They looked at each other, and she was reminded

of the day she first knew she loved him. She was ten and he was seventeen. He was branding cattle and she was watching. She'd gotten too close to the irons heating in the fire. He grabbed her just before she burned herself.

"Are you...all right?" His voice brought her back to the present. To her surprise, he brushed the hair away from her face, gently, as if he was almost afraid to touch her. "You were pretty dazed this afternoon. Jed really let loose on you, didn't he?"

She shrugged. "It wasn't the first time."

He looked at her as if he was just now really seeing her. As if he, too, remembered the days they'd spent together that summer in the fresh air, in the high open meadows and thickets choked with aspen, where once she'd helped him rescue a stray calf.

"A man has no business beating a woman. Wife, sister, doesn't matter. It's not right."

After the accident, after Jeff had buried his father, he'd changed. He'd told her to stay away from him. None of the Mayberrys were welcome on Langworthy land, but that hadn't stopped her from riding out in good weather to the hiding place where she'd secretly watch him work.

Years later, when she was fifteen, she saw him there with a girl. Katherine McCall was her name. She was rich and beautiful, and Clarissa used to dream of trading places with her. One day Katherine kissed him, and Clarissa thought she'd die. She never rode out after that. It was the last day she ever saw Jeff Langworthy, until today.

"Why'd you say I did it?"

"Hmm? Oh." Clarissa knew what he meant. "That nice man, Mr. Chaitlain—he misunderstood me. I was so exhausted, so terrified that Jed would come after me… I meant that I needed your help, not that you'd done it.''

He *harrumphed* in disbelief.

"They mean to hurt you, Jeff." His hand rested on her chair back. She covered it with hers and squeezed. "I'm telling the truth."

He looked at her intently, as if he were weighing her words in his mind. In the end, he pulled his hand away and smirked. "Yeah, and I'm a sheep rancher."

"Here's the iodine!" Mrs. Langworthy breezed into the kitchen. Her smile faded as Jeff stormed past her out the door.

CHAPTER TWO

CLARISSA AWOKE the next morning feeling wonderful.

Yes, she was sore from yesterday's long walk to the Bar L and hours clinging first to her brother, then to Jeff, on horseback. Her arm hurt where Jed had grabbed her, and her lip was still tender, but none of that mattered now. What mattered was that she was here, with Jeff, with all of them.

"Just about ready?" Mrs. Langworthy called through the bedroom door.

"Yes, ma'am. I'll be right down."

Clarissa couldn't remember the last time she'd attended Sunday services at the church in town. The Langworthys made the trip together each week as a family. This Sunday Clarissa was expected to join them. She gazed at her reflection in the mirror atop the walnut bureau in Agnes's bedroom. Despite her bruised cheek and split lip, she smiled.

"Here it is!" Frances burst into the room waving a velvet reticule, Mary on her heels. "It's perfect for your outfit."

Last night Mrs. Langworthy had rifled through Agnes's wardrobe, forcing Clarissa to accept the loan of some clean clothes. The dress they'd chosen for her to wear to church that morning was the most beautiful thing Clarissa had ever seen. The blue calico set off her eyes and, indeed, was a perfect match for the reticule and cloak Frances had scavenged from among her castoffs.

"You don't need to fuss over me like this. I'm fine, really."

The girls crowded around her, giggling. Frances went to work on her hair—now dry and squeaky clean thanks to Mrs. Langworthy's insistence on a long, hot bath last night—arranging it into a soft twist on top of her head. Clarissa wasn't used to wearing her hair up. In fact, she wasn't used to worrying about her appearance at all.

The Mayberry ranch was remote, and in recent years her brothers rarely allowed her off the property. Her mother disapproved of any sort of affectation, her father barely noticed her and Jed reminded her, almost daily, that there was no sense in dressing up, since there was no one there to see her. No one who gave a hoot.

"What's taking so long?" Jeff's broad shoulders filled the doorway.

Clarissa's gaze connected with his in the mirror. His breath caught, loud enough for all of them to hear. His sisters giggled, then scattered like flushed quail, darting past him out the door.

Clarissa held her breath as he entered the room.

"You look different."

She felt herself blush, and had to grip the edge of the bureau to keep from looking away. He was right behind her now. "It's the dress. It was kind of Agnes to loan it to me."

His gaze swept over her body, lingering for the barest moment on her breasts, fully aware that she watched him in the mirror. "It wasn't Agnes who was kind, it was my mother. If my sister had had her way, you'd still be wearing those rags.''

She looked away, embarrassed by the mention of her clothing. Even had her one good dress not been torn—it had happened during the beating, when she was trying to get away and Jed grabbed her—it was still old and threadbare, nothing like the fine garments the Langworthys wore.

She mustered her pride and turned, assuming he'd step aside and let her pass. He didn't. He was dressed in his Sunday best—a dark suit and fine white shirt, silk vest and tie. She was so close she could smell his shaving soap.

''L-let me by,'' she said.

''No.'' He hemmed her in, resting his hands on the walnut bureau behind her.

She looked up, and it proved to be a mistake.

He looked different, too. Different than last night when he'd done little but scowl at her. He wasn't scowling now. Not exactly. His jaw was tight, his expression hard, but those green eyes of his were on fire. She was on fire, too.

''What do you want from me?''

''The truth.''

''I—I told you. Jed and Papa and the others…they don't want things to change, and they don't want you to change them.''

''Statehood, you mean.''

She nodded. ''Not that they really care about politics. They just don't want you to profit from it.''

''Everyone profits from it. Cattle ranchers, sheep ranchers, businessmen, everyone.''

''And that's fine, as long as *you* don't. See what I mean?''

He ground his teeth.

"I had to warn you, Jeff. I had to."

"Why?" He looked at her, and she was suddenly aware of his size and strength, the way his suit jacket pulled tight over the muscles in his arms. His breath felt warm on her face.

"I…" She pushed past him, her heart suddenly pounding, and made for the door. He grabbed her.

"You forgot these." He nodded at the forgotten cloak and matching reticule lying on the bed. "Here," he said, letting go of her arm. "I'll help you."

She forced herself to breathe as he slowly, and with great care, wrapped the cloak around her shoulders. No one had ever treated her with such respect before, or with such suspicion, and all at the same time.

She gave up a tiny smile—she couldn't help it— and her gaze darted to his as they moved into the upstairs hallway. Boisterous chatter sounded from the parlor below, where the rest of the family assembled to leave for church.

Jeff didn't smile back, but in his eyes she read undeniable interest.

"Entirely different," he said, escorting her to the staircase.

Maybe someone did give a hoot, after all.

THERE WASN'T ROOM for all of them on the buckboard, which suited his little brother just fine. "The men of the house will have to ride." Abe grinned as he mounted the even-tempered mare Jeff had broken for him a few years ago.

Jeff helped his mother and sisters into their customary places, then turned to Clarissa.

"There's not enough room!" Agnes twisted her normally pretty face into another of her famous scowls. "Can't she walk?"

"Oh, Agnes," his mother and sisters chorused.

"I think she's done enough walking for a while." Jeff offered Clarissa his hand, and she took it, smiling up at him like an angel. His throat constricted.

Last night he'd looked beyond her bedraggled state, the cuts and bruises, the dark circles under her eyes from what he suspected was hard work and lack of sleep, and had seen the pretty young woman beneath. But after some hot food, a bath and a good night's sleep—and his younger sisters' fussing, which came with the territory in the Langworthy household— Clarissa Mayberry was downright beautiful.

She placed her foot on the buckboard's wheel and he helped her up, his free hand curling around her waist. He must have looked like a smitten fool, because Agnes rolled her eyes. Jeff ignored her.

"Let's go," he said, and mounted up.

The weather was cool and crisp as an autumn apple, their ride into town uneventful. The miles gave him time to think about yesterday's events. He'd lain awake most of the night thinking not about Dan Chaitlain and the other sheep ranchers whose support he desperately needed at the upcoming convention, but about Clarissa.

His gaze strayed to her every few seconds. He couldn't stop himself. She stole glances at him when she thought he wasn't looking. She'd been his shadow when they were growing up, before his father's so-called accident, before his view of the Mayberrys had irrevocably changed.

Now he didn't know what to think. She could be

telling the truth. The beating she'd received was real enough, he'd decided. He'd forgive Jed Mayberry a lot of things, but never that.

He knew for a fact Clarissa's brothers hated him and, from their way of thinking, they had reason to. They'd come up short in the last round of negotiations on local water rights, and blamed his political dickering for their loss. Every rancher in the county had given ground, sheep breeders and cattlemen alike. Jeff had convinced them it was necessary for the greater good. The vote had been unanimous, save for the Mayberrys.

Clarissa insisted her brothers were out to pay him back, and what better way than to sabotage his political future. He hadn't seen her for years. Why had she challenged Jed? Why had she walked nine miles over rough terrain to warn him? That's what he couldn't figure.

As they approached the small white church, his mother maneuvered the buckboard into line with a half dozen others, then pulled up short under some shade. He stole another glance at Clarissa. She met his gaze, and the warmth shining in her eyes grew suddenly hotter, more intimate, until he, himself, began to burn.

"Oh, honestly!" Agnes stood and stepped over her in a most unladylike way, then jumped to the ground, not waiting for Jeff to dismount and assist her.

Clarissa grinned.

None of this was lost on his mother. She gave him one of her *it may be none of my business, but…* looks, when he helped her from the buckboard. She herded his sisters toward the church, Abe in their wake.

Clarissa remained behind. "I know you don't want to be seen with me."

"It isn't that. Come on." He took her arm and moved onto the gravel path crowded with townsfolk exchanging pleasantries. All of them stared as he escorted her into church.

"You have a reputation to uphold."

She was right, he did. But in his mind he was doing exactly that. A neighbor, cast out by her family, needed his help. So he was doing the neighborly thing. He was helping her.

Dan Chaitlain and his wife were already seated inside, along with several of the other sheep ranchers who'd been at the Bar L yesterday afternoon. From the murmurs sweeping like wildfire through the congregation as he strode up the aisle, Clarissa on his arm, he suspected everyone in town knew what had happened.

"Morning, Dan," he said, as he passed. "Mrs. Chaitlain."

Chaitlain's wife returned the greeting, but her husband did not.

Sam McDonald and his family were seated in front. Sam had witnessed Clarissa's arrival at the Bar L, too, and Jed's prompt retrieval of her. His oldest son, Tom, was just a few years younger than Jeff, but still had an awkwardness about him that he couldn't seem to grow out of. Or maybe he was just awkward around Agnes.

Jeff's sister beamed a smile at him brighter than a harvest moon, and Tom all but tripped over himself making space in the pew beside him for her to sit.

"He's sweet on her," Clarissa whispered, as they squeezed in next to them.

"How do you know?"

"It's plain as day. Look at them."

He didn't look at them, he looked at her, and felt instantly punch drunk from gazing into those warm blue eyes. The pew was cramped, and his thigh was pressed up next to hers. She blushed, as if suddenly aware of their proximity, and his heat. Much more of this and he'd have to loosen his tie.

An hour later when they joined the procession leaving the church, he was still on fire. Clarissa paused at the entrance to speak with the reverend.

"Why, Clarissa Mayberry, it's been how many years? I almost didn't recognize you."

He *hadn't* recognized her, Jeff suspected. He'd heard about what had happened at the Bar L. His sister Frances chattered incessantly both before and after the service, making sure everyone knew how he'd ridden out after Clarissa and Jed, and had brought Clarissa home with him.

Some of the ranchers eyed him with suspicion, but others greeted him as if nothing was out of the ordinary. The story was likely so twisted by now, there was no telling what people thought. *He* didn't even know what to think. As far as Clarissa Mayberry was concerned, his own personal jury was still out. Still weighing all the evidence.

"I'm pleased to see you, Reverend." Clarissa shook his hand, then waited for Jeff to pay his respects.

Agnes brushed past them, her arm wrapped snugly around Tom McDonald's. She nearly knocked Clarissa out of the way.

"Miss Mayberry!" Tom said, and all but jerked Agnes to a halt. "I'm pleased to see you."

"Thank you." Clarissa smiled, and Jeff watched in amusement as Agnes's eyes blazed murder. He was reminded of a political cartoon that appeared in the *Rocky Mountain News,* showing the territorial governor so enraged that steam blasted out of his ears.

"That's a beautiful dress, if I may say so."

"Tom McDonald!" Agnes stamped her foot like a jealous child.

"The compliment rightly belongs to Agnes," Clarissa said quickly. "It's her dress, and I can't thank her enough for the loan of it." Agnes started to interrupt, but Clarissa kept talking. "She was so kind to me last night when the Langworthys took me in."

"Was she really?" Tom looked at Agnes with new eyes.

"Oh, yes. She gave up her bedroom so I'd have somewhere to sleep, and has treated me just like a sister."

Jeff suppressed a laugh, for the last part was no fiction. Agnes had behaved every bit as shrewishly toward Clarissa as she did with Frances and Mary.

"Well, that doesn't surprise me one bit," Tom said. His arm tightened around Agnes's. "She's an angel, I've always said. Agnes Langworthy is a pure angel."

Agnes practically melted in his arms. She shot Clarissa a tiny smile, then pulled Tom down the steps toward their waiting families.

"Well done," Jeff said. "I believe you've won her over."

Clarissa sighed. "What else could I do. She's in love with him. He loves her, too. He just doesn't know it yet."

"Is that so?" Jeff slipped his arm under hers and

moved them into the crowd outside the church. "And how do you know so much about love?"

"Well…"

He grew hot again watching the color rise in her cheeks.

"I don't, really. I just imagine what it would be like."

"Do you?"

She looked up at him, and it dawned on him that Clarissa Mayberry was either very innocent or very good at pulling the wool over a man's eyes.

"Sometimes," she said, a little breathless. "Yes, I do."

Jeff sucked in a breath and did some of his own imagining.

His mother waved them toward the buckboard and waiting horses. "I've got a nice roast for Sunday dinner. It should be just about done by the time we get home."

On the ride back out to the ranch he forced himself not to look in Clarissa's direction. It was easier that way. If he was going to get to the bottom of what she and her brothers were up to, he had to remain objective. And the only way to do that, he admitted, was to keep from diving headlong into the deep blue pools that were Clarissa Mayberry's eyes.

An hour later they turned onto the long road winding up the high mountain meadow to the Bar L. Jeff swore silently under his breath. Cattle that should have been grazing in the upper pasture were scattered along the road.

"Someone must have opened the gate," Clarissa said.

Jeff spurred his horse ahead of the buckboard, a bad feeling curling in his gut.

Abe ignored his command to stay with the women, and trotted along beside him through the entry arch bearing the Bar L brand that his father hand-carved some twenty years ago. Abe's eagle eyes fixed on the shocking panorama Jeff would have spared him if he'd had any warning. The boy's breath caught.

Dozens of this year's spring calves lay slaughtered in bloody heaps, buzzing with flies, lining the road leading to the ranch.

CHAPTER THREE

"BUT I DON'T WANT TO GO!" Abe stood in front of
the stagecoach, his arms crossed over his chest. "I
want to stay here with you and catch the bad men
who killed our cattle."

"I know you do," Jeff said as he handed his
brother's suitcase to the driver. "And I want you to
stay. You'd be a big help to me. But I can't send
Mother and the girls off to Colorado Springs alone,
now can I?"

Abe wouldn't look at him.

"Can I?"

The boy drew a curlicue in the dirt with his foot.
"No, I guess not."

Clarissa stepped back, allowing them a moment
alone. Mrs. Langworthy and Jeff's sisters were already aboard the stagecoach. They waved at her—
even Agnes, who'd instantly warmed to her following
yesterday's church service and their conversation with
Tom McDonald.

Finally, Abe climbed in beside his sisters.

"You're sure, now, Jeff?" Mrs. Langworthy said.

He approached the coach's window. "Dead sure. I
want you and the girls somewhere safe until I get to
the bottom of this dead cattle business."

"It was a massacre!" Abe cried. "Maybe it was
Indians."

"It was *not* Indians." Jeff shot Clarissa a hard look.

Her brothers' animosity ran deep, and their intent to discredit Jeff was real. While she didn't want to believe they'd do something so grisly as slaughtering those calves, she knew that Jed, at least, was entirely capable of such devilry.

Jeff was convinced they'd done it, but couldn't prove it. No one had seen anything. Most of the cowhands he employed had Sundays off, and the family had been at church. Clarissa kept circling back to the same question. If her brothers weren't responsible, then who was? No one else had any motive, and killing cattle was a serious crime.

The driver cracked his whip, pulling Clarissa back to the present, and the stage lurched forward. The girls cried out their goodbyes, and Mrs. Langworthy waved. Only Abe sat pouting, slouched down in his seat.

"Take care," Jeff said. "And give Aunt Penny my love." He watched until the stage turned the corner and rumbled out of sight.

"It's a warning," Clarissa said, at last.

"What's a warning?"

She'd resigned herself to it this morning, after a fitful night's sleep peppered with bad dreams. Yesterday she'd argued with him that her brothers weren't responsible. Today she knew in her heart they were. "The cattle. You were right. It was likely Jed's idea. The others would just go along."

He looked at her with renewed suspicion. "You knew about it, didn't you?" Grabbing her arm, he pulled her, not gently, toward the buckboard. "It was all planned."

"Let go of me!" She tried, but failed, to wrestle out of his grasp. "No, I didn't know about it. How could I? I was at church with you, remember?"

He turned on her, and out of habit she cowered, one hand raised to protect her face. Her reaction was not lost on him. Townspeople stopped on the street and stared, and Clarissa was embarrassed.

He let her go, then ran a hand through his hair in a gesture she recognized as frustration. "I'm sorry. I didn't hurt your arm, did I?"

"No." He didn't know what hurt meant. He'd never suffered one of Jed's beatings.

"I didn't mean to…" He cocked his head, searching for words. "I'd never lay a hand on you, Clarissa. You know that, don't you?"

Only once had she seen Jeff Langworthy raise a hand in anger against anyone. Years ago when one of the Langworthys' hired hands had caught her in the rocks above the meadow, spying on the family. He'd started to wallop her, and Jeff asked him to stop. He wouldn't. She could still recall the spectacular shade of violet that wrangler's eye took on after Jeff's fist had connected with it. Jeff had later joked that it was the same color as her eyes.

He was studying them now, waiting for her response.

"I know you wouldn't. But I want you to believe I had nothing to do with what happened yesterday. If it was Jed, he's just trying to provoke you. He knows the last thing you need is a battle with a neighboring rancher—especially a sheep rancher. It's exactly the kind of thing that could ruin your career."

"What do you know about my career?"

"Not a lot. Just that you've worked hard and made a name for yourself in the territory. Jed wants that name tarnished. Permanently."

"And what do you want?"

"Me?" She looked into his eyes and knew exactly what she wanted, but never in a million years would she have told him. Butterflies danced in her stomach. "I don't know." She turned toward the buckboard and, without waiting for him to help her up, pulled herself onto the seat and took the reins.

Jeff watched her. When it was clear she wasn't going to say any more, he tied his horse up to the back, then climbed on up beside her. He grabbed the reins. "Get up!"

She didn't say a word as he drove them back down the street, passing the dusty road leading out of town to the Bar L. She knew where he was going. It had all been decided that morning before they'd left the ranch.

"Mr. and Mrs. McDonald are fine people. Under the circumstances, I'm sure they'll take you in."

It wouldn't be proper for Clarissa to stay at the Bar L, not now, with the family gone. There was already enough talk. Her own reputation aside, she knew it was best for Jeff, too. Besides, he didn't want her there, not after what had happened with the calves.

"I could stay right here in town. Get a job at the boardinghouse to pay for the room."

"No. Town's not a place for a single woman, especially that boardinghouse. I've told you that."

They'd been all over it this morning. She couldn't stay at the ranch, and he wouldn't hear of her staying anywhere else, except with a good family. He cared about what happened to her, what the townspeople thought of her, and it thrilled her.

Nearly an hour later they reached the McDonald place. She waited while he walked to the front door and rang the bell. Mrs. McDonald peeked out the curtains at her while her husband spoke with Jeff. Neither man was smiling. Finally, the front door closed, and Jeff returned to the buckboard.

"Well?" she said.

Jeff didn't look at her.

"Did you tell them it would only be for a day or two, until I can find some work and a place to live?" She didn't want to be a burden on the McDonalds— or on anyone. They seemed like nice people, from what little she'd seen of them at church.

"They're expecting company. Family out from Denver."

"Oh."

The answer was the same at the next ranch and the next. Company was expected, kin coming over from the Springs, in-laws arriving from out East. They'd love to have her, but they just didn't have the room. If she were Katherine McCall instead of Clarissa Mayberry, she suspected they'd have found it.

All the same, she refused to feel like a homeless pup that no one wanted. Despite her family's best efforts to beat it out of her, she still had her pride. Late in the day, she finally put her foot down.

"Take me back to town. I'll not have you begging on my behalf. I'm young and I'm strong, and a good worker. And Lord knows there's plenty of work to be had here."

Jeff pulled up short on the reins, and the buckboard slammed to a halt. "We've been over this, Clarissa."

She wasn't going to argue with him. Despite the weather, which had become more and more threatening the past few hours, she grabbed the small suitcase of clothes Agnes had loaned her, and jumped to the ground. Jeff swore.

She started down the road. It was barely three miles back to town, an easy stretch of the legs.

"Come back here."

She ignored him.

"Damn it, Clarissa!"

She kept on walking, even when she heard his boots hit the ground and his heavy breathing when he stormed up behind her. He grabbed her arm and spun her round. This time she didn't cower.

"Before you start, Jeff Langworthy, I'll say my piece."

She could tell he was angry. His green eyes flashed like lightning, and he ground his teeth as if to stop himself from speaking words he'd later regret. She remembered that careful control from when they were children. She also remembered that, at any moment, it could snap.

"I came to you to warn you, and I've done that, though you've made it clear you think I'm part of whatever scheme Jed's cooked up." He started to say something, but she went on. "I needed your help and you gave it, and for that I'm grateful—to you and your family. But I don't want your charity, and I certainly don't want it from your neighbors."

"They're your neighbors, too."

"Maybe, but you saw how they looked at me, and you know what they think of me and mine."

It wasn't lost on her that he'd only taken her around to the local sheep ranchers with whom he was friendly. All of them had been at the Bar L yesterday, and by now they would have known that Jeff wasn't in any way responsible for her situation. Her own family was. If neighboring sheep ranchers wouldn't have her, the prominent cattle ranchers Jeff knew certainly wouldn't, either.

"You're not staying in town, not alone."

"I can't stay with you, now can I?"

He looked at her, and she could tell by the flare of rebellion in his eyes he was considering exactly that. "Why not?"

She didn't bother hiding her surprise. "You know why not. It'd be bad for your reputation."

"*My* reputation? What about yours?"

She almost laughed. "Apparently I don't have much of one, if my own neighbors won't even shelter me."

He snatched the suitcase from her hand. "Come on. I'm taking you home."

She argued with him about it all the way back to the Bar L. Not because she didn't want to stay there with him. Lord help her, she did. And not because it had started raining and they were both wet. Her own reputation didn't concern her, and his was flawless enough that she didn't think a little thing like this would harm it. The real reason she argued with him was that deep down she suspected he simply didn't want her around.

And that hurt. More, perhaps, than it should have.

She was still in love with him.

"Are we clear on this now?" Jeff maneuvered the buckboard to a stop in front of the porch. One of his dogs barked a greeting.

The house was dark inside. Valentina and the other household help had been given time off to visit their families until Jeff's family returned from the Springs. Paid time off, Clarissa had noted. Jeff Langworthy was a generous man.

He looked at her, unmoving, waiting for her answer. Water sluiced off his hat onto his slicker. His hair was wet and his cheeks ruddy from the cold. Those green eyes burned into her. She would have given her last bit, if she'd had one, to know what he was thinking.

"All right," she said at last. "For now. Until I decide what to do."

"Good." He jumped down from the buckboard and offered her his hand. She took it.

The ground beneath them was a river of mud. Noting it, he swept her off her feet and carried her to the porch. As he set her down, his gaze fixed on hers, she got the strangest feeling that perhaps Jeff Langworthy did want her around. He just didn't want to own up to it.

IT RAINED ON into the evening. Jeff tended to the horses, fed his dogs, then checked in with the ranch foreman who, on his order, had herded all of the stock into the mile-long pasture above the house—just in case the Mayberry boys had any other bright ideas.

He'd known the second he'd seen the slain cattle who'd done it. He'd also known he'd find no evidence pinning the crime on Jed Mayberry and his brothers. His first instinct had been to exact revenge, but he had his family to think about, and in the day it took to get them safely away, he'd reconsidered.

Clarissa was right. Jed was trying to provoke him into doing something stupid, something that would threaten the progress he'd made in rallying the local sheep ranchers' support for Colorado's statehood and his own election to office. His father had worked long years to see this dream made real. Jeff had worked, too, damned hard, and wasn't about to throw it all away for the brief satisfaction his petty vengeance would yield.

He recalled the look on Clarissa's face when she'd seen the bloody carcasses along the road. Her rosy cheeks had paled, her violet eyes had stormed. She'd been as stunned as the rest of them. At first he'd thought she was acting, but now he believed her. She'd had no foreknowledge of her brother's misdeeds.

So what was he going to do with her?

The moment they'd arrived at the ranch she'd retired to her room, and he hadn't seen her since. Standing, now, in the darkened parlor listening to the rain, he recalled the feel of her in his arms as he lifted her from the buckboard, the faint scent of lavender on her skin.

They were alone together in the house, and would be for several days, maybe longer. The thought of it should have weighed heavy on his mind, but it didn't, and that's what bothered him.

Shaking off his unease, he lit a couple of lamps in the parlor, then made his way to the kitchen. Soft light spilled out from under the door, and delicious smells greeted his nose as he opened it. He remembered that Valentina had left him a savory stew and some freshly baked bread for his supper. He hadn't eaten since breakfast and was starved. Clarissa would be, too.

To his surprise she was there, already engaged in preparing their meal. Bent over the stove, she was trying to lift the stew from the oven. Jeff grabbed a pot holder and came to her aid.

"Stand back," she said. "I've got it."

"Let me help you. That cast iron pot is heavy as sin."

She ignored him and whisked it to the table. "There! All set. Are you hungry?"

It was cold outside, but the room was warm. Clarissa's cheeks blazed a pretty pink that, together with the blue dress she wore, set off her violet eyes. He sat down without thinking about it, as if it was the most natural thing in the world for him to be sharing a meal with her in his kitchen.

His father would have been shocked. The family ate only in the dining room, set up proper with china and silver. Even when alone, Jeff ate there, but not tonight. Convention be damned! Tonight he'd eat in the kitchen with Clarissa Mayberry. Already he felt himself relax.

The awkwardness of the afternoon had vanished. Though the business between him and her brothers still lay between them, she didn't mention it. It was as if she'd put it out of her mind for the time being. He decided to do likewise, not that he could have helped it. Just watching her move around the kitchen was distracting to the point he couldn't have fixed his mind on anything else.

The stew was good, and they ate heartily, drifting into conversation about the long years since their families had been, if not exactly friendly, at least on speaking terms. She told him how her father had taken her out of school as soon as she'd been old enough to shoulder chores around the ranch. He'd also meant to keep an eye on her. Her brothers had discovered she'd been visiting the Bar L—and him. Anger twisted in his gut when she matter-of-factly talked about the beatings she'd suffered because of it.

"Yet you still came."

She put down her fork and looked at him. "What do you mean?"

"After your father forbade it. Even after I forbade it. You still rode out to the upper pasture and watched us work. I remember."

"You do? I mean…you knew I was there?"

He smiled, remembering the little blond waif spying on him from the rocks above the house. Overnight, it seemed, she'd grown into a woman. A woman he couldn't take his eyes off.

"I had no idea. You never said anything."

"Why'd you keep coming?" His gaze pinned hers and he wouldn't let go.

She blushed hotly—exactly the reaction he'd hoped for—then abruptly rose from the table. "It's warm in here. I think I'll step outside and cool off."

He followed her out to the porch and stood behind her as she watched the rain. She was aware of him, the way a woman is aware of a man who wants her. He could tell from the way she gripped the porch post, from the deep breaths she took to calm her nerves. He did want her, he realized, very much.

"Clarissa."

She turned and looked up at him.

Moonlight bathed her face. The clean scent of the rain coupled with her fragrance made his head spin. He meant to kiss her. He wanted to kiss her, but the look of innocent expectation in her eyes stopped him. That, and the weight of a dozen reasons why he shouldn't.

To begin with, she was a Mayberry, and too many unresolved things lay between their families. His father's "accident" chief among them. And then there was his career. He was a cattleman, and he was going to be a statesman. He had a name and a reputation to protect.

She was uneducated and all of eighteen, the daughter of a sheep rancher whom even other sheep ranchers didn't respect. And somewhere in the back of his mind he thought of Katherine McCall, the woman his father had chosen for him to marry. A suitable choice, under the circumstances.

The problem was the circumstances had changed. Clarissa Mayberry had changed them, had changed him in ways he couldn't quite put his finger on. Why else would he be standing here with her in the moonlight, his hands drifting to her waist, hers lighting on his shoulders.

"Jeff," she breathed.

He kissed her.

JED MAYBERRY crouched in the brush above the house and watched as his sister let Jefferson Langworthy paw her. His brothers snickered. Jed trained his rifle first on Langworthy, then on Clarissa. He didn't know which one he hated more.

CHAPTER FOUR

DAYS LATER she still recalled the kiss, and the thrilling seconds she'd spent in Jeff's arms. He'd been gentle with her, but determined. His hands had circled her waist, drawing her close. When he'd deepened the kiss she'd melted into him. His tongue darted into her mouth, taking her breath away.

"Clarissa?"

She nearly flew off the rocker at the sound of his voice. Scrambling for the forgotten sewing in her lap, she rose to greet him. His cool eyes and stony expression told her nothing had changed since that night. She loathed remembering how it had all ended.

Abruptly he'd pulled away from her, apologizing for his bad behavior. The kiss had been a mistake. He'd lost his head, wasn't thinking. But he *had* been thinking ever since. His polite but cool treatment of her in the days following their moment together in the moonlight told all.

She simply wasn't suitable, not for a man with his prospects. At least she was smart enough to know it. Sheep and cattle would graze together and hell would freeze before she ever made a fool of herself over him again.

Despite that, she knew he wanted her.

Even now she felt his desire, carefully banked but burning hot below the surface like embers in an old fire. She was on fire, too, and had been since the rainy night he'd whisked her home to the ranch. But it was a desire he wouldn't act on. Or, if he did, he'd regret it. She'd felt that regret tenfold the other night in his arms.

"I thought you'd gone up to the pasture," she said with a casual air that didn't betray her feelings.

"I was just about to. Would you like to ride along?"

The invitation surprised her. She'd spent the past few days cloistered at the house while he worked behind closed doors in his study and on the range with his stock, though he'd made certain never to leave her unattended. One of his cowhands or the ranch foreman was always close at hand, stationed near the barn, when he left the house.

"I'd like that," she said, and risked a smile.

He didn't smile back, though she could swear he wanted to.

The day was cold and clear, and as they rode out over the grassy meadow above the house, she shivered in anticipation of the coming winter. What was she going to do? She couldn't stay here forever, and she couldn't go home. She wouldn't go home. She had to start over somewhere, make a life for herself.

"You ride well," he said.

"It's been a while. I don't have my own horse. Jed sold it."

"He didn't want you riding?"

She laughed. "He didn't want me riding away."

"Oh." He did smile, then, and it shot right through her like Cupid's arrow. "You've had a rough time of it."

"That's behind me, now. It's time to think of the

future." But it wasn't behind her, and wouldn't be until she knew for certain what kind of trouble her brothers were planning to unleash on Jeff. Somehow she had to find out. She'd come this far and wasn't about to back off, regardless of how he felt about her.

"I like that kind of spirit."

"Even in a woman?"

He laughed. "Especially in a woman."

She laughed, too. It felt good, along with the cool breeze, after so many days of being shut up inside the house.

He looked at her, shading his eyes against the afternoon sun. His smile faded, and she knew the light-hearted conversation she'd hoped for was not to be. "There's something I need to tell you."

Her stomach did a slow roll. She knew what he was about to say, as surely as she knew the kiss they'd shared in the moonlight four nights ago would be their last.

"A statesman's expected to uphold certain traditions. Like...marriage, for instance."

She looked away, toward the horizon, wishing she could bolt right now, before he set in stone with words what she already knew in her heart.

"Some say a politician's the same as any other man, and that it doesn't matter if his wife's a prominent figure in her own right or not. But, my father—"

"Prominent?"

"You know. Respected, from a distinguished family."

She felt sick inside. "Like the daughter of one of those big cattle ranchers down Denver way."

"Exactly."

Drawing in a breath of autumn air, she turned to him and displayed a smile. "You're obliged to Katherine McCall, have been for years. Everybody around here knows it."

"They do? I mean, you do?"

"Of course." She kicked her mount and lurched forward, making for the small rise a quarter mile ahead of them.

Jeff followed. He caught her just as she came up over the hillock, grabbing the reins and pulling both their mounts up short.

"Clarissa."

She mustered the fortitude she knew was inside her. If it couldn't be beaten out of her, why did it fail her now when the only weapon the man beside her brandished was words?

"It's not so much a marriage as a business arrangement. Between the families. We haven't spent time together in years. For all I know, she—"

"I understand."

"Do you?"

She willed herself not to cry. "Perfectly."

"Well…" He nodded, as if he were convincing himself he believed her. "Good. Good, then."

"Yes," she said. "I'm happy for you, and for her."

"Are you?"

She met his gaze and read a flicker of disappointment in his eyes.

"Why wouldn't I be? It's what you want, isn't it?"

He didn't answer right away. He gazed out over the high pasture, where cattle grazed in the distance. "It's what my father wanted for me. So, yes."

She maneuvered her mount onto a dusty cattle trail,

and Jeff fell into place beside her. One of the hired
hands, a cowpuncher Clarissa recognized, waved
them over to where he was inspecting the fence line.
Clarissa picked up the pace.

Jeff stayed with her. "I know I've said it once, but
I'd like to say it again. I'm sorry about the other
night."

"You may be," she said. "But I'm not."

He didn't have time to reply, and she was grateful
for it. Their conversation ended abruptly when the
cowhand showed Jeff a dozen or so breaches in the
two-mile stretch of fence line between the Mayberrys'
ranch and his.

"It's been cut," Clarissa said.

Jeff's face turned to stone.

THEY LOST over a hundred head of cattle, give or
take. When Jeff and his men rode out to retrieve them,
they were greeted by the Mayberry boys, almost as if
they'd been expected.

All three of them rode new horses and carried the
latest firearms. Jeff recognized the mounts from a trip
he'd made the previous week to a horse breeder south
of town. He didn't have to ask where they'd gotten
the money.

Jed pointed the business end of an 1873 Winchester
at him and smiled. "Nice to see you, Langworthy.
How's my sister?"

He wanted to take the bait so badly he tasted blood.
Remembering Clarissa's bruises and split lip, and her
admission of similar beatings, he was barely able to
hold himself in check.

After a conversation about the lost cattle, which got
them nowhere, some choice threats on Jed's part and

some carefully worded warnings on his, he and his men returned to the Bar L. Jeff was fuming.

"Did you get them back?" Clarissa asked.

"No." He brushed past her into the house, and they didn't speak of it again.

Nearly every day that week his cowhands encountered more petty vandalism and evidence that someone had been on the ranch at night. Jeff posted sentries along the fence lines, but hadn't enough men to go around. The Langworthy spread was just too big.

After five days he realized the Mayberry boys had already accomplished part of what Clarissa had warned him of. They'd drawn his attention away from his political work, had kept him from urgent business in Colorado Springs and Denver, and they'd done it practically overnight.

He could have hired more men. He could have entrusted the Bar L to any one of a half dozen local cattle ranchers, capable men who knew how to deal with the likes of Jed Mayberry and his brothers. He could have gone to the Springs to visit his family and take care of forgotten business, then on to Denver to meet with influential men he hadn't spent nearly enough time with since Clarissa Mayberry had walked back into his life.

He could have, but he didn't. He watched her sewing in the parlor and knew she was the reason he hadn't set foot off the Bar L in over a week. His father, God rest his soul, was likely rolling in his grave.

Jeff put it out of his mind.

A stack of mail lay on the secretary in front of the window. He rifled through it, finding the letter from his mother and sisters he'd started to read earlier that day....

They missed him, but were enjoying their extended visit with his aunt in the Springs. Abe had added a long postscript about the soda fountain he'd been haunting since their arrival. Agnes inquired after Tom McDonald—at least three times in the text.

Jeff chuckled.

Clarissa looked up from her work. "Are they well?"

"Here." He handed her the letter. "They seem to be having a fine time." He watched her as she read it, slowly, her finger moving over the words as she silently mouthed them.

It occurred to him that her father had pulled her out of school the same year he'd forbidden her to ever again visit the Bar L. She'd have been about ten at the time.

"Sasparilla," he said, realizing from her frown and her tapping finger that she was stuck.

"Oh!" She smiled up at him, and his knees went weak like a schoolboy's. "Thank you."

"You're welcome." He sat down beside her on the brocade settee, then reached behind them to the bookcase and chose a volume. "I've noticed you looking at my father's books. Would you like to read some more?"

"Oh, yes. But I'm afraid I'm not very good at it."

"I'll help you." He opened the volume to the first chapter and handed it to her.

"Sheep ranching, a primer," she read, then laughed.

"What's so funny?"

"I thought you'd choose something more exciting."

"Like what?"

She turned toward the walnut bookcase, and in the process her knee touched his. It sent a shiver clear through him, but she seemed oblivious, so fixed was she on reading the spines of his father's sizable collection.

"Hmm," she said, frowning. "History, politics, animal husbandry…"

"And a score of books on ranching. I know. My father wasn't an advocate of frivolous reading." Joshua Langworthy hadn't been an advocate of frivolous anything.

"Sheep ranching it is, then." She settled back into her seat, opened the book to the middle and began to read.

Jeff caught himself staring at her mouth. He'd deliberately kept his distance from her since the night he'd kissed her on the porch. Their one ride out together had been his sole digression, until now.

He wanted to kiss her again, hold her close, watch her bloom in his arms, as he had that night. He ran a hand through his hair and muttered a self-rebuke under his breath.

"Hmm?" Clarissa said, looking up from the book. "Did you say something?"

"Uh, no. I was just…"

Their eyes met, and for the briefest moment he considered abandoning his political future, his father's dying wish, his own conscience and good sense.

"This book is silly," she said, jolting him back to the subject at hand.

"W-what?" Get ahold of yourself, Langworthy.

"And most of it's wrong. Look what it says right here, page eighty-five." She pointed to a long passage, one he remembered underlining a few days ago while researching a topic critical to his political dealings with the local sheep ranchers, Dan Chaitlain in particular.

"Who's the author?" She flipped to the frontispiece and frowned at what she read there. "Mortimer P. Fogg, professor of animal husbandry, Harvard University. Where's that?" She turned to Jeff.

"Boston."

Clarissa's brows shot up. "Are there sheep ranches in Boston?"

"Not likely."

She paged back to the underlined passage and tapped her finger on the words. "This kind of stock rotation hasn't been used for fifty years. It's wasteful. No sheep rancher worth his salt would consider it."

"Really?"

He'd recommended Fogg's stock management program, quoting the passage almost word for word, in a letter to Dan Chaitlain he'd just finished writing last night. It lay on the secretary along with other correspondence waiting to be delivered to the post office in town.

Clarissa snapped the book closed. "He'd be a laughingstock."

Jeff glanced at the letter on the walnut secretary. "I'd have been the laughingstock."

"What?"

He retrieved the letter, ripped it in half and stuffed it into his pocket. "How do you know all this?"

She shot him an incredulous look, as if his question wasn't worth a response. She was a sheep rancher's daughter and granddaughter. She'd lived her whole life on the Mayberry ranch, but he'd never once considered that she might be able to help him with his work.

Though he was a cattleman through and through, he'd studied sheep ranching in order to deal with the prominent men whose votes were desperately needed to elect delegates that would ensure Colorado's statehood. Those votes were also needed to secure his future.

"What else do you know?"

"About sheep?"

He sat down again beside her on the settee, this time closer, heedless of the warnings flashing in his mind. "Yes."

"Lots. What do you want to know?"

He smiled at her and thought for the dozenth time that day how beautiful she was. Beautiful and smart, and courageous and... Hell, he was falling in love with her, and there wasn't a damned thing he could do about it.

"Everything," he said, holding her gaze. "Tell me everything."

LATE THAT NIGHT, unable to sleep, stimulated by all he'd learned, Jeff sat in the glider on the front porch and thought about his life.

He'd recrafted his letter to Chaitlain, this time with Clarissa's help. She'd been eager to assist him, excited about the prospect of him unifying the ranchers in their political thinking, about Colorado's statehood and his own aspirations for the future.

Her excitement had fueled his own, and his mind was abuzz with new ideas. Radical ideas that would bring Colorado the recognition it deserved, ideas that would change people's lives. His life would change, too, for the better, and he wanted Clarissa Mayberry to share it.

Katherine McCall would understand. Hell, she'd probably be relieved. The last time he'd seen her was in Denver six months ago, at a dinner hosted by the territorial governor. She'd been cordial to him, and he to her, but there'd been no real spark between them. There never had been.

He'd spent the past eight years honoring his father's memory by carrying out his wishes, striving for the things Joshua Langworthy had deemed important. But he was a grown man now, and had some wishes of his own.

Tomorrow he'd ask Clarissa to be his wife. He'd make peace with her family. If not with Jed, then with her father. And for Clarissa's sake he'd lay to rest his suspicions about his own father's unresolved death.

The night was clear and cold, the sky a starry froth that lit up the pasture. Crickets and cicadas sang their nighttime songs, and for the first time in over a week, since the day Clarissa Mayberry appeared at his door, Jeff felt at peace with himself.

He rose and readied for bed, slid between cool sheets, and just as he began to drift off, secure in his decision, he heard a noise. The sound of a door closing, soft footfalls on the porch. Slowly he sat up in bed. It was nearly midnight. Perhaps Clarissa couldn't sleep. He reached for his trousers, a smile spreading through him like warm honey. He'd ask her tonight. Why wait?

A minute later he was dressed and out the back door. He expected to find her sitting on the glider looking out across the pasture, a pastime he knew she enjoyed. But she wasn't there. Twice he circled the porch surrounding the house, thinking he'd simply missed her. "Clarissa?"

A low growl sounded from somewhere behind him, near the barn, then a yip. One of his dogs. He stood at the edge of the porch, peering into the darkness, and listened. Cricket song was all he heard. Two of his cowhands were asleep in the bunkhouse along with the foreman. The others were out on patrol.

No one had reason to be in the barn at night. No one who didn't spell trouble. If those Mayberry boys were fool enough to think they could waltz right up to his house and steal his horses... "Damn!"

His rifle lay in its usual place in the gun rack in his study, his pistol in a drawer in the desk. It would take him a couple of minutes to—

The barn door creaked opened.

Like lightning Jeff slid into a shadowed corner of the porch, his gaze fixed on the opening. A dark figure stepped from the barn leading a saddled horse. He was small, the same size as Jed Mayberry's youngest brother, and was dressed in a long leather duster and a hat pulled low over his eyes.

The ranch dog Jeff had heard earlier pranced out of the barn behind the horse, tail wagging.

What the—?

The intruder mounted, paused to adjust the horse's livery, then went stock-still, as if he feared someone was watching. A sliver of moon slipped out from behind a cloud, and he saw the rider's face.

Jeff stood silent in the shadows and watched as Clarissa Mayberry rode away.

CHAPTER FIVE

HE KNEW, even before she cut across the meadow and galloped onto the open range, where she was going. Home. A sick feeling twisted inside him, one that would not subside until he knew, beyond a doubt, her intent.

He tracked her, undetected, for miles under a starry sky, losing her once in a dry wash that twisted and turned for a heart-pounding eternity, during which he thought hard about the events of the past two weeks.

Days ago he'd dismissed the notion of Clarissa being in league with her brothers. It surfaced now, against his will, but he refused to let it take hold of him. She had defied her family to warn him, suffered their abuse to protect him. He simply wouldn't believe it was all an act.

Why, then, didn't he stop her? Why didn't he sweep her off that horse and into his arms? A larger question loomed: how could he love a woman he still didn't trust? If he had trusted her, completely, as a man would trust his wife, he would have stopped her the second he saw her in the moonlight by the barn, questioned her about her actions.

But he hadn't.

And now his suspicions were back in spades.

The weather was clear and the trail dry. Soon he was riding past small flocks of sheep, clumped to-

gether on the open range. He smelled them before he
saw them, silent and silver in the moonlight. The
Mayberry house was just ahead. Lamplight shone
from an undraped window, silhouetting Clarissa as
she dismounted and tied her stolen mount to a post.

Jeff slid from his horse and crept closer, moving
from bush to bush, crouching, at last, behind a boulder not twenty feet from the house.

The door opened before she stepped onto the porch.
He recognized Jed Mayberry's tall, lanky figure,
framed in the doorway, rifle in hand, pointed directly
at Clarissa.

His own rifle, cocked and ready, was aimed at Jed.
If the son of a bitch so much as raised a hand in her
direction, he'd blow him to kingdom come.

"I'm back," Clarissa said as her other brothers
crowded into the doorway.

Jeff held his breath.

"I have news."

Her words knocked the wind out of him as if he'd
been punched.

"About what?" Jed hadn't lowered his rifle.

"About the Langworthys. You do want to hear it,
don't you?" She marched up the steps. Showing none
of the fear he'd seen in her past dealings with Jed,
she matter-of-factly pushed the business end of his
rifle to the side. "You'd be a fool, Jed Mayberry, if
you didn't."

Frank and Cyrus, smaller, leaner versions of their
brother, guffawed at her sharp-tongued comment. Jed
smacked them both upside the head. Clarissa brushed
past them into the house. Frank and Cyrus followed
like whipped pups.

Only Jed remained on the porch, eyes narrowed,

scanning the weed-infested yard for movement. Jeff didn't have to work to avoid being seen. He was so stunned he couldn't breathe, paralyzed with a dark fusion of anger and disbelief.

"Looks like little sister's changed her stripes," Jed said to no one in particular. "'Bout time she's come to her senses." He lowered his rifle, retreating into the house, and kicked the rickety door shut behind him.

Jeff collapsed cross-legged onto the ground. He ran a hand through his windswept hair, closing his eyes for a long calming moment, working to regain control.

The words he'd just heard from Clarissa's mouth— a mouth he'd kissed, savored, plundered as if it were a treasure trove—didn't register. The ramifications of her deception, her guilt and his stupidity, were too dizzying for him to comprehend. There'd be time enough later to dwell on it. Now he had to act.

It had been years since he'd been to the Mayberry house. It was smaller than he remembered, and the whitewash was all but worn off. Trim paint peeled from the porch railing, coming off in his hand as he silently mounted the steps and moved, catlike, to the undraped window. It was closed, but a rock-size shard of glass was missing near the bottom.

Clarissa's soft laughter drifted out on stale air that reeked of tobacco. Jeff sank down beside the broken window, sweating now, not from exertion but from rage. His rifle in hand, he settled in to listen.

"You don't say?" Frank said.

"I'm telling you true. He doesn't know a whit about sheep, not the first thing."

"That's a boon, then, ain't it, Jed?" Cyrus's voice

was still edged with the strains of adolescence. Jeff figured he was barely nineteen, a year younger than Frank, four years younger than Jed, if he remembered rightly.

"Don't know. Depends on whether she's telling the truth or not."

Jeff couldn't help himself. He edged to the window and peeked inside. Clarissa sat at the head of the bare kitchen table, Frank and Cyrus flanking her. Jed stood behind her, toying with a lock of her hair.

For the barest moment he thought he read fear in those pretty, violet eyes. Then it was gone, and the confidence he'd seen her display on the porch returned.

"Stop that!" She turned and batted Jed's hand away, her eyes flashing annoyance.

Jed laughed. "Well, are you?"

"Of course I am. Why would I lie?"

Frank and Cyrus looked to their brother, expecting him to answer. He didn't. All was quiet for a moment. Clarissa drummed a finger absently on the table. Cyrus yawned. Jeff heard a concerto of snores coming from another part of the house, and concluded that Mr. and Mrs. Mayberry didn't keep the same late-night hours as their wayward sons.

Jeff watched, on edge, as Jed grabbed a jug of corn mash from a shelf and poured each of them a glass. He slid Clarissa's across the table into her hands.

"Drink it," he said. It wasn't a request, it was an order.

"I'm not thirsty."

"Drink it." Their gazes locked, and Jeff expected a battle of wills to ensue. It didn't. Clarissa grabbed the glass and knocked back the corn mash like a seasoned poker player at a card game she knew she'd win.

"There," she said. "Happy?"

Jed smiled. Frank and Cyrus laughed. Jeff tried to remember what she'd felt like in his arms that night on the porch, but couldn't. He was numb.

Clarissa slapped her hands on the table, then sat up straight. "All right. You want to know how you can hurt him? Here's how."

"Wait just a good goddarned minute." Jed leaned in close, nearly nose to nose with her. "What's changed you? Why are you so hell-bent on turning redcoat all of a sudden?"

Clarissa shot from the table, her empty glass in hand. She turned toward the window but didn't see him, her mind working. She gripped the glass so tight, Jeff thought it would shatter in her hand. Her face was stone, her eyes daggers.

Without warning she pitched it toward the window as hard as she could. Jeff lurched sideways. Window glass shattered all around him on the porch. The whisky glass landed with a thud on the weedy ground beyond the porch, nearly spooking the horse. Inside he heard all three of her brothers cackling like hens.

When the laughter died, he edged back to the window and peered inside. Clarissa was turned away from then, arms crossed, a slim hip hiked onto the table.

"He don't want you. That's it, ain't it?" Jed didn't try to disguise his satisfaction.

"Shut up!" Clarissa's cheeks blazed.

"Geez, Jed, you hit the nail square on the head." Frank stared at her, and Jeff was stunned to see sympathy shining in his eyes.

"Seems I did." Jed sidled up next to her and slid an arm around her shoulder. Clarissa tensed. "Don't matter, though, cuz Langworthy's a dead man, just like his pa."

Jeff bit off a curse, nearly revealing himself to the Mayberrys. He sank back onto the porch and closed his eyes, counting to ten, telling himself to bide his time, be smart, hear all that Jed Mayberry had to say before killing him.

"What do you mean?" Clarissa's voice was sharp.

"He means," Frank said, "any grand notions Langworthy's got about politics is over. And if he ain't hanging from a tree when all's said and done, Jed'll arrange a little accident, just like he did the old man. I was still a kid, but I remember when he done it. You remember, too, Cyrus, don'tcha?"

Jeff shot back to the window, blood pulsing through his veins in a searing torrent. He looked at Jed Mayberry and saw red.

"I remember his eyes," Cyrus said. "They was dead. I ain't never seen eyes like that. I nearly—"

"Enough!" Jed slapped his brother across the face. Frank cowered, waiting for his turn.

"I told you damned fools never to mention it, and I mean it!"

"J-Jed." Clarissa slid from the table. Her face was white with what Jeff believed was genuine shock. "You didn't?"

"You, too," Jed said to her, pointing his finger at her threateningly. "Not now, not never."

It was all Jeff could do to stop himself from launching through the broken window like an animal and tearing Jed Mayberry apart with his bare hands.

He did stop himself, because Jed wasn't finished.

There was more on his mind and he was ready to spill, and Jeff would hear it all before acting.

Clarissa sank into a chair, her eyes dull, her expression blank. "What are you planning, Jed?"

The drama over, Jed and his brothers took their places at the table, and he revealed his plan to them. Jeff listened, committing to memory every detail. Bloodlust raged inside him, but he worked to quell it and let rational thought prevail.

He knew in his heart that, no matter how fierce his thirst for vengeance, he wasn't a man who'd do murder, not even to avenge his father. Joshua Langworthy had lived by the letter of the law and had raised his son to do the same. Jeff would get his revenge, but not this way. Not in the middle of the night with a lever-action Winchester repeater.

He also knew that no jury in the territory would convict Jed Mayberry of a murder that happened eight years ago, and that had been officially recorded as an accident.

But there was another way to see justice done. If not for his father's murder, then at least for the mayhem they were planning. He'd just have to catch them red-handed. He and Dan Chaitlain and Sam McDonald together. All of them, along with the sheriff and his men. If it was the last thing on God's good earth he did, Jeff vowed to get them.

"Tell me again about the poison." Clarissa was animated now, noting every point as if her own life, and not just Jeff's, depended on it.

"Milkweed. It'll kill them sheep deader than door nails. I seen it work. Once they got it in 'em, there's no savin' 'em." Jed drained the last of the corn mash from his glass.

"Mr. Chaitlain will lose his entire stock." Clarissa's eyes widened.

"That's the point." Frank was grinning like a fool. "McDonald, too, and the rest of 'em."

"They'll think Jeff did it."

"*That's* the point," Jed said. "No damned way, after that, he'll be elected to anything, except maybe swabbin' floors at the county jail before they hang him."

"What if they don't believe he did it?" Cyrus asked.

"They'll believe it. I'll see to it. A man desperate for votes might do anything. Besides, ain't no love lost between them ranchers and Langworthy. Chaitlain's looking for any excuse not to back him." He glanced at Clarissa. "That little scene at the Bar L just about did it on its own. We got you to thank for that, little sister." Jed grinned at her.

"When are you planning to do it?" Clarissa asked.

"The poisoning?" Jed's smile faded. "Tomorrow night. Dark of the moon."

"Good," Clarissa said, then rose from the table. "I'll be there." She turned to where she'd dumped her borrowed coat, one of *his* coats, Jeff realized, and put it on.

"Where you going?" Jed grabbed her arm.

Clarissa shot him a nasty look and pulled away. "Where do you think? Back."

"What the hell is going on out here?" Old Mr. Mayberry staggered through the doorway leading from the hall. Jeff hadn't seen him in years. He looked bad, yellow and withered the way old people get with a lifetime of drinking behind them.

"Go back to bed, Pa." Jed grabbed the jug of corn

mash from the table and handed it to him. "Here, take this."

"What's she doin' here?" The old man nodded at Clarissa. "Thought you'd gone."

"I'm about to." She headed for the front door.

Jeff scrambled to his feet and shot to the side of the house where he wouldn't be seen if they came out onto the porch.

"Oh no you ain't," Jed said.

The front door opened, and Clarissa stepped outside. "Are you crazy? I've got to. If Jeff wakes up tomorrow and finds me gone, he'll know something's not right. He might even come out here."

"Why would he do that?" Jed let her get as far as the steps before stopping her. "I thought he didn't want you. He ought to be pleased as punch you're out of his hair."

"You don't understand. He's not like that. He's... decent."

Jed snickered.

"You're right, he doesn't want me. But he doesn't want me manhandled by the likes of you, either. This is the first place he'd come looking if I've gone missing." She marched down the steps and untied the horse she'd stolen from his barn.

This time Jed didn't stop her.

"She's right, Jed." Frank looked at his brother. "We've come too goddarned far to ruin this thing now."

Jeff waited, wondering if he could make it back to where he'd tethered his horse, undetected, before Clarissa retraced her steps.

"Go on, then," Jed said. "But I'm warning you right now, little sister." He slid his buck knife from its sheath and waved it at her. Moonlight glinted off the blade. "You turn on us again, I'll rearrange your face permanent this time. Understand?"

Jeff had never wanted to kill a man more in his life.

Clarissa mounted, adjusted a stirrup, then sat there, glaring at her brother. "Perfectly," she said, and rode off.

HIS LUCK HELD. Clarissa returned to the Bar L by a different route, avoiding altogether the thicket where he'd left his horse. Jeff followed her, making sure she didn't get into trouble, and used the time to plot his revenge.

Not on Jed and the others, but on her.

The pain he felt at her betrayal was almost more than he could bear. His feelings were so raw, so convoluted, he couldn't make sense of them. The crazy thing was he still loved her. How that was possible, he didn't know. The realization cut him to the quick, so he buried it deep inside himself and fixed his mind on how he'd make her pay.

And she would pay. Just as her brothers would.

At first he thought to confront her, threaten every last detail of their sick little plan out of her. He wanted to know everything, from the very beginning. How she and Jed had planned her arrival at the Bar L just at the right moment, knowing Dan Chaitlain and the other ranchers would be there. How she'd kept him tied to the ranch like a smitten schoolboy, while his political life had gone to hell.

Confrontation would provide him with satisfaction. He wanted her to know he knew everything, but not yet. What he wanted more was for her to feel what he'd felt as he'd watched her betray him to her brothers. He'd been fool enough to think she loved him. Maybe she had in the beginning, and just maybe he could use that against her. Now there was an idea with merit.

They came up over a rise, Clarissa in front of him some hundred yards, oblivious to his presence. The Bar L was just ahead. They'd not encountered any of his sentries on the ride out, nor did Jeff see any now. No wonder the Mayberry boys had so easily trespassed. He'd fire them all in the morning and hire new ones.

At the top of a hill overlooking the house he paused and crouched amongst the rocks, as he'd seen Clarissa do so many times when they were young. He watched her as she returned his horse to the barn, patted the dogs who ran to greet her, then silently slipped into the house. She had no idea he wasn't there, sleeping.

By the time he opened her bedroom door a few minutes later, stripped to the waist, wielding a single candle and his deadliest smile, Clarissa was undressed.

When she heard him enter the room she turned and gasped, holding her nightgown in front of her like a shield. But this was not a battle she would win. Jeff knew it with certainty as his gaze washed over her fair skin and waist-length hair, a mantle of gold in the candlelight.

"Jeff," she said, recovering herself. "You're awake."

He stepped into the room, closing the door behind him. Clarissa didn't so much as breathe. He set the candle down on the night table by the four-poster bed and took her hand. "I had a dream."

"A-about what?" She held the nightgown in front of her as best she could, but already it was slipping.

He felt himself grow hard. Gently he pressed her palm to his mouth and kissed it. "About you, sweetheart."

CHAPTER SIX

HE WASN'T THE ONE dreaming, she was.

Clarissa forced herself to draw air as Jeff trailed a delicate spray of kisses across the pulse point of her wrist, caressing her bare arm as he worked his way higher.

"I—I'm not dressed," she managed to say. Her clothes lay in a heap on the floor, forgotten.

"Oh." He paused as if he'd just noticed. "That makes you uncomfortable." The way he looked at her was strange, as if he weren't himself, or perhaps had had too much wine.

The double shot of corn mash she'd been forced to drink a couple of hours ago had not entirely worn off. She felt herself sway on her feet, but wasn't sure if it was the liquor or the dizzying effect of holding Jeff's heated gaze.

"Well, then," he said, letting go of her hand.

She immediately stepped back, bumping up against the window sash. Wrapping the dressing gown snugly around herself, she waited to see what he'd do next. Had she the presence of mind to do something herself, anything, she would have.

Her eyes widened of their own accord as he slowly unbuttoned his trousers and let them slip to the floor. She sucked in a ragged breath, and her shock was not lost on him.

"Is this better?" His smile was the most wicked she'd ever seen in her life. "Now we're both undressed."

She was all at once conscious of her heart beating in her chest, the icy air of the room around her, and the heat he gave off as he stood there drinking her in.

"Are you unwell?" It was a ridiculous thing to say, but it was all she could think of.

"On the contrary," he said and stepped closer, his hands lighting on her shoulders. "I'm quite well. In fact I've come to my senses."

"A-about what?"

He leaned in to kiss her, and she held her breath, waiting, knowing she should stop him, but wanting it to happen.

"About us."

Her experience with him on the porch in the moonlight was not to be repeated. His kiss was harsh, almost savage. He pulled her to him, his hands slipping to her waist, groping her backside as he deepened the kiss.

All rational thought fled her mind. She gave herself up to the moment and kissed him back, relishing the taste of him, the feel of his hands on her body. How many times had she dreamed of this? She grew bold, her hands sliding over the steely muscles of his back, moving lower, mimicking his.

"You like it?" he whispered between kisses.

"Yes," she heard herself say. Her response was shocking, but she didn't care.

He lifted her into his arms, and hers slid around his neck. The dressing gown fell away and they were skin to skin. He was hot, on fire, and so was she. He kissed her again, giving her no time to protest. Not that she would have. A moment later she was on the bed with him on top of her. Her legs twined round his hips as they kissed more deeply, as if her body already knew what to do, even if she didn't.

"Do you love me?" he said, stunning her.

She looked into his eyes, and for a moment she read something there that was more than raw desire. It flickered between them like magic, then it was gone.

"Yes. Oh, yes."

"Good," he said, and rolled his hips provocatively into hers.

She gasped at the feel of him against her.

"And you want me?" he said.

"Yes." She did, God help her. She'd always wanted him, and now he would be hers and she would be his.

He suckled her breasts, each in turn, until she thought she'd go mad. She kissed him with all that she felt for him, drunk on his words and his caresses, his heat and hardness, the way his tongue teased her and plundered her mouth.

A hundred unrelated thoughts blazed through her mind, among them a question. Why this change in him? Why tonight? What of his plans for the future, his career, the woman to whom he's pledged? All were obliterated by his kisses. All save the unthinkable things she'd heard in her family's kitchen.

"Jeff," she said, pushing against his chest.

"Hmm?" His eyes were half-closed, green and cat-like, reminding her of a predator.

"I went out tonight, left the ranch. There are things I...I need to tell you."

His lips silenced her. "Tomorrow," he breathed, and slid into her with no warning.

The shock of it knocked the breath from her. He was big, and she was virgin-tight, and nothing in her experience prepared her for what she would feel. He was the only man she'd ever kissed, and now he was inside her. Her pain vanished in an instant, and then there was only him.

"Easy now." He moved slowly, exerting enormous control, she realized, allowing her time to recover. "That's it. Like that."

She gave herself up to pure instinct, emotions so new, so raw, that her pleasure, melding body and soul and heart, was nearly unbearable. She opened her eyes and looked at him. His were full of wonder, his face an intense fusion of all that she, herself, felt.

"Do you love me?" she breathed, losing herself in his eyes.

In answer he slipped his hand between them and drove her to madness.

HE LAY THERE watching her sleep till nearly dawn.

When the sun rose he'd have his revenge. He'd cart her off to the sheriff and make her tell all. But there was no joy in his victory, only regret.

He toyed with a lock of her hair, smoothing it across her bare shoulder. Clarissa sighed in her sleep. A powerful urge to make love to her again possessed him, but he fought it. What he'd done last night was wrong, no matter what she'd done to him. And somewhere in the back of his mind was the nagging thought that perhaps the only thing she was guilty of was love.

He was guilty of much more.

He'd hurt her, and she'd lashed out in the only way she knew how. For that he'd punished her, if one could call what they'd shared last night punishment. But in his lust to have her, he'd miscalculated one critical truth—the effect she continued to have on him.

As planned, he'd allowed his ardor to go unchecked, but so had his emotions. The seduction had been easy—he knew it would be—but the reality of their coupling left him questioning his motives and what he'd felt last night in her arms. Also what he felt this morning in that gray sleepy hour before dawn.

What *did* he feel?

"Jeff," she whispered at the edge of sleep. She rolled away from him, half-dreaming, but he didn't follow.

His head pounded with conflicting information, random thoughts, impossible feelings, his plans of the past eight years dancing in his mind in a muddle.

Last night Clarissa had admitted to him she'd been out. She'd wanted to explain, but he hadn't let her. Either she'd been about to tell him the truth, that she'd been to the Mayberry ranch, or she'd been prepared to spin a lie. Which was it?

He was ashamed, now, to admit to himself why he'd stopped her from speaking. He'd wanted her, more desperately than he'd ever wanted anything, and her apparent guilt was the excuse he'd used to have her.

Running a hand through his hair in frustration, he gazed at her sleeping form. She looked like an angel at rest, her hair a froth of spun honey, her face glowing with contentment in the candlelight.

If she *was* innocent of all he'd accused her of in
his mind, what he'd done last night was unforgivable.
It took all of his willpower to ignore his confused
feelings and rise from the bed. After pulling a quilt
up over her shoulders, he dressed and slipped silently
from the room.

WHEN CLARISSA AWOKE she was alone. Perhaps it
had been a dream. But the twisted sheets and the
scent of him on her skin told her it wasn't.

Squinting against the sunlight streaming in through
the lace draperies, she sat up in bed and took stock
of the room. A candle, burned to nothing, sat on the
night table where Jeff had left it. Her dressing gown
lay discarded on the floor.

It had *not* been a dream. Neither had her midnight
visit home and all that she'd learned there. She'd
wanted to tell Jeff last night, she'd tried to tell him,
more than once, but had given in to his lovemaking
each time, putting all thought of it out of her mind
until this morning.

But morning had come and gone. She could see
that from the position of the sun. Clarissa shot from
the bed. Her hair was a tangled mess, she had laundry
to do and needed desperately to bathe, but all of that
could wait.

A few minutes later she was dressed and flying out
the door, hurrying down the hallway toward the staircase. As she descended the steps, the same unsettling
questions she'd wondered at last night, paraded into
her mind.

Why had Jeff come to her? Why this sudden
change of heart? It went against all he'd led her to
believe about his feelings and his intentions. He'd

wanted her declaration of love, and she'd given it wholeheartedly, yet he hadn't reciprocated, at least not in words. What did that mean?

More confusing still was his absence this morning. He had work, yes, but after what they'd shared, she thought it strange he'd abandon her without a word.

She paused on the staircase, another, more urgent question pressing in on her. What would he do when she told him her brother had arranged his father's accident? She felt sick inside, remembering.

Jeff was a man of reason, but murder was beyond reason, and she feared his reaction would be, too. If he went after Jed, there was no telling what terrible thing might happen. She not only feared for his life, but for his reputation, his career, should he carry out some awful revenge, however justified.

No, she wouldn't tell him, not yet. Nor would she tell him what Jed and her brothers planned for tonight. Jeff's involvement, even in trying to stop them, might be misconstrued. The rift between cattlemen and sheep ranchers ran deep, steeped in years of hatred, acts of violence and revenge.

Jeff was in a precarious position with both sides, each ready to withhold their support for his life's work should he step off the narrow path they'd laid out for him. He couldn't get involved.

But she could.

"That's it!" she said, and hurried down the stairs.

Late this afternoon she'd ride to town, warn the sheriff of Jed's plans. She'd leave Jeff out of it entirely. The sheriff would notify the ranchers, they'd be ready, and her brothers would be stopped. If only she could slip away from the Bar L, once again, unnoticed....

"Clarissa."

She nearly jumped out of her skin at the sound of Jeff's voice. "Oh! You startled me."

"Sorry."

Their gazes met, but his eyes were unreadable. The raw emotion she'd read in them last night was either vanished or carefully shielded. She blushed, then looked away.

"You'd wanted to tell me something last night."

Her heart skipped a beat.

He took her hand and led her into the parlor, sat next to her on the settee. "Tell me now."

"I…" She swallowed hard, her mouth dry. His hand was warm and so was the room. She felt suddenly light-headed.

"You said you'd gone out. You know I don't like you leaving the house on your own, especially at night. It could be dangerous with your brothers on the loose."

"I know. I just…"

His eyes softened, and the feelings she was certain they'd shared last night, came rushing back tenfold.

"Oh, Jeff."

"Tell me," he said again.

He hadn't even kissed her. He was holding her hand, but he was also holding himself back, and she wondered why.

"I…went for a walk," she said, gathering her resolve.

"A walk." His hand stiffened in hers.

"Around the pasture above the house. I didn't go far. One of the dogs was with me all the time." The lies tumbled out of her now that she was committed.

"I see." Abruptly he stood.

"Can we talk about…the rest of last night?" She needed to know how he felt about her, here and now, in the light of day.

"The rest?" He was pacing now, his jaw set, his green eyes cool. "Oh." He waved a hand in the air as if dismissing the whole event, and her. "Later. I've got work to do." And with that he quit the room.

Clarissa sat there, stunned, tears pooling in her eyes. She told herself that for now, for today, his behavior was for the best. She had to get to town, warn the sheriff, and to do that, she needed Jeff occupied elsewhere. That seemed to be his intention, so she forced herself to view it for what it was—a stroke of luck—and refused to dwell on what it implied about his feelings.

She sprang to her feet and rushed back upstairs, intent on carrying out her plan. Her brothers wouldn't dream of setting out till well after dark. She had time, and she meant to use it.

JEFF SAT on the porch watching the sun set like a fireball in the west, rocking back and forth in the glider as if he hadn't a care in the world. By his father's way of thinking, he shouldn't have. His plans were in place. He'd done what needed doing. All that was left now was to wait.

Clarissa peeked out at him from the dining room draperies for the third time in the past hour. He pretended not to see her. She'd attempted to leave the ranch twice that afternoon. The first time one of his foremen had caught her trying to saddle the very horse she'd stolen last night. The second time, he'd caught her himself.

She'd given him a poor excuse about needing exercise. He'd told her to take another of her walks around the pasture with the dogs. He'd done it coolly, and with a forced lack of emotion that was tearing him up inside. Why had she lied to him about last night? More important, why hadn't he called her on it?

He knew why. He feared he'd lose what little control he still had over his emotions. Would he take her in his arms and shake her or kiss her senseless? He didn't know, and that scared him.

His father had been a man who held his feelings, good or ill, in check. Jeff had spent his life emulating his stoic example, until now. In two short weeks Clarissa Mayberry had flayed him open, left him vulnerable in a way that was completely foreign to him.

That vulnerability threatened all that he'd become, made him question his own actions, his motives, his dreams for the future and the very tenets on which he'd built his life.

If she truly meant to join her brothers in an act they thought would ruin him, then damn it, perhaps he should just let her go. Then he might believe her passion had been contrived, that her love for him wasn't real.

The next time she peered through the draperies he feigned sleep. It was time to find out the truth.

While she readied her horse, he instructed his men to ignore her, allow her a wide path, make her believe she'd gotten away unnoticed. As soon as she set off, he sent them on ahead to Dan Chaitlain's ranch to be of whatever help they might. The sheriff would already be there. Jeff had seen to it that morning. Dan and his men would be ready, too. Jed Mayberry had no idea what he was walking into.

Meanwhile, Jeff retrieved his gun belt from the desk in his study. He couldn't remember the last time he wore it. He had two good rifles, and slid them both into saddle holsters, then mounted his horse.

Nightfall ate up the quarter mile of trail separating him from Clarissa as he watched her gallop away. He rode in shadow, just inside the heavy tree line edging the pasture, in case she happened to turn and look back.

And that was his mistake.

The cool end of a gun barrel nudged the back of his neck.

"Howdy, Jeff."

CHAPTER SEVEN

THEY COULD HAVE just killed him, but they didn't.

Tossing a sack over Jeff's head so he couldn't see their faces, they jerked him off his horse and bound him to a tree. It didn't matter. Jeff would know that voice anywhere.

Jed Mayberry was smarter than he'd given him credit for. It would be cleaner this way and more satisfying, he supposed, from Jed's sick point of view. The Mayberrys didn't simply want him dead, they wanted him publicly ruined first.

He worked at the ropes binding him. It was dark now, and there was no moon. The Mayberrys had taken his horse and his guns, so even if he managed to free himself—which he was close to doing—he'd have to make his way on foot back to the Bar L for another mount.

"Damn it!"

He wondered if Clarissa had known about the ambush. He didn't think so. It wasn't mentioned last night in the Mayberrys' kitchen. In fact, not much of anything was mentioned, outside of Jed's plan to poison the sheep.

He recalled Clarissa's words: *I've got news—about the Langworthys. You do want to hear it, don't you?* That's how she'd gotten inside, on the promise she would tell them something they could use against him.

Only she *hadn't*.

The realization hit him like a bucket of cold water.

He wrestled himself free of the ropes, shot to his feet and took off at a run, back the way he'd come. Hoofbeats sounded in the distance, but he paid them no mind. His head spun with random recollections of Clarissa's exact words, her expressions and behavior, now seen in a new light.

She'd talked in generalities, mostly about how little he knew about sheep. It had fueled her brothers' obsession with belittling him, but had served them in no other way. She could have told them any of a dozen useful facts that would have aided them in their cause, but she hadn't!

The afternoon he and Clarissa had spent reading in the parlor, they'd talked for hours about local ranching, water rights, territorial politics and the quirks and passions of each of the prominent sheep breeders and cattlemen he was working to sway to his cause. She'd mentioned *none* of these facts to Jed.

She'd been acting, all right, just as he'd suspected, but with her brothers, not with him!

Last night when he'd held her in his arms and asked her if she loved him, she'd answered truthfully. He'd known it then, but hadn't wanted to believe it. He knew it now, and something else. He loved her, too.

The hoofbeats were close, now, just over the next rise.

"Son of a—" He tripped over a loose rock in the trail and went sprawling.

"Jeff! Is that you?"

He scrambled to his feet as Sam McDonald and two of his men rode up over the ridge.

"Sam! What are you doing here?"

"Recognized your horse running like a streak of lightning past the Chaitlain ranch. No rider. Figured something happened." Sam tossed him the reins.

"Where's the sheriff?"

"With Dan and the others. Chaitlain's flock's the closest. Sheriff figured Mayberry'd hit him first."

"Did you see Clarissa?" His gut twisted into knots thinking about what Jed might do to her when he realized his scheme had been blown to hell. He'd blame her first and ask questions later.

"Nope. Haven't seen her. Her brothers, neither. Not yet, at any rate."

Jeff leaped onto his horse. His saddle holsters, as expected, were empty. "Got an extra rifle with you, Sam?" McDonald tossed him one. "Much obliged."

If Jed Mayberry so much as touched her...

"Let's ride."

CLARISSA RODE HARDER than she ever had in her life. Twice her mount faltered in the dark. Once she nearly took a spill. Halfway to town, with miles still to go, she realized she'd never get there in time for the sheriff and his men to ride back out to the ranches and stop Jed. If only she'd managed to get away from the Bar L sooner!

She cursed, then pulled her horse up short on the trail. "Whoa! Easy boy."

She had to think! Where would Jed go first?

The Chaitlain ranch was the closest, but she'd heard her brothers speak often about how fortresslike it was, backed up into a canyon with a view of the range that went on for miles. It was too risky this time of night. Jed would wait until after midnight to poison the Chaitlain stock, when everyone was sure to be asleep.

"Where, then?" She recalled the ranches she and Jeff had visited the day he'd sent his family to visit their aunt. "Of course! The McDonalds'."

Their spread flanked Chaitlain's on the west, but the terrain was hilly, and the stock had a tendency to gather at night in the winding arroyos and washes peppering the property. That's where Jed would start. It was the easiest of the ranches to penetrate.

Clarissa turned west and set off cross-country, driving her horse as fast as she dared, praying to God he'd keep his footing. An hour later she galloped past the high arch bearing the McDonald brand and raced for the house.

She never got there.

A horse sprang out of the darkness and cut her off.

"Whoa, little sister!"

"Jed!" Her stomach did a somersault.

Before she could react, he snatched the reins from her hands and guided them both off the road into a deep wash. Cyrus and Frank were there, waiting.

"You was movin' mighty fast there, Clarissa." Frank offered her help dismounting, but she ignored him.

Her legs were shaking when she hit the ground.

"Too fast," Jed said. He grabbed her chin and jerked it upward so he could see her face. Her eyes had adjusted to the starlight, and she had no trouble discerning his scowl.

"I...was trying to find you. I said I would, remember?"

"She did, Jed," Cyrus said, trying to be helpful. Of the three of them, he'd always been the kindest to her. "I remember it plain as day. Well, it was night when she said it, so—"

"Shut up!" Jed turned his attention back to her. "How'd you know we'd be here?"

She could smell the whiskey on him. That, together with the reek of sweat and stale tobacco made her want to retch. "Let me go!" She slapped his hand away and stepped back into the wall that was Frank. He grabbed her arms and held her.

"How'd you know, Clarissa?" Jed inched closer.

She was never very good at lying or hiding her emotions. She wore her heart on her sleeve for all to see, and her brothers knew it. Last night had been a rare gamble that had paid off. She gathered her courage and gambled again.

"Do you think I'm stupid?" She wrestled out of Frank's grip but stood her ground. "Where else would you start? You bumble around over at Chaitlain's this time of the evening and you'd be in the town jail before midnight."

"That's exactly what *you* said, Jed." Cyrus grinned.

Jed glared at her, not buying it.

She snorted for effect. "Makes no sense to start east and work west. It would take twice as long."

"That's what I told him," Frank said.

"Yep, you did," Cyrus said. "I remember it, Jed."

Jed spun toward him, his fist raised. Cyrus cowered.

"Oh, stop it! We're wasting time." Clarissa grabbed the burlap sack she'd noticed sitting on the ground and opened it. "Is this the tainted grain?"

Jed backed off. She could tell by his stiff posture he was still on the fence about whether or not he could trust her.

She didn't give him time to think about it. "Show me what to do."

They spent the next few minutes dividing up the poisoned grain and crafting their plan. Jed wanted them to work together, moving from one flock to the next, but she convinced him they'd go faster if they split up. After a tense argument during which Cyrus and Frank were swayed to her side, Jed finally gave in.

Clarissa breathed.

"You're not back here in a half hour—" Jed drew his buck knife from the leather sheath at his hip. "You'll be sorry."

"I'll be back long before that." She would, too. Just as soon as she raised Sam McDonald and his sons up at the house. Another thought occurred to her. "What about McDonald's night men?" Every flock had round-the-clock protection.

"Took care of them, already," Frank said.

Cyrus started cackling, and Jed thumped him.

"They meet each night after supper out at that shack up yonder." Frank nodded up the ravine. "It's a cold night, and I reckon their whiskey went down extra smooth."

"You drugged it," she said, guessing.

Frank smiled.

Clarissa grabbed her bag. "Let's get this over with."

She mounted her horse, anxious to get away from them now that they'd bought her story. Jed, still wary, insisted she work the flocks farthest from the house. She rode back the way she'd come, until she was out of sight. Then, keeping to the deepest washes, she circled back.

It was early yet. Sam McDonald and his sons would surely still be up, though the house was strangely dark as she approached it. Tethering her horse in a stand of aspen some hundred feet away, she stole quietly on foot to the back porch.

"Mr. McDonald!" She kept her voice to an urgent whisper. No one answered, so she tried the back door. It was locked. "Mr. McDonald! Tom, Thaddeus," she said, trying the boys' names. Still no answer. Were they not home? Where could they be?

Rounding the corner of the porch, she stopped dead, her gaze narrowed on a soft light edging the door of the barn across the yard. Someone was in there. She stood there for a moment, rigid, working up her courage to cross the bare expanse of gravel between the porch and that door. What if Jed were close by? What if he saw her?

She had to take the chance, and she'd best do it quick, before she changed her mind. She stepped off the porch and shot across the yard toward the barn, gravel crunching beneath her feet loud enough to raise the two generations of McDonalds buried in the plot behind the house.

She cursed, grabbed for the door and yanked it open. Slipping inside, she pulled it closed behind her, then gasped. A kerosene lantern backlit the figure pointing a double-barreled shotgun directly at her chest.

JEFF REINED HIS MOUNT to a halt at the fenced section-line bordering Dan Chaitlain's ranch. Something wasn't right.

"What is it, Jeff?"

He peered up the hill into the night, toward Chaitlain's darkened ranch house. Flocks of sheep gathered in the long valley below, spread out for a half mile in both directions. All was quiet.

"They're not here."

"Not yet, but they will be," Sam said. "Dan and the sheriff and a dozen men, including my boy Thaddeus, are right up there in those rocks, waiting." He pointed.

"They'll be waiting awhile, I suspect. The Mayberrys aren't here." He knew it, felt it.

Clarissa had ridden off in the direction of town. Several large ranches bordered the deeply rutted wagon trail, but Dan Chaitlain's wasn't one of them. Where had she been going?

"I think we ought to go up there," Sam said, "and join them."

Jeff shook his head. "I don't think so. Think I'm going to ride on and check things out up ahead."

"Waste of time. Them Mayberrys aren't smart enough to plan it all out proper. They'll dive right in to the first place they come to."

"Maybe," Jeff said. "And if so, just call me over-cautious. If I'm not back in a half hour, you'll know they were smarter than you thought."

"Suit yourself." Sam motioned to his men. A second later they were gone in a cloud of dust.

Jeff rode on. The farther he got from Chaitlain's spread the more convinced he was that he was right. The McDonald ranch was just ahead. If *he* was going to poison sheep, this is where he'd start. But he wouldn't send two bumbling brothers off on their own to do his dirty work for him. And that was Jed Mayberry's mistake.

He found Cyrus first, tripping over himself in the dark, chasing a single sheep into a dead-end ravine. It took Jeff less than a minute to disarm him, gag him and hog-tie him to the nearest tree.

Frank was next. He was smarter than Cyrus, but not any quicker. Jeff found him on the open range a quarter mile away, sprinkling something from a bag onto the ground. Frank saw him coming and went for his gun. He never got the chance to draw it. Jeff shot him in the leg, and he went down yelping like a pup.

"Nasty wound," Jeff said. "Let's hope the sheriff's got the doc with him." He stuffed Frank's dirty handkerchief into his mouth to stop his groaning, then bound him where he lay.

He knew from the trickling blood flow that the bullet had gone clean through and hadn't hit an artery. And while the thought of Frank Mayberry bleeding to death didn't cause him much distress, especially after a stunt like this, it *would* distress Clarissa.

"You're a lucky man, Frank. If I didn't think so much of your sister, my aim might have strayed."

He left him lying there and rode on.

There was still no sign of Jed or Clarissa. He'd found three of Sam McDonald's hired hands passed out in the range shed, and took note of the empty whiskey bottle on the table. He couldn't rouse them, and knew why when he caught the distinct whiff of laudanum in the air.

Sheep clustered in flocks in the dry washes and along the road dividing the McDonald spread. The ranch house was just ahead. One of Sam's bird dogs stood at attention in the yard, barking up a storm. The house was dark, as expected. Sam had sent his wife and daughter to town that morning when Jeff had warned him and the other ranchers of the Mayberrys' plan.

It was the light burning in the barn that bothered him.

He slid from his horse, rifle in hand, and approached on foot. The barn door was cracked. Someone was inside. He heard voices, then a skirmish, as he drew closer.

"You won't get away with this, Jed. I won't let you!"

Clarissa!

He burst inside. "What the—?"

Before he could react, Tom McDonald spun toward him, his face pure fear. Tom checked himself a split second away from blowing Jeff's head off with a double-barreled shotgun.

"Whoa!"

Tom nearly collapsed in relief. "Jeff!" He lowered his gun. "I thought for sure you were—"

"Where's Clarissa?" He scanned the barn, every shadow, but she wasn't there.

"Don't cross me, little sister."

Jed!

"Th-they're out back." Tom motioned with his gun to the barn's double doors leading out to the pasture. "I—I was hiding here in the barn, watching, just like Pa told me to." Jeff could see he was shaking.

He snuffed the lantern, then moved to the double doors and peered out. Their voices were far away now, but he could still hear them.

"C-Clarissa busted in here looking for Jed. I—I reckon I surprised her."

"Is she all right?"

"Looked all right. Said she'd come to warn us, that I should ride for help."

"She did?" He motioned for Tom to stay behind him as he followed the sound of Clarissa's voice.

"Yes, sir. Told me everything. Said she hadn't breathed a word of Jed's plan to you for fear you'd get tangled up in the whole mess."

"She said that?"

"Plain as day. Said she didn't want you to look bad, or do anything that might compromise your chances, whatever that means."

His career. That's what it meant. Clarissa had taken it upon herself to stop her brothers. She'd done it for him. She'd likely gone to the Mayberry ranch last night specifically to learn their plans.

He felt like a fool. She *had* been on her way to town that afternoon—to raise the sheriff—but she'd gotten a late start. It was his fault she was here now, in danger.

"I told her you'd already warned us. That you and Pa and Mr. Chaitlain were fixing to—"

"Quiet!"

They crept forward. His head was throbbing. He could just make out Clarissa's willowy figure. Jed was holding her arm, and not gently.

"I'm not gonna let you do it, Jed. Besides, Jeff knows. The sheriff's been told, and he's on his way."

"Why, you little whore!" Jed dropped the sack he was toting and backhanded her across the face.

Jeff exploded. He launched himself at Jed. Clarissa screamed, and all three of them went down. Jeff's rifle lay forgotten in the grass. Had he used it, she might've been hurt. It was too damned dark, and the quarters were too close.

His fist connected solidly with Jed's face. He was out of control, his mind filled with images of his father lying dead in a dry creek bed at the base of a cliff, of Clarissa beaten and dazed. His cry of rage split the air.

Jed went for his Colt.

"No!" Clarissa screamed.

"Run!" Jeff said, but she didn't.

As he struggled with Jed for the Colt, he was aware of Tom McDonald yelling, trying to drag her away. Good man, but she fought him like a wildcat. "Jed, don't!"

Sam's dog leaped into the fray, and for a heartbeat Jed was distracted. Jeff grabbed the gun. It went off when Jed wrenched it away.

Everyone froze. Hoofbeats sounded all around them.

"Jeff?" Sam McDonald's voice.

Clarissa broke free of Tom's hold and was suddenly there, weeping, pushing Jed's body off of him. He worked to catch his breath, his arms sliding around her as she clutched him.

"You all right, Langworthy?" The sheriff knelt beside them and rolled Jed Mayberry over.

Jeff could smell the blood. "I'm fine," he said, "but he's not."

"You…" Jed's whisper was like a soft wind. His head lolled toward Clarissa, his eyes, near lifeless in the starlight, sought hers. "…love him."

Jeff held on to her. Her tears felt hot against his

cheek as she pressed herself closer. "I do," she whispered, turning her face upward, her eyes seeking his.

"Marry me," he heard himself say.

Her breath caught.

Jed grabbed for her hand. She didn't take it. A moment later he was gone.

"Well, damn," the sheriff said. "I was looking forward to the hanging."

"W-where's Cyrus," she said. "And Frank."

"Found 'em both squirmin' around, hog-tied, on the ride in. Much obliged, Langworthy."

He nodded at the sheriff, then helped Clarissa to her feet. She was shaking.

"Let me take her inside," Sam said. "Tom, get some coffee going."

"No," Clarissa said, still clutching at him. "I—I want to stay with you."

Jeff placed her gently into Sam McDonald's arms. "Go with Sam. I'll be right there. I need to speak to the sheriff."

"You'll need to come on in to town with me, Langworthy."

He looked at Sam, who nodded in answer to his unasked question. The McDonalds would take care of Clarissa until he returned.

She stood there, mute, staring at him in the dark.

"Tomorrow," he said. "Wait for me."

SHE DIDN'T WAIT. She couldn't.

At her request, Sam McDonald brought her home. She had to tell her parents about Jed. They didn't seem to take the news hard. After a sleepless night, she took one last look around the dilapidated house she'd grown up in, said goodbye to her parents, who merely looked at her with a mixture of apathy and contempt, then rode away.

She never looked back.

Just before noon she reached the Bar L. The house was in an uproar. The family was back, along with Valentina and the rest of the hired help. One of the hands was unloading their luggage from the buckboard.

Agnes met her as she rode up, and barely let her dismount before she hugged her. "I heard all about it from Jeff! You poor thing!"

"Where is he?" She couldn't wait to see him and hear the words again, in the light of day, that he'd breathed in her ear last night.

Marry me.

"Still in town."

Clarissa hid her disappointment.

"We arrived on the stage last night. No one knew we were coming, so we stayed at the hotel."

Agnes babbled on as Clarissa climbed the steps to the porch and collapsed into the glider. She could hear Abe inside, arguing with Frances and Mary, then thundering footfalls on the stairs as Mrs. Langworthy shooed them to their rooms.

"Is it true about Tom?"

"Hmm?" She wasn't listening. She was thinking about Jeff and the night they'd made love. His arms around her, his kisses, the feel of him inside her.

"They say he was awfully brave. That he pulled you out of the way when Jed drew his gun. He might have even saved your life."

She forced her attention back to Agnes. "Um, yes. Tom was there when I arrived, guarding the ranch all by himself. He was very brave." She didn't tell her he'd hidden in the barn while she'd gone out to her brother alone. Thank God Jeff had come when he did.

"Oh, I wish I'd been there to see it!"

Agnes prodded her for details, but all Clarissa could think about was Jeff. Had he truly meant it when he asked her to marry him? He'd never once said that he loved her.

"Did he say when he'd be back?"

"Tom?"

"No, Jeff!" Her patience was at an end.

"Oh." Agnes frowned. "No. He said he had some things to clear up with Mr. Chaitlain and Mr. Mc-Donald. They were both pretty mad. Some of the McDonalds' sheep got poisoned after all."

"It's my fault," she said. "I should have told Jeff the second I found out what Jed was planning."

"Speaking of Jed…" Agnes hesitated. "I—I'm sorry."

"I'm sorry, too," she said, a bittersweet feeling curling inside her. "He wasn't always bad."

"We heard that Frank and Cyrus are going to jail— for a while, at least."

"That might just straighten them out." She was glad they wouldn't hang. They were young, and deserved a chance at life without Jed corrupting them.

"Jeff told Mama he was gonna marry you. Is it true?"

"He said that?" Joy shot through her.

Agnes took her hand. "But I suppose I ought to tell you. There's been talk."

"What kind of talk?"

"About you and Jeff. Mr. McCall was in Colorado Springs while we were there. Do you know him?"

Katherine McCall's father. One of the most influential cattle barons in the territory. Clarissa's heart sunk. "Not personally."

"Well, I do, and I've never seen him half so mad as he was the day before yesterday. News travels fast around here. Somebody told him Jeff was sweet on you, and that you were staying at our house."

"Oh, no."

"It gets worse. He said if Jeff even thought about marrying you, he'd personally see to it his career in politics was over."

Clarissa let a breath out. "He's supposed to marry Katherine."

"Lord, no!" Agnes screwed up her face. "It was Father who wanted that match, not Mr. McCall. Why Jeff went along with the idea, I'll never know. Besides, Katherine's sweet on someone else. Has been for months. That was the talk in the Springs, at any rate."

"Then why—?"

"You ninny! Don't you see?"

Clarissa shook her head. She didn't see. Why, if his daughter's future wasn't at stake, did Cal McCall give a whit whom Jeff married?

"You're a *sheep* rancher's daughter. It's politics."

The truth struck her like lightning. "Of course." Jeff had spent his career trying to unite both sides— sheep breeders and cattle barons. Every public action he'd ever taken had been fair and unbiased, but the past was the past. "The cattlemen are afraid if he marries me..."

"Exactly," Agnes said. "That you'd use your... feminine wiles was the term Mr. McCall used...to sway Jeff's mind in political matters."

Clarissa was stunned. "He's serious, then. He'll ruin him if he…"

Marry me. Jeff's words burned in her ears.

"Mother said I wasn't to tell you. That Jeff was a man, now, and could make his own decisions. And that if you were his choice, it was good enough for her and ought to be good enough for the likes of Cal McCall."

"Your mother's a kind woman."

"She is. All the same, I thought you'd want to know." Agnes's eyes filled with regret. "Was I right to tell you?"

"Yes." She rose from the glider on unsteady legs. "Thank you, Agnes."

"W-what will you do?"

Clarissa stood on the porch, gripping the railing, and looked out across the rugged land. Wind whipped at her hair, carrying with it the scent of sage and the chill of autumn. Winter was close at hand. All her life she'd wanted to live here, in this house, with this family, married to the man she'd loved since she was a girl.

"I don't know." The lie came easy. If she was quick, she could get away before he returned.

CHAPTER EIGHT

"SHE WHAT?" Jeff backed Agnes into the bookshelves, upsetting a half dozen volumes that thudded to the parlor floor. "When?"

"This morning. I had no idea she was going to take off like that. If I had, I wouldn't have told her."

"I swear, if you weren't my sister…" Jeff counted to ten.

Meanwhile, his mother shooed Abe and the younger girls out of the room—for all the good it did. They crouched like wide-eyed elves, peeking around the doorway from the hall. Jeff ignored them.

"Where would she go?" his mother asked. "Did she give you any idea?"

Agnes shook her head. "She didn't say a thing. Only that she was going for a ride."

"And you believed her?" Jeff paced back and forth, looking to hit something.

"Calm down, Jeff." His mother tried to make him sit, but he wouldn't. "She couldn't have got far."

"You don't know her like I do." Every second he delayed, she'd get farther. "Damn it!"

"Don't swear."

"S-sorry, Jeff," Agnes squeaked, and backed into the hall.

"I'll deal with you, later." He stormed past her,

and the rest of his siblings scattered like spooked quail.

"You're sure it's what you want," his mother called after him.

"I'm sure." He shot down the front steps and headed for his mount.

"Then bring her back, son."

"I intend to."

HE TRACKED HER as far as Denver. God knows where she'd gotten the money for the train. He'd searched everywhere, queried hundreds of people, but no one had seen a fiery blonde with striking violet eyes.

Jeff stood in the middle of Lawrence Street and rubbed his eyes. He'd been wearing the same clothes for three days—cowpuncher's denims, tattered coat and a shirt sprayed with Jed Mayberry's dried blood. He'd neither shaved nor bathed, and was running on a few hours sleep.

"Jeff Langworthy?"

He shook off his exhaustion and turned toward the familiar voice. A well-dressed man in a three-piece suit descended the steps of the Odd Fellows Hall and walked toward him. It was John Amesbury, a prominent cattle baron who was active in politics and had been a good friend of his father's.

"By God, it *is* you! I hardly recognized you, Jeff. What's all this?" He nodded at his clothing and disheveled appearance. Cattlemen always dressed when they went to town.

"Nice to see you, John. I, uh…I'm looking for someone."

"Rustlers? Looks like you just rode in off the range. Told you a hundred times to join the association. Got some damned good investigators I could send your way.''

''Thanks, John, but no. I'm not here on Bar L business.''

''Politicking, then?''

He could tell by Amesbury's sudden frown that he was thinking no would-be statesman in his right mind would come to Denver looking like he just got dragged off a cattle drive.

If he'd had time to explain it all, he might have, as John had been a mentor to him since his father's death.

''No, I, uh…''

Amesbury arched a brow.

''Oh, hell, I'm looking for a woman.''

''A woman!'' Amesbury's face brightened. ''Well then, she must be either mighty important to you or of no consequence whatsoever, seeing as how you left the house looking like a brush popper.'' The older man looked at him hard. ''I suspect the former.''

''I won't deny it. There was no time to change clothes or pack a bag. I've been searching for three days.''

John Amesbury wasn't a man to pry, but he'd always been there for Jeff.

''Can I help?''

He let out a long breath and shook his head. ''Don't think so. I've just got to keep looking.''

''Where you staying?''

He hadn't even thought that far ahead. The past two nights he'd spent searching boardinghouses and hotels. He'd caught a few hours sleep at one of them. ''Nowhere yet, but—''

''Come on up to the town house, then. Get yourself

cleaned up. I'll loan you a suit.'' Amesbury clapped him on the shoulder.

"Thanks, John. I appreciate it."

"Come to think of it…"

"What?"

"Didn't you get Routt's letter?"

Jeff frowned, then it dawned on him. There'd been a letter from the territorial governor among the rest of the mail, sitting on the secretary in the parlor. He hadn't had time to read it.

"There's a public debate tomorrow about statehood and state's rights. Some mighty important men will be there. Cal McCall among them. You've been invited to speak."

"Tomorrow?"

"If I were you, Jeff, I'd be there."

He cursed under his breath. The last thing on his mind right now was politics. He had to find Clarissa, damn it! He had to find her and set her straight about his feelings for her. He was a fool not to have done it sooner. None of this would have happened if he'd trusted her from the beginning, if he'd trusted his own heart.

As for Cal McCall, he could go to the devil as far as Jeff was concerned. He'd paid him a visit yesterday. They'd spent the entire time arguing about Clarissa. Jeff hadn't backed down, and didn't intend to now.

He'd also seen Katherine. Before he could tell her what was on his mind, she'd blurted out that she was sorry she couldn't marry him because she was in love with someone else. This came as no surprise to him. Katherine was a fine woman, and no doubt had many suitors.

They'd talked about Jeff's father, and how he'd pushed the match on them all those years ago. Her father had gone along because he'd thought that's what she wanted, but in her heart she hadn't. Neither had Jeff. He told her about Clarissa, and in the end they wished each other well, parting on good terms.

John Amesbury's words pulled him back to the present. "You've spent a lot of years doing what your daddy thought was right, and that's all been fine and well, Jeff. But you're your own man, with your own ideas. You've got some damned good ones. Now's the time to share them."

Jeff knew he was right. He'd walked on eggshells with these ranchers—sheep breeders and cattlemen alike—wooing and currying favor, taking moderate positions on most issues to insure everyone's support. But that had been his father's way, not his. It was time to take a stand.

"Trust your instincts, Jeff. It might be the most important speech of your career—if you intend on having one. Be there."

CLARISSA PEERED out the lace-curtained window of her room at the ladies-only boardinghouse in which she'd secured a job as a housemaid. It was a fine, clear morning. She had a place to live and a fresh start. Jeff's career was intact and, in time, he'd see she'd made the right decision for both of them.

Why, then, was she so miserable?

"Best get going!" her employer called up the stairs to her.

She'd promised Mrs. White she'd go to the market for her this morning to purchase some nice winter squash for supper.

"Be right down." She smoothed her old gingham dress over her petticoat, grabbed the cloak Mrs. White had loaned her until she could afford one of her own, and hurried downstairs.

"There's a political meeting in the city proper. You'd do best to avoid Champa Street. The crowd's likely to be a nightmare."

"A political meeting?"

"A debate. Some notion about a territorial convention. But you've no time for that. I've got supper for sixteen tonight, and need you back here lightning-fast."

"Yes, ma'am." Clarissa pocketed the coins Mrs. White handed her and was off.

The streets were a mess. It had rained last night, and this time of year, sun or no sun, the ground never seemed to dry. Carriages rattled past her, horses kicking up mud. In the first block her borrowed cloak was spattered with more spots than a firehouse dog.

Clarissa sighed and hurried on. Mrs. White had said to avoid Champa Street, but that was the fastest route to the market. Besides, that's where the political meeting was, and in the back of her mind she wondered if Jeff would be there. If only she could get a glimpse of him. It would be enough, she told herself. It had to be.

She pushed her way through the crowds, trying to get nearer. An outdoor stage had been set up, and somber men in fine suits crowded onto it, milling about in small groups. They were landowners, mostly. Among them the territorial governor. All powerful men. Clarissa recognized some of them, but others she couldn't see. She had to get closer!

A man approached the podium, and as Clarissa maneuvered her way to the front, she recognized him. Cal McCall, Katherine McCall's father. He spoke at length about the evils of mixed-use grazing, but Clarissa was no fool. What he really was against was sheep ranchers buying up land he thought belonged to cattlemen by right. The crowd cheered wildly.

Where was Jeff?

She searched every face, but didn't see him. Then, as McCall took his seat, a tall, broad-shouldered man in an ill-fitting suit approached the stage.

"Jeff!"

He looked tired, not himself, as if he bore the weight of the world on his shoulders. He should have been happy, relieved. This whole mess with her family was over, and he was free, now, to get on with his life.

As he began to speak, the crowd quieted. She stood amongst them, captivated by his voice. He talked about statehood and all it would bring to Colorado. Of politics and range wars, land battles and water rights. There was a passion in his voice she'd never heard before, save once, when he'd said to her the words she'd never forget.

Marry me.

He spoke plainly and with a conviction that aroused the crowd to his no-nonsense way of thinking. He didn't mince words or skirt issues. Some of his positions were controversial. At one point Cal McCall instigated a ruckus in the crowd, but Jeff was undaunted. His words and the sheer power of his presence brought them back.

"I've one last thing to tell you. It concerns my personal life."

Clarissa sucked in a breath.

"There's a rumor going round that I'm to marry."

"Go get her, Jeff!" a man cried. The crowd erupted in laughter.

"Every word of it's true."

Clarissa exhaled, in a state of shock. The laughter died down. Perhaps he'd changed his mind about Katherine. Maybe what Agnes had told her wasn't true. She scanned the faces of the women on the stage, most of them wives of cattle barons or politicians. One face stood out. Katherine McCall sat quietly next to her father. To her right was a young man who gazed at her in adoration. Clarissa noticed he was holding her hand.

"I'm in love with a sheep rancher's daughter."

Clarissa gasped. The crowd erupted again, this time in chaos. Jeff stood silent, waiting for them to calm. Clarissa barely heard their banter as she pushed her way forward like a sleepwalker, aware that she was moving but unable to stop herself. She approached the stage, her gaze riveted to Jeff's face.

"Her name is Clarissa Mayberry. Not many of you have heard of her, I know. But you're about to. She's a fine woman, brave and true. With her I hope to be a better man. Maybe one day a better congressman." He paused and the crowd grew silent. "If she'll have me."

"I will," she said, loud enough for him to hear her.

He drew a sharp breath, stunned to see her standing right before him. Without preamble, he walked around the podium and lifted her onto the stage.

"Jeff!"

The crowd began to buzz, and Clarissa's head began to spin. Somewhere at the edge of her awareness she heard Cal McCall make a snide remark. Katherine rebuked him.

Jeff held her close. "I love you, Clarissa."

She looked into his eyes and saw her own joy reflected back at her. "I've waited a long time to hear you say it."

"I'm saying it now. I love you and I want you to marry me." He kissed her so tenderly she thought she would melt.

"That's all I've ever wanted." She grinned. "That and my own horse."

"Done!" he said. "We'll buy you a thoroughbred on the way home."

"Our home." How good that sounded. "The Bar L."

"For now." He looked out across the crowd, and saw that they were cheering. Well, enough of them, he supposed. He'd have plenty of time to convince the rest of them that he was their man. And hers.

"Your father would have been proud," she said quietly.

He lifted her off her feet and spun her around. Clarissa laughed with joy.

"You know…I believe you're right."

EPILOGUE

The Bar L, 1880

"CONGRESSMAN?"

Jeff looked up from his newspaper as Valentina entered the parlor. "You don't have to call me that, you know."

"She likes calling you that," Clarissa said. "I like it, too, *Congressman*." Her smile was like sunlight.

He loved the weeks when the legislature was out of session, when the family retreated from their house in Denver back to the Bar L. His mother and Abe and the girls usually stayed in town. There was more to do, Abe always argued. And more eligible men, Frances and Mary would say. Clarissa would simply shake her head.

Agnes and Tom were married, and had their own spread, now, not far from the Bar L, a wedding gift from Sam McDonald. There was a family picnic planned there for tomorrow.

"Supper's ready," Valentina said. "The dining room table's all set."

Jeff put his paper down as his four-year-old son climbed into his lap. Clarissa handed him the baby and he bounced them both on his knees. "Why don't we eat in the kitchen tonight, Valentina?"

"Mr. Langworthy..." She cast him a disapproving look.

"Oh, come on, don't be so stodgy. It'll be fun."

"I seem to recall someone else who was stodgy once." Clarissa nudged him. "Do you remember our first meal there?"

"No, but I remember what happened afterward." He grinned at his wife, and knew that she, too, was recalling their first kiss. "You're a beautiful woman, Mrs. Langworthy."

"Why, thank you, Congressman."

He carried their children to the kitchen, Clarissa on his arm. In 1876 Colorado had become a state. It was the year of the Centennial, and that's how he'd always think of her, as his Centennial bride.

"I never expected to be this happy," he said as they took their seats at the table.

Clarissa shot him a mischievous grin. "I did," she said, and dished him up some stew.

* * * * *

To read more about the origins of
COLORADO CONFIDENTIAL, be sure to pick
up Harlequin Historicals from bestselling
authors Judith Stacy, Carolyn Davidson and
Debra Lee Brown, beginning January 2004.

Don't miss the exciting continuation of
COLORADO CONFIDENTIAL
coming next month.

Turn the page for a sneak preview of
COVERT COWBOY *by Harper Allen*

CHAPTER ONE

He was going to have to lie to her, U.S. Marshall Conrad Burke told himself as he carried Marilyn Langworthy to the couch in the corner of her office. Against the creamy pallor of her cheeks her lashes stirred, and his self-disgust intensified. Damn. The lying was going to have to start now.

Dark lashes fluttered open. Eyes as blue as heaven gazed blankly up at him, and for a moment Con forgot everything. He recovered smoothly.

"Not the way I meant to introduce myself, sugar," he said with a quick, and he hoped, reassuring smile, his gaze steady on her suddenly widened one, "but it seems I walked in just as you fainted. You feeling all right now, cher'?"

He hadn't planned on introducing himself at all and he certainly hadn't walked in only minutes ago, so even if he didn't count the fact that he needed no introduction to Marilyn Langworthy, those were lies number one and two right there, and the guilt rippled unfamiliarly through him. And the lady wasn't buying them, he realized as he saw that heaven-blue gaze focus and begin to harden.

She was going to ask him how he'd gotten past security and into her locked office. He needed to plant other questions in her mind, and fast.

"New Orleans P.D." He slipped two fingers into

the inner pocket of his suit jacket and extracted a leather identification case, complete with gold badge. Deftly he flipped it open in front of her. "Detective Connor Ducharme. I'm investigating—"

"Is he *safe?*"

Under his open jacket he was wearing a waist-coat—what those unfortunate enough to be born north of the Mason-Dixon line and west of the Missouri River called a vest, he supposed. Before he'd known what she intended she'd grabbed its lapels. Slim fingers gave a surprisingly strong tug and she repeated her query, those perfect features of hers etched with strain.

"Is he safe? Have you found him? Dear God— New *Orleans?* Why in heaven's name did they take him there?"

"Cher', I'm not here about the little one," he said, as gently as he could. "The case I'm working involves a certain Tony Corso, wanted on fraud charges in Louisiana. I wish I had news of your nephew for you, but I don't."

She closed her eyes. When she opened them again he saw the urgently hopeful light in them had disappeared. Her fingers slid from his lapels.

"I—I thought maybe it was all over. The nightmare, I mean. I thought Sky might be on his way home right now."

Her head still bowed, she took a deep breath. Letting it out, she sat up on the couch. She swung her legs to the floor and met his look with a suddenly flinty one of her own.

"How did you know my nephew had been kidnapped? Since it's not common knowledge in Denver,

I can't believe every last man on the New Orleans force has been alerted.''

"Probably not." He shrugged easily, more sure of his ground now. "But when I discovered Corso's trail led here the local law brought me up to speed."

He flicked a glance at her still-white face. Something prompted him to add, "From what I hear, the rest of your family's sticking pretty close together these days. Why aren't you with them?''

He'd gone too far, he realized immediately. She stiffened, and when her gaze locked on his he could have sworn the temperature in the room dropped several degrees.

"My personal life can't be part of your investigation, Detective, so I'm going to pretend I didn't hear that question.''

She smoothed her skirt down her thighs and stood, and despite the perceptible chill emanating from her, Con felt sudden heat slam into him. Not everything he'd told her had been a lie, he thought, trying to school his features into impassivity. He *had* asked questions before coming here, and the answers he'd gotten had all been the same. Marilyn Langworthy was a bitch. She was an ice queen. Nothing touched her—not the kidnapping of her tiny nephew, and certainly not the breakup of her relationship with Tony Corso.

Maybe some of what he'd heard was true, but he'd already seen enough of the woman to put the lie to at least two of the labels that had been pinned on her. She cared about the child—cared enough that she was being torn apart by Sky's abduction, judging from what he'd witnessed moments ago. And if she was an ice queen, it was only because the right man hadn't come along to melt her yet.

You gon' be the one who does that, Cap?

The jeering voice inside his head held the same scepticism he'd heard from the late night denizens of the Canal Street clubs he'd trolled when he'd been young enough that even hardened gamblers had felt a momentary pang of conscience before dealing a tough Creole urchin in on a game of five-card stud. He'd taken them and their consciences to the cleaners, Con recalled without regret. But back then all he'd been risking was money.

The stakes were higher here. And the odds were more overwhelmingly against him than they'd ever been in his life. *F'sure. One of these days I'm gonna come back here and give it my best shot,* he answered the jeering voice with a determination that disconcerted even himself. *But whether she knows it or not, tonight the lady just needs someone to be with her. And maybe if that someone gets her good and angry it'll ease her pain for a few hours. Before I leave I can do that for her, at least.*

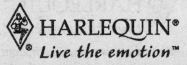

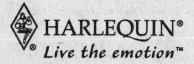

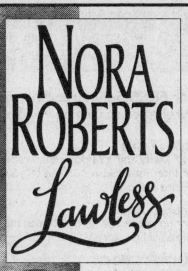

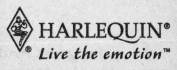